Also by Christina Dodd

CHRISTINA DODD

Lost In Your Arms

AVON BOOKS

An Imprint of HarperCollinsPublishers

AVON BOOKS
An Imprint of HarperCollins*Publishers*
10 East 53rd Street
New York, New York 10022-5299

*This book is dedicated with thanks to
Luke Skywalker, for his constant assistance
in writing my novels.
Luke, no other cat could sit on a keyboard,
shed into a computer, or chose such
inopportune moments to demand to be petted.
May the force be with you.*

Chapter 1

London, 1843

"Please, Mrs. MacLean, won't ye tell us about *yer* wedding?"

Her mouth full of cake, Enid stared around at the circle of feminine faces in Lady Halifax's parlor, all bright with happiness, and at the blond, round-cheeked girl in whose honor they were gathered. The girl who had asked the question. The girl who, in less than a fortnight, would become the blushing bride to Lady Halifax's underbutler. Swallowing, Enid took a breath. "My wedding? Oh, you don't want to know about *my* wedding."

"We do!"

An eager chorus answered her, a chorus from Lady Halifax's upstairs maids, her downstairs maids, and her scullery maids, all girls with their heads stuffed with puff pastry dreams of love.

Enid, at the ripe old age of twenty-six, was at least five years everyone's senior in age and five hundred years their senior in cynicism.

"Was yer wedding as wonderful as mine is going t'

be?" Kay clasped her hands at her bosom. The girl was resplendent with flowers and ribbons in her hair, surrounded by gifts given by her friends, and glowing with the light of love.

So Enid tried desperately to divert the conversation. "Nothing could be as wonderful as your wedding is going to be. That lace Lady Halifax asked me to bring as your wedding gift will make a lovely collar for your wedding gown."

"Aye, it will." Kay patted the fancy, machine-sewn lace Enid had delivered. "Lady Halifax is a grand mistress, an' ye must convey me thanks t'er. Mrs. MacLean, did ye have lace on yer gown?"

The problem, as Enid saw it, was that she was a woman of mystery.

Oh, not really. For three years she had lived in the London town house as Lady Halifax's nurse-companion. At first she had done little more than pass Lady Halifax her cane and make sure she had a clean handkerchief. But as time had gone on and the wasting disease had weakened Lady Halifax, Enid had become her mouth and ears in the household. She had reported the household activities to Lady Halifax and given Lady Halifax's instructions to the servants. But never, ever, had she confided her past to anyone.

She knew speculation had run rampant. Because of Enid's upper-class accent, her education and manners, the maids thought that she was a lady who had fallen on misfortune and had turned to labor to support herself. She had done nothing to dissuade them of that notion.

Now they had her trapped with their offer of tea and cake, their high hopes and fabulous imaginings.

"Please, Mrs. MacLean?" Sarah, the upstairs parlor maid, begged.

"Please?" Shirley, fifteen years old and fresh from the country, clapped her hands and tipped her cake plate off her lap and onto the carpet.

Everyone jumped to their feet, but Enid hushed the horrified exclamations and helped clean up the mess. "It's all right, dear. See? There's no harm done." Trying to distract the tearful Shirley, she said, "Stop crying so you can hear the details of my wedding."

Shirley snuffled into her handkerchief. "Aye."

"Tell us," Kay urged.

Enid could never confess the truth—so she would have to tell them a lie.

"Did ye get married in a big church?" Ardelia, plain, plump and brown, dabbed up the last crumbs of cake with her thumb.

Putting down her fork, Enid put the plate on the end table beside her and made the decision that, if she was going to tell a lie, she might as well tell a colossus. "*I* was married in a *cathedral* by a *bishop.*"

"A cathedral?" Sarah's brown eyes grew huge.

"I was wed on a beautiful, sunny morning in June, with wild pink roses in my arms and all my friends in attendance."

"Did ye wear white like Queen Victoria?" Ardelia quivered with excitement.

"No, not white."

The maids groaned with disappointment.

"Her Majesty hadn't married yet, and it wasn't the style. But I did wear a blue dimity, very fine"—turned only twice—"with a splendid full skirt and black lace gloves"—loaned by the vicar's wife—"and a blue velvet hat with a black veil"—given by Stephen and acquired heaven-knew-where and hopefully by legal means. Carried away with her enthusiasm, Enid added, "And my black boots were polished so brightly, I could see my face in them."

"Wi' yer blue eyes an' yer black 'air, ye must have looked splendid, Mrs. MacLean." Gloria, a rather nondescript girl who extravagantly admired Enid, flattered her now. " 'Ow did ye dress yer 'air?"

Enid touched the loose knot gathered in a black net snood at the base of her neck. "It's so flyaway, I can never do much more with it than this."

Wide-eyed with innocence, Ardelia asked, "Why didn't ye 'ave yer maid dress yer 'air?"

Bent on making the tale the best, most dramatic story they'd ever heard, Enid told them, "I didn't have a maid."

The girls exchanged sympathetic looks.

"My family had had setbacks . . ." Enid dabbed at her perfectly dry eyes. Dear, dear, these girls would believe anything!

"Oo." Sarah loved a good theatrical better than anyone, and she knew how this story should end. "Yer family 'ad lost their money, then yer Stephen rescued ye."

Love never rescued anyone. If Enid were kind, she would have told the truth and disillusioned these girls. But she knew they wouldn't believe her. Young people never did. *She* hadn't.

"Yer 'air's pretty that way, Mrs. MacLean," Shirley said.

"Thank you, Shirley."

Ardelia leaned forward, eyes shining. "Did yer Da give ye away?"

"No, my father was dead." *Good riddance.* "But I needed only Stephen."

"Was yer 'usband a tall and 'andsome gennaman?" Dena's ample bosom heaved at the thought.

"He boasted a head full of golden hair, so bright it almost outshone the sun, and fine pale skin." Enid stared out the window at Lady Halifax's city garden, not seeing the summer blossoms, instead trying to remember how Stephen MacLean had looked on that day nine years ago. Her memory produced a portrait tarnished by time. But that answer would never do for girls who wanted to believe in love ever after. "His eyes . . . I will never forget the color of his eyes . . ." That much was true, at least. "His eyes were the deepest green, almost like the sea on a stormy day, and shot with gold, like lightning bolts."

"Sea green lightning bolts," Ardelia said in tones of awe.

"But he wasn't at all vain." Stephen had been the vainest man Enid had ever met, but in this fairy tale he became a prince. "He would chortle and say that no man whose ears stuck out as his did"—she demonstrated with her hands—"could be handsome, but he carried with him an air of adventure and excitement that never flagged."

" 'E was an adventurer?" Shirley breathed in quick little gasps.

"Indeed. He was the son of a noble family, unjustly dispossessed by his wicked cousin, so he roamed the byways of England, helping the old and bringing justice to the poor."

"Like Robin 'ood," Sarah said.

"Just like that." Enid's narrative carried her away.

"Did 'e sweep ye off yer feet like me Roger did?" Kay asked.

"He did. He met me, and right away he claimed I was the very woman he was looking for." That, sadly, was the truth. Enid just hadn't understood the underlying reason why. "He proposed that very night, but I was determined to be wise. I refused him for a fortnight." She laughed at her youthful foolhardiness. "I was only seventeen. Two weeks was a very long time."

"I'm seventeen, too!" Kay exclaimed. "An' it seems like forever until I marry me Roger."

"Time will pass," Enid promised.

Kay grimaced. "Ye sound like me mum, Mrs. MacLean."

Kay's words pricked Enid's bubble, and like Cook's tall soufflé, she wanted to collapse in a wretched heap. Twenty-six years old, and this child proclaimed Enid to be just like her mother? How had Enid gone from youthful indiscretion to aged wisdom so quickly? How had she become like someone's mother when she'd never even cradled a babe in her arms . . . and because of Stephen, she never would?

She strove never to think of that, yet here she was, glaring at a silly gaggle of girls who gradually straightened in their chairs and looked down at their feet.

"Mrs. MacLean, are ye . . . well?" Kay asked timidly.

Rising, Enid strode to the window to hide her expression. "I'm just lost in memory." Too true, and too bad.

Sarah broke the brief, fearful moment of silence.

"Mrs. MacLean, if ye don't mind me asking, what 'appened to yer 'usband?"

Enid hesitated, turned her head away, and considered how to end the tale. Finally, with delicate understatement, she said, "He rode out one day on his charger, and he . . . and he . . ."

"Was 'e rescuing some old poor lady?"

Kay furiously turned on Ardelia. "Sh!"

"Just so." Enid smiled with tragic courage. "Now he is forever gone from me."

Dena elbowed Shirley in the ribs. "I told ye she was like one o' those tragic 'eroines ye like so well."

Her lies condemned Enid to hell. She knew it. But hell or not, she couldn't resist one last, theatrical—and in its way truthful—declaration. "There isn't a day that goes by when I don't think of him, or a night where I don't wish I could see his face one more time." Facing the maids, she struck a dramatic pose, her hands clutching the gold fringe of the curtains on either side of her. "I would give anything to see him one more time."

The maids sighed in gusty, thrilled unison.

Lady Halifax's quavering voice spoke from the doorway. "Enid, dear, Mr. Kinman has arrived to fulfill your dearest wish."

Caught! In outrageous dramatizations, and by Lady Halifax, a woman Enid most admired.

There was more than one route to hell.

Enid snapped out of her affected pose. Pain-ridden and confined in her rolling chair, Lady Halifax observed her with sorrowful, incredulous eyes.

Behind her stood an officious-looking stranger,

dressed in the brown tweed proper. He, too, wore a solemn expression on his florid, prizefighter face.

Fear caught at Enid's throat. What had Lady Halifax said? *Your dearest wish . . .*

A whisper of concern rose from the maids.

Dropping a curtsy, Enid asked, "Ma'am? What do you mean?"

"Mr. Kinman?" Lady Halifax gestured at the gentleman. "Would you explain the situation to Mrs. MacLean?"

"It's true." Mr. Kinman stepped forward, twirling his brown derby in stubby fingers. "We have found your husband, Stephen—alive."

Dressed in her sturdy, dark traveling clothes, Enid placed her case on the floor outside Lady Halifax's bedchamber. With a soft knock, she entered the shadowy room. The new nurse rose from her chair beside the bed and came to her. "Lady Halifax is resting," she said softly, "but until she's seen you she refuses to sleep." With a sympathetic pat on Enid's shoulder, the nurse left the room, shutting the door behind her.

While Enid waited for her eyes to adjust to the dim light, she breathed in the familiar scents of lavender, cough syrup, old age and pain-wrought courage. Then with a rustle of petticoats, she slipped to the bedside.

Lady Halifax lay flat on her back, the counterpane pulled up under her chin and held in clawlike fingers. Her dark eyes glittered. "A *husband*, Enid? Why didn't you tell me?"

Trust Lady Halifax to go right to the heart of the matter.

Enid placed a pillow under Lady Halifax's bony

shoulders to ease her labored breathing. "A failed marriage is nothing to swank about, and a woman who can't keep a husband is at best an object of pity."

"Pity? You?" Lady Halifax laughed until she coughed, then rested until she could finish her thought. "You've survived and prospered. Nothing to pity about that."

Enid straightened the bedside table while she thought about that. She could see that where some women would have given up, she had succeeded. She was an independent person. Of course, she had lost a great deal of the girl she had been, too. She was cynical. Sarcastic. She never allowed herself to indulge in the softer side of her nature, didn't even know if the softer side still existed.

But of course it did. The proof reclined right before her eyes. Lady Halifax, skinny, sharp-tongued, ill-tempered at the best of times, held a piece of Enid's heart. In a low tone, Enid said, "My lady, I don't want to leave you."

"But you must, dear." Lady Halifax trailed a trembling finger over Enid's cheek. "No matter what he has done, this Stephen is your husband."

During the painful interview in Lady Halifax's library, Mr. Kinman had told Enid she'd been sent for, and when she demanded to know more, he would say only that her husband was injured. Clearly, he'd imagined she would rush to her husband's side. Such was, after all, a wife's duty.

Lady Halifax obviously agreed. "It is proper that you go to your Stephen. He needs your loving care."

"Love." Enid invested the word with scorn.

"You must have loved him when you wed."

"Infatuation, easily cured. Nothing kills love like having to listen to a man whimper that the world treats him badly, nothing that's happened to him is his fault, it's all bad luck and the fact that the laird of the MacLeans doesn't like him." Without realizing it, Enid slipped into a Scottish brogue. "And he's a MacLean, by God, and not just any MacLean, but a MacLean of the Isle of Mull."

Lady Halifax's mouth dropped open, and she struggled to lift herself on her elbow. "You . . . you married one of *those* MacLeans? I know them. I used to hunt in Scotland."

Enid tucked the blankets tighter about Lady Halifax's legs. "Are they as grand and proud as Stephen said?"

"Proud, at least. They've survived by playing along with the English rule, but when they come face to face with one of us, they look as if they'd been presented with a bowl of bedbugs and cream. I'll wager your marriage angered the laird."

"Yes, indeed. He wrote me a most scathing letter, informing me a greedy orphan like me would never partake in the life or the fortunes of the Clan MacLean." Enid clenched her fists as she recalled that old humiliation. "As if I cared whether I was part of that family."

"I would have thought an orphan would want to be part of a family."

Lady Halifax was right, of course. Enid had dreamed of meeting Stephen's mother, his aunt, his cousins. Of staying in Castle MacLean, of knowing this clan had been on this land for hundreds of years, and fancying herself a part of that tradition. Tight-lipped, she shook her head and admitted to nothing.

Lady Halifax moved her head restlessly on the pillows. "That new nurse doesn't know what she's doing. You know I don't like the hairpins sticking me while I rest. Take my hair down."

Enid did as Lady Halifax commanded, then pulled a brush through the ends and braided the long gray locks.

Lady Halifax sighed with relief as she settled back once more. "You work very hard, Enid. You don't smell as bad as the last girl I had, and you don't often weary me with your petty complaints."

Praise indeed from Lady Halifax.

"Yet you're thrifty. You save every ha'penny. You dress plainly, without a hint of furbelows." Lady Halifax peered at Enid from beneath wild graying brows. "What are you saving for?"

Enid glanced at Lady Halifax out of the corner of her eyes and thought, *Why not?* "I want land."

"Land? Like . . . an estate? You want to marry a rich man?" Lady Halifax *tsked* in disbelief. "You're an intelligent girl, but you haven't the looks or the youth for that."

"Pah! What would I do with two husbands? I want *land*. An acre or two, that's all, but it has to be the right acres. A little marsh, a little mountain, with good soil and sunshine."

"What are you going to do with your acres?"

"Have neighbors who'll visit occasionally. Go to a village church built five hundred years ago and listen to the same vicar for the rest of my life. Grow herbs. Make ointments. Potions. Sell them and never work for someone else again. Have a home." A superstitious shiver worked its way down Enid's back as she ex-

pressed her deepest desire. Was this like wishing on a
star? When she spoke aloud the dream of her heart,
was she setting the furies on her trail . . . or had they
already discovered her when they'd happened upon her
husband?

"You'd be smarter marrying a rich man," Lady Halifax declared.

"I'm already married." Enid hadn't wished for
MacLean's death—she wasn't so far gone into acrimony—but she had dared to dream that someday free-
dom would be hers. "If I should be widowed, I see no
reason to repeat the wedded experience."

"You young girls these days have no sense of propriety." Lady Halifax's mouth puckered as if she'd
sucked a lemon, and the wrinkles on her upper lip cut
like ravines into her skin. "Make ointments, indeed.
Silly plan."

"Not so silly. I would be the master of my own fate."
Enid's chest tightened as she contemplated the facts. "I
fear when I discover the true extent of MacLean's
debts, I will find myself impoverished again."

"You worry for nothing. You'll be compensated for
doing the right thing, if not here, then in heaven."

Enid had heard those promises years ago from the
charity workers who'd urged resignation to her fate,
and she rejected resignation just as vigorously now as
she had then. "I'm a poor, wretched creature of the
flesh who wants to reach heaven, but not yet, and not
by starving to death."

Lady Halifax risked a brief pat on Enid's hand. "I
promise that won't happen. You'll get that land of
yours."

Enid imagined herself walking through her gardens,

scissors in her gloved hands, basket on her arm. "Yes, I will. I just hope that MacLean—"

"There's no use worrying about it now." Lady Halifax moved restlessly on the pillows. "You'll discover the truth soon enough."

Enid saw the shadows under Lady Halifax's eyes and smoothed the covers in a futile effort to bring comfort through tidiness. "My lady, I don't want to leave Halifax House." Enid realized her voice quivered and realized, too, that she had formed an attachment not only to this place but also to its mistress.

"Yes, well, needs drive." Lady Halifax wouldn't allow for pity, not for Enid, not for herself.

Yet their attachment had developed from wakeful nights and pain-filled days, and for Lady Halifax, too few of those remained. Enid would probably never see the old woman alive again. Both of them knew it. This was the hell Enid feared. The pain of separation, the heartbreak of unwelcome duty.

Enid blinked the tears away. Lady Halifax wouldn't thank her for coming maudlin. "I've left you a jar of the rosemary cream. Have your new companion rub it on your back every night, and make sure she frequently turns you." Lifting her hand, Enid pressed a farewell kiss on the bony knuckles. "God grant you peace, my lady."

"Don't be so sloppy and sentimental, MacLean. It's not attractive." Lady Halifax turned her head away, but not before Enid saw the shadows under her eyes.

Quickly, before Enid could allow the doubts to stop her, she hurried from the room and left Lady Halifax alone.

Chapter 2

A black wrought-iron gate with the initial T worked into the metal in ornate curlicues guarded the entrance to hell. Hell's coach was well sprung, with padded velvet seats and matching curtains, which Mr. Kinman had insisted remained closed throughout most of the journey. Only now, as they waited for the gatehouse keeper to approach, did Mr. Kinman allow Enid a glimpse outside.

Hell much resembled Suffolk. Summer flowers blazed on the undulating hills, and a rural sense of isolation clung to the road before them. Suffolk—and hell—had a reputation for remoteness, for the fens to the north and Epping Forest to the south made rails difficult to build and roads scarce. If Enid was capable of surprise—and at this juncture she didn't believe herself capable of any marked emotion—she would have marveled to discover hell was difficult to approach. After all, she had always heard all roads led there.

As the gatehouse keeper walked to the carriage, Mr.

Kinman lowered the window. "Greetings, Harry." His voice contained faint traces of an east London accent. "I've got the wife."

Enid thought that sounded ominous, almost as if she were a parcel, wrapped neatly in brown paper and tied in string.

Harry leaped onto the footman's perch and peered inside. He was handsome, young, with a hard face. He scanned the corners of the vehicle, but the floor of the carriage contained nothing but four feet and Enid's pocketbook, so he nodded and in an educated accent said, "All right, then. Go right to the garden." His gaze lingered on Enid, on her neat brown traveling costume, her straw bonnet and her tan kid gloves.

Mr. Kinman stared at Enid, too.

Their mixture of wariness and hope gave her a queasy feeling—not that she wasn't feeling queasy anyway at the thought of seeing Stephen once more.

Harry jumped down. "Drive on."

"A very odd sort of gatekeeper," Enid said, making conversation as they rumbled through a small pine wood and up over a hill.

"Harry's a good man. You can trust him." Mr. Kinman's meaty face was heavy with sincerity. "Anyone I introduce to you will be a man of good faith, but please, Mrs. MacLean, don't put your trust in strangers."

"How many strangers will I meet?" Enid asked.

Mr. Kinman's starched white collar apparently strangled him, for he ran a finger around it in a half-circle. "None, ma'am. You should meet none at all."

Except MacLean, and he was the strangest of all. She feared that, like a runaway train, he would once again rush over her, crush her, and leave her writhing in the destruction of her life before he rolled on to another adventure, another conquest.

The thought of seeing MacLean again gave her a pain in the gut, and that, combined with the rolling motion of the coach, made her wish that the journey would be over, and soon.

As they passed a hill topped by a ruined castle covered by ivy and honeysuckle, Mr. Kinman said earnestly, "Blythe Hall is a lovely spot, close to the coast and on the banks of the River Blythe."

"I would have sworn it was the River Styx," she said.

Mr. Kinman's broad forehead puckered as he struggled to comprehend her enigmatic reference to the river that flowed through hell. "No, ma'am, I don't know why you would think that. It is the River Blythe. The estate is Blythe Hall. Your host is Mr. Throckmorton, a gentleman of substance and one of Her Majesty's loyal subjects."

"He will tell me the details of my husband's injury?"

"Yes, ma'am."

Her questions and comments made Mr. Kinman frankly uncomfortable, and at any other time and in any other circumstances, she would have taken pity on him. But not here, and not now. She had left a dying woman to come here and see Stephen MacLean. This had better not be one of MacLean's tricks, or she would personally see that he *was* given an injury.

"Mr. Throckmorton has commanded that you be given anything you want, anything at all," Mr. Kinman continued. "We—all of us who serve Mr. Throckmorton—

will do our best to provide for your needs. We'll see that your stay here is at least tolerable."

Tolerable? She turned her head away and stared out the window. No, this duty would not be tolerable. The marital mistake of her youth would haunt her forever.

The drive turned and twisted through groves of trees and handsome gardens, and once she caught a glimpse of the manor, tall and glorious in the late afternoon's summer sunshine. Yet they drove to a walled garden. There the carriage stopped, and a gentleman stepped from beneath the arbor. Tall, dark and raw-boned, he wore authority like a second skin.

"Mr. Throckmorton's a straight-shooter," Mr. Kinman told her as the footman opened the carriage door.

But Enid didn't move. This wasn't a moment she wanted to rush to embrace. No, not with Mr. Kinman nudging her from behind and Mr. Throckmorton looking grim as death as he advanced to offer his hand.

But she had no choice, and with a sigh and a wince she climbed from the carriage.

The muscles of her thighs ached. Ever since they'd left London, she'd been digging her heels into the floor in a vain, compulsive attempt to stop the onward rush toward her fate.

"Mrs. MacLean, it's a pleasure to meet you." Mr. Throckmorton bowed formally, his gray eyes seeming to appraise her. To Mr. Kinman, he said, "Stay with the carriage. We'll be back soon, and you can take her to the cottage."

Mr. Kinman touched his forehead like a soldier to his commander, then, to Enid's surprise, gave her a like salute.

Mr. Throckmorton led her into the garden, where vivid yellow daisies nodded beside the paths and tall lavender stocks bloomed against the ivy-covered walls. "Kinman likes you. That's good; he's a fair judge of character, and knowing of your estrangement with your husband, I had qualms about contacting you."

"How did you know of our estrangement? How did you find me? Is MacLean a friend of yours?"

"Your husband? Yes, a friend and colleague." He indicated a bench beneath an arbor. "Won't you sit down?"

"I've been sitting." Obviously, Mr. Throckmorton knew much about MacLean. Therefore, he knew about her, and she didn't like that. Anonymity, she had discovered, beat notoriety any day. "With your permission, I prefer to stand."

"As you wish." Taking her arm, he walked her along the small circle that made up the path within the garden.

"I imagine you found the news of MacLean's injury unsettling."

"It was the worst possible news." She had left Lady Halifax. "Mr. Throckmorton, how long do you foresee I will be here? I left a beloved patient who is near her moment of crisis, and I would like to be back at her side as soon as possible."

Mr. Throckmorton lifted a haughty brow. "The Distinguished Academy of Governesses arranged for another nurse to care for her, did they not?"

"Lady Halifax is failing badly, and I know what she needs, how she thinks." Enid's heart ached as she thought of the old woman who had so bravely sent her on her way. "I would like to be with her."

Mr. Throckmorton observed her closely, then passed judgment. "You are a good nurse."

"I am."

"Your husband needs a nurse now."

Her skirt swirled over the tops of the nodding flower heads, and in her present mood she would just as soon have ground them beneath her heel. Poor flowers, to be a substitute for that rotter Stephen MacLean! "What did MacLean do?" she asked caustically. "Crawl into the wrong bedroom window and get shot by an irate husband? Wager he could race his horses along the turnpike and overturn the carriage? Get drunk and tossed by his erstwhile companions?"

Her bitterness didn't shock Mr. Throckmorton. On the contrary, he answered as if her censure was the most natural thing in the world. "He was involved in an explosion."

Enid thought she should be ashamed of her accusations. She was not. They weren't unreasonable, not where Stephen MacLean was involved. "An explosion. He was playing with fireworks?"

"It was a bomb. He was in the Crimea. At the wrong place at the wrong time. A Russian agent set the explosive. MacLean's companion was killed."

"A Russian agent?" She halted, and, wide-eyed with comprehension, she stared at Mr. Throckmorton. No wonder he carried with him such a sense of authority! No wonder he had so easily discovered the state of her marriage and her direction! She had never actually met anyone like this before; after MacLean she had assiduously sought the quiet life. But tabloids and newsprint had fired her imagination with stories of spies at home and abroad. Now she stood next to just such a man. Then it occurred to her—"MacLean was *spying?*"

Mr. Throckmorton started, and cleared his throat as if her acuity displeased him. "No. The other man . . . but I can't say more."

Her brief hope collapsed. "It was too great a thing to hope MacLean had performed an honorable service for Her Majesty's government. Yet I would have thought such a hazardous activity would appeal to my husband."

"He was an innocent passerby," Mr. Throckmorton assured her. "Nevertheless, he needs you now."

"You don't understand. My husband would not wish for me to come and care for him. He wishes never to see me again." Enid drew a careful breath before adding, "Nor I him."

"Yes, we do understand, but MacLean is in no condition to refuse." Mr. Throckmorton stopped walking and took her gloved hand in his. "Mrs. MacLean, your husband is dying."

Chapter 3

"Dying?" Enid covered her mouth. Funny, for all of Mr. Throckmorton's descriptions, she hadn't thought MacLean could be dying. Possessed of a child's energy and a child's carelessness, MacLean never walked, he ran. He never talked, he yelled. He never smiled, he rolled with hysterical laughter. Death to him would be the ultimate adventure. Sometimes she thought he had wished nothing more than to embrace death in a final, dramatic *coup de théâtre*.

"The accident happened four weeks ago." Mr. Throckmorton led her to the seat she had previously scorned.

She sank down upon it. "What's wrong? Has he lost limbs? Why . . . dying?"

"The broken glass sliced his face and his chest. He's suffered a broken leg. The bone, they tell me, stuck through the skin."

She winced. Compound fractures usually killed a man. "How did he get back to England?"

"A ship transported him, a terrible journey through rough seas. He returned to consciousness at least once a day, but now . . . he's so weak, those moments are less frequent." Mr. Throckmorton watched her steadily. "Unless we can give him sustenance, there's no hope. We aren't asking you to do the heavy work. He has a nurse, and the doctor comes once a day."

"Then why am I here?"

"We hope the sound of your gentle voice might bring him back."

"From the brink of death? There's little chance of that. I'm telling you the truth. He has no fondness for the sound of my voice." But Enid fought a losing battle, and she knew it.

"I refuse to give up hope. All of us who know him refuse to give up hope."

"Of course." She understood hope. She'd been blessed, or cursed, with a soul wherein, regardless of her travails, hope sprang eternal. No matter how often she scolded herself, no matter how frequently she demanded good sense of herself, she always believed in a better life . . . tomorrow. Her vicar in London had told her she had an unending capacity for faith. She told herself she suffered a relentless supply of folly. "But, if as I suspect, I can't help him—"

"If you cannot help him and he's condemned to a death he doesn't deserve—if that is the case, the family will wish the body transported back to Scotland. As his wife, you, of course, will accompany it."

Worse and worse. Raising her voice in furious defiance, Enid said, "Lady Halifax needs me. And . . . and the clan MacLean wants nothing to do with me."

"Stephen MacLean might have left you a legacy."

Livid with the insinuation that greed drove her, Enid rose and faced off with Mr. Throckmorton. "I was wed to Stephen MacLean, and I assure you he more likely would leave me a load of debt."

Mr. Throckmorton acknowledged that by saying, "The MacLean family is wealthy. They might be willing to help you."

"And I would take any help, Mr. Throckmorton, for I supported my husband during the three months of our marriage. It would be nothing more than a repayment long in arrears. But I don't look for help from the MacLeans. After the wedding, their laird made it clear in the letter he wrote—my husband had no money of his own, and Kiernan MacLean would rather I rot than support such an opportunistic creature as I am."

For the first time in their conversation, Mr. Throckmorton appeared nonplussed. "I'm sure the laird didn't mean—"

"He meant exactly what he said. No, Mr. Throckmorton, I am a single woman with nothing standing between me and starvation but my own hard labor, and I'll not trouble his Scottish relations."

Mr. Throckmorton drew himself up to his full height and stared down his nose at her.

She stared right back. "If we are done with our discussion, Mr. Throckmorton, I would like to go assess my patient. The sooner he's returned to health, the sooner I may leave."

Settling back to his normal size, Mr. Throckmorton observed, "Mrs. MacLean, you don't intimidate easily."

"No." She walked toward the garden entrance.

Mr. Kinman paced beside the carriage, an overgrown, shambling bear of a man who wore clothes as if they were small, uncomfortable and restrictive. His face lit up when he saw her, and he leaped to assist her into the carriage. "I told you Mr. Throckmorton would explain everything," he said proudly.

"He certainly did." Enid settled herself in the carriage.

The carriage dipped as Mr. Kinman swung his great bulk inside. "Do you think you can help MacLean?"

"I'll have to examine him first." Furious and upset, she stared straight ahead.

"Mrs. MacLean!" Mr. Throckmorton hurried out of the garden to the open door of the carriage. "Let me assure you—you're performing a service for Her Majesty's government. You will be paid. Regardless of your husband's legacy, you'll not be left destitute at the end of your service."

Mr. Kinman looked shocked to hear money discussed, but Enid wanted to sag with relief. "Thank you, Mr. Throckmorton. That's good to know."

"While you're here, if you need anything, anything at all, you are to ask Kinman."

"Glad to do anything," Mr. Kinman said gruffly.

"We placed MacLean in one of the estate's cottages. I am going to be married the first of September." Mr. Throckmorton gave a brief, genuine smile, then sobered at once. "The cottage is quieter and more conducive to a recovery than the house, which is bustling with every kind of tradesman."

The cottage is easier to defend, Enid found herself thinking. And she remembered how, on the train from London, two guards had stood outside her compartment.

Mr. Throckmorton and Mr. Kinman were worried about something—or someone.

Had they lied to her? Was she in some kind of danger?

But she didn't ask those questions. These were men. The best of men believed a woman should be protected from unpleasant truths, and the worst of men believed women would gossip if told a secret. She judged Mr. Throckmorton and Mr. Kinman to be the best of men, and if they had lied once, they would lie again.

So she said only, "Don't worry, Mr. Throckmorton. I will protect myself—and my patient."

The carriage drove to a charming stone cottage surrounded by a white picket fence and covered with pink climbing roses. Leaning close to the window, Mr. Kinman scanned the area. "We transformed the attic into a sickroom. London sent us the best doctor to care for MacLean, but I don't believe—"

The carriage lurched to a stop. Before Mr. Kinman could finish, Enid stood. Before the footmen could descend, she opened the door. Now that she understood the extent of MacLean's injuries, she was anxious to see for herself what kind of dire situation she faced.

She noted how the footmen scurried to set the step, how Mr. Kinman steadied her from behind as she descended. Servants stood on either side of the gate, curtsying and bowing as she passed. Enid nodded, but she didn't stop. Only the wounded man inside mattered now.

She crossed the threshold into a large, bright room. The windows were opened to the summer breeze. A table with benches stood by the fireplace, where a small pot bubbled and steamed. A bed occupied one corner. Yet nothing interested her here; all her concentration focused on the wooden stair that rose in the middle of the room, straight and broad, to the dim opening in the ceiling. She put her foot on the bottom step and thought where these stairs would lead her. Back to Stephen MacLean and the turmoil of being his wife . . . or his widow.

As she climbed, the atmosphere grew still and stifling, rife with the smells of illness. She stepped into the attic. Curtains hung over the windows, allowing in only slivers of light. As her eyes adjusted, she saw the bed and the still form lying there. The floorboards creaked as she groped her way to MacLean's side.

As Mr. Throckmorton had promised, bandages swathed his face and chest. The counterpane covered the rest of him. He lay so still, so silent, that she couldn't even see the rise and fall of his chest. Fearfully, she leaned over him and touched his arm. He was still warm. Still alive. "MacLean," she said.

No response. His flesh was *too* warm; the muscles beneath her hand hung slack. Death hovered very near, and in a rush of fury she strode to the window, flung the drapes aside and opened the sash. Sunshine and fresh air rushed in.

A female voice squawked, " 'Ey!"

Enid turned on the unnoticed attendant as she rose from her place in the corner.

"Ye can't do that!" the beefy, drowsy-eyed woman said. "Th' doctor—"

"Is a fool if he commanded this," Enid finished. She heard a thump of boots as Mr. Kinman topped the stairs. "Go open that other window. You can't rouse a man if he doesn't know the sun is shining!"

Mr. Kinman's mouth hung slack, but he slapped it shut. "I don't know if I should."

"Mr. Kinman, do as I say!"

He did.

Returning to MacLean's side, she pulled the heavy covers back.

" 'E's got a fever!" the attendant protested.

"I would say he does. Who wouldn't, wrapped like some Egyptian mummy?"

"Look, miss, I don't know 'oo ye are, but I'm tellin' ye—"

"I'm his wife." Enid spaced the words, made them a threat.

The woman shrank back. Then her confidence rebounded, and she advanced on Enid. "Ye're th' wife? Ye're 'ere t' talk t'im, not tell yer betters 'ow t' do their jobs."

Her odor made Enid step back a pace. "Mr. Kinman, remove her, please. She smells of gin, she sleeps at her post, and this room is dirty and disorganized."

Mr. Kinman bowed and took the woman's arm.

"Ye can't remove me. I work fer Dr. Bridges!" the female yelled as she followed Mr. Kinman. "Ye'll hear about this!"

Enid didn't listen to the fading protests. Instead she leaned over the prone body of her husband and examined him. His forehead and the side of his face were bandaged, but no matter; she would never have recognized him. His nose had been broken. Swelling disfigured every visible part of his features. Blood seeped through the linen strips on his chest, and as she slowly pulled the covers back, she saw that the bandages extended all the way to his stomach and below the loose, short breeches he wore. His leg . . . his leg was splinted and raised on pillows, and every bit of him stank of sweat and sickness.

What had they been thinking, to treat him like some wayfarer felled on the road of life? If this was the best Her Majesty's government could do, then philistines and charlatans populated Her Majesty's government. Going to the stairs, she shouted, "Mr. Kinman!"

"Ma'am?" He sounded amazed by her ferocity.

"I want hot water immediately!"

"Yes, ma'am." He came to the bottom of the stairs and stared up at her with something akin to awe. "Mr. Throckmorton is on his way, ma'am."

"Good. I have a few words to say to Mr. Throckmorton." Indeed she did. As she peeled back the first of the bandages, she practiced those words. "If you want to save a man's life, you don't hire some slattern of a nurse and use some ignorant bumpkin of a physician. Incompetent, uncaring . . ."

Dear heavens. Her hands slowed as she revealed MacLean's face. She would never have recognized him. The explosion had obviously come from the right side, for that side of his face had been sliced and cut by a dozen shards. Each injury had been neatly stitched, but the swelling and bruising disfigured his cheek. He'd lost his earlobe, but his scraggly beard hid any injuries to his jaw. The fever had cracked deep grooves into the fullness of his lips. "MacLean?" Leaning close to his face, she looked again. She touched him using just her fingertips. That heat wasn't just his temperature. That heat was his will to live. If he could have moved, he would have grasped life in both hands and held it tightly.

She would have to do it for him.

But she didn't like the look of his wounds. "Mr. Kinman!" she called.

"Ma'am?" He had sneaked up the stairs and even now moved toward her on tiptoe, towels draped over his arm, extending the basin as if afraid to bring it closer.

"Put it on the bedside table."

He did.

She peeled away the bandages from MacLean's neck, chest and arms. Some of them stuck, and she glanced around. "Clean rags," she said. "Towels."

Mr. Kinman thrust them at her, then scuttled as far away as he could be and still remain in the room.

Dipping the rag in the warm water, she stroked MacLean's still face and sought some remnant of the man he had been. Beneath the swelling she discovered the broad cheekbones and forehead and angular jaw that had made her husband such a handsome man. But his nose, smashed as it was, looked larger and sharper than she remembered. The passage of time, the effects of the explosion, her own memories betrayed her. "MacLean, what have you done?" she murmured.

She dropped the crimson-stained bandages onto the floor in an ever-increasing pile. "Mr. Kinman, I need a bucket to dispose of these, and when I'm done washing him, I'm going to need help changing the sheets."

Mr. Kinman made an odd noise, and she glanced toward him.

With horrified fascination, he gazed at the dreadful

wounds she had revealed. Color washed from his cheeks, his eyes rolled up like those of an unbroken horse, and he hit the floor with a thud.

Too bad. She could have used the assistance. But she didn't have time to worry about him now. Mr. Kinman would stir by himself; her patient lay motionless beneath her hands. "Your friend is useless, did you know that?" she asked MacLean in a conversational tone. "A pleasant man, and probably good in a fight, but he's fainted clean away. I'm amused. Are you?" She watched MacLean for any sign that her words reached him.

Nothing.

"This explosion of yours did an amazing amount of damage." She gently probed his ribs. "Yet you were lucky. Perhaps you have some cracked ribs, but none are broken and stabbing you." As she washed each part of him, she dried it carefully and placed it beneath the blanket.

Each time she touched him, the sense of connection between them expanded. When he'd been healthy and her husband, she had never felt like this. Perhaps this tragedy had altered him—or perhaps the years had matured him, permeated his essence to such an extent she discerned them. Perhaps she'd changed, softened, grown forgiving. Or she realized that death hovered above them like a great dark raven, ready to snatch him away before they could write more of their history.

She could hear men moving below, a greeting, then the sound of footsteps on the stairs. Behind her, Mr. Kinman stirred and groaned, a great hulking man who feared the sight of blood. But only one thing was important now. To give MacLean a fighting chance. "MacLean."

She repeated his name, thinking surely he would respond to that above all else. "You could have lost an eye to the flying glass, but you were lucky there, too. And the break in your leg was dreadful." As the sound of booted feet grew closer, she began the torturous process of unwrapping the limb. "But somehow you've thrown off any infection. You'll walk again. So tell me, MacLean, why are you still asleep?"

"He's asleep, young lady, because of the blow he sustained to the head." A bewhiskered gentleman stood at the top of the stairs, dressed in brown tweed and smelling of tobacco. A superior gentleman, and from his expression, one given to scorn and an unwarranted haughtiness. "I'm Dr. Bridges, and I demand to know what you think you're doing!"

Mr. Throckmorton stood behind him in the shadows, and for all that he allowed Dr. Bridges to take the lead, Enid addressed only him, "Mr. Throckmorton, I'm washing MacLean. He was filthy." Enid tossed her rag into the basin. "Mr. Kinman, could I prevail upon you to discard this and bring more warm, clean water?"

Mr. Kinman groaned again, then crawled toward her and held up his hands.

She placed the basin in them and admonished, "Don't spill it."

"I won't," Mr. Kinman whispered. Staggering to his feet, he headed for the stairs.

Dr. Bridges's luxuriant mustache quivered with indignation at being ignored. "Young lady, I am a trained physician, a graduate of Oxford, and what you're doing is wrong."

"Perhaps it is, but what *you're* doing is killing him."

She kept her voice low, for if she didn't, she would have started shouting again, and that might disturb the patient.

She glanced at MacLean's slack features.

Although she might come to shouting yet, if that would wake him.

"Even a sick man deserves to be washed and to rest on clean sheets," she said.

"Those bandages were the only thing keeping the swelling down." Dr. Bridges gestured toward MacLean. "Look at him! Now that you've removed them, he's puffing up like a toad."

He was, and Enid's heart sank. If only she'd had time to finish assessing MacLean before facing her opponent and her judge. "I'll pack him in ice to keep the swelling down. Mr. Throckmorton, can you commandeer me ice?"

"Indeed." Mr. Throckmorton walked to the stairs, called down and gave the order, then returned to watch Enid and the doctor, weighing them both with austere resolution.

Mr. Kinman returned, looking a little less ill and a great deal more interested in the conversation. He set the basin on the bedstand and offered clean rags and a small towel filled with ice. When she took them he offered a quick nod of encouragement.

He didn't like the doctor, either.

Mr. Kinman stepped back to stand by Mr. Throckmorton.

She placed the towel across MacLean's nose and over his eyes, taking care that it should not block his airway. Wetting the rag, she stroked it over MacLean's thigh. She could clearly see the scarring where the bone had protruded through the skin. Yet the bone had set straight and true. If he survived, he would walk again, and she recognized that miracle.

"Fresh air. While you bathe him!" Like a spectator in a tennis match, Dr. Bridges looked from window to window. "The chill will kill him."

Enid's indignation rose anew. "This chamber was like a mausoleum, not a sickroom. How is MacLean to know when to wake if he's held in a prison?"

"Wake? You think he's going to wake? We can scarcely get water into him, and I'd like to know how you'll do better, young lady!" The doctor's whiskers quivered with resentment. "You've unwrapped his leg. I hope you haven't ruined that, too."

Dabbing the leg dry with a towel, Enid considered the situation. Mr. Throckmorton had no reason to trust in her skill, while Dr. Bridges held a degree from the most prestigious medical school in England. But Enid *had* to stay with MacLean. He needed her if he was to survive. More than that, the unconscious, emaciated form on the bed tugged at her soul. She didn't know why; he should be no more to her than any other patient.

In fact, if MacLean lived, she would still be bound to him, and if he died while in her care, she would be free. Yet something about this man tugged at her senses. Even unconscious, he exuded an aura of strength, of power, of irresistible allure. So she would do anything—beg, fight, even appease the doctor—for a chance to drag MacLean back to life. Nothing else was acceptable.

So although conciliation stuck in her throat, Enid offered an olive branch. "You did an excellent job with the leg, Dr. Bridges." Amazing though it seemed, he had. "A difficult break. Congratulations."

A profound silence settled on the room, and she glanced up from her ministrations.

"An Arab physician set the bone," Mr. Throckmorton said.

Dr. Bridges whirled to face Mr. Throckmorton. "He's going to die anyway! What difference does it make?"

Mr. Throckmorton's expression stilled. His eyes grew so cold that the temperature in the room dropped perceptibly. "Do you mean to tell me you've been treating *my friend* inattentively because you believe he can't be saved?"

Dr. Bridges wasn't an intuitive man, for he dared to answer, "I've done what I can for him, but I've never seen such dreadful wounds. Of course he's doomed."

Mr. Throckmorton snapped his fingers, then moved to stand beside Enid.

Taking the protesting doctor by the arm, Mr. Kinman hustled him down the stairs.

"I requested the best," Mr. Throckmorton said, chill fury in his tone. "And that's what I got?"

The anxiety that clutched at Enid's throat relaxed, and in a careful, nonjudgmental tone, she said, "Dr. Gerritson, the man who trained me, used to say trouble comes when the physicians believe in their own infallibility."

"Your Dr. Gerritson sounds like an intelligent man. How did you come to train with him?"

"After MacLean abandoned me, I had to pay off his

debts. So I assisted the village doctor with all manner
of injuries and illnesses. I didn't faint at the sight of
blood—I'd seen too much at the orphanage to get
queasy about anything. After I helped him set the
hostler's collarbone, he offered me a place working
with him. His wife said he was too old to work so hard.
She was right. He died three years later, and here I am."

Mr. Throckmorton watched in silence as she
bathed MacLean's wounds. "Will *you* be able to save
MacLean?"

"I don't know." MacLean was so ill. "I don't even
know if I can keep him alive through the night. But I
will try."

He didn't reproach her. Instead he asked, "What can
I do to assist?"

If only all men were so astute! "I need an attendant,
a sturdy woman of good size and sense who'll help me
move him, give him water and feed him should he
come to consciousness."

"I'll send Mrs. Brown to you. She's our nursemaid,
and a more sensible woman I've never met."

"I hate to deprive your children of their nursemaid."

"My daughter and my niece, and I assure you, my
fiancée will be thrilled to have the children to herself."
Mr. Throckmorton's smile twisted up on one side and
down on the other, and he looked like a man who
didn't know whether he was delighted or deprived.
"My fiancée was formerly their governess, you see."

Enid didn't see, but she didn't care, either. As long
as Mr. Throckmorton filled her needs, he and his be-
trothed could do and be whatever they wished. "If Mrs.
Brown is the best to be had, I'll take her and gladly. I
want maids to clean this room so I can bring some kind

of order to the unguents and linens and . . ." She gestured at the clutter about her. In the face of such a vital task, she needed sanitation and organization or her methodical soul would rebel.

"Maids. Immediately. I need herbs."

"My gardener will attend you."

She nodded, well-satisfied, and leaned over MacLean again.

"I would ask while you're here that you stay within the confines of the cottage unless accompanied by one of my men."

She glanced at him sharply. More precautions. "I can't imagine I'll have the desire to go anywhere until MacLean's on the mend."

"A walk in the garden every day will be a requirement, I think." Mr. Throckmorton took off his jacket and rolled up his sleeves. "Since Mrs. Brown is not yet available, I'll help you change the sheets."

As they worked, sliding the dirty linens out from beneath MacLean, replacing them with clean ones, rolling MacLean from side to side with utmost care, the late afternoon sun shone in the window and slowly climbed the bed, at last reaching MacLean's face and resting on the rugged features.

And with a long, rasping gasp, MacLean opened his eyes.

His distinctive, green-and-gold eyes.

Chapter 4

Each time MacLean awoke, he could see her, shining like a candle in the darkness. At first she hurt his eyes, glowing as she did with that inner radiance, but he looked as long as he could before sliding back into the void.

Later he heard a woman's voice talking to him, and he knew it was her. She filled his mind with images of trees pink with blossom, of people gruff and joyous, of songs sung on a Saturday's eve. Each image slipped away as soon as he tried to grasp it, and any effort brought pain. Pain in his leg, his chest, his face. He was tired of fighting the pain, so he sought refuge in the void.

Then she scolded him, called him, and the memory of that glowing face brought him back. Each time he opened his eyes, there she was.

Always she pounced on him, lifting him, filling him with fluid of every sort. Such activity vaguely troubled him. His body didn't crave anything. But his mind demanded to see her, and if being fed was the price he had to pay, he would do it.

He always fulfilled his obligations.

Usually he came back in the sunshine, but once he heard the roar of thunder, and he opened his eyes to the night.

She was beautiful then, too, the brightest flame in a room full of candles. She moved with such grace, leaning over him, her ruffled pink wrapper loosely tied, her hair braided into an ebony ripple. Her very skin gleamed like fine pale velvet, with a shimmer of pink about the cheeks, a deeper rose dusting the full lower lip, a faint golden sheen on the vee of her chest. Each lightning flash illuminated more of her: the delicate shells of her ears, the divine compassion of her fingers.

That night, for the first time, he discovered he wanted to be raised up and given water, or broth, or anything she chose to stuff down him. For if she held him, his head against her bosom, her arms around him, he could die happy.

He frowned.

Die? He wasn't going to die.

There was never a question of that.

"A beautiful morning, miss, after that storm last night." Mrs. Brown bustled into the sunlit room, white apron smoothed over her brown cotton dress, Enid's breakfast tray in her hands. "The old men in the clouds were playing hard at ninepins last night."

Arms raised, Enid turned from the small mirror on the wall and faced the woman who had been her greatest support during the long, grim fortnight. "I was awake." And she couldn't wait to share her news—although not all her news. Some things were meant to be kept secret.

Mrs. Brown placed the breakfast tray on the table by the window and hurried to help Enid put up her hair. The dark, abundant fall, which extended past Enid's hips, waved with a life of its own, but Mrs. Brown hadn't raised nineteen children for nothing. The tall, sturdy woman twisted the tresses in her strong hands until Enid's eyes slanted and she came up on her toes from the pain. She didn't complain, though; the novelty and joy of receiving motherly care far exceeded her discomfort.

As Mrs. Brown arranged the snood and secured it with pins, she asked, "Did the storm disturb him, miss?" Her broad face was serious as she nodded toward MacLean, silent and unresponsive on the bed.

Enid grinned with excitement. "I woke at midnight, and his eyes were open."

"Ah, is that the truth, then?"

Mrs. Brown acknowledged the report with her typical serenity, but Enid saw the satisfaction in her kind eyes. Mrs. Brown's endless good sense and cheery attitude had kept Enid going when exhaustion and discouragement would otherwise have brought her to tears. Mrs. Brown looked after Enid, too, sending her on walks, directing the undermaids to fetch and carry, to carry the linens and laundry and iron Enid's gowns.

"That's good news." Grasping Enid by the shoulders, Mrs. Brown steered her toward the breakfast tray. "He's never come awake without ye talking at him before."

"Very good news, I would think." Enid glanced at his still form as she seated herself.

"Your letter is here," Mrs. Brown said.

Enid snatched up the white sheet of paper and broke the seal. She scanned the first few lines. Lady Halifax claimed to be well, and, in fact, was well enough to make acerbic observations about her new nurse, the household and the state of the world in general. The weekly missives kept Enid's conscience at bay and the old lady's wit always made her laugh. She placed the letter on the table. "I'll write her this afternoon." Shaking out her napkin, she said, "I think MacLean is improving."

He *was* improving, for when she had finished feeding him his broth and she'd leaned over to tuck him in, he'd slid his hand inside her wrapper and cupped her breast! Not tentatively, not with trepidation, but with the smooth confidence of an aficionado of women.

She had jumped back and gasped, and as if the effort had exhausted him, his hand had fallen to his side and his eyes had shut.

She'd stood well away from the bed, holding the edges of her wrapper and saying aloud in a shocked tone, "Sir! That is uncalled for." As if he could hear her. As if he would care if he did.

And where had MacLean learned a move like that? His rampage through life had included a rampage in the marital bed, and he had usually left her behind in his frenzy and his rush.

"No doubt he is getting better, miss. He responds to ye. Yer voice." Mrs. Brown pulled out the chair and removed the covers from the food. "Yer touch."

"I believe you're right." An uprush of joy buoyed Enid. She had succeeded. MacLean had touched her. MacLean was definitely going to live.

"Eat yer breakfast. Esther sent along the season's first peach just fer ye."

Esther, the cook, sent the best produce and the finest cookery to Enid three times a day. Sometimes a plate of warm biscuits or a cool slice of pie arrived in between meals. Milford, the gardener, brought whatever herbs Enid required for her medicines, and every day the sickroom received a bouquet of flowers. Mr. Kinman appeared frequently to check on Enid, although he never stayed long enough to observe any sickroom rituals, and the three other gentlemen who guarded the cottage were deferential and kind.

But Enid concentrated on her patient. Even now, as she ate pork and potato pie and washed it down with apple cider, her gaze lingered on MacLean. He came to consciousness usually once a day, usually in the evening when sunshine touched his face. He stared fixedly at her but never spoke. He drank whatever water and broth she poured down him, but he never lifted a finger to help himself. It was as if his body demanded attention and he responded, but never did his mind surface to perform the functions necessary to his continued existence.

Mr. Throckmorton was frankly discouraged.

But MacLean was in there. Enid knew he was. She sensed a life in him, a spirit of strength and determination. She spoke to that spirit every day, telling him the story of her life, reading him the newspaper, commenting on the weather, giving her opinion on politics. At first Mrs. Brown had acted as if Enid were a little touched, then slowly the ample woman with the graying hair and the soft face had become convinced he did hear. When Enid would go for her daily walk, Mrs. Brown would converse with him about events on the estate and in the village. "But he likes to listen to ye best, miss," Mrs. Brown said often. "I can just tell."

Going now to the bed, Mrs. Brown laid her hand on his forehead. "No fever." She frowned down at him as she poured her palm full of oil. "My fingers itch to wash his hair, really wash it in a basin. 'Tis so filthy I can scarcely tell the color."

"It used to be a rather sandy blond."

Mrs. Brown squinted down at it. "Underneath all that oil, it looks to me to be an auburn."

"I suppose it's darkened as he aged." Memory brushed at her, and Enid chuckled. "He always thought he was losing his hair. He used to stare at the hairs in his brush and complain vociferously."

"It appears he was wrong."

"When he wakes and can move, we'll give him a bath in a tub." Enid brushed the rosy skin of the peach with her fingers and sniffed the ripe, sweet smell. "I imagine he'll be happy about that."

"Men are odd creatures. I had a son who went a month without changing his underwear, and protested when I burned them afterward." Mrs. Brown spoke in a slow, measured tone, like a guide providing a tour of male peculiarity.

Enid wrinkled her nose at the thought. "MacLean will be so weak he won't be able to fight us."

"I imagine he'll be so weak he'll scarcely be able to lift his own head." Picking up his arm, Mrs. Brown massaged the limp muscles. "We've got to get ye into shape," she addressed him. "A big, strong man like ye alyin' in bed for nigh on to two months. Ye must be bored to tears with yerself." Her big hands moved up to the shoulder and across the scarring of his chest, then moved and stretched his arm. They exercised him twice a day to slow the inevitable atrophy of muscle.

Enid watched pensively. Even now, with the weeks of service, she still scarcely recognized him as her husband. The swelling in his face had subsided under the steady application of ice. The scars on his chest and his right shoulder had faded from red to pink, and occasionally a shard of glass worked its way to the surface. All his bruises had healed, and she moved his leg cautiously, but with more confidence every day.

But his features, mangled by the explosion, had changed almost beyond recognition. Only the curve of his cheek and the set of his ears, always too big and far too protuberant, were the same. And his eyes, of course. She could identify those eyes anywhere— as pale green as spring grass, shot through with rays of golden sunlight. It was his eyes that she'd first noticed nine years ago, and his eyes that she prayed, every day, would open and gaze on her again with cognition.

"Ye'd be happier, sir, if ye'd wake and eat, too." Mrs. Brown gently hefted him onto his stomach and rubbed his back. "A man like ye wants potatoes and beef, not these tit-baby cups of broth we keep pouring down ye."

"Mrs. Brown!" Enid choked on a bite of the peach.

"He would not like being called a tit-baby, I can tell you."

"Then he should wake up and tell me so."

"Yes, he should." Still eating the fragrant fruit, Enid wandered over to the bedside. His head was turned sideways on the pillow, his cheek crushed into the clean linen. "I think he could tell us a lot if he only would wake." She waved the peach under his nose. "Smell that, MacLean. Doesn't it smell like summer mornings in the orchard? Don't you remember what it's like to pick a bushel of peaches, and feel the fuzz float down your back and collect in the creases of your neck and itch? Don't you wish you were out there, stretched in the grass, eating a peach fresh from the tree and watching the sun filter through the leaves while a faint breeze dusts your cheeks?"

Mrs. Brown's hands moved slowly along his back as Enid talked.

Caught up in the picture she had created, Enid knelt beside the bed and spoke softly, insistently, into his ear. "It's so beautiful outside. A summer like no other has been before, or will be again, and you're wasting it in the sickroom." She brushed his hair back from his face, wanting nothing so much as to see him open his eyes and hear him speak. She had worked too hard to return him to health to let him languish in this unconscious state. Beneath the surface his mind was stirring, and she longed to communicate with him, to discover if his aura of power and honor was a true representation of his being . . . or whether she had stitched it up from fragments of longing and threads of loneliness. She tried to lure him with voice and words and touch. "We could laugh together—lazy fools that we are—and tell stories about other summers more grand than this, but we would know we were lying, because this is the best time in the world. The sun is ours, the sky is blue, the scents are lush and full of fruit so ripe it hangs from the trees and flowers wild with bloom. Come back to me, MacLean, and I'll take you there."

Then he opened his eyes and said, "All right, you can take me there. But first, tell me—who are you?"

Chapter 5

The female stared at him, her startling blue eyes unblinking, her rosy lips slightly open as if she were surprised. She inhaled, long and slow, and in a measured tone repeated, "Who . . . am . . . I?"

If she were a man, he would have snapped her head off for such inanity, but he had a softness for women, all women, and this lass was a fetching piece. So fetching, in fact, he was surprised he didn't remember her name. He'd seen her before, and he'd wanted nothing more than to touch her, but he'd contented himself with just looking because . . . because . . . why didn't he remember her? He searched his memory. His excellent memory that had never failed him before. Why didn't he remember her?

What had she done to him?

In a voice harsh with suspicion, he demanded, "Who *are* you? I remember you, glowing, your hair tumbling about your shoulders, but . . . I can't recall . . . your name."

"Praise be, he's awake!" Another woman spoke from behind him.

He tried to fling himself around, to see who stood behind him at his unprotected back.

Pain struck at his joints, at his muscles, at his leg. With a vicious curse, he fell back on the bed.

The female kneeling beside the bed leaped to her feet and clutched his shoulders.

The other female grabbed at him. "Muscle cramps, sir, not surprising in yer condition," she said.

The women, whoever they were, were all over him now, chirping, holding, easing him onto his back. His leg, the center of that lancinating pain, dragged until the second wench lifted it and placed it on a pillow. Then he fell backward, panting.

The other female was older, plump and sharp-eyed, to all appearances a proper English villager. No threat. Not now. He glanced about the room. Treetops waved outside the open windows, the ceiling had open rafters and sloped down . . . so they kept him in an attic room. For what purpose?

What was wrong with him? Where was he?

Who was he?

Panic rose in him. Panic, which he subdued at once, and fury, which he allowed to grow. For he didn't know the answer to the most basic question of all. But he would get that answer, and now.

He looked again at the young woman. She watched him, eyes wide and shining. He knew her, damn it, but he couldn't remember her name. He remembered hearing her gentle voice regaling him with tales of her day. He remembered seeing her heart-shaped face leaning over him when he woke. He remembered how her eyes lit up when she smiled, how her tender hands smoothed his covers, how her rich, dark hair tumbled about her shoulders and brushed his cheek. He remembered the delightful curve of her breast peeking forth from her wrapper.

But he didn't remember tumbling her onto the mattress, and why else would he have seen her in such dishabille? What was happening? What did he remember?

Nothing. *Nothing.*

He struggled to raise up—*why wouldn't his body work?*—and demanded, "Who the hell am I?"

The female exclaimed and slid an arm under his head.

Behind him, the other woman said, "Whoa, dear sir, ye're in no shape fer wrestling," and caught at his shoulders.

"I want to sit up." His annoyance at his weakness could scarcely be expressed. This thought-blankness grew and grew until it filled his mind. No matter how he tried, no matter how he searched for memories, he found nothing.

He took command as he always did, giving orders in that clipped tone that got instant results.

But how did he know that?

"Women, you will tell me who I am and what I'm doing here right now." He'd make their lives hell if they didn't answer him, but how?

Who was he?

"Calmly. Move slowly."

The sweet-faced woman, the one with those extraordinary blue eyes and the sprightly breasts, leaned over him as he maneuvered on the bed, trying to find a comfortable position.

"You've been very ill," she said.

"I deduced that, you silly wench."

With a small offended huff, the female straightened hastily.

But he had no taste for tact. "I'm in bed. It's daylight. I don't lie about unless I'm ill. I've got too much to do."

But what did he do?

The other female, the gray one with the motherly face—*he recognized her, too, but why?*—leaned down close to him. She looked him in the eyes, and in a tone of voice she must have perfected through countless scoldings, she said, "Ye ha   look of trouble about ye even when ye were unconscious. Now ye listen to me, my lad. I'm Mrs. Brown. I'm going to get the master. He'll explain everything to ye, but in the meantime this young lady will care for ye. Don't ye do anything stupid. Don't try and get up, ye're not capable. Ye listen to me, and ye do exactly what this kind lady tells ye."

Like a sulky boy, he said, "Why should I?"

"Because she's the one who pulled you back from the brink of death, and I'm the one who's been wiping yer bare bottom."

He stared at her.

She stared at him.

He knew he was a warrior, and a warrior acknowledged when he'd been defeated. He nodded grudgingly, and with a shuffle of leather soles, the older female left.

The younger female laughed, one hand over her eyes.

"What's so funny?" he snapped. As if he didn't know.

She lifted her head. "We were so worried you would never wake up, and now that you have, you're more boorish than you ever were."

Two things caught his attention. She'd called him boorish, so she knew him. And her eyes were wet. She'd been laughing, but she'd been crying, too. A funny sort of a thing for a damsel to do.

But everything seemed odd today. His body, which usually performed as he required, throbbed with pain. His face hurt when he spoke. And his leg . . . what had he done to his leg to make it hurt like this? He could scarcely lift his hand, and when he did, he stared at it. Skeletal. Wasted. The precariousness of his physical condition became more and more clear, and it infuriated him. Infuriated him almost as much as this vast blankness. He turned his gaze on the lass and found her watching him, her eyes grave. "I've got little mind to wait for this master," he said. "You know who I am. Tell me."

Without hesitation, she told him, "You're Stephen MacLean of the Isle of Mull." She stopped there, waiting while he tasted the name on his tongue.

"Stephen MacLean." Were the syllables familiar? Were the sounds a compilation of him? He shook his head. "I dinna ken."

She chuckled, but her laughter wobbled with emotion. "You *have* been sick, if you're speaking a bit of the Scot. You had nothing but scorn for Scotland before."

"The best place on earth," he said, and frowned. He had no memory of ever saying those words before, but he spoke them with involuntary fervor. "Who are you?"

She stared at him as if weighing his strength.

How dare she even consider that she had the right to make decisions about his well-being? He, who was the . . . who was he? Spacing the words like a slow, measured threat, he said, "You will tell me who you are at once."

With a scornful smile and a toss of her pretty head, she announced, "I am your wife."

Never taking his gaze off the woman, MacLean ignored the pain in his body and gradually lifted himself onto his elbows. "Liar."

Her eyebrows lifted. Her mouth opened slightly. She stared at him, then threw back her head and burst into laughter.

If he could have stood, he would have strangled her.

But she stopped laughing almost at once. "Well, I've imagined this scene many a time, but I never imagined that response." Drawing nearer in a slow, cautious pace, she asked, "Why do you think I'm a liar?"

"I don't remember you."

"You claim you don't remember anything at all."

This woman, this female, this liar did not believe his assertion that he had lost his memory. No one ever doubted his word, because . . . he didn't know why, but he knew he was the pillar of honesty and integrity. He *was*.

White with fury, he demanded, "You dare . . . doubt me?"

"So we're even."

His gaze measured her from top to toe. She wore a dark green cotton gown almost military in its severity and buttoned up to the neck. Her waist was trim, and if her petticoats hid the curve of her hips, well, he had an imagination and he used it now. A fine-looking woman. A little too thin, but she'd done something right in her childhood to grow into such a fine lass.

If his appraisal perturbed her, she showed no sign. Nor did she show earthy enthusiasm or spicy interest. She stood with her hands clasped at her waist, looking at him with calm interest, waiting for his verdict.

His wife? Not likely. His wife, if he looked her over with frankly carnal attention, would damned well respond with a smile and a flutter of sooty eyelashes.

He sank back on the pillows. Married. No. Not to her.

Without a qualm, he said, "You're not my wife. No man would forget making love to you."

She didn't blush or stir, and her voice contained all of the chill of the wind off the North Sea. "Apparently *you* have."

So they were at quits, and at odds.

Why did she lie to him? Why was he here? A faint unease crawled up his spine as he tried once more to remember . . . remember . . . what? Something bad, something perilous. His instincts warned him of danger, and he always trusted his instincts.

"What's your name?" he demanded.

"Enid MacLean."

"Enid." A good name. He liked it, even as he wondered if she lied about that, too. "Where am I?"

"In Suffolk, in England."

She answered him readily enough. "What happened to me?"

"You were visiting the Crimea."

In his most neutral voice, he questioned, "Without you?" He detected a moment of hesitation in her.

Then, "Yes. There was an explosion. You were hurt, another man killed."

The Crimea. He didn't remember such a trip, although he well knew the Crimea was a bit of soil and sand sticking out into the Black Sea.

Why did he remember that?

An explosion. He tried to sit up and look down at himself, but he had exhausted his strength in his earlier, feeble struggles. And that enraged him yet again. "Are all my parts intact?" he demanded.

"Yes."

He didn't believe her. He wiggled his toes. Painfully moved his legs and his arms. Told her, "Turn your back if you have any modesty."

She did, but when he'd got done groping himself, finding the important parts were indeed still there, he noted a fiery blush climbing the back of her neck. "I can't believe you're embarrassed, lass. You've got me in nothing but a pair of trousers cut off at the knee, and drafty it is."

"It was easier for us to tend your wounds," she defended herself stiffly.

"You can turn around now."

Cautiously she peeked around, and when she saw his hands on top of the covers, she faced him again.

"If you were really my wife, you would be glad I still possess the wherewithal to bring you to bliss."

"If you were much of a husband, I would be."

"If I could rise from this bed, you wouldn't say that to my face."

"You don't know me at all." If she had any affection for him, any feeling at all, she hid it behind those expressionless features, schooling herself like some military sergeant in charge of supplies.

More proof she was not his wife. "When was the explosion?"

"Six, almost seven weeks ago."

He snorted. "Come, miss, you don't expect me to believe that. In six weeks, I'd be dead."

"You should be dead."

She didn't look deceitful, but he'd met beautiful liars before . . . *where?* And suspicion haunted him because . . . *why?* What made him watch her so cynically, when everything about her shouted sincerity?

"You want something to drink." Hurrying to the pitcher, she poured him a mug of water.

"Aye, that I do." His stomach rumbled, and he realized the demands of his body had overridden the demands of his mind. "And eat!" Craftily, he inquired, "Have I been in prison? Was I starved?"

"In a manner of speaking." Coming to his side, she eased her hip onto the bed and slid her arm behind his shoulders to lift him. He tried to take the mug; she held it up out of his reach. "You'll drop it."

"A mug?"

"What do you think?"

He thought he liked snuggling up against her bosom. He thought he'd been here before. He recognized the faint scent of gardenias that clung to her. Intimacy . . . familiar intimacy.

Letting her bring the mug to his lips, he drank greedily, the taste pristine in its purity.

Was it possible that he was wrong? That he had forgotten making love to her, that she was his wife?

No. By God, he couldn't have forgotten that.

"Mr. Throckmorton has had water brought in for you from a spring in Yorkshire," she told him. "You've come to consciousness occasionally, long enough to let us fill you with water and broth, but you didn't talk and you didn't seem to hear us." Her hand shook, and the mug clattered against his teeth. "Do you remember now? Are the memories coming back?"

He gasped as he finished drinking—even that bit of activity exhausted him. "No." Making the effort, he grasped her wrist to keep her in place. "Who's Mr. Throckmorton?"

"He's the master of Blythe Hall, the one Mrs. Brown went to fetch. He's . . . your friend?"

She was implying a question. *Do you remember him?* MacLean shook his head in answer.

"Mr. Throckmorton owns this estate, where you have been recuperating." She disengaged herself from his hold. "Let me get you something to eat."

She walked toward the stairway, leaving him incensed that she had eluded him with so little trouble, desolate from the loss of her touch, and resentful that he depended so much on a female, even a female who claimed to be his wife. "What do you mean, boorish?" he demanded.

Swinging to face him, she shook her head as if confused. "What?"

"You said I was as boorish as ever."

"Oh." She glanced at the stairway as if longing for

escape, then took a slow step back toward him. "You and I are estranged."

"Nonsense." He spoke without thinking. "I would never be estranged from my own wife."

"Again you call me a liar. As I said—boorish." With a flounce, she walked to the stairway and called to someone below, "I need a cup of broth. Don't dally!"

As she returned to his side, he saw the flame in her burning so brightly that she brought a memory back. The night. The lightning. The weight of her breast in his hand. The sharp sense of possession, of rightness.

All right. It was possible. She could be his wife. A lying Jezebel kind of a wife, but if he had wed her, he had tamed her before. He would tame her again.

"Come here," he said softly, wrapping her in a blanket of command.

If she was impressed, she hid it well. With her hands on her hips, she inquired, "What do you want?"

He didn't think she'd be easily manipulated, but this weakness prevented him from going after her, so he had to try. "You're afraid of me. A big, strong lass like you, and you're afraid of me."

"I am not!"

"Then come here. It's not as if you can't leave whenever you wish."

"Oh, for heaven's—" She knelt beside the bed, taking the same position she'd been in when he'd awoken. "What?"

Ah, she was a girl with no experience of a man's guile. A girl he could play like a little silver fish on a hook. Rolling onto his side, he caught her face in his hands.

She pulled back.

"I want to kiss you," he said.

"Why? I'm not your wife. I'm a liar."

"Sarcastic lass!" He caressed the curve of her cheek. "And you say I'm a liar, too, who remembers and doesn't admit to it. A couple of right suspicious sorts we are. But the truth is, I don't remember anything. Not my name, not my place, not why I'm in pain or how it happened. So I'm searching for a memory, and if you're my wife, you are the key. The only thing here in Suffolk in England that is familiar to me. So grant me the kiss I want, because I need to know who I am, and I'm too weak to hold you."

Guilt purchased him what force could not. She bit her lip, then sighed with extravagant petulance, closed her eyes and pursed her lips.

He laughed softly and tilted her head to his. Ah, the touch of her tender mouth against his! No matter that she was unwilling or exasperated. Just as he knew where the Crimea was located, that he was a warrior and a Scot, and that he had reason to be suspicious of his circumstances, so he knew how to gentle an unwilling woman with kisses.

He kissed Enid over and over, small, gentle, swift busses that landed on the corner of her mouth, on her lower lip, even on the tip of her nose. Her cherished pucker of disdain relaxed as she tried to keep up, to understand his strategy. That's when he pressed his mouth exactly on hers. He learned the contours of her lips, their plush texture, that sweet indent at the top, the width that made a man plot erotic joys. All the while, she caught her breath repeatedly as if startled by his every advance. For a moment he thought of pulling back and asking how long they'd been estranged. Then he diagnosed such a deed as insanity and slid his fingers around to cup her head.

She noticed at once he'd imprisoned her. She tried to draw back, but he wasn't as feeble as she would have liked. At least not when he had good and rightful reason to use his strength. He held her, coaxed her, coerced her . . . deepened the kiss. Her mouth opened under his, and she jolted him with her sweet wetness, the taste of spice and the warmth of wonder. She withheld her tongue, so he went seeking it, little forays into the depths of her mouth, searching for and finding all her secrets, and showing her how well he could use those secrets against her. She responded tentatively at first, then as he got her used to him and his wickedness, she brought her hands up and cupped his face just as he cupped hers.

Held captive by a female. By a female who claimed to be his wife and, even if she weren't, would soon thrash beneath him in delight.

The world held no greater pleasure than coaxing an unwilling woman.

He wanted to laugh aloud when his body—aching, wounded, weak—stirred to life. He could scarcely lift his head, his leg burned, and as far as he could tell, he'd been near death. But his pecker, valiant, aggressive, none-too-bright, still reared its impudent head and demanded to be serviced. Ah, it was good to be a man, to be alive on this sunshiny day . . . to be kissing this bonny lass who gave him such incentive to thrive.

But not now. Anything he tried now would end in ignominious collapse. Besides . . .

Withdrawing by degrees, he brought the kiss to an end. He kissed her wrist, smoothed her hair back from her face, and waited until she opened her eyes. Her heavy lids and dazed expression fueled his masculine pride, and for a moment he almost returned to the chase. But he hadn't the strength, and so instead he said, "Dearling, we have company."

Chapter 6

Gasping, Enid came to her feet in a rush and covered her hot cheeks with her hands.

Mr. Throckmorton. Mr. Kinman. Mrs. Brown. Sally, one of the scullery maids who had so often come bearing a meal. That gatehouse keeper with the hard face—what was his name? Harry. And a strange man she had never met before. All lined up staring as if they'd never seen a man kiss a woman.

Mr. Kinman's jaw dropped.

How long had everyone been standing there—and why had she not heard them walking up the stairs?

As if she didn't know.

Because she'd been experiencing the most delicious, exotic, erotic kiss she'd had in years.

All right. Ever.

Even now her hands trembled, her breath caught, and the heat in her face was not solely from mortification. MacLean had set her ablaze, and if they'd been alone and he'd been healthy, she would have . . . and really, how healthy did a man have to be to perform between the sheets? Lady Halifax claimed that men were capable of every kind of licentious behavior regardless of their age, intelligence or vigor.

Dropping a curtsy, Enid stammered, "Mr. . . . Mr. Throckmorton! Excuse me. I'm sorry. I didn't see you."

"I'll say you didn't," Mrs. Brown muttered.

"No, please, Mrs. MacLean, excuse *us*." Mr. Throckmorton proved his discretion when he bowed and without so much as a sly wink, said, "We thoughtlessly interrupted a long-awaited reunion."

No, you didn't, Enid wanted to say. *I haven't been waiting for MacLean at all.*

She saw no graceful way out of this embarrassment, and when she heard an indulgent chuckle from the bed behind her, she wanted to turn and land MacLean a blow. Perhaps he'd forgotten how many pugilistic skills she'd learned at the orphanage . . . well, of course he had if he didn't remember anything, but she'd be glad to jog his memory.

"MacLean." Mr. Throckmorton strode to the bed, took MacLean's emaciated hand gently in his and shook it. "You had us worried."

"I would imagine." MacLean didn't appear gratified to have a man of such importance drop everything to attend him. Instead he watched Mr. Throckmorton coolly, taking his measure before bestowing his confidence.

MacLean had his nerve . . . but Enid had already discovered that.

Mr. Kinman shambled over next, a big, overgrown

man who stood looking down at MacLean with a grin on his face. " 'Bout time you woke up," he said.

Perhaps MacLean didn't remember him, but such was Mr. Kinman's unadulterated delight that MacLean returned the smile. "Lazy as an old yellow dog, that's me."

Mr. Kinman hit him gingerly on the shoulder. "That's you," he echoed in a rumbling voice choked with emotion.

Enid's stomach tightened on seeing MacLean's importance to these men. These last few weeks, everything in her mind and soul had been concentrated on MacLean. Ill, unconscious, wounded as he had been, he had been *hers*. Now he was awake, he spoke, he listened, he looked at everyone else. She had been demoted to the role of caretaker. Which is, of course, what she was. She preferred the part.

At least he didn't kiss the others, she thought, and promptly blushed at her own foolishness.

"How do you feel?" Mr. Throckmorton asked him.

"As if I've been beaten and starved." MacLean gestured to the maid. "Is that food on that tray?"

"Aye, sir." Mrs. Brown hurried to him, Sally in her wake. "Let me slide another pillow beneath yer shoulders and we'll get some broth into ye."

MacLean's eyes narrowed. "Broth! I don't want broth, I want real food."

He had come awake with a vengeance.

"Mrs. MacLean has the final say on yer care." Mrs. Brown courteously turned to Enid. "Mrs. MacLean, what have ye to say to that?"

"Hm?" Enid wrenched her mind away from the turmoil of her emotions and back to the business at hand.

"Oh! Broth now, and once we see if he holds it down we'll start him on soft foods."

He groaned. "I have a taste for peaches."

"Tomorrow," she promised, but she didn't look at him. *Couldn't* look at him. Smug, self-satisfied. When had he learned to kiss like that? And with whom? And why was she jealous of some faceless woman now when for eight years all she'd asked of fate was that MacLean stay far, far away from her?

She moved to help Mrs. Brown raise him on the bed but found herself supplanted by Mr. Throckmorton and Mr. Kinman, both of whom assisted Mrs. Brown effortlessly. Enid watched as Mrs. Brown lifted the mug of broth off the tray, and decided she wasn't needed. Decided she was glad of it.

"I'm Throckmorton," he introduced himself. "This is Kinman, my right-hand man. That's Harry over by the door, he's in charge of the gatehouse, and that fellow with the crossed arms is Jackson. I've hired him as your valet, to care for you and your clothing, to shave and bathe you as you wish."

A valet? Enid looked at Jackson, who moved to the bedside and bowed. Jackson was of medium height and age, with brown hair, slightly stooped shoulders, gold-rimmed glasses, and the most impressive set of side-whiskers she'd ever seen. He might have been innocuous except for his superior air, which many valets considered so much a part of their nature.

A valet. Enid's duties were swiftly disappearing.

Enid moved back toward the stairway, back to Harry's side. "MacLean's awake," she said unnecessarily.

"He is." Harry never took his gaze off the bed. "Will he recover?"

"It's too early to tell." She hesitated. "But yes. I think so. If sheer willpower can make it so, he'll recover."

"Willpower." Harry sounded skeptical. "Does it mean so much?"

"It means everything. I've cared for a great many patients, and it's their will that keeps them alive past their time. Willpower that drives them to recover. Or a lack of will that brings them to an untimely end."

"MacLean has always had the most fortitude of any man I've ever met."

Fortitude? Stephen MacLean had fortitude?

"I would never have recognized him." Harry turned his remarkably large brown eyes on her. "Would you?"

She didn't like Harry, she realized. She didn't like him or trust him at all. He watched too intensely. He dressed in dark clothing. He stood too tall, and with the coiled tautness of a steel spring. His size, his strength, everything that should have made him a good bodyguard instead exuded a faint sense of threat.

But she didn't know him. Certainly Mr. Kinman trusted him, and more important, Mr. Throckmorton.

And she . . . she had suffered too many changes in her life lately. She'd had too little sleep and too much worry. She should remember—she had proved herself to be a poor judge of character. She had married Stephen MacLean. So she contented herself with a mere, "MacLean is greatly changed."

"Enid!" MacLean sounded testy. "Come here, Enid. You know I'm too weak to hold this mug by myself."

She did, but that he would confess such a weakness filled her with suspicion. She approached. The crowd around his bedside parted. Like an Eastern potentate, he lolled on the pillows. How easily he had moved from a coma to dominating a room full of people. And he was trying to extend his domination to her.

Her steps slowed. She badly wanted to defy him.

He scowled at her, commanded her attendance with his gaze.

Who did he think he was?

Her husband.

But no. He'd said she'd lied to him. He'd said he didn't believe they were married. She knew the truth. He was her husband, Stephen MacLean—reprobate, gambler, knave. Probably *he'd* perjured himself when *he'd* said he didn't remember anything. Stephen MacLean had always been the kind of man who would rather tell a lie when the truth would do. But there was something about him—the brief show of panic, the irrational fury—that made her think that in this matter, at least, he told the truth.

She owed him nothing except the care for which she was paid to provide—and he did need care. He had just come to consciousness. He might slip away from them at any moment.

Accepting the mug from Mrs. Brown, Enid sat beside him on the bed. She slid her arm behind his head and lifted the mug to his lips. He drank that as greedily as he'd swallowed the water, and she extended the mug to Mrs. Brown for a refill.

He glanced up at her, then around at the assemblage. "Now, dear lass, are you going to burp me?"

The men laughed, relieved from the tension created by seeing one of their own fed like a baby.

The women exchanged exasperated glances.

Enid accepted the broth and held it for MacLean.

This time he sipped more slowly and with a great deal more caution. She observed him as she had observed him these last weeks, hoping he would keep everything down, praying that this time he would sleep to wake again.

Now he was awake, and she couldn't seem to cease her vigilance.

It wasn't healthy for a man to be the center of anyone's existence; men already had exaggerated ideas of their own importance.

Mr. Throckmorton looked around at his minions. "You know this, but I must impress on you the importance of silence. No word of MacLean's recovery must be allowed to leak out. My wedding is fast approaching. There will be guests aplenty at Blythe Hall. A single mistake could put his life in jeopardy."

All faces looked solemn. All heads nodded. All except MacLean's; he watched Mr. Throckmorton with cynical interest.

Nor did Enid nod. Instead she again wondered why such a protective net extended over the person of her husband.

"I will speak to MacLean alone," Mr. Throckmorton said.

Sally left first with a bob of a curtsy. Mrs. Brown followed. Jackson bowed again, then descended the stairs. Mr. Kinman headed for the door and paused beside Harry, who stood still, his brown eyes dwelling on MacLean, then on Enid, with sober intensity.

The way he watched them made her uncomfortable. She realized MacLean's head rested in the crook of her arm. That she must appear protective and . . . affectionate.

She tried to remove her arm.

Catching her hand, MacLean held it firmly in his grasp.

She could have gotten free, of course. His wasted muscles had no power. But from the little she knew of this MacLean, he wouldn't give up without a fight. Such a struggle would be undignified.

Mr. Kinman clapped his hand to Harry's shoulder. "Come on, man, we'll go have a drink to celebrate. Then it's back to work. We've got a lot to do in the weeks before the wedding."

After a final, measured stare, the gatehouse keeper descended the stairs.

Enid moved to put the mug down so she could leave, but MacLean squeezed her fingers gently and challenged Mr. Throckmorton with his tone. "Not you, you're my wife."

"Now I'm your wife?" Enid mocked. "Quite a change from an hour ago."

"Of course you're his wife," Mr. Throckmorton said. "And you should stay."

MacLean rubbed his cheek against her hand. "There. We have a ruling from an authority. We are married."

Enid wanted to reply smartly, but she became a shadow in the chamber as the two men sized each other up. Their concentration, the sense of power each man exuded astounded Enid. Of course Mr. Throckmorton possessed that indefatigable air of command, but MacLean seemed to possess it, too, and when had that happened?

"So there's going to be a wedding here," MacLean said. "Who's getting married?"

"I am." Going to the hole in the floor, Mr. Throckmorton shut the door on the stairway and the room below. "Mrs. MacLean, I would like you to keep this locked at all times when you are alone with your husband."

"Why?" Enid and MacLean demanded together.

"There will be a great many strangers here for my wedding, and I would rest more easily if I knew you to be undiscovered."

Mr. Throckmorton's answer was no answer at all, but before Enid could question him further, MacLean said, "Congratulations on your upcoming nuptials. I can't imagine what sort of lass would be so foolish as to tie herself to a morose bastard like you." MacLean looked startled at his own joking, friendly comment.

"Wait until you see her," Mr. Throckmorton said. "Celeste is beautiful. She's charming. She's too intelligent for her own good. You'll really wonder what she's thinking then."

"You're rich?"

Mr. Throckmorton nodded.

"Is she of like circumstances?"

"Poor as a church mouse. But she loves me for myself." Not a hint of sarcasm colored his tone; Mr. Throckmorton was a happy man and didn't care who knew it.

MacLean's mouth turned down. "You *believe* that?"

Appalled, Enid chided, "MacLean, how rude!"

MacLean picked her hand off his shoulder and kissed it. "I'm a rude lad, I think."

But Mr. Throckmorton didn't seem to be offended by MacLean's insolence. Placing his fists on the mattress, he leaned over MacLean. "Even if I didn't, I wouldn't care. If I had to bribe her to marry me, I'd do it. I would do anything to have Celeste."

"Then you're a fool," MacLean said.

Mr. Throckmorton grinned. "You lied—as a safeguard, no doubt. You *do* still have your memory."

Anticipation gripped Enid. *Did* MacLean remember?

"No." MacLean looked him right in the eyes. "I don't."

Hope faded again, and Enid sighed.

A silence fell on the chamber. Not a silence such as had wrapped them 'round for the last fortnight, but a thoughtful silence. A guarded silence.

Enid watched the two men, wondering how Mr. Throckmorton would take the disappointment, seeing how MacLean waited, apparently relaxed, while waiting for the reaction.

Straightening, Mr. Throckmorton said, "You're a suspicious sort. You always have been. That's one of your qualities that first attracted my attention."

"Am I? I don't remember."

"You say you don't remember, yet you always were pessimistic about marriage."

"I still am, although I can't tell you why." MacLean glanced up at Enid. "Especially when I've taken such a bonny lass to wife."

Mr. Throckmorton's gaze flicked from one to the other.

"Of course, she tells me we've been estranged."

"I . . . yes, you were." Mr. Throckmorton paced away.

"Perhaps that's the reason for my cynicism." MacLean closed his eyes for a moment as if the excitement had tired him.

In a tone so noncommittal as to be dry, Mr. Throckmorton said, "I had to bring Mrs. MacLean here in the hopes you would revive for her sake."

"As I have. It was her sweet voice that guided me to consciousness." MacLean's thin face creased as he smiled at her with an edge so sharp it cut her like a razor. "But not to memory."

Mr. Throckmorton paced back to the foot of the bed and grasped the rails between his fingers. "I will tell you the truth, MacLean. I can't shake the suspicion that you remember everything but fear I may have betrayed you. Yet if I'd had anything to do with the explosion, you'd be dead now. You're on my land; it would have been no problem at all to have had your life snuffed out."

"I may have information you need," MacLean said flatly.

"You do."

Enid shrank from their intensity.

Mr. Throckmorton said, "We believe—we hope—you have some knowledge of who set that bomb, killed our man and injured you. If I didn't want that information known, I could have had you killed. Knowing this, I have to ask you again—is it true you remember nothing?"

Enid found herself holding her breath.

"Nothing," he whispered, as if grieved, and his eyelids drooped. "I remember nothing."

"Very well," Mr. Throckmorton said. "I believe you. I have no choice."

"Where . . ." MacLean seemed to be struggling to stay awake. "Where are my things?"

Enid was startled. "Your things?"

"I must have something that is mine. If I could see and touch and smell the pieces of my past, perhaps I could remember . . ."

"You came away from the bombing with only your kilt and your sporran."

"My sporran. Yes. I want my sporran." As quickly as MacLean had awoken, he slumped on the pillows.

In a panic, Enid leaned close to his face. His breath dusted her cheek. She placed her fingers on the pulse of his neck. His heart beat strongly beneath her touch. Easing away, she answered Mr. Throckmorton's unasked question. "He's fine. Just exhausted."

"He'll wake again?"

"There are no absolutes in human health—but yes, I think so."

Mr. Throckmorton sighed. Walking to the window, he stared out at the garden. "How long will this loss of memory last?"

"I don't know. I have no experience with riddles of the mind." She put the mug on the tray and noted that her hand trembled. "I've heard of patients claiming they didn't remember anything, but I always thought it was silly, a story concocted by the guilty or the insane."

Mr. Throckmorton faced her. In a voice of displeasure, he said, "MacLean has no reason to feel guilty."

"I hope not." No recent reason, anyway.

"And he's not insane."

"Heavens, no!" She shook her head with a little more calm. "No, he is not."

"All right." Mr. Throckmorton took her hands. "Feed him. Make him better. When his body is healthy, his mind will heal, too."

"I hope so." Although she liked this enfeebled husband better than the physically whole one she'd had before. "I think so."

"I'll send Mrs. Brown to you." Mr. Throckmorton went to the trapdoor and opened it. "Lock this behind me, and open it only to one you know."

Enid stared after him, then hurried to obey him. The sturdy bolt slid into place with a click. The quagmire in which she found herself grew deeper and more perilous by the moment. She feared she would be sucked below the surface. More than that, she feared, despite Mr. Throckmorton's assurances, that MacLean might be in danger, and she knew herself only too well. While he was helpless, she would do anything, even risk her own life, to save him.

She would do the same for any patient, she assured herself. She would; nothing about MacLean and that kiss could remove the sting of eight years of poverty and debt.

"What is your impression of Throckmorton?"

At the gravelly sound of MacLean's voice, Enid almost jumped out of her skin. She faced him and saw how he struggled to keep his eyes open, how his skin had bleached to the shade of parchment, how he remained awake only through the exercise of his will. "You need sleep," she said. "You haven't the strength for this kind of exertion."

"What do you think of Throckmorton?"

Weak as a lamb, stubborn as a mule! MacLean wouldn't stop asking until she'd given her opinion, and so she said, "I like him."

MacLean wheezed with laughter. "But is he telling the truth?"

"Yes. I mean, I think so. He has given me no reason to think otherwise." She came to MacLean's side, lifted his head and gave him another drink of water. "He's right. He could have had you killed at any time."

"If I've discovered information he wants, and the information exists only within my mind, then Throckmorton would wish to keep me alive until I've given up that information. When he has the information, then he can kill me."

"Oh." She hadn't thought of it that way. "I never excelled at logic."

"That's what you have me for." MacLean's eyelids drooped and his voice became slurred. "Throckmorton might not be an ally. He might well be my executioner."

"So you really don't remember."

Smiling, he shook his head.

But she began to comprehend the labyrinth of distrust and skepticism through which they wandered. "But I work for Mr. Throckmorton, and you don't remember that I'm your wife."

"Not so awful at logic, after all." He smiled at her with that cruel, sharp smile. "You could be my executioner, too." His eyelids slid shut. "And there isn't a damn thing I could do about it." He was asleep.

She stood looking down at him. The swelling on his face had subsided, leaving the harsh bone structure unsoftened by a padding of healthy flesh. Instead his skin was slashed and scarred, his blade of a nose hooked where it had been broken, his beard was scraggly and colored blond and auburn with sprinkles of gray. His lips . . . when she'd first come, they'd been cracked with fever. She'd rubbed them with ointment, bringing them to a state of wide, pale smoothness. Truth to tell, she'd fallen a little in love with his lips. Not that she'd gone so far as to imagine another kiss, but she had found pleasure in their shape, their velvety texture, the way they might feel if they brushed her neck, her chest, her . . . well, she found pleasure in their velvety texture.

She still didn't recognize Stephen MacLean, but as each day passed and she concentrated solely on the man in the bed, the old memories faded. He would never again resemble the man she'd married, but perhaps that was a good thing, for he gave every appearance of wanting . . . things she wasn't ready to give.

He'd kissed her. More important, she'd kissed him back. That kiss had succeeded because MacLean had caught her by surprise. Yes, that was it. He'd caught her unawares, and her response had been a reaction more to years of deprivation than to real passion. She needed to remember who he was. What he had done. To her. To others, too. Stephen MacLean had never been too concerned with telling the truth or allowing others to retain what was theirs. They'd fought about that, and many a time he'd taunted her, called her an orphan who didn't understand how her betters lived.

When this man's memory returned, his old, feckless personality would return. She knew it. No man changed as MacLean had changed. She needed to remember that because . . . because if he stayed the man he had been for this brief hour, she could develop a passion for him.

She'd suffered through infatuation once, and the results had almost brought her to her knees. The thought of springing that trap again frightened her as she hadn't been frightened for eight long years. Her gaze fixed on the unconscious man, she freed her fingers from his and retreated from the bed.

Plagued by sleep terrors, he jumped. He groaned. His eyes fluttered open and glanced wildly about him. His gaze found her, and he sighed. "Stay with me."

She heard the undercurrent of desperation in his voice. She didn't want to feel sorry for him. She didn't want to make promises.

He tried to struggle up on his elbows. "Stay," he insisted.

"I'll be here when you wake."

He extended his hand.

Helpless to resist, she returned.

He grasped her fingers. "I need you."

Surely there could be no harm in promising such a simple thing. "I won't leave."

On that assurance, he was asleep. Really asleep this time. But even in slumber, he clung to her.

Sighing, she hooked her foot around the straight-backed chair and brought it around so she could sit. "I want you to understand something," she told the sleeping man. "I'm not promising forever."

Chapter 7

MacLean opened his eyes to candlelight. He knew where he was immediately. In an attic room in Suffolk, his body torn by an explosion, his mind blank and still—and the woman who called herself his wife hovering close over him like a restless spirit. "What is wrong, woman?" he snapped.

Enid straightened and backed up a long, slow step, her spine stiff with displeasure. "You've slept long, ten hours since this morning. We feared you wouldn't again wake."

"You'll not be so lucky again." His leg hurt, his butt ached. He groped for another pillow to put under his shoulders.

Enid sprang to his assistance. "You're a more pleasant man when you're unconscious."

The village woman he'd met earlier—Mrs. Brown, her name was—stood at the foot of the bed, and she gave her unwanted opinion. "Most men are. Most babes, too."

Enid's smile came as suddenly as a spark to flint. "I suppose there's a lesson to be learned there."

For all that he wanted to nip at her for her insolence, he was so stricken by the dimple in her chin, the lilt in her voice, the sparkle of her teeth, that he could do no more than stare. Gads, when she was happy everything about her shouted her joy.

She hadn't smiled at him before. Not once. Not ever.

He couldn't have forgotten her.

Damn it. Damn it! His name. His home. His mother, his father, his kin. What had this explosion done to him? He'd forgotten all. Oppressed by lucid despair, he pressed his hands to his forehead.

Gently, Enid pushed them away and looked into his eyes. "Do you have a headache?"

She wasn't staring at him with romantic interest; she was watching his pupils, checking to see if they were normal. His wife. She had claimed to be his wife, yet—how had his wife become this woman of cool blue eyes and steady voice? She said they were estranged; did she cherish no sweet memories of their mating?

Mrs. Brown handed her a steaming cup, and the rich scent smelled of parsley and beef.

His mouth watered, and he found himself reaching out.

Enid steadied the mug.

He swallowed so quickly that it burned the roof of his mouth, and the broth tasted salty and rich on his tongue.

"Do you have a headache?" Enid asked again.

He glanced at Mrs. Brown. She stood across the room, folding linens at the table, too far away to hear him speak, so in a low tone he admitted, "More of a heartache. I don't know who I am." Then he cursed himself for showing Enid his soft underbelly. Women scorned a weak man.

But Enid didn't show her contempt. She answered just as softly, "I'll take care of you until you know who you are."

She still wore the dark green gown, a little more wrinkled than before, with the sleeves rolled up to the elbow. The candlelight caressed her, but tiredness ringed her eyes and curling wisps of hair straggled from the snood that bound her locks. He caught her hand. "And after," he demanded rather than asked.

"If you want me." Her tone made it clear she doubted that.

Again a memory slipped from the mists of his mind. Enid, leaning over him, her wrap loose about her shoulders, golden candlelight gleaming on the upper swells of her breasts.

Why couldn't he remember what happened after? Just that wisp of memory brought his member stirring to life, and he needed to remember everything about her more than he needed to remember all the rest of his life.

He wanted to press a kiss on her fingers, slip an arm around her waist, carry her off to some private place and love her until that tight expression of concern and control slipped and became tender passion.

He wanted to do all those things, but he gazed on their intertwined hands, and the difference jolted him. Her fingers were strong, her nails short, her skin pink and healthy. His hands were skeletal, pasty white, the hands of an invalid. He hadn't the strength to take her, but more important, no woman would want him like this.

A thought occurred to him, and panic abruptly escaped from behind its prison bars. "How old am I?"

"Let me think." Her brow wrinkled, and she counted on her fingers. "You're thirty-five."

Relief swept him. "Not an old man, then."

"Not at all."

"Just contrary as the devil," Mrs. Brown said.

He smirked at her. "Do you recognize your master?"

Mrs. Brown went on about her work, not at all offended. "Ah, ye're a wicked one, Mr. MacLean."

Enid brought him a hand mirror.

The scars struck him first. Pale lines crisscrossed one side of his face. "I look like Frankenstein's monster."

She didn't answer.

Glancing at her still, set face, he asked, "What?"

"You've read *Frankenstein*?"

"Yes."

"Who wrote it?"

"Mary Shelley." He understood Enid now, and he said, "I don't know why I know that, I just do. I can quote Bible verses, hundreds of them, and do all of Hamlet's soliloquy." He gestured grandly and proclaimed, "To be or not to be, that is the question. Whether 'tis nobler in the mind to suffer the slings and arrows of outrageous fortune, or to take arms against a sea of troubles—"

"—And by opposing end them," she interrupted. "I do believe you when you say you remember your *Hamlet*."

He continued, "I can tell you how to trap a rabbit

and clean it, and how to make at least a dozen knots. But I don't remember who I am, and that's what I want to know."

"All right."

He didn't believe she had accepted his explanation, and silently he demanded she do so.

"All right!" She spread her hands wide. "I don't understand how this works, I admit it. You'll allow me my moments of doubt."

"You can doubt anything you want, but don't doubt me. I'm the only man here who is telling you all the truth."

"How do you know that?"

"I have an instinct." Let her make of that what she would.

Lifting the mirror again, he touched the scars lightly with his fingertips. They explained why his cheek felt stiff and sore when he spoke. He widened his eyes, flexed his jaw, tilted his head. The man in the mirror made the motions, too, but he didn't recognize him. Nothing about the juxtaposition of harsh lines, pale scars and dark beard looked familiar to him.

Yet Enid seemed to find nothing unusual in his features. "Do you know yourself?"

"Not at all."

"Ye're a man quite in your prime," Mrs. Brown commented as she moved back and forth in the room, putting the linens away.

He teased, "If you have to wipe a bottom, you're glad it was mine, heh?"

Enid gasped. "MacLean!"

But Mrs. Brown positively cackled. "I'm getting

old, sir, but my eyesight's fine and I got quite a pleasant eyeful."

"Mrs. Brown!" Enid sounded even more shocked by the older woman than by MacLean himself.

MacLean and Mrs. Brown exchanged grins.

Handing Enid the mirror, he said, "For a moment I wondered if I'd slept my life away."

"Gambling it away would be more your style."

He frowned. He didn't understand her. "I don't gamble."

"It is your vice."

He didn't understand that, either. He knew about cards, he knew about men who spent days and nights in smoke-filled rooms betting their livelihood on a single toss of the dice, but that wasn't him. He resented her insinuation that he was a weakling like . . . the thought slipped away almost as soon as he formed it. Like who? Whose face did he see, garish with agitation, as he wagered everything on an illusion?

MacLean's excitement subsided before it had a chance to develop. Faces paraded across his mind in no more context than they would in a dream, and until he could bring the memories up from the depths, he would be helpless to understand them.

Helpless . . . he was helpless, damn it! Extending the mug, he said, "I want more broth, and this time put real food in it."

She mimicked his deep voice. "Please, Enid, may I have some more broth?"

"If I don't beg, will you starve me more?"

"I don't want you to beg, I want you to treat me with a modicum of courtesy. But I forgot!" She snapped her fingers. "You don't possess manners unless you'll profit from the effort."

The trouble was, he rather thought she was right. Command felt right to him. Impatience felt right to him. Words like "please" and "thank you" felt alien. In a tone of grinding rage, he said, "Please, Enid, may I have some more broth?"

Taking the cup, she said, "I'd be delighted to get you more broth."

"And this time, put some real food in it."

The flame in her burned vibrant and restless, yet contained by her strength of will, and her smile blazed with hauteur. She tossed her head. A few more errant curls drifted from the snood and settled around her shoulders. Her skirts swished as she descended the stairs.

He watched her until the last strand of hair disappeared from sight. "Where is she going?" he asked Mrs. Brown.

"Downstairs we have a cookfire with someone always ready with food should you wish for some." She came to the bedside, her arms full of linens, her simple, kind, wrinkled face set in smiling lines. "Mr. Throckmorton has gone through a great deal of trouble for you."

"I'll wager he has. Are there guards below, too?"

"Night and day. A great deal of trouble, indeed."

"He considers me worth the trouble."

"Ye're an arrogant bear of a man." She studied him until he thought she could see right through his skin. "Scared to death, aren't ye, m'lord?"

He flinched, and the movement shot pain through his whole body. "What do you mean?"

"Everyone wonders if ye're playing a game, saying ye don't remember. I know that ye aren't, for if ye did ye'd not be shouting and nasty to hide yer terror."

"I'm not terrified." He wasn't!

"Of course ye're not. I've raised a dozen boys, and I don't know a thing about men." She placed a stack of towels on the table beside his bed. "For yer bath tomorrow."

"I'm not taking a bath."

"We've already discussed it, Mrs. MacLean and I, and we're going to give ye a sponge bath, just like we do every other day."

"The hell you are." He refused to expose this white, emaciated body to anyone, certainly not a female who had once fawned over his strength and masculinity. Fawned enough to marry him, if he was to believe her.

Mrs. Brown's smile widened. "See, there it is again. Ye're so terrified, ye're snapping about every little thing."

"It's not a little thing," he said from between clenched teeth.

"My point is, I'm right fond of Mrs. MacLean. I've watched her bring ye from the brink of death, talk to ye when I thought her addled to do so, turn yer big, limp body so ye wouldn't get bedsores when she's just a slip of a thing who shouldn't be lifting her own teacup." Mrs. Brown placed her hands on her broad hips. "Now I understand a man having his fears, and I understand ye're a man used to command, but when I hear ye being so nasty to Mrs. MacLean, I think to myself that I ought to explain to her how frightened ye are so she'll not take offense."

He stared at Mrs. Brown, seeing the iron beneath the

kindness. She threatened to tattle to Enid that beneath his gruff exterior lay a scared little boy. Enid would be nice to him, of course, but he knew that beneath her courtesy would be the lash of condescension all women felt for puny men.

He wasn't weak. He wasn't scared of the great, gaping hole in his mind, or that he would never find himself again. It wasn't true—but it didn't matter. Mrs. Brown would say it was, and his denials would fall on deaf ears.

"Of course, I'm just a servant. My place is to keep my mouth shut." Mrs. Brown's face lost all kindliness and gleamed with demonic determination. "And I could keep mum if ye could find it in yer heart to be a little bit more civil to our dear Mrs. MacLean."

A deal. Mrs. Brown was offering him a deal! And he spied a way to sweeten the pot. "You'll get me out of taking a bath."

"Ye smell."

"Females are too fussy about cleanliness."

"Ye haven't had a real bath for at least seven weeks. The cows in the barn have complained of the stench."

In slow, succinct tones, he said, "I'm not having *her* bathe me."

"Ah. It's *her* you object to." Mrs. Brown nodded. "Ye don't want *her* to bathe ye. Now, that I can arrange."

She moved away before he could say more, and he heard Enid's footsteps on the stairs. By the time she entered, Mrs. Brown stood across the room wiping off the dining table.

Enid held a cup and, under her arm, a package

wrapped in brown paper. Coming to his side, she extended the cup. The same cup as before.

He wouldn't take it. He glared at that cup as if it were possessed of unnatural powers. "No more broth."

"Thickened with gruel," Enid assured him.

Excellent! To him, gruel now sounded like manna from heaven.

She let him take the mug, balancing it as if he were a child who might slop all over himself. As he well might, he admitted. His hands trembled with weakness, and he wanted to swallow every bit at once.

She wouldn't let him. She removed the mug after every swallow and gave him water instead.

And his stomach filled rapidly. He couldn't believe half a mug of broth and thin gruel satisfied him.

Enid understood without him saying a word. Mrs. Brown hovered in the background, watching with an anxious gaze that belied her previous curtness. Enid handed her the mug. "Don't take it too far."

"Ye'll want more soon," Mrs. Brown told him. "Yer stomach's shrunk, and that gruel's more than ye've had in weeks."

He looked at his hands again. He stretched out his arms before him, then to the side, then back to meet in the middle. His muscles trembled from the effort, but his muscles could be trained to work his will again. It was the other he didn't know about. His mind. "Will my memories return to me?"

"When your strength has returned," Enid assured him.

"Is that what the doctor says?"

"I threw the doctor out."

"So you know what you're talking about."

"No."

He stared at her. Audacious female, to think she knew better than a learned physician.

Yet he'd known some physicians in his time—not that he remembered any specifics—and they'd been fools, and supercilious into the bargain. He'd rather trust his life to her slender hands than to those idiots. "Right," he said briefly.

She relaxed, and he realized she'd been waiting for him to rail at her. Handing him the package, she said, "Mr. Throckmorton sent this to you."

She had to cut the string that bound it, but when he spread the brown paper flat, he didn't recognize the charred remains of the kilt. The plaid was red, a green so dark as to be almost black, and a thread of yellow. The sporran's fur was scorched, and the leather clasp had been so mangled as to be impossible to open, but this was his sporran, although he didn't know why he knew.

Picking up the towels off the bedstand, Enid waved them before his nose. "We're going to give you a bath."

He shot a glance at Mrs. Brown, who nodded at him. Folding the brown paper back over the remnants of his past, he laid the package on the night stand. "I'm not getting naked in front of you, lass."

Her eyebrows shot up. "I don't know why not."

"You're not the brightest, and you're not bathing me."

"I'm not the brightest?" Enid's eyes narrowed. "At least I know when I stink."

He did feel filthy, and since Mrs. Brown had mentioned it, he'd noted a bit of an odor about him, but he wasn't about to admit it. "It's a good, manly smell."

"If men smell like something out of the rubbish heap," Enid said briskly. "Maybe you can't smell yourself, but tell me the truth"—her voice held a coaxing note—"doesn't your skin feel crusty?"

He wouldn't have some young female handling him as if he were a piece of meat. Especially not Enid, who had already proved she could bring him to aching readiness with a feeble bit of a kiss. Enid, a female who claimed to be his wife, whom he suspected of lying while hoping she told the truth so on some future date he'd have the right to tumble her beneath him on a bed. Craftily, he said, "A bit of a wash won't do the trick. If you're going to embarrass me, then give me a real bath in a tub."

"We can't. You can't walk. You're thinner, but you're still too big for us to lift, and that's what it'll take to get you into a tub."

"Get the men to do it. That Kinman and that Harry chap, and the valet Mr. Throckmorton hired for me. Jackson."

"They'd hurt you. Hurt your leg." But she was yielding, which showed him how badly he must indeed smell.

"Mrs. Brown can stay and supervise them," he decided. "They'll do as she tells them."

Obviously tempted, Enid hesitated.

"He's right, Miss Enid." Smoothly, Mrs. Brown took her cue. "We can get the big tub from Mr. Throckmorton's bedchamber. Mr. MacLean can almost stretch out in that. The maids will get the water boiling, the men will bring it up, then I'll make sure nothing'll hurt Mr. MacLean."

"Well . . ." Enid chewed her lip and stared at him.

"We'll do it tomorrow in the heat of the afternoon." Mrs. Brown removed the towels from Enid's hands.

"There we are." Everything had fallen out just as he'd planned, and he smiled at Enid, sure she would be glad he had taken charge. "It's all fixed."

She didn't smile back. Looking straight at him, she demanded, "Why Mrs. Brown? Why not me?"

MacLean exchanged an exasperated glance with Mrs. Brown.

"Because he'll not be pointing anything at me," Mrs. Brown answered.

"Oh, for heaven's sake! It's not as if I—" Enid bit her lip.

"It's not as if you . . . what?" *It's not as if she hadn't seen it before.* He could almost hear her speaking the condescension-laden words. But she hadn't finished the sentence, and he detected a faint blush on her cheeks. She might have seen it during their marriage, but that had been years ago. And she might have seen it while he was unconscious, but even a lass as tight-laced as Enid must realize there could be a huge—and he did mean *huge*—difference.

"You can't even hold a mug. Who's going to hold the bedpan for you?" she asked in a tone so cocky he ached to throttle her.

"I will piss on the floor," he snapped.

Mrs. Brown interrupted their mutual fury with a chuckle. "Just give a good shout, sir, and someone will come to care for ye."

Enid stopped glaring at him to glare at Mrs. Brown. The older woman withstood that with good humor, and just when he thought he'd won a round, Enid got her revenge.

She spoke to Mrs. Brown as if he weren't there. "Since we're not going to bathe him, we'll exercise him."

All remnants of relaxation vanished. "You make me sound like a horse," he declared. "What do you mean, exercise me?"

Picking up his hand, she rotated his wrist first one way, then the other.

Mrs. Brown did the same with the other side.

He couldn't pull his hands away from the women, knew to try would be foolish. He understood they worked his limbs to keep him mobile; he even appreciated the care they'd taken of an unconscious man. But how he hated this weakness! To be pushed and pulled, shifted and shoved. To be incapable of moving himself.

Like a spectator, he watched as the women lifted his arms above his head in a slow rhythm. His muscles ached as they stretched. His gut twisted at his helplessness, and even though they made the effort for him, he found himself gasping for air.

"Let's give him some water," Enid said.

"Yes, let's," he replied sarcastically.

They glanced at him as if surprised to hear him speak, and he swore to himself this would never happen again. Starting tomorrow, he would exercise himself. He would push himself to the limit of his endurance. He would stop worrying about the workings of his mind and concentrate on the workings of his body until each joint and muscle moved with the strength and dexterity of well-oiled steel.

Grimly, he accepted the water, gulping it down, and watched as the women moved to his lower body. They draped the sheet over his hips, lifted his legs, and first moved the ankle up and down, then pressed the knee toward his stomach. Enid held the broken leg; she moved it slowly and steadily, but the pain made his eyes half-close and sweat roll off his body. When they stopped at last, he asked, "Will I be able to stand on that leg?"

"Yes!" The question seemed to surprise Enid. "Unless there's some damage I can't see, you'll be able to stand and walk."

He mopped the perspiration off his brow with the towel she handed him, and watched as they wiped him down with damp cloths, then dried him piece by piece. He wanted to cavil about that, too, but except for his leg, which really hurt, his muscles ached with pleasant tiredness, and he found he enjoyed the attention. "I'll hold you to that promise, lass."

"You do that." She smoothed the covers over him. "You do that."

Chapter 8

Enid sat alone in the rocking chair, listening to the creak of the floorboards as she rocked, pretending to read her well-worn copy of *Northanger Abbey*. The late afternoon sun warmed the attic room, the breeze blew through the open windows, and for the first time in six weeks—no, in eight years—she had leisure time for herself. And she didn't know what to do with it.

Her gaze wandered to the bed where MacLean sprawled. His bath had exhausted, but not hurt, him. Mr. Throckmorton had ordered the procedure, and all had gone as planned. Mrs. Brown had supervised. Harry, Mr. Kinman and Jackson had carried him to the tub. He had soaked in the warm water while an army of servants had stripped his bed, cleaned the floors, even changed his mattress for a fresh one packed firmly with feathers.

Now, as daylight caressed the polished woods and lingered to illuminate every corner, Mrs. Brown had gone visiting, the attic no longer smelled like a sick-room, and MacLean slept the sleep of the innocent.

They'd done it without Enid. Every bit without her. She had walked in the garden, enjoyed the sunshine, smelled the flowers . . . watched the window, wrung her hands, waited to be called . . .

How odd to feel betrayed by the fact that the man she had hovered over for six weeks had recovered enough to do without her for an hour.

He looked so much better. Already his cheeks had filled out, and his eyes were no longer sunk in their sockets. His newly washed dark auburn hair gleamed, and the scars that crisscrossed his face were pale and healed. Jackson had trimmed MacLean's beard close to his face, and she could see now that his square jaw jutted forward, giving his face a bulldog determination. His cheekbones were starkly high, and his poor broken nose had a hump that gave him the look of a ruthless thug. Perhaps when he'd had a shave and a haircut, he would look like Stephen MacLean, and not like some stranger who tugged at her heart.

She smiled as she looked down at her hands. Tugged at her heart when he was asleep, anyway. When he was awake, he remained an arrogant, unpleasant jackass.

She thought she must feel the turmoil a mother feels when her sweet, happy baby takes its first steps and says its first word—and that word is *no!*

A groan from the bed brought her head up.

MacLean stretched in slow, careful increments as he watched her. "Now there's a smile to make a man uneasy."

Her fingers tightened on the book. When MacLean

was awake, the blood raced through her veins, the air hurt to breathe and every moment she lived in fear of the hurtful things he would say. Lived in fear . . . and anticipation. Because something in her, some remnant of wildness she thought long crushed by life, relished their repartee. She gave him as good as she got. Never again would he treat her with thoughtless insensitivity. There was nothing of the invalid and the nurse between them, nor of the wronged wife and reckless cad. They were MacLean and Enid, opponents who shared a goal—the return of MacLean's health and memory.

When he had remembered . . . then everything would change.

He finished stretching, but he still stared at her, observing her as she rocked her chair back and forth with slow, gentle motions.

She refused to speed up just because he made her nervous; she would maintain an air of serenity if it killed her.

"How long have we been married?" he asked.

She froze. The rocking chair stopped. She balanced her toes on the floor and wondered if his mind, gone for so long, ever now halted in its insatiable demand for information. "Nine years."

"Infidelity?"

"I don't think so"—her eyes narrowed as she stared at him—"although I'm sure there's been plenty since."

"I meant you!" he roared.

"Oh!" She lost all equanimity and started rocking rapidly, serenity vanquished. "No, of course not. As if I would care enough to cheat."

That piqued his manly pride, she could see it in the

way his mouth tightened. She didn't care. In her opinion, he had a great deal too much manly pride, and no great reason for it.

She knew. She'd shared a bed with him. The experience was nothing to brag about. Yesterday's expertly applied kiss couldn't alter the truth of that, and she, and her body, had best remember what had happened last time she had yielded to this man's entreaties. She'd ended up married, and at the start of a long, lonely, poverty-stricken road.

Yet the way MacLean had watched her last night . . . he hadn't slept right away, as she'd thought he would. Instead he had observed her as she'd moved about the room, tidying up before going to bed. When she'd gone behind the screen to change into her nightgown, she'd been aware, every moment, that he'd listened to her movements and the rustle of her petticoats. She had found herself undressing carefully, slipping the nightgown over her head and removing her undergarments so as to show as little flesh as possible. As if he could view her!

Donning her robe, she had crept on bare feet out from behind the screen and across the floor, never quite checking to see if he was still scrutinizing her, yet knowing that he was. She'd blown out the candles, all except one. That she'd left burning in case he woke in the night and needed her. And that, she'd known, had given enough light for him if he'd wished to watch her discard her robe and slide into bed.

He had watched, of course. She never doubted that.

The memory drove her to her feet. "I can get you something to eat."

"Yes." Apparently her lecture the day before had had a bracing effect, for he tacked on, "Please."

"Good." She placed the book in the chair and made polite conversation. "I'm glad you're hungry."

"Why?" He lolled in the bed and sneered at her. "If you feel such indifference about me, why should you care if I live or die?"

So much for polite conversation. "The more you eat and drink, the farther the spectre of death slips away from you, and for all that you are an out-and-out rotter, that pleases me. I worked too hard to bring you back to life to accept anything less for you." Let him chew on that! "I'll be back."

The trip downstairs took only a minute, and for all that she had not liked being away from MacLean while he'd had his bath, now she found herself loathe to return to him. Why did he have to be so disagreeable? If he truly didn't remember their marriage, fine. But why did he have to interrogate her, then blatantly distrust everything she told him? He imagined himself a better person than he was, and therefore accused her of being worse than she was. It wasn't fair, and as she ascended the stair carrying a bowl of stew and a ladle, she straightened her shoulders and stiffened her spine.

He didn't even wait until she was all the way in the room to start on her. "We're estranged," he said.

"Yes." She put everything down on the table and reached for one of the mugs Mrs. Brown had left her.

"Do you live in my home?"

"No."

In a voice rife with irritation, he said, "Women like to talk. They never shut up. Why won't you talk?"

She smacked the mug with the ladle so hard she cracked the cup.

"Speak to me, woman. Where have you been? What have you been doing?"

With more patience than was reasonable for any much-maligned woman to possess, she took another mug and filled it. "I've lived in England."

"Alone?"

She halted, cup in hand, and glared at him. "Are you accusing me of having a lover?"

His gaze lingered on her lips, and his mouth quirked. "No. Not likely."

What did he mean by that, and why was he smiling?

"How long have you lived in England?"

"My whole life."

"You can't be more than twenty-five."

"Twenty-six."

"How old were you when we were married?"

"Seventeen."

"You were a child!"

"That's an excuse." She used her smile like a prod. "I usually just call myself a fool."

"We were together less than a year?"

"Very good," she congratulated him. "Despite your loss of memory, you can still do arithmetic. We were together for three months."

Despite her rudeness, he had the cheek to sound smug. "*Now* you're talking to me."

Standing there with the cupful of steaming stew, she considered spilling it on his groin. But she wouldn't. Only because it wouldn't be fair. Not when he couldn't leap up and pour cold water on his pants. But once he could stand . . .

He didn't even realize his danger, or how great her restraint.

"Could this be any worse? This goes to prove an alliance between English and Scots is impossible." Then, like a donkey, he brayed the same song. "I don't believe we are married. I'm too smart to have wed a Sassenach."

Stupid donkey. Stupid man. "If Mr. Throckmorton is in a conspiracy to trick you, why would he try to dupe you by presenting you with a wife so palpably distasteful to you?"

"You are not distasteful to me." He had the gall to stroke his hand down her arm as if reassuring her. "You are simply difficult and sharp-tongued."

"While you are the voice of wisdom and courtesy." She moved away from his touch. "We had no reason to believe you would wake without your memories."

"There is nothing worse than a female who has logic," he allowed.

"Unless it's a male who has none."

He didn't acknowledge her hit. Of course not. A male, concede that a female was smarter than he? Never!

Pretending she hadn't even spoken, he said in an imperious tone, "I'll eat now."

"Your manners have disintegrated again."

"Please, ma'am, may I have more to eat?" He watched her lift the spoon, and craftily suggested, "A little piece of mutton wouldn't come amiss, or some cabbage and a wee dram of wine."

"There are some mashed carrots and mashed potatoes to thicken the broth today." She fed him until he snatched the mug from her and fed himself. "If you tolerate that, you can have a bit of minced beef tomorrow."

He finished and blotted his mouth on the napkin she handed him. "Later today."

"Maybe." She refilled the mug.

He ate until he sighed with repletion and placed the mug on the nightstand. "When can I have a peach?" he asked. "I dreamed of peaches while I slept, and I have a mighty taste for their sweet, tender flesh."

And although he looked in her face, she would have sworn he spoke of something else entirely.

Then, with a grin, he said, "The fastest way to a man's heart is through his stomach."

"The fastest way to a man's heart is through his chest." Enid leaned closer, and just in case he didn't understand, she clarified, "With a dagger."

"Virago."

"Never forget it." He had recognized her as a force to be reckoned with, and that thrilled her. His green-and-gold eyes locked with hers. And she found herself trapped in an unwavering match to see who would look away first.

She stared resolutely at first, seeing this as a minor skirmish that would show him, once again, that she could not be intimidated.

Then, with each passing moment, the silence between them thickened, and she realized theirs was more than a contest of wills. It was a seduction. He gazed at her as if she were a morsel and he a starving man . . . and worse, she knew he was a starving man. Starving for food. Starving for love . . . no, not love. For fornication. Eight years ago, MacLean had wanted adoration and obedience, not love.

Knowing that, why did she want to slip forward into the void of their silence, touch the burr of dark hair on his jaw, and taste his lips? Why did she imagine how it would feel to rest her breasts against his chest, to indulge in long, slow, deep kisses, to have his hands on her bare skin?

Her mouth parted as her breath quickened in heady anticipation. Her flesh warmed in a generous flush. The tension she had felt every moment since his awakening grew and skittered along her nerve endings, settling in her womb like a burden that breathed and moved and demanded attention.

She would look away now—if she could. She would gladly concede him the victory in their small battle if she could only save herself from this . . . this what? This humiliation? This trap?

This pleasure?

"Madame MacLean?" an unknown feminine voice trilled from the room below.

The spell broke. Enid blinked. Her hands rested on the mattress, she was leaning over him . . . her head jerked back.

"*Bonjour, Madame!* Are you up there?"

Enid glanced around, bewildered to be brought back to earth so abruptly, thankful someone—a woman, a stranger—had rescued her. "I'm here," she called and started toward the stairs.

But MacLean caught her hand and wouldn't let go until she looked at him.

He watched her, unsmiling.

"Saved," he whispered. "But not for long."

Chapter 9

Enid pretended she didn't understand, but MacLean didn't care. She understood, all right. She knew what had almost happened. The passion between them pulsed and burned with fresh blood and new fire.

He slid a deliberate, carnal finger down her arm and over the pulse point in her wrist.

Yanking her hand away from his, she stalked toward the stairs, where the patter of footsteps sounded.

A head popped up, a beautiful female who dazzled with a smile, who wore joy like a garment and made everyone around happy to be with her. Seeing Enid, she asked, "*Madame* MacLean?"

"Yes, I'm Enid MacLean."

As the woman climbed into the room, he saw she was petite and pretty, and even without introductions he knew she was the woman Throckmorton was taking to wife. No other woman could have made that solemn old son of a bitch marry without money or title.

MacLean blinked. What a revelation! He *had*

known Throckmorton before, and he'd been a friend, too, or MacLean wouldn't reflect on him with the cheerful amusement of one trapped male about another.

Trapped . . . he slid a glance at Enid. Married. To her. He might not want to think he would marry an Englishwoman, but she was right. If Throckmorton wished to deceive him, he would have presented him with a beauteous maiden with honey on her lips, not this termagant.

Anticipation mixed with the bitterness of knowing he had failed to keep his mate happy. He didn't remember, but Enid was his wife, and he would make new memories with her. Her seduction was something to plan, and something to look forward to.

Celeste wore her honey gold hair done in one of those intricate styles that irritated any sensible man, with braids going here and there, wrapping around her ears and over her head, and diamond-headed pins sticking about and sparkling until MacLean wanted to tell her to blow out the lights.

Enid, silly girl, took one look and touched her hands to that black net snood in an ineffectual attempt to straighten that magnificent mane of flyaway hair.

"Don't," Celeste cried, the faintest of French accents coloring her words. "Wait!" She hurried forward, her wide, vividly pink skirts flying, a listing bouquet of flowers clasped in her arms. "Let me." Pulling the hairpins free from Enid's hair, she snatched the black net snood away.

The curly mane fell about Enid's shoulders in total disarray, and she lifted her hands and caught the strands. With her upswept arms and startled expression, she looked so much like a female caught at her toilette that MacLean almost groaned from desire. Bending one knee, he hid his blooming thistle beneath the tented sheet and watched with a voyeur's bliss as Celeste pushed Enid's hands away and fingercombed Enid's hair. It reached Enid's waist. He'd caught glimpses last night in the candlelight, and now he wanted to stroke each strand, kiss her lips, cover her . . .

"Look at this!" Celeste exclaimed. "You are so lucky. My hair is straight and fine, but this—this is magnificent!" Turning to MacLean, she said, "*Monsieur*, don't you love her hair?"

Today. Last night. Tomorrow, stretched across his pillow in a tumbled disarray. But he said no more than, "It's gorgeous."

Enid glanced at him, wide-eyed and startled, and the passion he hid with his bent knee must have sounded in his voice, for she blushed a fiery red and snatched at that ridiculous snood.

"I would say so!" Celeste laughed, and charm oozed from every pore. "*Madame* MacLean, I have not introduced myself, and you're wondering who I am. I am Celeste Milford. I'm going to marry Throckmorton."

Celeste's joy was infectious. MacLean smiled, and even Enid, intent on stuffing her hair into that hair-snare, chuckled with her and said, "I know."

"Did he tell you?" Celeste hopped up and down, little hops that expressed her delight.

"He told us," Enid said.

Celeste clasped her hands at her knees and chuckled. "Isn't it wonderful that he should love me?"

"I would say he loves you because you're wonderful," Enid answered. The two women looked at each other, and some kernel of friendship leaped between them, for they burst into laughter, and hugged.

They reminded MacLean of his sister and her silly friends, always giggling for no reason and talking when they had nothing to say. He could see them now . . . he clutched at the sheets as the picture rose in his mind. His sister, standing on a rock at the seashore and waving her arms like a bird as the wind tore through her auburn hair . . .

Celeste babbled, "Throckmorton told me not to bother either of you because you were busy and didn't need me to interfere."

MacLean glanced up. He'd remembered something. He'd really remembered, but the women hadn't noticed.

"All that means is that he wants me to mind my own business. So I brought the bouquet of flowers my father clipped for you just so I could meet you." Celeste thrust the flowers at Enid. "Do you like them?"

Nor would MacLean tell them that a golden piece of past had floated up from the depths of his mind. Not yet. Not until he knew what it meant, if it was just a single treasure he would be granted, or if it was the beginning of an ever-widening lode.

Enid accepted the rather droopy flowers with such enthusiasm that it seemed she must never have received flowers before.

"Also, I have a letter for you." Celeste delved into her pocket and presented Enid with a folded, sealed sheet.

Enid glanced at it, and, as if it contained some precious message that couldn't be shared, she slipped it in her pocket. "Thank you! I've been waiting for this."

"Who is it?" MacLean demanded. "Who's writing you?"

"An old friend." To Celeste, Enid said, "I don't have a vase, so we'll fill a bowl with water for the flowers."

"That will do very well," Celeste answered.

The letter. Enid was avoiding the letter, and that letter provided a link to Enid's former life. The one MacLean knew nothing about. "Aren't you going to read it now?"

As if she were embarrassed, Enid frowned fiercely at him. "We have company."

MacLean subsided, but he wouldn't forget.

Celeste filled the bowl from the pitcher. Enid put the flowers into the water, and MacLean saw his straight-faced, prickly wife chuckle when they fell over.

So Celeste cut and arranged them, and Enid took instructions with eager attention and without a hint of belligerence. MacLean had never imagined this transformation from responsibility-laden nurse to carefree girl.

"MacLean," she called, "do you need anything?"

He wouldn't dream of interrupting, not when he had a window into Enid's behavior with someone she could call a friend. "I might sleep a little."

"We must be quiet," Celeste murmured as she tiptoed toward the chairs near the window and gestured Enid to a seat. "Sh, sh."

Luckily for MacLean, he had a hunter's hearing.

"You are from the Distinguished Academy of Governesses," Celeste said.

"Yes, Lady Bucknell found my last job for me."

Sheer curiosity swept MacLean into speech. "The Distinguished Academy of Governesses? What's that?"

"I thought you were sleeping." Enid sounded as if she knew very well he'd planned to eavesdrop.

"Not yet." He thought he gave a reasonable imitation of innocence.

"We call it the Governess School. It's the business which Lady Bucknell directs, and she finds jobs for many young women," Celeste advised him. Then, as if he were of no importance, she turned back to Enid. "I'm from the Distinguished Academy of Governesses, too. Lady Bucknell taught me to be a governess, then she sent me to France, then I came back here because Throckmorton needed a governess and I wanted to marry his brother."

Confused, MacLean asked, "So you're marrying Throckmorton's brother?"

"No, she's marrying Mr. Throckmorton." Enid shook her head as if he were obtuse.

Yet he knew very well he'd just heard Celeste say she'd returned to Blythe Hall to marry Throckmorton's brother. How did women communicate in such a haphazard way?

"When did you return from France?" Enid asked.

"Only a few months ago, but Throckmorton courted me, although he did not wish to, really, but now he has changed his mind and desires to wed as soon as possible. His mother, chère Lady Philberta, didn't want us to stay in the house together, for she worries we will have a baby too soon. I could tell her we are, but that would spoil the surprise."

"Oh!" Enid leaped to her feet and hugged Celeste. "Such good news! When?"

"Well done, Throckmorton!" MacLean grinned. Who would have thought Throckmorton would bend the rules enough to slip into this girl's bed?

"I am sure our other babies will take nine months, but this one will be no more than seven." Celeste dimpled. "You won't tell Throckmorton, will you?"

Shocked, MacLean lifted himself on his elbow. "You haven't told the father?"

Celeste flushed. "Go to sleep!"

"I am, but you should tell him immediately. You've already told us, and he doesn't know."

The two women looked at each other, and in unison, they shrugged.

"A woman likes to tell another woman this kind of news first," Enid explained. "Men don't understand."

He massaged his forehead with his fingertips. "Of course we understand. She's having a babe. It's a natural occurrence."

"That is what men don't understand." Celeste shook her head sadly. "They say it is a natural function. They even think they have something to do with it."

"We . . . something to *do* with it? Yes, we do," MacLean sputtered. "I'd like to see you do it on your own!"

Enid touched her bodice as if her heart spoke to her. "Babies are a miracle of God."

Celeste agreed and dismissed him at the same time.

"Exactly. So my chère Lady Philberta whisked me back to Paris, where we bought my trousseau." She spread her skirt wide. "This is the newest style. Do you not like it?"

"It's lovely." Enid touched the fabric with her fingertips. "Voile, I think."

How did a woman know that? MacLean wondered. They looked at some other woman, dressed in some gown that looked just like all the rest of them, and pronounced the color as being peacock or foam or cream or some other substance that was a thing, not a color. They could tell the material, the weave, whether the lady wore ruffles on her drawers and the number of seamstresses who had sewn on it. All for a dress!

Now, if they could talk that way about horses, it would be worth something.

"The sleeves and the bodice are velvet. I don't know if I like such a material in the daytime, but the couturier insisted it was chic and Throckmorton likes the feel of it when we—" Celeste clamped her mouth shut and glanced at MacLean.

He closed his eyes and pretended to be asleep.

"I have little experience with men, but Throckmorton is very virile," Celeste announced in a loud whisper. "Very passionate all the time. Is your husband like that, too?"

Oh, he couldn't wait to hear what Enid said to that!

"He was always more interested in cards and dice." Enid didn't bother to whisper, and he would wager she knew he was awake.

"I'm surprised. Throckmorton thinks the world of your husband, and he doesn't approve of gambling or wild living." Celeste sounded disappointed, then brightened. "Now that Mr. MacLean forgets everything, maybe he will remember how to make love."

"Maybe." Enid inveighed the word with doubt. "But never mind him. You were saying you're from the Governess School, too."

"Yes, and do you know who I met here at Blythe Hall? The founders of the Distinguished Academy of Governesses!"

Enid gasped. "Really? They're legends. What did they look like? What did they say?"

"They are young, they are pretty, they are smart—of course—"

Feeling drowsy, MacLean listened to the prattle with one ear. He was clean, he'd just been given a glimpse into the mind of his wife, and he had remembered his sister. A good day. Tomorrow would be better. Tomorrow, he would find out about that letter, and he would remember everything about himself, his family—and his wife. His difficult, complex, enticing little wife.

Chapter 10

This time when he woke, it was the middle of the night. A single candle burned low, elongating the shadow. On the bed by the wall, Enid lay, her braid draped across the pillow, her pale hand open and softly curled. She snored in complete relaxation.

He grinned. She snored—softly, to be sure, but still she snored. How good to know his perfect wife possessed at least one human vulnerability.

On the other hand, he hated to wake her from so deep a sleep, and he badly needed a drink. His gaze measured the distance between his bed and the table where the pitcher rested. Five steps, no more. Except for a few aches and pains, and the persistent weakness in his leg, he felt healthy. Only five steps. Surely he could walk it and could pour himself a glass.

Swinging his legs over the side of the bed, he leaned a hand on the night table. His head swam for a minute but cleared.

Yes, he could do this.

He stood—and his damnable leg gave way. He toppled over. He hit the floor with a thud that reverberated
through the floorboards and every bone and muscle in
his body. The night table came with him. Towels flew.
The porcelain washbowl smashed into pieces and scattered everywhere.

The shards had not yet settled when Enid appeared
at his side.

Furious, embarrassed, in pain, MacLean said, "I'm
fine. I'm fine!"

Enid was having nothing of it. "Are you hurt? Is
anything broken?"

His pride. Nothing of importance. "The washbowl,"
he snapped.

"I mean you." Her voice lashed at him. "Are you
hurt?"

"I'm fine," he repeated. "Have a care of the broken
crockery."

Two men appeared at the top of the stairs, pistols
drawn.

Reacting on instinct, MacLean grabbed Enid and
thrust her to the floor.

She squawked like a chicken.

The men glanced about the room, and MacLean realized that they were his bodyguards. Relaxing his grip
on Enid, he allowed her to sit up.

"What are you doing? Are you crazy?" She glanced
at the men as they put their pistols away. "Oh." She
switched back into the role of caretaker. "Don't worry.
It's just Harry and Sandeman. They won't hurt you."

MacLean wanted to tell her that he did not appreciate her soothing him like a child who had woken from
a nightmare, especially not in front of the men, but she

had wrapped her arm around his shoulders to assist him as he pushed himself up to a sitting position, and her arms constituted a first-rate place to be.

Holding him as if he were a child that had tripped and cracked his head, she directed the gunmen. "You! Harry, Sandeman! Help me put him back into bed."

MacLean possessed the strength to push her away. "Go put on some shoes first. You'll hurt yourself."

"We'll take him, miss."

MacLean recognized the man who spoke. Harry.

"You do as MacLean says and put on some shoes," Harry said.

"I want to help—"

MacLean observed that both men were staring fixedly up at the ceiling. He glanced at Enid.

Dear Lord, but for the long, sheer summer night-gown, she was almost naked.

He looked, because he couldn't help it. He enjoyed, because a man would have to be dead not to enjoy. Then, using small words and speaking very slowly, he said, "Go put on a robe."

Glancing down at herself, she said, "Men!" in a tone that expressed her total disgust for creatures that could think of a woman's nudity in such a crisis.

MacLean could have told her that men could think of a wench's nudity during the most gruesome of tortures, during an audience with the queen, during a direct lightning strike. But sometimes too much knowledge was bad for a woman.

She flounced away, the men still looking elsewhere, and as soon as she'd left, Harry knelt at MacLean's side. "Break anything?"

"No."

"Bleeding?"

"No."

"All right, then." The two men hefted MacLean back onto the bed with a minimum of fuss.

MacLean grunted as he assimilated the various aches and pains he'd added, but he'd done no permanent damage, so he cast his gaze on his bodyguards. Harry had been in the room that first day when MacLean had opened his eyes, and although Harry had put his pistol away, MacLean wouldn't soon forget how at home he looked with it in his hand. "Are you always downstairs?" he asked.

"Someone is." Harry glanced behind him. "Here she comes."

Enid had gotten her pink cotton robe and shoes on in record time, and Harry and his friend stepped aside for her. She leaned over MacLean, all anxious concern. Her braid fell over her shoulder, and he caught the scent of flowers and spring breezes, captured during her walk. "Did you fall out of bed?"

"No, I tried to get up for a drink," MacLean said.

"Don't be silly. There's nothing to be embarrassed about falling out of—" She shook her head as if his sentence had finally penetrated her mind. Somehow she realized he told the truth, and there, right before his eyes, she transformed from a tender caretaker to an outraged wife. Squeezing the ties of her robe in her hands, she asked, "Do you mean to tell me after two days of sustenance and with your injuries, you thought you could walk to the table?"

"Couldn't be more than three steps." He subtracted two from his original estimate.

"You haven't walked for two months! Your leg is

broken!" She took an outraged breath. "Don't you have any sense at all?"

"No!" he roared at her. "I don't! I'm just a stupid man who doesn't understand where babies come from, remember?"

The silence that fell in the room was awesome in its magnitude. The men with the guns looked at each other, then at the floor.

Enid stared at him, then at the men. She looked at him again. And she started to laugh.

He gave a sigh of relief. He detected a note of hysteria in her merriment, but hysteria was better than the alternative—he had thought she would re-break his leg herself.

Covering her forehead with her hand, she said, "You thought you could walk to the water." She staggered toward the window, laughing again.

"What were the guns for, lads?" MacLean asked in a casual tone.

"Someone tried to kill you in the Crimea, and that makes Her Majesty's government unhappy," Harry answered.

"Only three steps," Enid whooped.

MacLean found himself remarkably calm. "Is Her Majesty's government expecting a repeat of the attempt in England?"

"Perhaps." Harry nudged his companion, then they backed down the stairs.

"Don't know where babies come from." Enid's glee was dying a slow, bitter death.

It wouldn't last much longer. Too bad, because MacLean knew recriminations would be next. He allowed himself a glance toward the window.

She sat down on the windowsill, crossed her arms, and gazed at him.

He might not remember being married before, but he knew a few things about handling a woman. "I'm sorry," he said. "That fall was stupid, and my fault."

She fingered her braid.

He tried again. "You've made me feel well so quickly, I was overconfident."

Sighing, she stood and walked to the pitcher.

"Please, may I have water?" he asked.

She turned on him so quickly that she almost burned the floorboards. "Is that so hard to ask? 'Please, Enid, bring me water.' 'Water, Enid, water.' Even, 'Get up and get me water, woman.' I might not like it when you're a rude barbarian, but I don't ever refuse you anything, do I? Do I?"

The return of her fury caught him by surprise, and he used his most reassuring tone. "You are everything a man could want in a wife."

"No, I'm not. You always made sure I knew that. But I'm a wonderful nurse." Stalking toward him, she handed him the water. "Here."

He took a sip, then, when he noticed how forbiddingly she stared, he hastily swallowed the rest of it.

"Are you hurt?" she asked in a more reasonable tone of voice.

"Bruised," he admitted. "Nothing serious."

She took the glass and filled it again. "Are you hungry?"

"Please, may I have bread?"

She must have anticipated his request, for she removed the towel from a loaf on the table, tore off a small piece, and presented it to him.

He considered the golden crust. "I never thought you'd let me have bread. You told me I could only have broth and vegetables."

She reached for the bread.

He held it out of reach. "But I'll keep it."

"Take small bites," she advised, then she knelt to pick up the pieces of shattered crockery.

Prickles of discomfort ran up his spine. He didn't like to see her on her knees, cleaning up after him. It made him feel . . . uncomfortable. "Call a servant to do that."

"They're asleep." She sounded brisk and unaffected as she bent her head to her task. "Besides, I've done worse jobs."

The bread tasted yeasty, rich, and so wonderful that he wanted to stuff the whole thing in his mouth. Curiosity stopped him. He had questions he wanted to ask. "Jobs like being a governess?" he inquired.

"I've never been a governess."

"But you said you worked for the Distinguished Academy of Governesses."

"No, I said Lady Bucknell found me my last position." She tossed the big pieces of the washbowl in the dustbin and fetched the broom from the corner. "I'm a nurse."

He was a proud man. He knew he was. Yet he had allowed his wife to become estranged from him? And that woman had been forced to toil for her living among strangers? As a nurse? Nurses were little better than prostitutes.

Enid must have read his mind, for she stopped sweeping and asked, "Would you rather I'd had a man support me?"

"No." He looked at Enid. Slim, straight, with a clear gaze. She didn't look as if she'd ever been touched by a man. She certainly didn't look as if she'd ever been touched by the filth of a sickroom. He didn't believe she had worked as a nurse. He didn't believe he had allowed such a thing.

Yet . . . yet she exuded scorn, resentment, distrust— of him. Surely no female could simulate such intensity.

"You cared for . . . people. Who?"

"The ill." She knew what he was asking, and she taunted him with too little information.

"Men?"

"Yes."

He wanted to shout at her. Instead, he coaxed, "Enid, talk to me."

Leaning against the broom, she sighed and yielded. "I stopped caring for gentlemen. Even the most elderly would bring themselves back from the brink of death to offer me a position as their mistress."

He hated this. He could feel the fury coiling in his belly, but his fury was for the circumstances that stood between them, for his loss of memory, for his helplessness in her resentment. He didn't want to hear, and at the same time he needed to understand. "How did you come to be a . . . a nurse?"

"There was a doctor in the village where we lived for awhile."

"Where you and I lived?"

"Yes." She swept beneath the bed, beneath the nightstand, chasing pottery into every corner.

"A village in Scotland?"

"No, in Little Bidewell north of York."

"Why was I living in England?"

"You probably got thrown out of Scotland." She used the dustpan to collect the shards. "We're going to find bits and pieces on this floor for months."

"Enid." Silently, he demanded she tell him all.

"You aren't going to like this," she warned him, and she seemed to regret having to tell him. "You were an adventurer. A gambler. You moved about a great deal. We would live somewhere for perhaps two weeks, and then you would have worn out our welcome by beating the constable in cards or wagering the innkeeper out of his best silver. So we'd be off again."

"I can't give credence to this." If Enid were to be believed, he was the kind of man he despised. And yet . . . yet, he couldn't *not* believe her. He didn't know about himself. He didn't remember any of his past. And more than that, through the last few days of care and dissention, he'd grown to trust her.

A glow radiated from her like the clearest of candles. She did her duty without self-pity, cleaning up the broken bowl and replacing the dustpan and broom, feeding him at any hour, answering him smartly, her astringent replies like the slap of a crashing North Sea wave. She made him think, she made him feel, she made him want. He wanted to warm his hands on her, hold her against him until she filled him with her light—and he filled her with himself.

"Since you've come awake," she said, "I've thought that you have changed."

There had to be a reason that she so uncompromisingly disdained his former self. He could not be so wrong.

Staring at her, he saw a handsome female clad in a worn pink robe, beautiful in her intelligence and the force of her personality. The kind of female who would look on a situation, decide how it was, and stick to her opinion regardless of how mulishly wrong she was. That had to explain this discrepancy between who he was and who she recalled. She saw their relationship through the eyes of uncompromising youth, and what she remembered could not be the truth.

Yes, that had to be it. When his memory returned, he would discover their marriage had been a series of youthful errors, that for her, time had altered the facts, and that with the maturity of their years, they could mend old mistakes.

Her next words jerked his attention back to her. "I treasure the hope that in the years we've been separated, you reconciled with your family. You always said they weren't important to you, but your defiance of them guided your every action."

"I was at odds with my family?" He would have sworn he was the most dedicated of family men. Probably she was wrong about that, too.

"That's why you wed me. I was not the bride the MacLeans would have chosen." Her mouth curled in a bitter smile as she put the broom and dustpan away. "Your cousin, the laird of the MacLeans, was much opposed to our marriage."

"I had a cousin." His memory of the girl on the rock flashed into his mind once more, and he asked craftily, "Anyone else? Mother, father, sister?"

"A mother, but you dismissed her without interest. You spoke only of Kiernan. Kiernan was a stick. Kiernan thought he was so smart. You'd show Kiernan. You ate yourself alive with envy of Kiernan."

"Kiernan." He sat up slowly. The name rang a bell in his mind. "I remember him."

She hurried to his side, and her voice sharpened with hope. "Do you?"

"No. I mean . . . I recall the name, or something." He tried; he tried so hard, straining as he reached for the memory, but he couldn't quite grasp it. Kiernan, like everyone and everything else, hovered out of reach in the mists of his mind.

Exhausted from the effort, he collapsed back on the pillows. "He's not there."

Her forehead puckered. "Do you want us to let him know you're alive? I'm sure your family must be worried."

"It doesn't sound as if they would be." Perhaps he was cruel to so dismiss the clan which had given him being, but he wouldn't go and face strangers he didn't remember, or try to justify an existence spent in dissipation . . . if indeed he had so lived that life. "So tell me about this doctor. The one who taught you your profession."

"Dr. Gerritson was in his seventies, and he had lived in Little Bidewell his whole life, curing everything he could, human and animal. I stayed with him. I helped him treat his patients and learned everything he could teach me."

Catching the end of her braid, MacLean brought her closer to his bedside. "What have you done since then?"

"I've cared for the elderly, mostly, and the very ill."

He tangled his finger in the braid, marveling at its silky texture.

"For the last three years, I've lived with Lady Halifax as her nurse-companion."

Enid had been living with a female. "Is she a dear old thing?"

"I would say not. She is disagreeable, querulous, demanding, and difficult. Also intelligent, discerning, fair, and the best of women. I admire her very much."

"Did she send the letter you received?"

"Indeed."

He relaxed about one thing, at least.

"But she's very ill. She can't write anymore, but she dictates to the new nurse." Enid looked down at her interlocked hands. "I left her to come to you."

Her expressionless voice expressed better than anything else her obdurate resentment. Tightening his grip on her braid, he said, "You would rather care for an elderly woman than for me. You would rather clean up after the ill and hold a dying person's hand than live with me. No matter how disgraceful my morals, how could you have left me for such an existence?"

"You misunderstand. I didn't leave you." Stepping away from him, she yanked her hair free of him. "You abandoned me."

Chapter 11

"Ma'am, do you know what worm is eating at his gut?" Mrs. Brown watched from the rocking chair as MacLean pulled himself up on the bar over his bed for the dozenth time that morning. "He's working himself night and day building those muscles of his, like if he doesn't something bad's going to happen."

"I suppose he wants to be able to get up and walk again." Enid folded the towels in preparation for MacLean's bath. For the last three weeks, he had bathed every day—after his exercises. "Ever since he fell, he's been resolved that he'll get on his feet."

Mrs. Brown glanced sideways at Enid. "Ye're going to have to let him sooner or later, ye know."

"I know." Enid weighed the linen in her hand. "I'm worried about that compound fracture. I've never cared for one before, but old Dr. Gerritson had, and he said the patient should just be shot, like a horse, to save trouble. I don't want MacLean to die."

"Not after the trouble we've had bringing him this far." Mrs. Brown threaded her needle with silky white thread and set to work on a fragile bit of froth trimming a little girl's petticoat. "But if he was going to die, he would have already passed on, and knowing that man and his determination, there wouldn't have been a thing we could do about it."

"You're right. I agree." But that didn't ease Enid's mind. At night when she lay wakeful, she found herself imagining the worst: MacLean collapsing in agony, MacLean's leg swelling from a blood clot, MacLean's mind slipping away again. All absurd conjecture; she knew it, yet fruitlessly she chased phantoms of ill fortune through her dreams.

Without paying the women a bit of heed, MacLean lifted the iron weights Mr. Throckmorton had provided for him. Next he would work his legs, lifting them, flexing them, ignoring the compound fracture as if it had never been. Relentlessly he rebuilt his body as if he had a meeting with fate—as perhaps he did.

"He's looking better," Mrs. Brown said. "Filling out nicely."

An understatement. As the iron weights rose above his head again and again, the muscles in his shoulders and arms bunched and relaxed.

"Of course, as much as he's eating, he should be filling out," Mrs. Brown added.

Long, smooth, taut muscles had developed on his massive bones and changed him from a skeleton into a living, breathing, Greek god. And Enid had been on her own for too long if she compared Stephen MacLean with Apollo for any other reason except dissipation.

"He should wear a shirt," Enid fretted.

Mrs. Brown looked him over. "Why? It's not often a woman my age gets to pleasure her eyes with such a sight."

Shocked by the older woman's frank appraisal—women her age weren't supposed to be looking at men—Enid exclaimed, "Mrs. Brown!"

"A woman would have to be blind or dead not to appreciate him." Mrs. Brown chuckled. "I suppose that's why ye're wanting him to clothe himself, though. He's scarcely speaking to ye, so I suppose ye're not sharing his bed."

"That is not any of your business," Enid said loftily.

"No, then," Mrs. Brown decided. "I thought not. Ye'd both be a lot easier to be around if ye were dancing the bedtime minuet."

Enid didn't need a confidante, nor did she need an advisor. She was perfectly capable of managing her life without help from anyone.

Of course, she would have liked to tell someone MacLean's real problem, and see whether or not they thought he would ever forgive her. For it was she who had set off this frenzy of muscle-building. She had told him who he had been, and he hadn't liked hearing about his gambling, his cheating, his wandering. He had been infuriated by her recitation of his crimes. And when she had said he'd abandoned her he had called her a fraud. An imposter. A hypocrite.

She'd felt sorry for the man. He'd been so obviously flummoxed by her announcement. So she had let him abuse her and hadn't said a word, and what did she get in return? He could barely stand to gaze at her. They never held a real conversation any more.

See if she ever tolerated one of his tantrums again.

Worse, he worked to bring himself to the peak of fitness so he could go off and find out the truth, and confront her with it. She knew that soon he would demand to be on his feet, and despite her fears that his leg would buckle beneath him, she would let him. She was surprised he hadn't already attempted to stand.

But she couldn't confide in Mrs. Brown. Not that Mrs. Brown needed an invitation to comment on the tense situation in the sickroom. Apparently the older woman considered Enid a daughter, and she heaped wisdom on Enid's head whether Enid welcomed it or not.

"Ye don't know how to manage yer husband," Mrs. Brown began.

"I don't want to learn."

"Then ye're a fool. All women need to know how to manage their man. How else are ye going to get the big lummox to do what ye want him to?"

"I don't want him to do anything." Enid felt as if she shouted into the wind.

And Mrs. Brown sounded so quietly exasperated. "Ye've got to break that habit of telling falsehoods, Mrs. MacLean. It's bad for the soul. Now I don't know what ye told Mr. MacLean that set him into such a snit, but—"

"I told him he was a wastrel of Olympic proportions."

"There. Ye see? Ye don't have to tell him every little thing. If ye'd told him he was a prince among men, mayhap he'd act the part. Instead, ye allowed yer grudges to cause ye to blurt out every little difficulty—"

Enid put her hands to her aching head. "You said I wasn't to tell falsehoods, so why would I claim he was a prince among men?"

"Telling a falsehood to your husband isn't really a falsehood, it's more in the line of a stretching of the truth. The Lord will forgive ye that if it's in pursuit of yer husband's happiness."

"I don't care whether he's happy."

"Of course ye do! He's yer husband. Ye have no choice. Marriage is forever, and ye might as well settle down and make do, just like every other woman who wed."

Enid had never heard Mrs. Brown speak so frankly. "Is that what you did? Make do?"

"Yes, dear. I married beneath me. As do all women." Mrs. Brown had finished her sewing. Shaking out the petticoat, she nodded as if satisfied. "If ye don't need me any more today, ma'am, I'll be off to the nursery to care for Miss Penelope and Miss Kiki. With the wedding only four weeks away, they're wild with excitement."

"I imagine they are." Enid had enjoyed hearing the details of the arrangements every time Celeste had visited, and Celeste had come at least twice a week, always carrying flowers, a haircomb, and occasionally a book. Enid would have been grateful for Celeste's thoughtfulness, except that MacLean talked to Celeste. He teased her. And Enid was tired of being ignored, tired of being envious of a friend, tired of this anxious, vaguely guilty sensation whenever she saw MacLean concentrating fiercely on recapturing his strength.

She was, in a word, fed up, and she told Mrs.

Brown, "You go ahead and tend the children. *I'll* take care of Mr. MacLean."

"Ye sound a little frazzled." But nothing rattled Mrs. Brown's placidity. "Better not get too snappish with him. Ye'll not win with that man."

Enid would have argued that point, but while she thought she could vanquish MacLean and his silly resentments, she knew she would never win against the powerfully practical Mrs. Brown. Folding her hands and lowering her head in mock meekness, Enid said, "I'll read him the London newspaper."

"He likes that." Mrs. Brown rolled up the petticoat and placed it in her sewing basket. "It makes the time go quickly when he exercises."

"How do you know?" Enid asked.

"He told me." Mrs. Brown prepared to descend the stairs. "You ought to talk to him sometime, dear. He's actually quite a nice man."

A nice man. MacLean was about as nice as a Roman conqueror sacking a village. And in the space of one morning, Enid had compared him to a Greek god and a Roman conqueror. Next it would be a medieval knight, and he had nothing of chivalry about him. Nothing at all.

She glanced at him and found him watching her as he twisted one side to the other, putting his elbow to his opposite knee, back and forth, over and over. He had that expression on his face, like he wanted to pry open her head and peer into the contents.

Well, wasn't that interesting. MacLean had suddenly decided he could be interested in her. Wouldn't he be surprised to discover her thoughts?

Taking the *Sunday News of the World*—Mr. Throckmorton sent it every week—she walked to his bedside. "Would you like me to read to you?"

He nodded as he always did, for he exercised his mind just as he did his body. He listened to the stories, demanded explanations, and occasionally contributed a comment that proved he remembered . . . something. Yet he insisted his memory hadn't returned, and she had no reason to doubt him. After all, if he remembered, he would know who he was and who he had been, and he would be apologizing to her for doubting him.

Pleased to discover her sense of humor hadn't abandoned her, she grinned.

Placing a chair by his bedside, she sat, snapped open the paper, and read an article about the SS *Great Britain*, the first large iron-hulled screw-propeller steamship, and its launch on July 19.

He grunted. "She won't make it across the Atlantic."

She read about the statue of Lord Nelson being hoisted on the column in London's new Trafalgar Square.

"About time," he decided and curled up, then back down, then up again, until Enid's abdomen ached to watch him.

She was reading a story attacking Prince Albert for being a foreigner when, without ceremony, MacLean interrupted. "Who are your family?"

There it was. A prying question put in the bluntest of tones. Dropping the paper into her lap, she said, "That's the first personal thing you've said to me in three weeks, and you want to know about my family?

There's no, 'I'm sorry I've been a knave,' or 'It's been lonely without your gentle conversation.' Just, 'Who are your family?' "

Unimpressed, he lifted an eyebrow and his heaviest weights. "So who are they?"

Of course, he'd gone right to the heart of the matter. He wanted to know why she'd been deemed an unsuitable bride by the ogre leader of his clan.

Well. She could easily tell him that. "I don't have a family."

"Everyone has a family."

"Not bastards."

That got his attention. He stopped lifting his weights; he swept her with a critical glance.

What difference did it make if he knew? When he recovered his memory, he would taunt her with her illegitimacy. He always had.

"No mother? No father?" His bare chest rose and fell, powerfully pulling in enough air to feed his body.

She watched, saw the muscles that rippled beneath the skin, the layer of auburn hair that curled across his pectorals, and imagined how he would appear when he had recovered all his strength. "Not to . . . to speak of." She needed to concentrate on the conversation, not on the view. "My mother died in childbirth. My father paid my tuition to Mrs. Palmer's School for Young Ladies, and I attended until I was fourteen years old."

"So you *do* have a father. Who is he?"

"Was, MacLean. He was the honorable earl of Binghamton."

"You have noble English blood running through

your veins." His Scots accent strengthened. "Blood of the silly, vain, useless aristocratic conquerors."

"I'm English through and through, and proud of it, too," she said fiercely. "Nothing you can do will ever change that, but there is never anybody less noble than a female child raised among her betters."

"Your schoolmates were better than you?"

"They thought they were." In her mind's eye, she saw the long corridors of Mrs. Palmer's School, lined with dull, pimpled girls with bad teeth, and all of them contemptuous of Miss Enid Who Had No Last Name. "Legitimate daughters of earls and barons, legitimate daughters of clergymen and knights, legitimate daughters of wealthy upstart merchants. In society's eyes, they are all better than me."

"So if they attended this Mrs. Palmer's School, it was a fine, prestigious organization?"

"I believe it had that reputation."

"That explains much about you." He stared at Enid as if he could peel away the layers of equanimity and see the trembling child hiding within. "You speak with a high-class British inflection. You know the classics, you do needlepoint, and I heard you speak French with Miss Celeste. Very impressive."

She didn't appreciate the catalogue of her virtues as recited by a rude, most barbaric wastrel whose only real skill was dice games best played on the stable floor. Haughtily—and she had learned haughty from the best—she said, "Don't forget my light touch at the pianoforte and my skill at the waltz."

He flashed her a sharp glance. "In addition, you sport a quick wit—I imagine you developed that to fend off the other girls and their barbs. The earl of Binghamton made it possible for you to move in higher circles. You're surely grateful."

"Grateful." The word dripped with sarcasm; in Enid's early years, she'd been told often that she should be grateful that her father had supported her. Gratitude was not what she felt; instead, she experienced a vast impatience that a man unable to keep his trousers buttoned was deemed generous and even honorable. He certainly hadn't made provision for her support after his death, and he had taken care that she never lay eyes on him.

"Not grateful, eh? You're no dullard, Mrs. MacLean."

"Oh, please, Mr. MacLean. Such flattery will turn this poor girl's head."

He grinned at her, a sudden, brilliant slash of untamed amusement.

Enid caught her breath. He hadn't smiled for three weeks, and the transformation from brooding resentment to outgoing charm almost frightened her. If he acted like that all the time, she could forget all her grudges and, like an unwary maiden, fall in love with him as she had never been in love with him before.

Luckily for her, he couldn't consistently stay charming.

"You said you were at Mrs. Palmer's until you were fourteen," he said. "What happened then?"

"Binghamton died. I was expelled from school and sent to the Home for Indigent Waifs." A place that made Mrs. Palmer's snob-lined corridors look like the passageways of heaven. "His Lordship's wife and legitimate children didn't care to continue his benevolence."

Placing the weights on the table beside the bed, he said mildly, "That must have been a shock."

"To go from a school where the dancing master arrived on Tuesday and tea was served every day precisely at three, to a place filled with dirty children suffering from all kinds of disease, where stealing was the only way to get enough to eat and the steward slapped me when I used proper English?" Enid smiled tightly. "Yes, it was a shock."

To Enid's relief, MacLean showed no surprise or sympathy. "How did you survive?"

"The steward's wife saw a way to make money, and when I was sixteen sold me to the vicar's wife as a governess. The vicar's wife had pretensions of gentility; she wanted her children to learn to speak with an upper-crust accent, as she called it." Enid smiled with a more genuine mirth. "During my stay there I realized my vocation did not embrace teaching."

"Then you met me."

"It would probably be better if we both forgot how we met." She folded the paper and prepared to rise.

She'd never told anyone her story, had scarcely allowed herself to remember, but freed from the dam of reserve, the words had tumbled out. But pride and reserve stopped her from telling what was next. She had met MacLean, and no girl before or since had ever been so stupid. So gullible. She wanted to cry for the girl she had been, and she didn't want to tell anyone the tale of her marriage—not even the man she'd wed.

"You said I abandoned you." Leaning forward, he

caught her wrist, halting her flight before it could begin. "Tell me those circumstances."

"It would be better if we forgot those, too."

"I *have* forgotten those circumstances. I've forgotten everything, but you resent them so much you will never forget them." He held her wrist loosely, but she had no chance of escape. "So tell me so we can both know."

"No," she whispered, her gaze locked with his. "I don't want to." She wasn't talking about their discussion; she was talking about the fact that he inexorably pulled her toward him. "MacLean, don't."

"What?" He wrapped his arm around her waist and lifted her on top of him. "Don't what?"

Sweat made him sticky to the touch. He smelled like a working man. And still she slid her arms on the pillow beside his head and bent her face to his. "Why are you doing this? Is this some kind of revenge because I told you the truth about yourself?"

"You're my wife. The other half of me. If I take revenge on you, I hurt myself."

His breath whispered over her skin. His voice was low, deep. His nearness vibrated through her in earthy seduction, and like a fool she wanted to kiss him as he had kissed her all those weeks ago.

He continued, "Marriage is a vow made until death do us part. I can't kill you, no matter how much I might occasionally wish to."

She tried to lift herself away from him, came up against the cage of his arms, and weakly retorted, "More than occasionally for me."

He tightened his grip on her. "You and I can't escape from each other, so we will learn to deal with each other."

The light dawned. "You've been talking to Mrs. Brown."

"I have. So have you."

"Yes," Enid admitted without enthusiasm.

"She's right. I know it." He smoothed her hair away from her face. "You know it."

"I don't want to be stuck with you." She stubbornly preserved a few inches of space between their bodies.

"I'm going to tell Mrs. Brown you said that."

"You wouldn't!"

"Not if you give me a kiss." He was laughing at her. "A kiss, Enid. You know you want to."

She did, blast him, and she slid downward under his urging, her lips opening softly, her eyes closing. He slanted his mouth to hers so she tasted him at once. She relished the warmth and dampness of intimacy. Bliss echoed in her mind, her heart, her loins. She slid her tongue deep, and he sucked on it gently. He encouraged her with his hands, sliding up and down her back, and it felt so good . . . and so bad. Like temptation. Like sin. Like pleasure.

Those few inches between them that she had so carefully preserved disappeared, and her body collapsed onto his. She moaned softly at the sensation of another human form so close against hers. She'd never experienced this kind of toe-curling arousal; she wanted to eat him, drink him, absorb him into her system. She had to catch her breath, but she couldn't bear to think he might get away—as if he could or would!— so she held his head in her hands as she lifted her head . . . and caught a glimpse of his triumphant smile.

The ass. The unmitigated ass. He dared to appear . . . to appear smug. As if her passion was . . .

was surrender. As if he could command her when he was nothing but a vagrant, an adventurer, and a seducer of women.

And how could she have forgotten that?

Tearing herself free, she bounded toward the stairs.

Mr. Kinman was coming up as she dashed down. He grinned amiably as he always did when he saw her. He held a sealed white sheet of paper. "Mrs. MacLean, I brought a letter from Lady Halifax."

Snatching it from him, she bobbed a curtsy. "Thank you, it's good to know there is at least one gentleman left in this world." Without looking back, she fled.

Chapter 12

Kinman looked after her, hands on his hips, and in the puzzled tone of a happily unattached man, he asked, "What is wrong with her?"

"Must you ask?" MacLean sat up and turned himself around so that his feet dangled off the bed. "She's a female."

Kinman looked at MacLean, and his broad face slowly darkened. "That's not it. I know you. You've upset her again."

"I was trying to make her very happy." MacLean reflected sourly on the irrationality of all females, and his wife in particular. "She just doesn't know what's good for her."

Hurrying over, Kinman reached behind the night table, brought forth a cane and handed it to MacLean. "I don't know what's wrong with you, MacLean. You've got a beautiful wife who cares for you—as if *you're* worth saving—and what do you do? You make her run like the hounds are after her."

With deliberate movements, MacLean put his feet
on the floor and stood up. "We'll come to an understanding soon." He was determined on that. For the last
three weeks, he'd been punishing her for telling him
what she considered the truth. She'd allowed his sul-
lenness, caring for him regardless of his resentment.

Of course, she'd answered him smartly whenever
he'd snarled at her, and sometimes he'd scarcely re-
frained from guffawing when she'd snapped out some
witty comment.

Kinman's hand hovered beneath MacLean's arm as
he took his first steps, but eventually Kinman moved
away. "You won't need the cane for much longer."

"Don't really need it now." MacLean's feet tingled,
his hips ached and the leg that had been broken
throbbed, but everything worked remarkably well con-
sidering he'd been prone in that bed for over two
months. Hooking the cane over his arm, he began the
routine he'd established every day when Enid went on
her walk.

Enid . . . he now knew why, in some distant, unre-
membered past, he'd married her.

Much as he had tried not to, he liked her. In spite of
her tainted English heritage, if he met her today he
would pursue her with all his resolve. He knew the details of her form. Each night he waited for her to step
out from behind that screen clad in a sheer nightgown
and a tattered pink robe, and although he didn't remember any other women, he knew that he anticipated
that glimpse of her feminine form more than a mouth-
ful of pleasure from another.

Enid clutched him by the short hairs.

He would do his damnedest to make sure she never

knew it, for if she knew how easily she could manipulate him, she would hold the reins in their marriage. His wife already had a tendency to be domineering, when she should, as a female, be submissive, so he would take control. When he got close to her once more—and that time would be soon—he would cajole and seduce her, and make theirs a good marriage regardless of what it had been in the past.

Kinman dragged the tub out from its corner. "You want to make Mrs. MacLean happy? Tell her you can walk."

"Not yet." These last few weeks, MacLean's sense of jeopardy had been steadily increasing. Disaster hovered just over the horizon, he didn't know why or how, but he would be prepared, and his full strength eluded him. He didn't want people knowing what he could do. He needed the element of surprise on his side. "Where's Throckmorton?" For Throckmorton came every day to chat and apprise him of any events, and also, MacLean knew, to verify that his memory hadn't returned.

"He's on his way," Kinman said. "I thought he would be here by now, but guests have started arriving for the wedding. He's been busy today."

"Already?" MacLean paced back and forth across the room, counting laps. "The wedding isn't for another four weeks."

Kinman shrugged. "These aristocrats have nothing to do but visit the great manor houses, and Throckmorton's hospitality can't be faulted."

When MacLean had done as many laps as yesterday, he added another ten. "He serves good brandy?"

"The best."

MacLean jerked his head toward the stairs and Kinman descended. When he returned, he said, "The coast is clear."

Gripping the cane in his hand, MacLean climbed the stairs, up and down, until his muscles clenched. His thighs, especially, burned from the exertion, but he didn't give up until he'd exceeded his previous record. Then back and forth across the room again, pushing himself, always pushing himself. Only when he'd walked so long that he feared Enid would return did he sink onto a chair to rest.

"Are you ready for your bath?" Kinman asked.

MacLean nodded, taking deep breaths, pleased at his improvement and at the same time cursing the weakness. He needed to be prepared. For what, he didn't know, but he needed to be prepared *now*.

"I'll call for the water, then." Kinman leaned out the window and waved, and almost at once MacLean heard the sound of activity in the room below. At this time of day, the water was always boiling in the cauldron. Men's voices sounded, then the first of a long line of footmen clomped up the stairs, carrying up the heavy buckets of alternately hot and cold water. Two maids, Sally and Jennifer, dusted and swept, stripped the bed and remade it with fresh linens, and took his dirty clothing away. Jackson brought fresh linens and an ironed white shirt, sans collar and cuffs, and an ironed pair of trousers, cut off at the knee.

MacLean grinned as the valet made clear his opinion of the trousers with sniffs and disgusted head shaking. Jackson really was a stick, a slump-shouldered English fool. MacLean would have dismissed him with the scorn he deserved, except for the fact that he was a genius with a razor. Despite the scars that marred MacLean's cheek and neck, Jackson could shave him cleanly with never a nick, and MacLean refused to risk his skin just because the little worm suffered a misplaced sense of importance.

MacLean rubbed his hand across his chin. His day-old beard chafed his palm. That would never do. Enid's skin was as softly tinted and delicate as a peach, hinting at the delights within, and he wouldn't take the chance of marring it when he kissed her again, as he intended to do—and soon.

With a flick of the wrist, Jackson placed a towel on the table beside the basin and laid out his razor, his cup and his brush. He clapped his hands and pointed at one of the footmen. "I need hot water!"

The footman poured water from his bucket, slopping a bit on the table.

Jackson gave a long, suffering sigh and mopped up the mess. Then, with the efficiency that characterized all his motions, he shaved MacLean.

Throckmorton arrived in the midst of the organized chaos, greeting the men by name. When the tub was full, the footmen gone, and Jackson packed up and left, he said, "It's a rare valet whose work is as good as he claims."

"He is very good." MacLean rubbed the satin of his unscarred cheek. "But he's not much given to pleasantries."

Kinman's mouth twisted in disgust. "And if he's so good at shaving, why doesn't he shave himself? He looks as if caterpillars are crawling down his face."

Throckmorton laughed. "As long as he does his job, he can look like anything he wishes. Did you get your walk, MacLean?"

"A good one," Kinman said. "He doesn't need me here anymore."

"You'll stay with him, please," Throckmorton instructed. "I would not wish to face Mrs. MacLean if he falls."

"If I fall and hurt myself, just put me out of my misery at once, for if Mrs. MacLean finds out, she'll torture me to death." MacLean began to strip.

Throckmorton and Kinman turned their backs and stared fixedly out the window. When MacLean had eased himself into the tub, Throckmorton said, "We may have to move you."

MacLean had anticipated this. "Because of the wedding guests?" The warm water alleviated the pain in his muscles. He would have loved to soak, but he lathered himself immediately. He always feared Enid would return early and catch him still in the tub, and wonder why a bath should take so long.

"The more people who know you're here, the less I can guarantee your safety." Throckmorton rocked back and forth on his heels, his hands clasped behind his back. "With your permission, I've made arrangements to return you to Scotland."

MacLean dropped the soap with a splash. "Scotland?"

"I hope a return to your home will jog your memory."

"Aye." MacLean dug the bar out of the tub. "Though they won't welcome me back if I'm the wastrel Enid claims."

Throckmorton stopped rocking. During the long, thoughtful silence that followed, MacLean saw Kinman and Throckmorton exchange glances.

"I wouldn't call you a wastrel," Kinman said.

"Not lately," Throckmorton added.

They were cautious. Conspiratorial. *They'd been lying to him.* "What would you call me?"

"A gentleman who has reformed," Throckmorton said firmly.

How terrifically interesting. "I needed reformation?"

Throckmorton and Kinman exchanged glances again.

Before Throckmorton could speak, MacLean said, "It's time to tell me the whole story."

Throckmorton sighed. "Not yet."

The admission made MacLean furious. "Not yet? You're withholding information on a *whim*?"

"Not a whim. It's for your own safety."

"That's bloody hard to swallow." But if MacLean had learned one thing over these weeks, it was that Throckmorton wouldn't be forced or cajoled. "When will you tell me the whole truth?"

"In Scotland. Kinman will go with you. He'll tell you everything."

MacLean finished bathing himself with the vigor of rage. "Lying to a man with no memory is a damned dirty trick."

"We hoped we'd be done with this by now," Throckmorton said. "That you'd remember."

"*You'd* hoped," MacLean muttered as he hefted himself out of the tub. After that one, glorious moment when he had recalled his sister, he had had no stirrings in his brain. All of his straining toward remembrance had been for naught. All of his frustration had been worthless. The only thing he knew for sure was the nature of his character—and Enid claimed that memory faulty. So he had nothing.

As he wrapped the towel around his middle, he asked, "Is my wife lying to me, too?"

"Mrs. MacLean is just as she appears to be," Throckmorton assured him.

So the woman with the sweet face and tart tongue hadn't been lying to him, too. A part of MacLean's wrath—most of his wrath—died with the admission.

He dried himself and dressed. "So Enid is not in your employ?"

"Do you mean is she an actress playing a part?" Throckmorton asked. "Not at all."

"All right, I'm dressed." MacLean waited until the two men had turned to face him. Then, arms folded across his chest, he told them, "For the moment, we'll do this your way. But I want some assurances. I want some control. I want possession of some items. I expect that you will get them for me now."

Enid was returning to the cottage when she rounded the corner and walked into Celeste, walking slowly along the path arm in arm with an elegant, aged couple.

Celeste looked horrified.

Enid *was* horrified. She hadn't forgotten the warnings she'd received when she'd arrived, or that MacLean could be in danger, but in all her walks she had never come upon a stranger, and she'd grown secure in her surroundings.

She should have known better.

Ducking her head, she curtsied and stepped aside, hoping her plain garb would distinguish her as a servant, albeit one of the higher servants, and that the aristocrats would ignore her.

But aristocrats were ever contrary.

The tall, stout lady was clad in shimmering lavender shantung from the top of her ruffled parasol to the bottom of her full skirt, and her full chins quivered as she peered at Enid through her quizzing glass. "Who is this young woman, Celeste?"

"She is . . . one of my friends from the Distinguished Academy of Governesses," Celeste said.

Enid wanted to applaud Celeste's quick thinking. Not a lie, really, but a tale that should lead them astray.

"My lord, my lady, won't you come and look at the chrysanthemums?" Celeste said, gesturing toward the great display of gold and orange that blazed down the winding path.

"Introduce us to this lovely young lady first." The lord tottered forward, peered into Enid's face, and actually pinched her cheek.

When Lady Halifax had said there was no fool like an old fool, she might have been talking specifically about this man. Thin, tall, and wearing the highest black top hat Enid had ever seen, the gentleman smirked and waggled his eyebrows at her as if she were some green miss who knew no better than to flirt with a lord. And before his wife!

Enid wanted to smack him. But that would never do.

"Introduce you? Introduce you, my, yes, how silly of me." Celeste smiled like the silliest of girls. "Sometimes I just bobble the simplest courtesies. It's because

I'm the gardener's daughter. Yes, I should introduce you."

And Enid remembered—her last name would betray all.

Taking a breath, Celeste said, "Lord and Lady Featherstonebaugh, this is—"

In the brisk, no-nonsense tone of a woman not included to wait on the civilities, Enid said, "It's a pleasure to meet you, my lord and lady. I'm Enid Seywell."

Lady Featherstonebaugh frowned thoughtfully, then brightened. "Seywell? That's the earl of Binghamton's family name."

Enid started. Dear heavens, these people knew of her father!

"Are you related to the earl of Binghamton?" Lord Featherstonebaugh asked.

"I believe I may be." Enid kept her voice firm and her gaze steady, but she couldn't control the blush that scorched her chest, her neck, the tips of her ears.

Lifting her quizzing glass, Lady Featherstonebaugh examined Enid from toe to top, and lingered on her crimson cheeks. "I remember a scandal a few years ago when Binghamton died. Something about a bastard daughter."

"Yes." Lord Featherstonebaugh drew the word out with a denture-accented hiss. "I remember. His family discovered he'd been supporting the girl, and they were none too pleased."

Celeste wrung her hands.

"Lady Binghamton was such a pinchpenny, she could squeeze a guinea until the gold melted." Turning to Lord Featherstonebaugh, Lady Featherstonebaugh asked, "Was the child's name Enid, dear?"

"I believe so." Lord Featherstonebaugh looked harder at Enid. "By George, I think you've hit the nail on the head, my dear. She has the look of Binghamton about the eyes."

I do not. But Enid clamped her mouth shut. She didn't want to be recognized, didn't want to have this old couple gossiping about her before her face. And to have Celeste discover Enid's past, and in such a way! Mortification writhed in Enid's belly, and she didn't dare glance toward Celeste. She could do nothing, for scandal provided a screen behind which MacLean could hide.

"It's like seeing the old rascal alive once more," Lord Featherstonebaugh said. "Tell us, m'dear, are you Binghamton's daughter?"

For MacLean's safety, Enid could sacrifice this much dignity. She supposed.

But he would owe her yet another debt. "I am," she answered.

Enid had heard that couples who were long married frequently began to look alike. Lord and Lady Featherstonebaugh had obviously been married for a very long time, for their faces donned identical masks of delight. They blinked at the same rate, and they looked at each other at the same moment.

"Miss Seywell, I would be delighted to take you in to dinner," Lord Featherstonebaugh said.

"I have to return to the Distinguished Academy of Governesses," Enid lied smoothly.

Lady Featherstonebaugh straightened and said in a

stern tone of voice, "I'm sure that's unnecessary. You can stay another day."

Enid kept a smile on her face. "I can't. I'm sorry."

"She's a working girl, so she must leave." Celeste came to Enid's side and slipped her hand through Enid's arm. "I am so disappointed to lose my friend before the wedding, but duty calls!"

"Oh." Lady Featherstonebaugh adjusted her parasol. "How disappointing. I had looked forward to a cozy chat with you, Miss Seywell."

"And I," Lord Featherstonebaugh said.

Enid thought him a disgraceful old gentleman, but she nodded as they turned away.

"Go on, Lord and Lady Featherstonebaugh," Celeste called. "I'll catch up."

The young women wheeled about and marched as rapidly as possible in the opposite direction, keeping complete silence until they were far beyond the earshot of the elderly couple.

"I shouldn't have come out." Enid chewed on her lip and told herself she shouldn't worry about MacLean, that louse with the come-hither eyes that had enticed her to come thither.

"It's not your fault," Celeste answered.

"I didn't realize there were visitors to the estate, and I couldn't bear to remain in that cottage for one more minute." Because Enid would have been kissing MacLean, and a woman would have to be crazy to kiss him.

"It's not even my fault, although I'm sure Garrick won't see it that way."

"Who? Oh, you mean Mr. Throckmorton. MacLean

is absolutely the most disreputable of cads." And Enid was certifiably insane.

"Garrick accuses me of attracting trouble, as if I do it on purpose!" Celeste's eyes flashed. "I am not the fluff-brained little miss he might wish."

"I would say you are not! Nor am I a piece of feminine flesh to be petted or ignored." No matter how enticing the petting might be.

"They don't appreciate us." Abruptly, Celeste halted beside a bench at the trunk of a massive willow, looked at Enid and, in a voice filled with kinship, said, "Every trouble begins with a man."

Enid was tired of acting like an adult. She wanted to behave like a beast. Like MacLean. "Men are all alike," she said sulkily.

Celeste tapped her lip and considered. "If only that were true, but each is exasperating in his own way."

"I am done being a free finishing school for MacLean. Let him find out how to behave in civilized society without involving me." In anything. Enid didn't want to be involved in any more of MacLean's escapades. He was well. It was time to leave him. That's right, leave him as he had left her, and return where she was needed.

She slid her hand into her pocket and touched the letter from Lady Halifax. In those weekly missives, Lady Halifax had sounded as stout and brave as ever, but Enid knew the truth. Death hovered very near, and none of the sprightly letters she wrote in return were the same as being there for the dear, cantankerous old lady.

But her mind shied away from the scene in which

she told MacLean she was departing, so she abandoned her own problems and for a moment considered Celeste's. "Mr. Throckmorton adores you. I'm sure that's why he's irrational."

Celeste collapsed on the bench. "Do you mean men need an excuse to be irrational?"

Enid grinned and seated herself beside her friend.

Her irritation appeased, Celeste said, "The Featherstonebaughs are old family friends, kind old people—"

"I didn't notice," Enid said, cold with offended pride.

"No, they weren't kind to you. I'm sorry." Celeste glanced from side to side. "And to tell you the truth, I am not so fond of them as are the other members of the Throckmorton family. The Throckmortons excuse the Featherstonebaughs' ill behavior by saying they are the most terrific gossips in all of England, but I have been the brunt of their gossip, and it's not pleasant."

"Nor is it excusable." Enid tried to broach the subject delicately. "I must thank you for not spurning me. I know it's not agreeable to discover that someone to whom you have been kind is illegitimate, but—"

Celeste's eyes snapped with ire. "You are not to say another word, or I will be offended. I do not choose my friends by who their parents are, nor do you, or you would not be so generous to me, who is the daughter of a gardener."

"I would think nothing of—"

"Neither would I." Standing, Celeste shook out her skirts. "So that's settled. You're my friend, we have an affinity, and I think you will be leaving soon, but when your adventure is over you will visit me. Promise?"

"I promise."

Celeste touched Enid's shoulder. "Now I must find Lord and Lady Featherstonebaugh and divert their questions about you, and then I must tell Garrick you have been seen and listen to him complain." With a grimace and a wave, she walked off.

Celeste's declaration touched Enid's heart and made her remember the letter in her pocket. Digging it out, she stared at the familiar, noble Halifax seal, then turned it over to see unfamiliar handwriting. Lady Halifax had dictated to yet another one of her attendants. Carefully Enid freed the seal from the paper and unfolded the sheet.

She read the first line. Read the first line again. Then she scanned the remainder. Dropping her head onto her knees, she cried.

Chapter 13

MacLean recognized the tap of Enid's footsteps, and he didn't even wait until Enid's head cleared the top of the stairs before snapping, "Where the hell have you been?"

Enid stood aside as Sally slipped past her and down the stairs.

"In hell, of course."

The candles gave off insufficient light, but she looked unharmed, and that, as well as her cool tone and her reply, infuriated a man who had been remarkably patient after what had surely been a minor tiff. Punching the pile of pillows that helped him sit upright, he accused, "You made me wait."

"For what? There's always someone here if you need anything."

"Was it some kind of petty revenge because I tried to kiss you?"

She glared at him, then with a flourish slammed the trapdoor shut so hard that it shook the floor. "No."

And that made him even angrier. "Because you're being childish. You're my wife, and if I want to kiss you, I can."

She shot the bolt with her foot, then meticulously articulated, "Not if you can't catch me."

Lifting himself onto his elbows, he said, "You're damned saucy for a woman who, not six hours ago, had her tongue in my mouth."

"I didn't want to kiss you. I was being polite!"

He laughed. "Come here and show me how polite you can be."

"Rot first!" Going to the basin, she washed her hands, then groped for a towel. When she didn't immediately find one, she wiped them on her skirt.

He stared. Enid had wiped her hands on her skirt. This woman, so dainty in her habits that she scolded him for drinking out of the water pitcher, had wiped her hands on her skirt. Something very odd was happening.

Moderating his tone, he said, "You're being unreasonable. It was just a kiss."

She snapped her fingers and turned away. "It was nothing."

She dismissed him. Just like that. He wanted so badly to stand up, walk over, take her by the shoulders, and shake her.

But she was already shaking. Just a fine tremble in her fingers, which she immediately tucked into her pocket to hide from him. "If it was nothing, then why are you acting as if I demanded my conjugal rights?"

"You're not well enough to demand anything, much less conjugal rights."

He could have lifted the sheet and shown her proof

of her error, but either the shadows were playing tricks with her features or she had been crying. Her eyes were red. Her nose was blotchy and swollen.

Crying. Hell. He studied her. She had come in cranky. He knew of an easy explanation, but a man didn't live with a woman as closely as he had lived with Enid without knowing a bit about her, and she'd suffered through her monthlies a good ten days ago. So what was wrong now?

Turning her back, she said, "I don't feel like fighting with you."

He tested her. "That's a change."

She didn't bite. "I'm going to bed."

Glancing out of the west-facing window, he saw the faint red tint still staining the purple sky. "The sun has barely set."

"I want to go to bed."

Because he'd kissed her? He kept a watchful silence as she removed her snood and hairpins and slapped them on the table.

Her curly, dark hair tumbled around her shoulders. Tossing it back with a flip of her head, she ran her fingers through along her scalp, then clutched her head and closed her eyes as if she held in reason with her bare hands. Opening her eyes, she saw the way he observed her, and in the tone of a woman driven to the limit of her patience, she said, "You know, I didn't want to come to Blythe Hall and take care of you. I had a position with Lady Halifax. I had a responsibility to that lady. And I abandoned her to come and care for my husband. My worthless, good-for-nothing, cad of a husband who abandoned me nine years ago. There's an irony there if you care to examine it, but I don't." She unpinned her collar. "I don't."

She unpinned her cuffs, too, and threw them on the table atop her hair trinkets. She, who had never so much as unbuttoned a button in front of him before, removed clothing without a thought to the consequences. Kicking off her shoes, she sat down by the table.

"Aren't you going to pick up your shoes?" he asked.

"Why? They'll be there for me in the morning." She shoved the little pile of clothing aside. "It's not as if *you're* going to pick them up."

The woman was forever tidying the room, and folding towels and putting them away when five minutes later she had to unfold them to clean something up. *A place for everything, and everything in its place*, she always said.

"*You* never picked up anything even when you could walk."

And cruel. This woman who tenderly cared for him was being cruel. He would have asked her what was wrong—but she hiked up her skirt to her knees.

His mouth dried.

"Do you know who you were? You were a traveling player." She managed to imbue the term with stinging disdain. "You were handsome, dashing, older. You recited poetry with a Scottish burr, you lured me with the promise of adventure, and I was so feeble-minded, it worked."

He would have been offended and enraged if not for a peek at her white drawers, her sleek, stocking-clad calves and the garter perched close to her knee.

"I had a position as governess, and I ran away with

you so we could be married." She untied the garters and removed the stockings—all of which she dropped on the floor, too.

When she stood and shook out her skirts, he released an unsteady sigh. His heart pumped in deep, rapid throbs; he sucked in air in great gulps. "Enid, that happened a long time ago. You cannot still be upset . . . um . . . that . . ."

She dealt him a withering glance, her extraordinary blue eyes fierce with derision, then she marched to the dresser and pulled out one of her plain, white nightgowns. Clutching it tight against her chest, she said, "My position with Lady Halifax was the second job I have forsaken for you, but only because Lady Halifax said I had to. I had learned my lesson when I left my responsibilities as governess and got what I deserved. You abandoned me. There. I said it again. *You* abandoned *me.*"

She was goading him. That little woman with her slender ankles and her wild, black cape of hair was poking at him as if he were a bear to be baited! "Why?"

Her forehead wrinkled. "Why . . . what?"

He could have asked why she provoked him, but she wouldn't give him an answer. "Why did I abandon you?"

In an awkward, savage imitation of his Scottish accent, she said, "Because, dearling, ye're an anchor aroond my neck."

Interesting. "Were you an anchor around my neck?"

"I most certainly was. I wanted to settle down. Be married in a real home with a garden and a fence. Have children. Be normal."

He would like to do that with her, starting with the making of children.

She continued, "You wanted to be feckless, reckless and immature."

But first he would have to get to the bottom of this baffling, illogical temper that possessed her. They were alone, the door was locked, the room flickered with candlelight, and a warm, summer-scented breeze blew through the open windows. It was a good night for confessions.

"So in Little Bidewell, when you had gambled away your horse, you stole it back and ran like a thief—which you were—leaving me to pay your debts."

He glanced toward the pitcher of water on the table beside his bed. "Please, may I have a drink of water?"

She marched toward him. "That was a dirty trick, Stephen MacLean, and I have never forgiven you. Do you know how close I came to the workhouse?" She slopped water into a glass. "All those years of shame, knowing my husband cared so little he left me in dire straits and never even inquired after my well-being. Finally I get to a place where the mistress needs me, really needs me . . . and I have to leave to take care of you? I just can't"—her voice wobbled—"believe I let Lady Halifax talk me into coming here when she was so—"

Here it comes. Taking Enid's hand, he pulled her toward him.

"—So sick and near death—"

Although Enid set her heels, MacLean tugged hard and sat her on the bed with him, then removed the glass from her hand and placed it back on the table.

Her hip rested against his. She didn't look at him. Her voice was almost inaudible when she added, "And now I'll never see her again."

How could he have misread the signs? Enid struggled not against misplaced passion but against guilt and grief. Her Lady Halifax had died, and his proud, defiant wife crumpled before his eyes. "Come here, sweetheart." Wrapping his arms around her, he brought her alongside him so her head rested on his shoulder. "Sh." He kissed her forehead, smoothed her hair back from her face. "It's all right, darling. She sent you to do the right thing, and you did it, and now you've both proved your stout hearts."

"But she's dead," Enid whispered, and her voice broke. Her shoulders shook, and the tears she had fought against burst forth in a torrent. She pressed her mouth against his bare skin to muffle her sobs.

MacLean lifted her, adjusted her, brought her whole body up to rest on him. "God will care for her. Let me care for you."

She still held the nightgown tight in her arms, gripping it as if the pad of soft, worn cotton could provide comfort in a bleak world.

He tugged it free, then wiped her cheeks with the hem. Holding it up to her nose, he ordered, "Blow."

With sobs interrupting almost every word, she said in horror, "I'm . . . not going to . . . blow my nose on my . . . nightgown."

If she hadn't been so tragic, he might have laughed. As it was, he said wryly, "So Enid is still in there."

Sitting up, she grabbed a clean towel from the pile on the bedstand, lowered her face and sobbed into it.

She didn't understand. Even now, she didn't understand. Hauling her back into his arms, he pressed her cheek to his chest. "No matter how many times you pull away, I'll still be here to hold you."

Sobs wracked her. "She's . . . dead. Cold . . . alone in the grave. Dying . . . I've seen it."

Of course she had. She nursed the ill. But he hadn't considered how it would affect her.

Her fingers clutched at his skin, and she writhed as if the sobbing hurt. "Dying is so . . . lonely."

His heart ached for her. He slung his leg over hers to envelop her in solace. He smoothed his hands up and down her spine.

"I wanted . . . wanted to hold her . . . hand as she . . . she slipped away."

He stroked Enid, murmured disjointed bits of comfort in her ear—and marveled at the depths of her caring.

And she must be right. He must be a selfish pig of a man, or else he'd not be holding her as she sobbed, wanting to comfort her, at the same time wanting her fierce devotion for himself. By God, she would adore him with all the fervor and passion of her being. He would make sure of that. But for now he hid his intentions with comforting murmurs and long, slow caresses.

"I can't . . . help . . . her . . . now. I can do . . . nothing now." Enid's voice rose, and she hit him once, right on the chest.

He caught his breath. The lady railed at fate, held him responsible, and she packed a good wallop.

"I want to go back in time. I want to be with her." She rolled her head on his chest. "Fix it. Fix . . . it!"

"I will." Her hair caught on the stubble of his chin,

and the faint scent of gardenias and outdoors rose from the strands. "I'll fix everything."

At last her sobbing slowed. She hiccupped. Wiped her eyes on the towel. And her fingers smoothed over the place where she had punched him, and lingered to tangle in his silky chest hair.

She was distraught. She didn't know what she was doing, how her slightest touch would affect him.

For the first time, he held her willing body in his arms. His own body demanded he comfort her in a physical way. He knew well enough to ignore his body; his cock directed his other organs, and his cock never gave good advice. By concentrating hard, he retained a modicum of good sense. "Show me the letter."

Sitting up, she dug the crumpled sheet out of her pocket and for a moment held it as if she couldn't give it up. Slowly she handed it over. "Lady Halifax's solicitor wrote it. I wish you could have read one of hers. Witty and"—her voice wobbled again—"sharp." She settled back onto his shoulder.

Just as if she belonged there. He managed, barely, not to raise his fist in victory. Instead, he took a towel, wet it in the basin and blotted her hot cheeks. "Better?"

She nodded, took the towel and pressed it to her swollen eyes.

He perused the letter in silence, then folded it again and handed it to her. "She must have loved you. She left you a legacy."

Enid cleared her throat and thrust the letter back into her pocket. "I'm sure she left all of her servants a legacy."

She should not dismiss herself so easily. "You weren't her servant. You were her companion."

"I imagine she left everyone in her employ a gift."

"After all that you've done for me, if I were to die today, I would want you to have the world. I know you, Enid MacLean, and you gave Lady Halifax no less than your best." Taking the towel, he wet it again and stroked Enid's forehead. "Her legacy to you is no token, but a personal message of affection."

"I hope so. I would like to have her silver-backed brush. I remember"—her voice quivered again, and she steadied it—"I used to brush her hair in the evening before she slept. She said it made her sleep better."

Her hand followed the ridge of muscle that formed his pectorals. Absentmindedly, he was sure. "Then perhaps you'll have the silver-backed brush."

She circled his nipples with her fingertips.

Absentminded or not, she had to stop. Catching her hand, he lifted it off his chest. "I hurt for you when you cry. I wish I could make everything better for you." He took a deep breath. "But I am a man. I am your husband. I want to console you in the time-honored way. Do you comprehend?" With the ball of his thumb, he tilted her face up to his.

The signs of grief were fading, soothed away by the damp, cool cloth, and that inner light that had brought him back from death glowed in her glorious blue eyes and through her velvety complexion. "I comprehend," she whispered.

The light drew him. He wanted to warm his hands on her, absorb her into himself, and the strain of self-discipline made him gruff. "If you touch me like that, I will comfort you as a husband does a wife, and I will not have you accuse me afterward of taking advantage of your grief."

She stared at him keenly and frowned ferociously.

Good. She was taking solemn note of his good intentions. Perhaps he would get credit for them, for God knew he got no satisfaction from denial.

In a halting voice, she said, "I'm tired of being sad, and angry, and biting my tongue when you . . . when you lash at me."

He lifted his brows. "You've been biting your tongue?"

"I'm tired of doing the right thing, of being lonely, of suffering . . . a cold bed."

Everything in his unruly body rose to attention.

"I'm tired of longing for . . . for . . ."

She couldn't stop now! "What?"

Shoving him away, she scrambled out of bed and turned her back on him, rubbing her hands up and down her arms.

Damn. Damn! If she wanted to pay him back for his ill-temper, she was doing a hell of a job. He wanted to shout at her, yet her stooped shoulders and bent head stopped him. For all these weeks, she had been a tower of strength. Enid in a fragile state was a new experience, one that touched his heart as well as his body. "Don't run away. I won't jump on you."

"I . . . I know. It's not that." Turning back, she considered him, head cocked. "I just remembered . . . how much I loved you once."

Had it truly been such a horror?

Or was she coming to love him again? "You don't

have to stand there." He lifted the covers invitingly. "You can come back into my arms."

Sidling close to the bed, she took his hand and threaded her fingers through his.

He rubbed her palm with his thumb, noting the calluses caused by hard work.

"I've given up everything for you, because you are my husband. I've had all of the duties and none of the privileges. Not your financial support, not your affection, not even your presence." She lifted her chin. "So just for tonight, we're going to do things my way."

His heart thumped. He tugged her close.

She sat on the bed beside him. "All I want is you."

Chapter 14

"Do you mean as man and wife?" MacLean gently squeezed her hand. "Naked in a bed?"

"Both of us." During the days Enid had cared for MacLean, she'd come to know by the way he smiled, by the power of his kisses, by the roll of his muscles, that this man could give her pleasure.

"You're not thinking with any amount of clarity."

"Yes, I am. I'm thinking very clearly." Now that the bitterness and the sorrow had passed, she was profoundly aware of him. Of the hard plane of his muscles beneath her. Of the scent of mint soap on his skin. "I'm thinking you're too weak to do anything but lie there while I pleasure myself with you."

"As a threat, that fails to strike fear into my heart."

"It should." Scars on his chest parted the hair in sharp lines, but he had healed well—and he had filled out stunningly. The exercises he performed each day had created a man hard of muscle and sinew. With the flat of her hand, she stroked the dusting of curly auburn hair that grew over his pectorals, down the center of his breastbone and disappeared from sight beneath the sheet. "Because I intend to make you suffer."

Perhaps it was simply that she had been without the touch of another human being for so long that she wished to soak up every fragment of kindness. Perhaps she was a wicked woman snatching at any chance for happiness.

She circled his nipples with her fingertips.

Perhaps she needed him.

"We should be sensible." But his voice grew fainter as she slid off the bed. The closed curtains puffed at the windows, moving with the faint breeze, but night cloaked the cottage as she unbuttoned the first button at her neck.

"Who cares?" She didn't. Not now. She had drunk deep of sorrow, and she wanted a taste of life. "I want something more than duty and responsibility. What could be wrong about that?"

"You're distraught," he said hoarsely.

"Do stop your bloodless mutterings. This is no time to develop morals."

He desired her. She'd known for weeks, and not just because he'd kissed her. He watched her with a heated gaze. He resented it when she laughed with Mr. Kinman or Harry. More and more, he hated it when she waited on him as if he were an invalid.

She desired him. She didn't want to, but since the day she'd seen him unconscious, since the moment he'd opened those extraordinary green-and-gold eyes, she had craved his touch, his body, his approval.

She wore the simplest of undergarments, but by the way he watched she might have been dressed in silk and lace. The muscles corded in his neck. His hands formed fists. His mouth opened with awe at seeing her discard her clothing with a fine insouciance she could never match on a day when wisdom ruled.

She much enjoyed the sight of his amazement. "Besides," she said, "we're married. Remember?"

"No," he said. "I don't."

"Take my word for it."

"I do. I take your word for everything." His eyes were hot, but his voice was cool. "You are the reason I'm still here. Without you, I would have already gone seeking answers."

Tossing her dress on the floor, she leaned to slide her hands across his shoulders in a long, slow glide. "You're not really thinking of leaving?"

"I don't know who I am." He caught her wrists and brought them, one by one, to his mouth. "I don't know what I've done. I don't know who's after me." He kissed her pulse points, slow, warm, wet kisses that made her close her eyes to savor the delight. "A man like me needs answers. But you hold me here with your brief, brilliant smiles and your sharp, honest tongue, the sway of your hips and your assiduous attention."

Did he think she'd been beguiling him on purpose? "I haven't been trying to entice you," she said faintly.

"Oh, I know that." He rubbed his thumb across her damp skin.

Then what did he mean? "I just want you to get better."

"I am better." He stroked his tongue along the outside of her thumb, then lightly bit the tip. "I'll show you."

When he touched her like that, she could hardly

catch her breath. When he looked at her as if she were
a tidbit and he a hungry wolf, she wanted to flee in disarray. But more than that, she wanted to stay and feed
his hunger . . . and her own.

Turning her back on him, she removed her drawers.
When she put her hands behind her to untie her petticoats, his fingers brushed hers away.

She looked behind her. He had leaned off the bed,
his face intent. His wide, beautiful mouth was serious.
His eyes narrowed on his task, and he pulled her close
and efficiently freed her from her petticoats.

"Have you given up your feeble attempts at good
sense?" She laughed softly, an effervescence bubbling
in her veins.

"I have no good sense where you're concerned." He
stroked the length of her hip, caught the hem of her
white lawn chemise.

Turning on him, she put her knee on the bed and
pressed her hands to his shoulders. "I'm handling this.
You just stay quiet and do what I tell you."

His gaze feasted on the breasts that escaped the con-
finement of her corset and thrust at her chemise. She
suspected he could almost see them through the thin
cloth; she knew her nipples had come to attention at his
notice. She took a long, slow breath; she taunted him
with her body.

"Tell me to unlace your corset," he whispered, his
lips forming each word with loving precision.

She watched the motions and knew he wanted to
leap at her. But for once in her life she held control. He
would do what she wanted, because if he didn't, she
would walk across the room and he wouldn't be able to
follow. She was pitiless. She was unfeeling. She was

exacting revenge and the promise of ecstasy, and she loved every moment.

"Unlace my corset," she commanded.

His hands weren't quite steady as they rose to their task, but he loosened the strings and began, with long, slow motions, to liberate her from almost the last of her clothing. Beneath the corset was her chemise, and beneath the chemise was bare body. She knew it, and he knew it, and he wanted to see her so badly that the knowledge brought the flush of triumph to Enid's skin. All of Enid's skin.

So to show herself, she untied the ribbon at the neck of her chemise.

It drooped over one shoulder.

MacLean faltered.

She slid her hand along her collarbone and under the bagging garment. Without taking her gaze from his face, she pushed her chemise down her arm. The ribbon snagged on her nipple for just a moment, then her breast popped free.

MacLean gave a groan that fed Enid's pleasure-starved soul.

She floated her fingers back up her arm and over her own nipple, erect with excitement. She flicked it with her fingernail while he stared, fixated by the sight. She asked, "Aren't you going to finish with the corset?"

He jerked on the string so hard that he ripped the material around the eyelet.

She should have cared, for she didn't have another; she laughed.

The speed and strength he used to pull the corset down dragged the chemise off the other breast and halfway to her belly. She helped him push the corset

over her hips, and while she finished the job he managed to get ahead of her and shove her chemise down
her arm.

She was naked, he was in a hurry—everything was
just as she remembered. But before she could experience disappointment, he paused. With his hands fram-
ing either side of her, he looked. In a voice of absolute
worship, he said, "Dear God, you're beautiful."

What was a girl to say to that? "Thank you." She felt
beautiful. He made her feel beautiful.

Strands of his uncut hair shone auburn against the
white pillow. His eyes slanted softly, and one lid
drooped more than the other—a result of the explosion. The scars on his face were faded, but they, and
the jut of his jaw, lent him a toughness he had never
possessed before. For all that he couldn't walk, his
body glowed with muscled, muted power. She might
have been undressing for a pirate, a robber king, a
stranger, and the sense of muted danger made her
pause and—shamefully—thrill.

Nonsense, of course. He was no stranger. They *were*
married. Perhaps time had improved his character, but
she knew Stephen MacLean. He was an actor, and although he practiced an air of untamed menace, in truth
he was only a petty thief and inveterate gambler. She
was using him, and that was fine. He owed her.

With a shimmy of her hips, she shook free of the
chemise.

His gaze followed its descent, and he said hoarsely,
"So beautiful."

Her skin prickled, and she caught his wrist when he
would have buried his fingers in the thatch of hair at
her thighs. "Not yet," she said.

She thought he might cavil at the restraint, might even free himself and make a grab at her.

Instead he smiled a lopsided smile and waited until she released him. Then, not quite touching, he traced the shape of her hip with his hand.

She swallowed. His slow, sensuous pantomime fed her hunger and denied her thirst at the same time. His palm slithered up her belly—oh, not really, but just beyond touch—and traced the plumpness of her breasts. Her breath caught again and again at the hint of contact, the whisper of sensation. Each motion promised and didn't fulfill, and she, who had wanted only promises, now sought fulfillment.

She swayed forward, but his hand glided away, up to almost caress her collarbone, to almost stroke her neck, then to actually take a tress of her hair between two fingers and arrange it so it curled about her nipple, made coy by concealment.

Ah, but she could tease, too. Catching the sheet in her hand, she slid it off of him, tormenting him and herself with the slow revelation of his hard-won and reconstructed body.

His shoulders and arms bulged and rippled with imposing masculine power. Below, his ribs still protruded more than she would have liked, yet his hard work had layered muscle over the previously sharply defined ridges, and he was breathtaking. The distance between his collarbone and his waist seemed to stretch forever, and the spot where his flesh disappeared beneath the band of his shabby, cut-off trousers proved a provocation of the primal sort.

She had seen his torso many a time; it had been impossible to avoid the sight as he lifted weights and tortured his body. But she had never seen below the trousers.

She wanted to see below the trousers.

He chuckled. "Curious, dearling? There are answers to be had."

He failed to take her domination seriously. He seemed to think he could control her with charming smiles and smoking desire.

Two could play that game. She placed her hand atop the bulge in his trousers.

He stopped smiling.

The magnitude of him astounded her. Her hand could not encompass his length—and she tried. She stretched the tip of her longest finger toward the base and her wrist toward the tip, and realized she had forgotten more about MacLean than she remembered. Snatching her hand back, she glared at him. "Do you realize I haven't done this in eight years?"

"Damn, lass." He lunged for her, grabbed her around the waist and pulled her over and onto him. "For all I remember, *I* might not have!"

She laughed at his fierceness, then the impact of his bare chest on hers took her breath away. Catching the back of her head, he brought her lips to his. She met him eagerly. They pressed, open-mouthed, tasting each other, consuming each other. Her bare breasts against his chest seemed wicked and glorious, and she shifted back and forth, just enough to allow his curling hair to rasp at her nipples.

He tore away his lips from hers. "Lass," he said. Just that, but he moved with her as if the closeness delighted him, too. Sliding his fingers into her hair, he said, "I have wanted to love you since the first time I saw you. I want to pamper you, to see your face when you've indulged in love and you're soft and warm . . . and ready for more." He massaged her scalp in slow, circling seductions, and he tilted her head up to gaze into her eyes. "You're the reason I didn't die, do you know that?"

"No," she whispered. Smoothing her palms down his ribs, she wished he'd stop talking.

Yet she reveled in his praise. He didn't seem shocked at her licentiousness. He encouraged her. He didn't seem repulsed, he seemed proud of himself. Proud of her. And his pride showed itself in the arousal that prodded at her stomach.

Now he described her as if she were an angel. "Tell me," she urged.

"Every time I opened my eyes, there you were, feeding me, talking to me, bathing me—"

"You were so thin." She kissed his wrist. "You're so powerful now."

"Sometimes at night, you'd be wearing that ghastly pink wrapper of yours—"

Indignation drew her from her balmy nest of satisfaction, and she struggled to sit up. "There's nothing wrong with my robe!"

"—And when you leaned over, I could see down the neckline to your breasts." His gaze dropped to her bosom, and he caressed one with the lightest touch. "Your breasts have lured a man from the grips of death."

She giggled. A silly laugh, but he sounded so

earnest, and the day had been so dreadful, and this . . . this time was a time set apart, a dream to match her long-lost fantasy of love. She thought she had forever squandered that fantasy on this marriage, but tonight, for just a moment, this man was the prince she had dreamed of. He had provided her with fulfillment; she would return the favor. "Wait until you see what I can lure with my whole body."

Beneath her, the rod in his trousers flexed.

She kissed his shoulder and lingered on one of the scars there. "Does that hurt?"

"No, you've kissed it better."

"Oh!" She liked that. "How about here?" She kissed a scar on his chest.

"You've made that better, too."

"And here?" She loitered at his nipple, circling it with her tongue.

"You could raise the dead," he said fervently.

She kissed her way down his stomach, finding each scar and rib, treating each to her approval, until she reached his waistband. Tucking her fingers within, she glanced up at him.

He watched intently, his face still and bleak with need. "I feel as if I have waited for you forever."

Pressing her lips to the bulge in his trousers, she breathed the scent of soap, clean flesh, and MacLean. He was her husband. She wanted to make him happy, and in the process herself happy—and she knew how. Unbuttoning his trousers, she slipped her fingers inside. His belly rippled beneath her caress; she found his hardness at once, and explored him with a tender touch.

She had forgotten so much; the firm, smooth head, the marbled rod. His size, his heat, the way his hips rolled as she stroked him.

His trousers inched downward; he was removing them.

"We have all night," she chided.

"*I* have about five minutes before I expire from eagerness."

As the trousers slipped lower, she captured him in her mouth. He tasted good, a clean male animal, and when she sucked, and swirled her tongue, the flavor became the slightest bit salty.

He was close, so close . . .

He sat straight up and pulled her back so that she sat on him, on his thighs, her heels tucked under her buttocks. His trousers hit the floor. She thought he would tumble her on her back and thrust into her, and she braced herself for the discomfort. Instead, he lifted her, shifted her. Her breasts touched his chest. He stared into her face, his eyes aglow with demand and desire. She felt the tip of him touch her, seeking entrance. She caught at his shoulders; her body softened, grew damp with longing.

"Enid, help me." He held her hips. "I can't do it all. You'll have to do your part."

Realization—and trepidation—struck her.

He wanted her to guide him, to take him into herself.

She was an experienced woman. A wife. MacLean's wife. Yet she hadn't been with a man in eight years. MacLean was so close she could feel his breath on her lips, see his pupils expand as he watched her and waited for her to decide—would she take him?

In the softest of voices, he said, "You need to assist me. I can't do it without you. I would be lost . . . without you."

More important—would she keep him? For that was what he demanded.

The rush toward euphoria ceased. His still features might have been cast in steel; his scars, his broken nose, his harsh jaw proclaimed him a warrior, a man of savage strength held in check.

Only his eyes were alive. His unique gold-shot green eyes commanded that she come to him of her own free will.

"I need you to come to me," he said, "to stay with me . . . forever."

The silence in the attic room grew to immense proportions. She wanted, so badly, to run, to hide, to never have to make this choice. For when she did, she would be his wife, not just for the night, but forever. That was the price she paid for tonight's dissipation; if she refused, he would let her go. His character was strong enough to do that—but he would renew the assault another day.

Sooner or later, he would prevail.

She swallowed. All her fears rose in her.

No one had ever loved her. Not forever. And she could love—had loved—too many times, and been left standing on the wayside alone.

But MacLean was her husband. He had changed. He was different. He seemed honorable.

And, after all, if she was wrong about him, it didn't matter because she didn't love him. In the morning, as every morning, they would still be bound by the vows they'd exchanged nine years ago, yet she would not love him.

She could take the chance tonight because she wouldn't let herself love. She would never again be open to heartache and sorrow. She would forever be free of the ambush of love.

Slowly, she slipped her hand between them and positioned his penis in exactly the right place. She adjusted herself and pressed herself downward.

He smiled, a slight, hard, brief smile.

Then he proved the depths of his duplicity. For he didn't need her help.

He placed her hands back on his shoulders. His hands slid around her thighs. He opened her wider, pushing up with his hips.

And entered her. Inch by inch, he stroked into her. She grimaced, always at the point of discomfort, determined not to engage in a fruitless wrestling match as she tried to free herself. Eight years had been too long, she had been too young, her body had healed from his early assaults and closed itself once more.

But still he came into her, an inexorable march, stretching her so that she knew she would never find pleasure.

Just like before. She would be unfulfilled.

She tried to hide her disappointment, but he saw her distress. He observed everything. He was too perceptive, and she hated that, so she closed her eyes and turned her head.

And he slipped one hand between them. He used two fingers to adjust her. He touched her, the veriest whisper of voluptuousness.

She caught her breath. Her thighs flexed, and she

lifted herself just the tiniest bit. That had been . . . enjoyable.

His finger circled and touched her again.

Everything flexed.

She opened her eyes and stared at him, hope and passion blossoming together.

"Is that better, dearling?" His voice rasped a velvet seduction. "I felt that inside. You clutched at me, and you're already so . . . tight."

She half rose away from his touch. Then settled back.

His voice, smooth and seductive, rumbled in her ear. "You're like a velvet glove around me, caressing me. I'm in . . . ecstasy."

Everything fit a little more comfortably.

She rose.

"I'm going to possess you. You're going to know you're mine every minute of the day. You're going to want me inside you all night long."

At his husky warning, her knees gave out. She sank onto him, all the way down.

Then they were moving together. Violently, intemperately, a clash of bodies. He fell back onto the pillows. She leaned forward over him, hands braced against his shoulders. He guided her with his hands beneath her thighs. Her muscles ached as she moved on him. His hips pumped beneath her. He filled her. He watched her face, forced the pace, silently demanded with his voluptuous fury that she spend herself on him.

But she would not allow him to command her. Not about this. She had chosen to give herself to him. She was his nurse, his wife. She would force him to show his excitement. She moved with his rhythm, but she watched him in return. She ran her hands across his belly. She leaned back, placed her hands on his thighs, and proudly displayed her breasts.

His discipline failed. His eyes half-closed. His head tilted back. He breathed in great gasps, and his neck corded with the madness of passion.

She should have experienced triumph. Instead the sight of him beneath her, twisting in anguished pleasure, doubled and redoubled her own passion. She moaned with every stroke. To know that he found such ferocious delight with her—that was the true aphrodisiac.

The whole world was encapsulated in a bed with rumpled sheets, a stack of pillows, and a flushed, euphoric MacLean held captive between her legs. They moved together, more quickly, more quickly, and she could contain herself no longer. Her body, already warmed with passion, surged into orgasm. She threw her head back. Deep within her, her muscles convulsed, and she wanted . . . she sought . . . oh, God, she found.

She screamed her delight.

He held himself in check, stroking in the small, restrained movement. Then when she'd reached the crest, he released his restraint. He pounded into her, carrying her to another orgasm, and another, and at the same time, he poured his seed into her, a mighty, virile, majestic mating.

Gradually, her heart slowed. Lethargy took the place of passion, and she sank down on top of him, her head on his chest, her trembling thighs about his hips. The breath chafed in her lungs. She wondered briefly if anyone had heard them in the room below, then decided she wouldn't worry now. In the morning, perhaps. Then she would think about things like . . .

Like the fact that MacLean would assume she had promised him things she would never give.

The thought made her muscles tense. Lethargy fled, and she feigned a casual withdrawal. If she could just slip away and go to her own bed . . .

As if she could leave him and he would not notice.

Holding her firmly in place, he said, "You panic quickly."

How did he know?

"But you mustn't. You're mine now, and I'll take care of everything." He skimmed his fingers down her spine, caught the edge of the covers, and drew them over them both. "I'll take care of you."

Closing her eyes tightly, she pretended to be asleep.

In the wee hours of the morning, a pounding at the trapdoor and the shouts of men roused her from the depths of slumber.

"Fire! For God's sake, get out! The cottage is on fire!"

Chapter 15

MacLean. Enid struggled out of the covers. She had to get MacLean out of the cottage, and she didn't know how. She couldn't carry him, couldn't drag him . . . perhaps the guards below . . .

But MacLean was already up. Moving toward her, holding her pink wrapper.

With a cry, she tried to catch at him.

"Sh. I'm fine." He fed one of her arms into the sleeve. "Hurry. We've got to get out."

It was a miracle. Another miracle, one as great as when he'd opened his eyes and spoken. He could walk!

And the fire was going to kill him—and her.

The pounding on the trapdoor continued. "Wake up! Wake up! Fire!"

Fire. God, fire. Smoke oozed through the cracks in the floorboards. An odd light illuminated the west side of the room.

MacLean already had his trousers on. Kneeling at her feet, he helped her with one of her shoes while she stuck her arm in the other hole and tied the belt.

"I'm all right," she said hoarsely. "Go on!"

MacLean moved without any sign of distress, as if he saw no reason for haste, as if he dealt with crisis every day, as if he walked all the time.

She wanted to scream at him to hurry, then to be careful. This was too much for him. He might fall. His leg might break. He might die in the fire.

She pulled on her shoe while he tried to unfasten the latch of the trapdoor. Jerking his hand back, he shook it as if it had been burned.

Enid threw him a towel. He wrapped it around his fingers. He unlatched the door and tugged at it. Whoever stood below pushed at the same time. The door slammed back. Smoke rushed in. Enid heard a roaring from below as flames consumed the wooden walls on the interior of the cottage.

Holding a towel before his face, Harry bounded up the stairs and shut the door after him. "The way is blocked. We're going to have to go out the window."

"MacLean can't go out the window," Enid protested, and coughed as the smoke billowed around her face. "His leg—"

But the men weren't listening to her. They went to work, pulling a rope out of a bag MacLean had stashed beneath his bed. Before she knew it, Enid found herself crawling into the thicket of rosebushes beside the cottage. Hands from below caught her and pulled her out of the brambles.

Men shouted encouragement as MacLean started

the descent. She wanted to shout, too, but she couldn't. Terror closed her throat. She feared for him too much.

Then he stood beside her, grasping her arm. He led her to the picket fence, instructed, "Stay there until I come for you," and went back to help Harry off the rope and make sure no one else remained inside the cottage.

What did he think he could do? Mount a rescue? He'd been ill. She found herself crying again, she who never cried. The stone walls of the cottage glowed from the heat inside. Lady Halifax had died. Like a fool, Enid had consummated her marriage, letting MacLean assume all sorts of wrong things. Now a fire devoured everything while he stalked about like a man capable of performing rescues, going on adventures . . . abandoning her again.

Sobs shook her every limb. When she had allowed herself to think about MacLean's recovery, she had imagined she would lead him, slowly and carefully, back into the world of perambulation.

But he didn't need her. He wasn't her patient anymore. Everything had changed.

What was she going to do?

Someone gently took her arm and led her outside the gate, away from the gathering crowd who shouted and pointed at the flames shooting out of the roof. "Mrs. MacLean? Are you hurt?"

It was Mr. Throckmorton, his face illuminated in the weird, flickering light. He wore no cravat, his shirt had no collar and his hair stuck up wildly, but his tone was soothing and his gaze concerned.

She took a quivering breath. "I'm fine."

"You're crying." He offered his handkerchief. "Why are you crying?"

Oh, as if she would tell him that!

"It's all right." Gingerly, he patted her shoulder. "Everyone is safe, and that's all that truly matters. And I know you've lost all your possessions, but I promise we'll replace everything we can."

Her things! She hadn't even thought . . . her clothes, her letters from Lady Halifax, the shawl she'd been painstakingly tatting for over four years . . . she sobbed harder.

With a roar, the roof caved in. Men scattered in all directions. Enid forgot her own grief and wildly looked about, trying to locate MacLean.

Face smudged, smelling of smoke, he appeared at her side and pulled her into his arms.

She held onto him and sobbed.

This was getting to be a habit, one she shouldn't encourage, but she was tired and everything was horrible.

"Are you hurt?" he demanded.

She shook her head.

"She's a little concerned about her belongings," Mr. Throckmorton said.

MacLean hugged her, rocked her. "Don't worry about your things. The important thing is, we're safe."

Sharply furious at him, at Mr. Throckmorton, at the whole stupid world, she pushed away from him. "I'm not . . . worried about my . . . possessions!" Her voice hit such a high note that dogs were howling. She didn't care. "How can you think I'm so . . . foolish I would worry about my . . . things?"

Mr. Kinman had joined them, and Harry, and all

four of them had that distinctly uncomfortable mien of men forced to witness feminine emotion.

"It's just . . . the fire, and . . . you walking, and—" She caught herself before she mentioned that she and MacLean had spent the evening fornicating like rabbits. But she wanted to.

MacLean realized it, too, for he pulled her back into his arms and muffled her face in his chest. "I'm sorry. Throckmorton and I were wrong to worry about you."

"My letters from Lady Halifax." She hiccupped a last sob.

MacLean stroked her hair and wisely didn't answer.

Her fingers rubbed at his bare chest. She sniffled. "MacLean, why don't you ever wear a shirt? I'm tired of dripping on you."

Harry said, "She's irritable."

"I am not." But she muttered the denial.

In an amused tone, MacLean said, "Next time we have a fire in the middle of the night, we'll rescue her, but we won't wake her up."

Enid knew the men were nodding, and she wanted to slap them all. First MacLean, then Mr. Throckmorton, then Mr. Kinman, then Harry—then MacLean again. They didn't understand.

"The men are all accounted for," Mr. Kinman said.

Above her head, MacLean spoke in the sharp, commanding tone he usually saved for her. "So, Throckmorton, what caused the fire?"

Mr. Throckmorton answered, "We'll find out."

"Seems havey-cavey to me," Harry added.

A long silence followed his comment. Enid lifted

her head and saw MacLean, Mr. Kinman, and Mr. Throckmorton all glaring at Harry.

Harry's eyes glowed in the light of the dying flames, and he jerked his thumb toward her. "She's not stupid, you know."

"You think someone set the fire?"

Harry stuck his finger in his ear and jiggled it. She had hit that high note again.

"I think someone was careless, and whoever it is will be removed from his station," Mr. Throckmorton said firmly. "There's nothing for you to worry about, Mrs. MacLean."

She didn't believe him. Hadn't believed his assurances about her and about MacLean for quite a while now. An assassin, perhaps, would finish what the bomb had started. A killer would set a fire and trap a crippled man and burn him to death.

Harry was right. She wasn't stupid. She would be on the alert.

Mr. Throckmorton spoke gently to her. "We'll take you to the main house. The women can take care of you there." Then, to MacLean, he said, "I've sent for a carriage."

"Good." MacLean cleared his throat and lowered his voice so only she could hear him. "I don't think I can walk that far."

Guilt assaulted her. She'd been thinking of herself and her letters, for heaven's sake, while MacLean had risen for the first time in months and walked! And of course, being a man and as stubborn as a donkey, he didn't want to admit his fatigue in front of the other men. Enid gave a fierce scowl at Harry and Mr. Kinman, who backed off hurriedly, then she slipped her arm around MacLean's waist. "Come and sit on that bench."

On the other side, Mr. Throckmorton hooked his arm through MacLean's. "We'll get you clothes and everything you require for your trip."

His trip?

But MacLean sounded as if he understood. "Have you set the departure time, then?"

"As soon as possible. I don't believe in coincidence, and this . . ." Mr. Throckmorton trailed off, and when someone hailed him, he looked relieved. "Can you make it to the bench without me? It's not far." At MacLean's nod, he hurried away.

The stone bench stood only a few steps away. She was glad, for MacLean leaned his full weight on her.

His trip? She'd give him a trip! Dropping his arm, she shoved at him.

Off-balance, he toppled onto the bench. "Enid, be careful. My leg . . ."

She managed to keep her tone reasonable. "Your trip? Where are you going?"

"To Scotland."

"To Scotland." He was going to Scotland. He was leaving, and no one had said a word to her.

Of course, why would they? She was just the caretaker.

She was just his *wife*.

MacLean continued, "Throckmorton hopes I'll recover my memory at home."

"Too bad about the fire, isn't it?" She inveighed every word with sarcasm. "If not for the fire, you could have sneaked out of here without ever having to face me."

He did a good imitation of a man startled and offended. "Enid, you've misunderstood."

His weighty, commiserating tone made her want to retch. "Misunderstood? Not at all. You're abandoning me again. You can wrap it up in all the pretty words you like, but you're abandoning me again!" She put her fists on her hips, which made her look like a fishwife, but anything was better than giving in to the temptation of hitting him. "You've had your way with me, and you're running off home."

"No, dearling, listen—"

"I know I'm not the wife you wanted. I know I'm not particularly good between the sheets. But maybe that's because I haven't had enough practice, and whose fault is that?"

He glanced around at the people standing about, watching the dying flames. "Hush."

She raised her voice. "I will not hush! And what's wrong with my methods, anyway? You certainly seemed satisfied tonight!"

"I was. Enid, you've misunderstood!"

"Misunderstood what? That you're going to leave me here without a position to go to, thrust me into poverty once more, abandon me—"

"For God's sake, woman, would you clabber your maw?" he roared.

She stopped talking, crossed her arms over her chest, and glared at him.

He looked her over, then held out his hand. "Help me up."

She didn't want to. She didn't want to uncross her arms or take his hand. She suspected a trick. She suspected he would try and talk her around, and she would be forced to push him over again. But when he began to struggle to his feet on his own, she stuck out her hand. "Oh, here."

Taking it, he hefted himself up and wrapped her in his embrace all in one motion. "You're going with me."

She caught her breath. "Oh."

He rested his cheek on top of her head. "I wouldn't go anywhere without you. Not now. Not ever."

"Oh." She felt vaguely foolish. She wondered how many people had overheard her tirade. She wondered if she would care in the morning.

"Throckmorton and I discussed it today while you were gone. I had no time to tell you last night." His voice dropped to a whisper and warmed to an ember. "You know why."

Yes, she knew why. Standing here with his arms around her and her body stirring, she knew why very well.

"So I'm going to Scotland to meet your family at last." She wondered how they would welcome her. Whether Kiernan MacLean would disdain her. Whether Stephen MacLean would recover his memory and she would be once again alone.

MacLean tilted her chin up and smoothed the lines from between her eyebrows. "Don't worry. I'll take care of everything. I will care for you."

She looked at that strong, stubborn, determined face, and for the first time realized they could succeed as husband and wife. Even when MacLean got his memory back, he couldn't return to immaturity and selfishness. It wasn't possible for a character to regress so profoundly, and this new MacLean was everything she'd ever dreamed of. No—he was more than she had ever allowed herself to dream of.

"You look so dazed and so . . . pretty." He smiled at her with all the crooked charm his injured face would allow. "I was just thinking—when I was prone and you were bossing me around, I thought you a veritable giant, and you're only a wee bit of a thing. I assumed you were taller than this."

"Yes, well, I thought you were . . ." She caught her breath on a shard of dismay. *Shorter.* She thought he was shorter. Her husband, Stephen MacLean, was a bit under six feet tall. This man, this husband, was at least three inches taller.

"You thought I was . . . what?" He still smiled at her with his stranger's face.

Her desperate mind fumbled for an explanation.

She had forgotten his height as well as his face.

No, she hadn't. A woman always remembered gazing up at her husband during their wedding ceremony, and the top of her head had reached Stephen's chin.

He had grown.

Impossible. Stephen had been twenty-six when he'd wed her.

Only one explanation remained.

"What's wrong?" MacLean caught her shoulders in his hands. "Enid, what's wrong? You look as if you could faint."

This wasn't Stephen.

This man wasn't her husband.

Chapter 16

"Is there anything I can do for you before you leave, Mrs. MacLean?"

Enid stared around at the controlled pandemonium in the secluded drawing room, at the maids folding clothes and placing them in trunks, at Mrs. Brown, who carried linens, at Harry, who stood by the doorway, arms crossed, the epitome of belligerent suspicion. Then Enid looked up at Mr. Throckmorton.

She wanted to shriek, *Yes, tell me why you've done this.*

She breathed hard, trying to get enough air to save herself from fainting. Every time she thought of the dreadful deception, her stomach knotted, her hands shook, and she feared she would collapse in a blithering passion of hysteria. Because the man she had spent two months caring for, the man she had uprooted her whole life for . . . the man she had given her body to . . . wasn't her husband.

Yet those eyes. Those eyes were Stephen's. About that she could not be wrong.

But his face . . . not just battered from the explosion, but the wrong face. He was . . . he had to be . . . Kiernan MacLean, laird of the MacLeans. Kiernan MacLean, who on the occasion of her marriage to Stephen, had written to cruelly reject her.

She wasn't sure Mr. Throckmorton knew. Mac-Lean's appearance had fooled her, so maybe . . . oh, she didn't know. She didn't know if she should tell Mr. Throckmorton. She didn't know if her confession would cause more trouble and call forth more danger. So she said only, "I don't understand. Why are we going to Scotland *today?*" The sun had scarcely peeked over the horizon, yet they had been packing since they'd arrived at the main house.

"These are our normal precautions in a situation such as this," Mr. Throckmorton assured her. "Her Majesty's government does not take lightly the murder or the attempted murder of her subjects by a foreign power."

Perhaps, but with the far-flung borders of the empire growing ever larger, Enid had trouble believing Her Majesty's government exerted itself quite so much for each death. "Couldn't we at least wait until MacLean has recovered from the shock of the fire?"

Mr. Throckmorton seated himself in the chair opposite her. "MacLean seems to be thriving."

True. MacLean's color was good, his expression animated. He had demanded that his hair be cut, and the auburn locks she had slid through her fingers only the night before had been shorn to a more gentlemanly length. Clearly the inactivity of the sickroom had worn on him, and he welcomed departure. Yet he glanced at her occasionally, checking on her as if he were worried about her.

Well. She had almost passed out in front of the burning cottage. He didn't seem to know why. Indeed, she acquitted him of dissembling; he truly believed he was her husband.

But he wasn't. He wasn't.

"It's you I'm worried about," Mr. Throckmorton said. "Pardon me for observing, but you're pale and have dark rings under your eyes. We have a bedchamber made up for you. Won't you try to get some sleep?"

"I couldn't sleep." If she tried, she would see MacLean's green-and-gold eyes before her and know . . . know that she had committed fornication.

MacLean caught her looking at him, and right there, in front of everyone, he blew her a kiss.

Silly, romantic gesture. She wanted to duck and hide, for when he found out the truth, he would be furious.

Dear Lord, she had fornicated with Kiernan Mac-Lean.

"You're not to worry about your lost clothing." Mr. Throckmorton seemed to be trying to reassure her on every level. "Celeste is packing for you, and I know some of the gowns are from her own trousseau."

"I wish she wouldn't." Enid smoothed the skirt of the green tweed traveling outfit Celeste had insisted on giving her. Two seamstresses were sewing madly on a variety of costumes, clothes such as Enid had never dreamed of wearing, altering them to fit Enid's taller frame. "I can't ever pay her back."

Mr. Throckmorton looked pained. "Please, Mrs. MacLean. The fire which destroyed your belongings is my responsibility. I promise you I will replace every gown for Celeste." He looked at Celeste as she consulted with the seamstresses. "My fiancée is generous and clever, and you must not try to get in her way in this matter or any other, or she'll shoot you." He turned back to Enid, his mouth twisted in sardonic amusement. "I have the scars to prove it."

No matter what he said, no matter how hard everyone tried to make Enid feel as if this flurry of leaving was natural and wonderful, the rush of events battered at her. If only she could stop for a moment, think and reason, and decide the right thing to do. But Mr. Throckmorton wanted them out of here. Someone had attempted to kill MacLean.

She ought to send MacLean on his way, by himself, but if she did she would give up any right to know his fate. And perhaps, just perhaps, she acted as camouflage for him. After all, she appeared to be devoted to her husband. To Stephen MacLean.

Oh, why lie to herself? She *was* devoted to him.

Just . . . so frightened about what would happen if someone tried to hurt him again. And so appalled when she considered his justifiable rage when he realized he had lain with his cousin's despised wife.

His cousin, who was dead.

Stephen MacLean was—had to be—the man who had died in the explosion. She was truly a widow now, free to do as she wished. Except . . . she wasn't, because she was going to Scotland. She wanted to cover her face and cry in desolation and confusion, but she had sworn she wouldn't cry again.

She had one question. One question that desperately needed to be answered. In painfully polite tones, she said, "Mr. Throckmorton, I feel . . . peculiar about going to the Isle of Mull. As if I don't belong there."

Reading her confusion, Throckmorton examined her intently. "Mrs. MacLean, do you understand why I've wanted MacLean to recall, by himself, who he is and the events leading to his accident?"

"I . . . yes, I suppose so. You want him to remember without any prompting."

"That's right. I fear that if we tell him what to think, our influence will taint his memories."

She knew he had issued a plea—and a warning. *Don't tell MacLean about his past* . . . but what could she tell MacLean, except that he was not the man she had told him he was? That she was not the wife he believed? She didn't relish that conversation, and it would have to come, for sooner or later he would remember. If he didn't remember before they reached the Isle of Mull, she would face a highly uncomfortable situation. She would meet his family, and they would know the truth. They would tell the truth. More important, she might meet . . . She clasped her hands together, so hard her fingers tingled. "Tell me about the MacLeans. Who they are? What they do?"

Throckmorton answered readily enough. "They're a large family on an immense estate, with cousins and retainers galore."

Delicately, she angled toward the knowledge she wanted. "Is Stephen MacLean's mother alive?"

"Yes, she is. As I understand it, she's a beautiful woman who adores her son and thinks he can do no wrong." Mr. Throckmorton's face remained impassive. "Her name is Lady Catriona MacLean."

"Lady Catriona MacLean." Enid committed the name to memory. "But I know Stephen's father is dead." She found herself watching MacLean as she spoke.

MacLean caught her eye and grinned at her, a big, hairy man who thought her breasts brought him back to life, who had kissed her into ecstasy and made her his own.

She tore her gaze away. "What about . . . oh, his aunt?"

"That would be Lady Bess Hamilton. I met her once years ago. She's quite eccentric. She wears turbans and smokes cigars. When I met her I thought her charming." Throckmorton smiled. "Her son does not."

Enid's heart began a hard, steady thumping, as for the first time, knowing what she knew, she said his name. "Her son is Kiernan MacLean, the current laird?"

"Yes. There's a daughter, too, Kiernan's sister. Her name is Caitlin."

A light sweat dabbled Enid's forehead, and she leaned forward. "The laird himself? Is he . . . married?"

Throckmorton leaned back in his chair and looked hard at her. Slowly, drawing out the words, he said, "No. No, he's quite the ladies' man. He's never been married."

She sat back and let out a long, pent-up breath. "Good. That's very good."

* * *

The coach stood at ready with four matched horses to pull it. The trunks were loaded. MacLean stood on the broad steps, breathed in the fresh air and experienced the familiar sting of excitement. Then he laughed aloud. He didn't remember why that sting was familiar, but it was, and he loved it. He felt grand, in control of his destiny once more. He would mold events as he wished; soon the mysteries would be all solved, he'd have his memory back, and everything would be right in the world.

Then he caught sight of Enid, dressed in a traveling costume of a sturdy bottle green wool, a bonnet, a black worsted skirt with a bottle green velvet jacket, a glorious, brick red cravat, and a serene expression. She carried a capable air about her, and a smooth concern for him. She had gone away from him; before the fire, she'd been flustered, warm, a wife who'd been well pleasured. Now she smiled at him with impersonal kindness, acted like the kind of female who allowed herself to be hired rather than one who gave from the goodness of her heart.

She had even asked him if he felt married.

He had leered with exaggerated lust when he'd answered, "I do now."

She hadn't laughed.

Indeed, she'd indulged in no honest emotion at all, yet he saw the signs of tension; she had draped a handsome matching green wool cape, trimmed with fur, over her arm, and she clutched a large reticule so tightly that he was willing to wager that, beneath her black leather gloves, her knuckles were white.

Enid. Last night she had been everything he'd imagined. She had been wanton in her giving, generous in her caresses, and so heated in her loving that he had almost ignited with the pleasure. Of course, she had resisted his demand that she cleave to him, and even afterward she had not been convinced of the rightness of their union.

He was convinced enough for the both of them. While he knew on some level that she was not the most striking female in the world, when he looked at her, he saw perfection. She was his woman, and he would overcome her doubts. He only wished that when she looked at him she would manage a little affection. Her haunted blue eyes troubled him. It was almost as if she was saying good-bye.

In truth, he watched her closely, for he feared she would bolt.

Throckmorton strode up to him. "Ready?"

MacLean laughed a little. "Past ready."

"The items you asked for have been placed where you can get them. More than one stash, just as you requested." Observing him without a hint of amusement, Throckmorton said, "You're acting suspicious and wary, just as you always have. Are you sure you don't remember?"

"I don't remember, but yes, this feels natural to me. And my wariness saved my life last night, and my wife's."

Throckmorton lowered his voice. "Sally has disappeared."

"Sally?" MacLean remembered the girl who had waited on him, who seemed so eager to please. "The maid?"

"She came into the cottage last night to talk to the

guard. Harry found him unconscious, and the coals from the fireplace were spread across the wooden floor."

Thinking out loud, MacLean said, "Someone paid her. Someone wanted me eliminated."

"If they had known that you could walk, there would have been a more direct action."

"No wonder you're in such a hurry to get us out of here."

Throckmorton stuck his hands in his pockets and kicked at the step. "I'd go with you if I wasn't getting married."

"You must show up for the ceremony." MacLean rubbed his palm across the scars on his cheek. "You have no idea who is after me?"

Throckmorton lowered his voice yet again. "Not yet, but we're placing you in this carriage in full sight of anyone who might be watching. In a few hours, you'll stop at an inn to change the team. You'll remain there while another couple re-boards the carriage to go on. You—"

"And Enid."

Throckmorton nodded. "—And Enid will be left behind, there to transfer to a private train and go on to Edinburgh. After that we'll move you back to a carriage, and you'll go to Oban. Then a ferry to Mull. We've got men with you every step of the way. I can't promise nothing will happen—obviously, after last night, I cannot—but I've spread my protection as thickly as possible."

"Will my family know we're coming?"

"No one must know."

"So we're going to outrun trouble."

"Retreat is our first line of defense."

Belligerent with the need to know, MacLean said, "It's time you told me the truth."

Throckmorton hesitated, as if he were tempted. "You know most of the truth. You know what happened to you. You know that someone wants you dead. I harbor a great fear that if I tell you everything before you remember on your own, your memories will be confused. We need those memories. Whoever set the trap for you and killed the other fellow is very nervous, and if we could just find out his name—"

"I will tell you as soon as I know, but I like not that you are withholding information from me."

"If I told you now, you would just shout at me, and we can't afford a scene of that proportion." Throckmorton held out his hand. "Trust me a little longer. What I know can't hurt you."

MacLean clasped it. No other man here had his complete trust. Not Harry, black-clad and dangerous. Not Kinman, a sharp-eyed fellow who hid his intelligence behind a bumbling exterior. Not Jackson, the supercilious valet who wielded the razor so expertly. Someone was trying to kill him, and with him, his wife.

"So ye're going, sir?" Mrs. Brown stood behind them on the steps.

"I am." MacLean surveyed the woman whose wisdom he had come to cherish. "Will you miss me?"

"You and Mrs. MacLean." Mrs. Brown surveyed him with satisfaction. "I knew ye were holding out on us, sir. I knew ye'd been walking about the room."

"And how did you know that?"

"Calluses on yer feet."

"There's no fooling Mrs. Brown," Throckmorton grinned. "She's taken care of too many children."

"So she has told me." MacLean took her hand and kissed it, and in a spirit of mischief said, "I thank you, Mrs. Brown, for wiping my bare bottom."

Hand to her bosom, Mrs. Brown laughed and blushed.

Enid watched them as if she longed to come up and join in. He curved his hand to her invitingly, but she pretended she hadn't seen.

Mrs. Brown frowned at him. "Mr. MacLean, I thought I told you to have a care for your marriage."

"I have."

"Then why is she upset with ye?"

Irascibly, he said, "Why do you think her behavior is my fault?"

"Because ye're a man. It's always yer fault," Mrs. Brown answered roundly.

Throckmorton elbowed him. "You can't win with Mrs. Brown. I don't know why you try."

A familiar, faintly accented voice called from the top of the stairs.

Throckmorton's head snapped around, and at the sight of Celeste, he smiled a smile so fond and foolish that MacLean almost laughed aloud. She had the man wrapped around her delicate little finger.

With a smile and a wave, she bustled past them, a dynamo of energy and affection, and went right to Enid's side. Clasping her friend's hand, she said, "I wish you didn't have to go."

"Oh." Enid kissed her cheek. "I wish I didn't, either. I'll miss you so much!"

MacLean watched the women, wanting them to be

friends, yet jealous of the smile that lit Enid's face at the sight of Celeste. She had never looked at him that way, and ever since last night, she had acted as if he were bound to wound her.

"And I you. You must promise you'll return to visit me"—Celeste lowered her voice, but MacLean heard her—"no matter what happens."

"I don't know if you'll want me when you discover . . ." Enid's voice trailed off. She glanced at MacLean, and seeing him staring at her, she flushed scarlet.

She didn't glare. She didn't snap out a comment. She turned away as if humiliated by the sight of him.

He wanted to roar at her, to tell her not to be ashamed of what they'd done. He wanted to talk to her, to explain that they were husband and wife and they would be together always. He wanted to kiss her until she relaxed against him. Most of all, he wanted to tease her until his sharp-tongued wife retorted smartly and he knew, he *knew*, she belonged to him.

"Everything's ready." Throckmorton slapped him on the back. "It's time to go."

Chapter 17

Enid woke to hear the racket of the metal wheels on the track, to feel the jostling of the train. It had been daylight when she had finally succumbed to slumber in the specially built sleeping compartment. Now, a single candle burned in the sconce on the wall. When she parted the velvet curtains to look outside, she could see nothing but black night, without a star or a glimpse of the moon. They—she, MacLean, and their entourage— must be crossing a desolate region indeed; the northlands, she supposed, or they might even have crossed the border into Scotland. She didn't know how long it took to travel so far; she had never traveled by train before.

Blinking, she sat up in her bed. A light blanket had been pulled over her, by Kiernan MacLean, she supposed. She wondered where he'd wandered off to, then cursed herself for her curiosity. He had been with her when she'd gone to sleep; he had spent every moment with her since they'd left Blythe Hall, talking to her, stroking her hair, acting so much like a loving husband that she wanted to cry or shriek or cling to him and beg him to tell her everything would be fine.

She had not. She had maintained a serene façade—which she feared had not fooled him at all.

Sliding out of the bunk, she quietly performed her ablutions.

She couldn't nag him. She couldn't sob on him. She most certainly couldn't make love with him again. He was not her husband. She couldn't treat him like one.

Although—she faced the little mirror set above the table in the corner—he acted like a husband. He had untied the red wood cravat at her neck and loosened the buttons on her green velvet jacket, opening them and baring her neck down to the vee of her breasts. Perhaps he had done so to make her comfortable, but she knew he had taken delight in the sight of her bare skin, and in his right to make free with her clothing.

With a sniff, she brushed at her skirt, pulled on her sturdy black traveling boots, and arranged her garments to respectability again.

At least he hadn't tried to make love to her. She couldn't allow that. True, they had already taken a bite from the apple, but now she knew the facts. She knew right from wrong. She had clung to her morals through dreadful times when abandoning them would have made her life much easier. She could never make love with MacLean again—and she hated the pang that went through her.

She almost wished she could tell him, but Mr. Throckmorton had been quite specific in his instructions, and Enid feared he was right. Perhaps if they interfered with the return of MacLean's memories he would never find the truth that lurked beneath the surface of his mind.

She heard the murmur of men's voices in the compartment beyond the sleeping room, and she cautiously peered out the door.

MacLean sat with his legs propped up on the facing seat, talking to Harry.

Harry struck a similar pose, yet both men, for all their apparent repose, emitted an air of vigilance at odds with their postures.

They both wore black and brown, monotonous colors that gave them the appearance of morticians. Black jackets, black trousers, black boots that did not shine with polish, but rather were dulled as if the leather had been deliberately scuffed. Their waistcoats were dull brown, their cravats matched.

A small table sat between them, with five candles stuck in an affixed candelabra, an open bottle of wine, and two half-full glasses. They were speaking earnestly, and neither of them noticed her.

Enid sidled back toward her bunk, sat down and stared at the floor. She still didn't understand how MacLean had managed to change so quickly from invalid to man of action. He would be so much easier to handle if he remained trapped in a bed.

What was she to do in these next few days as they were whisked hither and yon by Mr. Throckmorton's men and MacLean came ever closer to his home? The knot in her stomach tightened. She considered herself a woman of good reason and logic, with a surfeit of etiquette and a healthy dollop of self-preservation, but she was allowing herself to be carried along by events because she didn't know what else to do.

Well, really, no precedent existed for her to follow. He needn't think that she lied to him. Either there had been a horrible mistake, or they both had been lied to, and MacLean would just have to listen to her explanations before he blistered her with his contempt.

Contempt she did not deserve and would not accept.

"I'll wake her." MacLean's voice sounded from right outside her door. In a humorous tone and in reply to Harry's murmured comment he said, "No, thank you, Harry, I can handle my own wife."

She stood up so quickly that her ankle boots struck the floor with a thud.

Pushing the door open, he considered her raised chin. "You heard that, did you?" His gaze ran over her too warmly. "You're looking beautiful as always." Before she could snap out a reply, he continued, "In a little more than an hour, we'll be coming into Edinburgh. We'll need to leave in a hurry."

She might have been surprised, except that she'd already been so buffeted by surprise that nothing could take her unawares again. "I'm ready."

He reached out his long arm and dragged her stumbling into his embrace. "There's my plucky girl."

Behind him, Harry chortled.

Harry. She still didn't like him, although for no more reason than the fact he made judgments where he shouldn't and carried caginess like a shield.

So, because she knew her antagonism was illogical, she smiled placidly at him while she freed herself from MacLean's grip. "I hope, if we're about to take another leg of our journey, that you gentlemen also slept."

Harry bowed. "Yes, ma'am. I'm a soldier. I sleep whenever I get a moment."

"And I. I slept with you until an hour ago." MacLean ran his finger over her lower lip. "You were exhausted. Do you feel better now?"

Everything about him shouted concern: his voice, deep and vibrant, his eyes, steady and warm, the way he touched her as if she were precious to him.

So she stepped away from him again. "I am better. I'll just make sure I have my things—"

Without warning, the train slammed to a halt. She staggered into MacLean. He tumbled backward, taking her with him. Harry flew over the chairs. Brakes squealed. Panels groaned. Glass shattered, and two of the candles pitched to the floor and went out.

The silence that followed terrified Enid. Two cars ahead, the engine chugged slowly, but no sound came from the forward cars, where the rest of Mr. Throckmorton's guard rested.

Harry got his breath first and swore, virulently and without regard for her delicate sensibilities—which satisfied a deep need in her, so she was grateful.

MacLean had just got out of his sickbed, and now he'd been flung violently to the ground. "MacLean, are you all right?"

"You're not as light as you look." He grunted and shifted her aside.

She tried to hold him still. "Your ribs? Your leg? Are you bleeding?"

Sitting up, he grasped her shoulders, held her still and looked into her eyes. "I'm well. And you?"

"Me? Of course I'm well. But you—"

"I am not an invalid." He said it so definitely and looked so forbidding that she subsided.

But she watched carefully as he rose without assistance and extended a hand to her.

"I'm fine, too, thank you for asking." Harry used a chair to help him to his feet.

"Blood?" MacLean asked.

"A little." Harry dabbed at his scalp, and his fingers came away red. "Wrenched my foot."

"That's bad." MacLean looked at the cars ahead. "I don't like this."

"Nor I." Harry limped forward through the car. "I'll go see what's happened."

MacLean waited until Harry opened the forward door and closed it again, then he sprang into action. He pulled on his greatcoat, handed her her cape and bonnet.

Frightened by his grim demeanor, she put them on without question.

"Gloves?" he questioned.

"I have them here." She didn't know what he planned to do, but she got a sick feeling in the pit of her stomach when he pulled a long-handled brown carpetbag out from under the bed.

He handed it to her. "Can you carry that?" It weighed so much that it dragged at her arms, but he didn't wait for an answer. Instead he brought forth another, larger one from beside the table. He took something out of it—she would have sworn he held a knife—then slung the pack over his shoulder. "Look at me," he said.

She did, and her mouth dried.

"This is an ambush. We're leaving, and pray God it's not too late."

She nodded.

"I'm going to the rear door. I need you to blow out those candles and come to me. Can you do that?"

"Of course I can." *And of course, I'm scared to death,* she might have added, but to what purpose? She eyed the distance between her and the door, then extinguished the candles. In a darkness as black and thick as tar, she moved through the debris to his side, glass crunching under her feet.

As if he could see her, he found her hand and clasped it. Pushing her against the wall, he whispered, "Stand there." He opened the door.

Fresh, cool air brushed her face. Not far away, she could hear men shouting. But back here, she could hear no movement.

"All right." Without making a sound, MacLean jumped onto the track. He whispered, "Jump, Enid. I'm here."

She obeyed without thought. He caught her and swung her off the tracks.

The shouting grew stronger, and a gunshot rang out.

She started and clutched at him.

Without a moment of hesitation, he led her swiftly away from the train and into the darkness.

When the sun finally lightened the dreary day, they were climbing a lonely hill at a great rate, and Enid was ready to collapse.

MacLean noticed, of course. On this jaunt through the dark countryside, he'd proved time and again that he noticed everything. He had successfully avoided the occasional farmhouse. He'd led her around cliffs and over rugged paths without pause. And when she'd said that he must be weary and need a rest, he'd found her a rock to hide behind so she could avail herself of the facilities.

She didn't like him understanding her so well.

And why didn't he need a rest, anyway? They'd come miles at a great rate and he moved ahead steadily, almost at the crest of the hill, while she . . .

"We'll stop here." He planted his walking stick beside a cluster of boulders. "You can rest and I can look out over the area, see where we're going, see if we're being followed."

Dropping her bag, she glared at him and panted, "You've been . . . sick. Why . . . aren't you . . . exhausted?"

"I'm a wee bit tired, lass." His Scottish accent had grown stronger the farther he'd walked into the countryside. "But you're doing well, too."

"I'm . . . wheezing!" Leaning against the boulder, she pressed her hand to the stitch in her side.

"English women don't exercise as they ought. Fresh air, there's the ticket, and brisk walks in the sunshine."

She tilted her head back against a boulder. "You're a jackass."

"If you can insult me, you're feeling well enough," he observed. "Here." He handed her a skin of water he'd filled at a stream at least ten years and half a continent ago.

"Thank you." But she just stared at the sack. "My arms hurt so badly from carrying that bag—what do you have in it, stones?—that I can't lift them."

Shaking his head, he uncorked the bag, then held it

for her to drink. She gulped eagerly at the water, and when she was finished she slid down the side of the boulder. The damp here chilled her bones, but her feet were up and her legs were outstretched, and she didn't have to move a single, aching muscle.

"A knife," he said.

She looked at him as he stood over her. "What?"

"You asked what was in your sack. A knife. Hardtack. Cheese. Dried meat. Blankets. Bandages. Ointment. Rope."

"You gave me the heavy bag!" Which she knew was nonsense, but she felt no need to be reasonable.

"I have the same thing, but more. I'm carrying my kilt and my sporran. Even scorched as they were, I couldn't leave them behind." Taking off his greatcoat, he rolled it up and stuffed it in his sack. "I brought you a comb, too."

If he expected praise, he shouldn't be telling a woman whose thighs trembled from exhaustion. Querulously, she picked the silliest thing to complain about. "We don't need two knives."

He couldn't have sounded more patient. "One to use. One to trade. It's a fair trek across Scotland, and the food won't last forever."

"We can't stop and buy something? You brought all that stuff and you didn't bring any funds?"

"There's a bit of the blunt, too, but any luck we'll avoid meeting anyone. If we do, we'll not show the cash around, and we'll save it for an emergency."

She wanted to groan, but she couldn't spare the breath. Instead, she watched as he made his way to the top of the hill and lay across the rocks to survey the land in every direction. The wind blew his auburn hair back from his familiar stranger's face. His eyes squinted as he looked back where they'd come from, then forward where they would go. His clothing blended into the landscape—ah, that explained the monotonous black and brown—but she could still see the broad shoulders, the narrow waist. And his legs—her lips tilted bitterly—they were muscled. How could she have been so foolish as to attribute those thighs and those calves to the exercises he had performed in bed? He had been walking, all right. No wonder everyone had insisted she take nice, long respites from her weighty duties.

Men.

What was she doing here? Last night—no, the night before—they had made love as passionately as ever two lovers had. She'd marveled at his strength, been astonished by his skill, learned his body as if she'd never learned it before.

Because she had never had him before. Because now, after eight years alone and innumerable offers from too many dissolute men, she had unwittingly become a wanton. They could never go back to the way it had been before: nurse and patient, abandoned wife and estranged husband. So she had made the resolution to be serene, strong, able to withstand the storm she saw hovering on the horizon.

The trouble was, she kept thinking that somehow she could avoid the storm.

If he never remembered, she could forever let him think they were married.

But his family knew the truth and would tell him.

But if not for his family, she could live a lie.

Although, why? She didn't love him.

But she had . . . feelings . . . for him, and she knew that when he discovered the truth, he would rage at her, or worse, stare at her with those green eyes as cold as ice.

But she wasn't a coward. It was his mind she worried about. His brain had had shocks enough, and she feared the consequences of such a blunt and dreadful truth . . .

She *was* a coward, and with low moral character to boot, for she still wanted him. Perhaps if she just gave a hint of the truth, that hint would be the trigger that returned all his memories. Yes, perhaps just a hint . . .

Just . . . she had to remain tranquil. No more repartee, no more teasing.

He jumped off the rocks and landed at her feet. "There's no one on the glen on either side. As long as the thugs don't have dogs, we've lost them. Stand up."

"What? Why?"

"You're sitting on the cold ground. Let's put a blanket under you so you don't get a chill."

She wanted to protest, to say it wasn't worth the pain of rising, but he had that look on his face. The *I know what's good for you* look. So wearily she climbed to her feet, allowed him to spread out a blanket, tumbled back down. "How many miles did we come?"

"Twelve, at least. We're not far from the tracks now."

"*What?*"

"We walked in a circle, backtracked a bit to throw them off the scent." He flung himself flat on his back right at her feet. "Lass, will you feed us some breakfast?"

"Of course." Pulling the stone-filled sack to her

side, she dug out the bread and cheese. "The man does the scouting, the woman does the real work." Tranquility would have to wait for another day. A day less fraught with danger.

He rolled onto his side, propped his head up with his hand. "Scouting's hard work. It takes years of training and expertise. Don't forget, I've been leading the way, too, forging a path through the dark and the cold."

Last night, for all his circling and backtracking, he had led the way so surely that he might have been able to see through the dungeonlike darkness. She could make out nothing, each step had been an adventure, and she had had to trust him not to walk her into a tree or drop her down a gully.

And she *had* trusted him. She had been impressed with his exploits. Now he made light of them. "I would trade places with you in a minute," she said.

He reached for the sack. "All right."

She hung onto the strap and glared at him.

Somehow, the balance between them had changed. She had moved into his territory, the land of hunter and hunted. She could never survive here, but MacLean had donned command like armor, and where before his life had been hers to save, now her life depended on him.

"I would lead," she said, "but not with the way my legs ache."

He grinned and relinquished his hold, and didn't point out she didn't have the foggiest idea which direction to choose.

"Besides, back at Blythe Hall you deceived me about your walking—"

He lifted his eyebrows, but didn't deny it, the louse.

"—But I presume you're tired now."

"I am," he admitted simply.

"I ought to give you the littlest piece of bread as punishment—when I think about the anguish I suffered over you taking your first step!—but I've cared for your body too long to jeopardize my work." She tore off a chunk of bread, placed it on a napkin and pushed it toward him.

"You did care for my body, most assiduously. I thank you." He smiled at her so salaciously she knew he didn't refer to her skill at nursing.

Finding the knife, she pulled it free of its sheath. She fingered the sharp edge and smiled in return. If she could have contained her blush, it would have been the perfect threat.

"Give me that, lass, before you're tempted to use it incorrectly." Sitting up, he took it and the cheese.

He handled the knife skillfully, she admitted, for the slices he placed on her bread were thin and even, just the way she liked them. And because she was compelled to worry about every little thing, she worried that he'd been watching her eat and remembering her preferences. A thoughtful man would do that for his wife.

Oh, heaven save her from thoughtful men! She took her first bites of the nutty bread and tart cheese, and hastily asked, "Who's tracking us?"

"I can't remember, lass, but from all appearances I'd have to say they're people who want me dead."

Rooting about in the bag, she found dried fruit. Not just apples, but more exotic fruits. Holding them up, she said, "Look. This is wonderful!"

"Your friend Celeste had her hand in this, I see." He

smiled at her uninhibited bliss. "When men pack, there's nothing so fine."

"Dear Celeste." She bit into an apricot and sagged in enjoyment of the tart, sweet flavor.

Snagging her hand, he brought it to his mouth and took the other half of the fruit in his teeth.

He fed her. She fed him. Much too primitive. Much too seductive. And the way he was looking at her, as if he planned to lean over and kiss her . . . those deep, fabulous kisses which led to sin and sorrow. She tried to snatch her hand back. He came along. He pressed her against the boulder, hand on her shoulder, and swooped in to catch her lips with his.

The kiss was everything she feared. Blatant entice-ment. He didn't force her compliance. The rat. He swept her lips with his, sweet, quick, smooth passes that made her quiver with the need to seize his hair and hold him for her kiss. The contact warmed her, made her heart hurry and her color rise. He smelled so good, like security, like husband, like love . . .

With her hand on his chest, she shoved him away and took a quivering breath. "See, this is just the type of trouble I feared."

"Trouble?" He cocked an eyebrow. "You call that trouble?"

"It could be, if we got carried away and the knaves chasing us found us *in flagrante delicto*—"

He chuckled. "With our trousers down and our skirts up, so to say."

"You ought to go on without me."

"Don't want to hang about with a man being pur-sued?" He sounded laconic and not at all worried.

"That's not it at all, as you very well know. I'm holding you back. You move more quickly, more quietly than I do, you blend into the countryside, you sound like a native—"

Reaching into the sack at her side, he brought out a slice of dried apple and tranquilly examined it. "I *am* a native."

"You could get home twice as quickly without me."

He didn't say anything for a very long moment, then he sighed. "Ah, the things you think of me."

"The things I . . . what do you mean?"

He looked up, and she changed her mind about his composure. His eyes glinted, his chin jutted; he was furious. "That I am the kind of man who would abandon his wife to cold and hunger in the middle of the Scottish wilds to save his own hide. That I would go without you to my home, never knowing if you lived or died." He held up his hand to stop her from speaking. "Maybe I was that kind of man before. I don't remember."

Distressed, she said, "No, not you!"

"But I know I'll not do it now, and you can just put it out of your mind."

"But what if I—" She swallowed.

"What if you what?"

In a rush, she asked, "What if I told you I wasn't your wife?"

His fury didn't roar. It arrived in a menacing whisper. "Then I'd say that two nights ago you did a damned good imitation of a wife." He took a breath. "We've got a long way to go. There's no use you attempting such tricks."

She couldn't believe it. She had taken courage in

hand and confessed the great deception—and he hadn't believed her!

"You are my beloved wife, and if they captured you, they would torture you until I gave myself up."

She hadn't thought of that, or that they—whoever *they* were—would believe her tale as little as MacLean did. "Would you give yourself up for me?" She blinked. Where had that come from?

"What do you think, lass?"

He stared into her eyes, and she caught her breath. Stephen MacLean would have given her up and never thought about it again. Kiernan MacLean would not only give himself up for the woman he perceived as his wife but he would fight for her—and die for her, too.

The differences between them were so great that she didn't understand how she could have ever been fooled.

Her stomach clenched as she realized how great an honor it would be to be Kiernan MacLean's wife, and she barely fought off the temptation to claim to be his. But if he had honor, she did, too. "As deeply as I feel about the tribute you bestow on me, I must insist—"

He slashed the air with his hand. "That's enough. How are your shoes?"

He had become someone she didn't recognize—a warrior determined to protect her and defend them. She didn't know how to convince him of the truth.

She didn't want to convince him.

She would convince him later. Surely in these circumstances cowardice was understandable. "They're . . . fine."

"No blisters on your heels? The boots don't leak?"

"They're comfortable. MacLean—"

"Good, then. We'll go on until midday, or until we find a likely shelter. We'll travel morning and evening at first, then when I'm sure we've lost them, we'll travel all day." Taking her hands, he stared earnestly into her eyes. "Trust me, Enid. Together, we'll find our way home."

Chapter 18

"Down you go, lass." MacLean grasped Enid about the waist, lifted her off the cart, and noted that her ribs were sticking out. In the twelve days they'd been on the road, Enid had lost too much weight, although she was still a fine-looking woman. So fine-looking, with her admirable bosom and her delicate features, that he had found it difficult to behave with any kind of discipline.

He shouldered one supply sack, handed Enid hers, and saw the farmer off with a wave of the hand and his thanks.

MacLean wanted to hold Enid in his arms and hear her moan as she had in the cottage in Suffolk. He wanted to teach her new pleasures and kiss her until they were both breathless and straining for fulfillment. He wanted all those things, and he had to content himself with holding her in his arms as they slept.

As soon as they got to his home, matters were going to change. Sooner, if he could manage it.

Taking her arm, he asked, "Shall we travel on?"

Enid looked around at this uninhabited corner of the Highlands: bleak escarpments, hills covered with gorse and heather, stands of pine forest and two narrow ruts for a road. "It's only noon," she said. "After such a comfortable jaunt"—she gazed pointedly after the rough-riding cart—"we should be able to go until midnight."

"Good idea. I'm glad you thought of it." But for all her sarcasm, he worried about her. Her complaints didn't have the edge he'd grown used to; she was flagging. That explained why, four days ago, he'd gone out of the wilderness and to the road.

Of course, most of what Highlanders called civilization probably looked almighty raw to a woman raised in England. A few huts huddled together on the shore of a loch constituted a town, and farms were few and far between. The first day they'd paid a young buck to ride on the footman's perch of his used English-style carriage, and gone many a mile before nightfall. The next day they'd crawled in a wagon of hay and slept most of the day. Last night they'd stumbled on a croft, a farm with a tiny garden, poor fields and a miserable hut. MacLean had bartered with the crofter to stay in their barn, and with the crofter's wife for two plates of thick shepherd's pie and two tankards of ale. Enid had eaten as if she'd never had such fine fare, and she had slept the sleep of the dead with a roof over her head. And today they had caught a ride with the crofter as he drove to market.

But they were nearing the west coast and the sea; MacLean caught the scent in the air and the change in the wind. More than that, he had spotted a likely track, far off the road and to the left. A sheep path, like most of the paths they'd traveled, but unlike other paths they'd traveled he vaguely recognized it. It, and the hill it ascended. And he thought . . . he suspected it would take them where he wanted to go.

Would he recognize what was on the other side?

He stepped off the road and into a grove of trees.

Enid didn't step with him.

Looking back at her, he said, "So let's go, then."

"Don't talk to me like I'm a hound!"

He caught his breath. She was about to throw a feminine tizzy.

In a desperate tone, she asked, "Let's stay somewhere with a fire and a bath. You haven't seen anybody suspicious for days now."

Coming back to her, he took her hand and looked into her large blue eyes with their fringe of sooty lashes. "No, I haven't seen anyone suspicious. I'm convinced we've lost whoever was following us. But I don't trust anyone from Suffolk, and I don't trust anyone I don't know, because mayhap they know me and are out for my blood. One night at an inn might kill us, for sure."

She was not in the mood to be reasonable. Her bottom lip stuck out, and it trembled.

Leading her into the trees, he asked reasonably, "How would we pay for it?"

"With the funds you brought."

Distracted by the growing sense of familiarity, he told her, "The funds are growing low, and they're for an emergency."

"I *stink*. How's that for an emergency?"

"I can't smell you," he assured her as they cleared

the trees. With one glance around to see that they were unobserved, he hurried her across the fields.

"That's because you stink, too." She sounded stiff and surly.

He examined her with the care of a lady's maid. Mud stiffened the hem of her cape up past her knees. Her sojourn under an overturned wagon had permanently warped her bonnet. She washed her face every morning, but invariably when they stopped she would collapse right where they stood, so dirt perpetually streaked her complexion. Her blue eyes were bright, her color good, she'd grown strong and even more beautiful with the exercise, but she'd come to think the trip would never end.

Such an attitude could lead to a careless disregard for her own safety. He couldn't have that.

As they struck the trail, she sighed dramatically and pointed behind her. "The inns are back that way."

He glanced around. He did know this place. He didn't know why, but he recognized the rocky outcrops, the steep incline at the top, the way the wind slapped their faces when they came over the top, the slow drop on the other side . . . and the way the path twisted and turned as it ascended yet another hill.

If he was right . . . if he remembered correctly . . . he could find her a bath. A bath and a soft bed and a willing husband, although she didn't wish for the last item. "I'll take you somewhere better than an inn," he said.

Although she trusted him to guide her, she didn't trust him with her love. She hadn't said so, but he couldn't forget that madness she had spouted the first day on the road—*I'm not your wife.* She could wish all she wanted, but saying the words would not make it so, and he intended to illustrate to her exactly how married they were. At first opportunity, he would turn his whole attention to Enid. He would make an opportunity, and he would by God discover why she pulled back from him when he asked about their past, why she had the look of a trapped rabbit when he discussed their future.

He moved swiftly along, on the watch as always, but also playing games with himself as he walked. Just over this ridge, he would see a waterfall off to his left. A weathered stone fence ran along the path up to the tree line. The green leafy branches of an orchard swayed in the glen below.

He was correct every time. They were getting close. He knew it in his bones. Soon he would be among his own family, and when that happened . . . oh, when that happened, he would be a whole man again, with memories and a mother and a sister . . . he would know his enemies, and he would exorcise them.

"There." Standing below the ridgeline, he pointed. "Can you see that?"

She shoved the brim of her bonnet away from her face. "There's a hollow."

"It's better than it looks."

She was so weary she didn't ask him how he knew.

A good thing, for he didn't know how he knew. He slid down the path just ahead of her, helping her with his hand beneath her elbow.

They swerved onto another, smaller track, nothing more than a rapidly descending impression in the grass. They threaded their way through a stack of boulders higher than his head, and abruptly they were there, in a little sun-warmed hollow surrounded by mountains.

He could almost remember running down here as a boy and visiting . . . someone. Someone old.

But he couldn't see her face . . .

Her face. It was a woman. She lived here alone in her little hut with a cow and a few chickens. She had a small orchard, protected from the worst of winter's blasts by towering granite boulders, where she grew plums and apples, and a garden where she grew vegetables. Ah, the most delectable spinach he'd ever eaten.

She was gone, whoever she was, and the animals had gone with her. All was neglected now. The stone house looked bereft, its shutters closed tight, the door latched from the outside, and no smoke coming from the chimney. Yet he experienced a sense that here he was safe.

He *was* remembering.

He almost dreaded to hear what Enid would say about the place; after all, she had lived with a lady in London, and with him at Blythe Hall, and the cottage at Blythe Hall was ten times the size of this shack.

But Enid gave a sigh of pleasure. "It's exquisite."

"Your standards have slipped."

"No, it really is a little piece of perfection. It's just . . . it's nice." She lifted her face to the sun. "It smells like apples, and it's warm here. I can hear the wind blowing over the top, but here we're protected."

As he gazed at her, he realized how very much their circumstances had changed. Enid was delicate and unused to physical challenges, yet she displayed as much pluck as any Scotswoman. She climbed hills and complained, slid down muddy paths and complained, hid in a hollow for two hours and uttered not a single word.

He could depend on her. More than that, he adored her.

"Why are you looking at me that way?" She dabbed at her face in obscure feminine alarm. "I've tanned, haven't I?"

He chuckled. "A few freckles, and charming they are. Come and look at the best."

Leading Enid along a short path that wove between slabs of stone, he followed the sound of trickling water and found a man-made basin, just big enough to wash dishes in. A bit of a stream dribbled off a rock into the clear, shallow, sandy pool, and another dribbled out and down to be lost around the bend. A sense of pride swelled in him as if this place was his, and a secret not to be shared with any but his heart of hearts.

"Oh, it's beautiful! It's clean! I could take a—"

"—Bath." He untied her bonnet, loosened her cloak.

She hugged her collar close as if she feared his intentions.

As she should. He'd said it before; women were much more impressed with cleanliness than men. He wouldn't have cared if they waited until they got to Mull to bathe, but she did. "It's warm now, but the mountains will obscure the light long before sunset in the rest of the land, so I had better dust out the cottage and start a fire. If you want a bath, you'd best move swiftly."

Still she stared at him.

"If you don't care, you can help me clean the hut."

She tossed the cloak aside, sat down on a rock and pulled off her mud-caked boots. She might be modest, but above all she was practical.

Whistling, he went to the hut and opened the door to the dark little hovel. He heard the skittering of mice, smelled the mustiness of long disuse, and the faint, lingering scent of a cow once in residence. Going to the windows, he opened the shutters and let the light and air in.

Wood was stacked by the fireplace. A shiny bucket rested beside the door. The bed was strung with ropes and covered in canvas, and at the foot blankets were wrapped in a linen envelope to keep off the dust.

He glanced about. The hut must be on some great man's land for it to be so well maintained.

Was this MacLean land? Did the laird of the MacLeans demand this place be maintained for the lonely wayfarer who wandered the hills? Justice, then, that he should find shelter here on his trek to the familial home.

MacLean took off his greatcoat and his jacket, and rolled up his sleeves. Taking the broom, he brushed the cobwebs out of the corners, then carefully swept the dirt floor. With a dry rag, he wiped off the table and the bench. He made up the fire, ready to be lit. Taking the blankets outside, he shook them hard, then carried them back and placed them on the bed. He picked up the bucket, but paused to look back at the place.

Everything was just as he remembered it. Clean. Dry. Cozy.

His.

He closed his eyes, and he saw her. The old woman with the dried apple face and the dark brown mole on her chin. "Coom anytime, lad. Th' place is yers."

Memories were claiming him.

He walked back to the stream without stealth, giving Enid a chance to scramble behind a boulder if she wished to—and, more's the shame, he supposed she would wish to.

But when he came around the corner, he stopped short. There she sat, cross-legged in the pool, eyes closed, wearing an expression of bliss—and absolutely nothing else. Her arms were graceful, her nipples softly blooming. She looked as fresh as a blushing rosebud. The clear water came to her waist, and between her strong, muscled legs, she was pink and glorious in her openness.

He must have made a stifled sound, for her eyes sprang open.

She had drifted off; he could see it in the sleepy droop of her eyelids, in the way she scrambled to comprehend the circumstances.

He didn't care. He dropped the bucket and started toward her.

She rose to her feet like Aphrodite rising from the waves.

Springing at her, he caught her around the waist as she turned to run.

"No!" she shouted. "We can't. I'm not . . . I'm not . . ."

"I don't give a damn what you think. You're mine." Lifting her out of the water, he carried her to a low slab of sun-warmed rock. Gently he tumbled her down on her back, her hips at the edge, her feet dangling off. The perfect position.

With one knee between her legs, he struggled with his fly.

"You planned this!" She tried to roll away.

"If I'd planned it, I'd already have my bloody trousers off." He freed his cock, shoved his pants down, and pinned her onto the stone. "I could accuse *you* of planning this. You were naked."

"That's how I take my bath!"

He wanted to grin at her; she was so damp and indignant. But he couldn't make his mouth move that way. All his muscle control went into not taking her now, at this moment. He needed to be inside her. His blood surged rich in his veins. He needed to know that she understood she *was* his.

"I am not your wife." She sounded as if she were pleading. Placing her hand on his shoulder, she looked him in the eye.

Well, of course. She wouldn't look lower.

"Listen to me," she said. "There was a mistake."

"Does this feel like a mistake?" Cupping her face, he kissed her. Desire burned in his gut. "Does this?" he asked gutturally, and slid his lips down her throat to her breast.

She whimpered when he caught her nipple and suckled. "You shouldn't—"

"And this?" He tangled his fingers into the curly bush between her thighs. Swiftly he slid his thumb along the crease, opening her.

When he touched her she brought her feet up onto the stone and lifted her hips. She said no, but she wanted him as he wanted her. And she was ready.

He couldn't wait. It had been too long. He stepped close and opened her with his fingers, positioned himself, and pressed into her.

Tight. She was so damned tight. And damp, and warm, and welcoming. No other men, she'd said. No doubt about that. The way her body held him, massaged him, was a miracle of delight.

He possessed her. He owned her. She was his. She had agreed to this that night in the cottage; he would not allow a display of nerves to ruin this union between them. In all the history of the world, there had never been such a marvelous fit between man and woman.

As if she had only just realized what was happening, she gave a convulsive shudder and tried to fight her way back from him.

He caught her thighs in his arms and held her, legs wide apart, so he had control. "Mine," he said.

"No," she whispered.

How dare she disagree? "All mine." Then he set up a rhythm guaranteed to rob her of her breath, to take her to ecstasy. He drove hard, rubbing his pelvis against her exposed femininity, pressing against her in open, basic lust.

She responded, as he knew she would. As her body demanded. She tossed her head, tendrils of her long black hair catching on the coarse surface of the rock. She moaned. She whimpered. She reached climax at once, spasming in forceful pleas, subsided, then shuddered and cried out again.

All the while he thrust into her. He made demands with his body and in return had his cock held and cradled in every erotic, carnal way. He couldn't make it last, didn't want to. Unhurried loving could wait for later; now she would recognize her master. His balls drew up tight. He plunged more feverishly.

"MacLean, dear heavens. MacLean!" Like winter storms off the sea, orgasms swept her continuously with strength and irresistible force.

He paused, on the verge, seeing what she looked like with her face turned to the heavens, her eyes closed, bliss written on every line of her straining body. Then he sped onward to take her, to fill her with his seed. To claim her as she deserved to be claimed—by him.

He didn't wait until he caught his breath, or even until the last of the spasms finished taking them. Leaning down, right in her face, he said, "Look at me."

Her eyes fluttered open, then in ready defiance, closed.

"Look at me!"

She was too weak to resist him. Those wonderful blue eyes opened and gazed on his face with much fondness. No matter how much she wished it different, she wanted him.

Holding her tight against him, he said, "I am the blood in your veins, the marrow in your bones. You'll never go anywhere without knowing I'm inside you, supporting you, keeping you alive. I am a part of you. You are a part of me. We are forever."

"Don't. Don't." But Enid felt him inside her, stretching her, filling her. He surrounded her with his scent, his body. He looked into her eyes, invaded her mind, held her captive in his arms. "Don't say things like that."

"I'm telling you the truth, love. You'd best accept it now."

That was the problem. She wanted to. She wanted to believe he could be a part of her forever.

Foolish, foolish woman. With her hand on his chest, she pushed him gently away.

To her surprise, he let her. Apparently, he believed he'd made enough of an impact with his possession and his words.

He could have been right—except she knew he wasn't her husband.

As he withdrew from her, she eased herself into a sitting position.

He steadied her with his palm under her elbow. "Slowly. We have all the time in the world."

She didn't want to look at him. Didn't want to see him, proudly naked and too pleased of himself to be borne. So she pushed back her hair with a trembling hand and looked around. The sunshine floated down and filled the little valley to the brim with warmth and color. The air had grown sharper and more flavorful, drenched with the scent of peaches from the orchard. Beneath her, the gray rock bristled like a pincushion. On a branch in the orchard, a lark sang in a gala celebration. This was what MacLean did to her; he made her blood pump through her veins, made her see and breathe and think as she had never done before, made every sense revel in the celebration of life.

She should hate him, but she didn't.

She should have resisted, but she hadn't. She had been tired of longing for Kiernan MacLean's touch . . . tired of loving him with her heart when her mind knew she shouldn't.

Love. Him. MacLean.

In a flurry of horror and disbelief, she leaped from him and scrambled to her feet.

"What's wrong?" He caught her before she could run.

Nonsense. She couldn't love him. He wasn't her husband.

"Enid? Did I hurt you?"

"No . . . no." She should have been self-conscious about her nudity. Instead she could only stagger under the weight of her thoughts. "I'm fine. I'm just . . . dazed."

"Did I frighten you?" He stepped close. "You needed to understand how it is between us."

"How you decreed it should be." *Blood in your veins, the marrow in your bones, we are forever.* Did he frighten her? Yes, but not nearly as much as her own musings.

Love Kiernan MacLean.

Some—Mrs. Brown, for instance—might tell Enid that she did love him, and that that was why she kissed him with such desperate longing, why she laughed at his jokes and hurt at his contempt. Love . . . oh, that would be an easy explanation as to why she couldn't resist him. She was besotted.

But she wasn't.

She couldn't be. She'd traveled that road before.

The trouble was, she had sensed a different sort of man in Kiernan MacLean, even when he was unconscious. A man made of steel, honor and fortitude. She had fought for him, made herself a part of him, demanded life for him. Even while she'd caviled at his unyielding character, she had admired it and his bullheaded determination.

If she loved him, she would suffer more than a simple infatuation. If she loved Kiernan MacLean, that love would be real.

"Why are you staring at me like that?" MacLean swept a lock of her hair off her shoulder. Slid his hand down to the narrow of her back. Marked her with his touch.

She hadn't realized she was staring. Staring at the broad shoulders, the strong hips, the thighs that bulged with muscle. Examining his broad face, his strong features, his scarred complexion.

Love always ended in pain.

But while that was true, she didn't love MacLean. She wouldn't allow herself to love MacLean.

So what difference would it make . . . if they made love tonight?

"I just . . . I like the way you look." *She wanted to love him again.* She needed closeness to chase away the sadness, the realization that soon they would part. She longed for the passion and the forgetfulness he could bring her. Making love to this man would mean nothing. Nothing.

So she would do it, over and over again.

"Come to the pool." With a smile composed in equal parts of seduction, uncertainty and passion, she said, "The water is almost warm and most . . . refreshing."

Chapter 19

Just before sunset, Enid crouched behind a coil of rope on the lonely, sea-soaked pier and stared at MacLean in horror. "We're going to steal that boat?"

"The fishermen have gone home for the day." He kept his voice down as he transferred all their belongings into a single sack. Rope, blankets . . . no food. Nothing since the morning, when they'd left the hut after eating the last of the hardtack. "They're all eating their supper right now."

Her stomach growled. "But it's *stealing*."

"Steal is a strong word. We're going to borrow the boat."

"Specious."

"I'll get the boat back to its rightful owner with a bit of a reward for his trouble." MacLean slipped the extra knife into his sleeve. "Do you have a better idea? Our pursuers know our ultimate destination. I would wager they're watching the ferry, and I've not come this far to be killed on my own front door."

"No." She couldn't bear that.

"Anyway, the ferry only goes out once a week."

Her heart gave a flutter. "How do you know that?"

Somberly, he looked up at her. "I remembered."

She shrank back, her hand at her throat. "Everything?"

"Not everything. Not yet. But it's coming."

It's coming. The words echoed in her mind. She didn't need to watch the slapping waves to feel queasy. The moment she had hoped for, the moment she had dreaded was upon her. Before too long, he would know the truth. "Good," she said.

He returned to packing the sack. "I started remembering at Granny Aileen's—"

"Granny Aileen's?"

Again he looked at her, but this time he grinned. "At the cottage in the dale."

She couldn't think of that hut without remembering how the afternoon of glorious passion in the sunshine had slipped into an evening of slow, soft loving, which had gone on to a night full of warm embraces, of whispered demands, of loving.

"I never knew I could rise to the occasion so many times, but you've needed care ever since I've met you, and I wanted to make you happy. Did I make you happy?" Standing, MacLean touched her cheek. "Enid?"

"Yes." She tried to smile at him, but her lips kept wobbling. "I'll always treasure what we had there."

After he had taken her the first time—after she'd broken her vow and lain with him—she had tossed ethics and good sense to the winds and helped him bathe. That had led to an episode in the grass, with him on the bottom this time because she was already scraped from the stone.

He got a rash.

They'd washed each other again. He'd brought a blanket out into the sunshine, and they'd drowsed there, soaking up the warmth.

They'd both acquired a bit of a burn and quite a few midge bites.

When the sun had disappeared behind the mountain and the chill had made her shiver, they'd gone into the hut. He'd lit the fire and brought out the cold pie he'd bought the night before. The crofter's wife wasn't much of a baker; half the crust was burned. But they'd eaten every bite, and when they had satisfied their hunger, they'd made the bed and explored another hunger. And in the night, she'd come awake to find him taking her again on an erotic journey such as she'd never imagined.

She should have been shocked at their dissipation.

She'd wished only that it could have lasted longer.

She didn't mind about the scrapes on her back or the sunburn that extended along the left side of her body. She cared only that she had memories laid by. Memories of a magic time, brief, glorious, and set apart from reality. She knew she had abandoned her morals. She knew the truth would lash her soon. But nothing that could happen would make her forget those brief hours at Granny Aileen's hut. They were hers. She would treasure them—for memory was returning to MacLean.

Now he slipped his hand around her waist. "It's a good day for the passage across the firth. A fair wind, a cloudy sky, and the surf is calm."

She looked out at the choppy bay and hoped never to see a stormy surf.

"I should be able to row it in five hours or so."

"You can't row for five hours straight. You just left your sickbed!"

He didn't laugh at her silly objection. He took it as seriously as any man can who has walked the breadth of Scotland. "I'll take a rest now and again."

"We don't have five hours before nightfall!"

"I can find the island in the dark." He bussed her on the lips. "I'll get the boat untied, then you come and jump in and push off. Can you do that?"

Stung, she said, "Of course I can."

"Good lass." He flung the bag over his shoulder and kissed her lips lightly, swiftly. "I can always depend on you." Coming to his feet, he leaped over the barrels and nets and jumped lightly onto the fifteen-foot boat. It rocked, but like a man used to the sea, MacLean stood with his legs astraddle. He loosened the moorings and gestured to her.

Her heart pounded as she rose, but she sauntered down the dock.

"What are you doing?" he asked. "Hurry!"

She stopped by the boat and extended her hand. "If I have to steal a boat, I will do it in a ladylike manner."

Taking her hand, he helped her down into the bow. "You're absolutely balmy, do you know that?"

"No balmier than a man who won't go to the minister of the Kirk and ask for help getting to his island."

They'd already had this fight.

"I'm going to get home on my own." He fit the oars in their collars.

She used an extra oar to shove away from the pier.

"Then I am going to observe the proprieties while thieving."

"You *are* balmy." He laughed, a great burst of merriment. "Absolutely mad. How am I going to bear a lifetime with you?"

"I don't think that's going to be a problem." She seated herself, facing him, as he bent his back to the oars.

The smell of fish permeated the wood. Water slapped against the sides. As they left the bay at Oban, the firth showed its true nature and tossed them from side to side. The afternoon slipped away, monotonous, frightening. The sun slipped below the horizon, gleaming pink and purple against the ever darkening ocean.

Gripping the sides of the boat, Enid scrutinized the horizon. "It's getting dark. Are you sure we can't miss the island?"

He was very, very firm. "I'll find it in the darkest night. I'm like a salmon going home to spawn. I don't need a map, I just know where it is."

Exactly what she feared.

"Relax, dearling, and rest your feet." He grinned at her. "Are they better for their massage?"

This morning, before they'd left the hut and over her very vocal objections, he'd insisted on massaging her feet. At first it had tickled. Then, as she'd relaxed into it, his fingers had taken on a magic of their own. She had moaned and twisted, and by the time he had finished the massage they were out of their clothes and into each other.

"Much better," she said primly, as if she didn't know what he was thinking about.

He just grinned more.

She watched the waves, the sky, then, when he was working the oars as hard as he could, she watched MacLean. These were her last hours with him. Once he remembered—and he was well on his way to remembering—she would be sent off in ignominy. So she hoarded memories of him: the way he grimaced as he pushed the oars through the water, the ripple of muscles beneath his shirt, the scruffy, week-old beard, the scarred cheek, his auburn hair ruffling in the breeze.

The wind rose as the sky turned dark purple, then to the blackest night. Her rear ached. She shivered with cold. She could see nothing, not the light of the stars, not the place where the land met the sea. The boat pitched through the waves, carrying her to a place where she had no sense of direction, no light to guide her. As dread closed her throat, she could scarcely give a shuddering sigh. She didn't want to arrive.

Yet—shouldn't they have got there by now? Had they overshot the island? Wrapping her arms around her knees, she huddled in her cloak at the bottom of the boat.

"Pull on my greatcoat." MacLean's deep voice came out of the darkness like a command from Poseidon.

She hesitated. "You're not cold?"

He laughed, a hard, dangerous laugh. A different sort of a laugh than she ever heard from him before. "Pull on my greatcoat and sit up. Watch for lights. We're getting close."

She heard the sound of waves crashing on the shore . . . or perhaps against rocks that would sink them. Light would mean a harbor. She scanned the horizon in every direction, desperate for any sign of land.

Then there it was. Feeble flickers of illumination. "Look." She pointed. "There!"

The splash of the oars stopped. "The harbor," he said with satisfaction. The oars started again, stronger.

"Is it dangerous?" she asked.

"I know the way." His voice sounded different, more commanding, absolutely confident.

Ah, the boat might not sink, but her heart certainly did.

The crash of the waves grew louder. The lights separated and grew square. Windows. Houses.

Suddenly the boat swerved away.

"You've missed it," she cried.

"We'll land to the west. It's closer to the castle."

She closed her eyes. That wasn't Poseidon speaking, or any other god. It was Kiernan, laird of the MacLeans.

The boat scraped on the sand, then pitched as he set the oars and leaped out into the surf. He dragged the boat onto the beach. His hand grasped her arm and pulled her to her feet. "Come on, lass. Come forward and step onto the gracious ground of the Isle of Mull."

In the dark, she stumbled across the nets and the seats.

With an impatient growl, he lifted her out and carried her onto the land. Setting her down, he said, "Stay where I put you."

As if she could leave. She still couldn't see, although he seemed to be doing well enough. "Where are you going?"

He didn't answer. He was already gone.

She wondered if this was some cruel jest; he would

walk away and leave her standing here in the pitch dark until morning. Perhaps she stood in a tidal basin and would be swept out to sea, and he would laugh cruelly as he sauntered home to his family. Perhaps—

He spoke right at her side. "The clouds are blowing away. The moon will be rising soon. We'll sit here until we can travel to the castle."

She clutched her chest and hoped she hadn't really made that stifled sound of terror. She wasn't so stupid as to think he really wanted to sit. He wanted to talk, and any admission of fear put her at a disadvantage. "So sit." She stayed stubbornly erect.

He, too, remained standing beside her, and when he spoke, that stern, resonant timbre sounded in his voice. "As I stand here, I feel the breeze off the ocean. I smell the smells of my home. In my mind's eye, I can see the way the road winds through the fences and over the hill to the other coast where Castle MacLean sits. I was born here. I was raised here, and I wonder how I could ever have forgotten any of it."

"Big bump on the head," she mumbled.

His tone changed, became a lash of fury. "I'm not Stephen MacLean, and you're not my wife!"

She took a deep breath. She'd been dreading this confrontation, but now that it was on her, she almost felt relief. Relief, because the worst had happened. He was angry and blamed her, and she could bolster her anger and shout back at him—and not dwell on the loneliness that would follow her into exile. "You're not, and I'm not."

"Do you know who I am?"

"You're Kiernan MacLean."

"You're right about that. Of course, you've got *that*

right." If only that fire he was breathing would light the night. "How do you propose to explain your part in this damnable deception?"

He'd had a shock, so she tried to be patient. "Once I discovered the truth, I did tell you. I told you I was not your wife."

"After two months of living together. After a night of the best bloody fooking I've ever had!"

Shocked by his crudeness, she sputtered, "You . . . you are a barbarian!"

"I could call you worse. Are you asking me to believe you didn't recognize your own husband?"

Patient? She had thought she could be patient? Not with that tone of voice coming from him. "It had been nine years since I'd seen Stephen, and when I got to Blythe Hall, you had a scraggly beard, bandages over half your face, and once we got rid of them, scars over that same half."

"I've been healed this last month."

"I don't know what you looked like before, but I imagine your family is going to be taken aback at the change in you." She shivered in the breeze. "As I was in Stephen!"

"We scarcely looked alike." He knelt.

She heard him rummaging about . . . in the sack, she supposed. "Alike enough. The eyes were the same, and for weeks, seeing you open your beautiful eyes was all that mattered. By the time you woke up, I was used to you, and I didn't think . . . well, I told you as soon as I thought it prudent."

"You told me we weren't married after we'd been attacked on that train!" He tossed a blanket over her shoulders. "It was a bit bloody late for confession."

She huddled into the woolen cloth. "Don't swear."

"Swear!" His voice rose. "You'd better ask me not to strangle you and leave your body on the sand."

About that she didn't worry. "I suppose this lets out the blood in my veins and marrow in my bones avowal."

"Damn it, woman, you are not my wife!"

She raised her voice, too. "I didn't know that until after the fire!"

The waves lapped at the shore, a cricket sang in the night, and MacLean said nothing.

She hoped that meant he was thinking.

"When you were standing next to me?" he asked with considerably more calm.

"Yes!" He *was* thinking.

"That night, you looked at me, wide-eyed and horrified, as if you'd been slapped by reality."

"As I had. I couldn't tell you then. I was confused. I didn't know what to think." She looked up to the place where she thought he must be. "I only knew Mr. Throckmorton asked that I let you recover without imposing my memories on you. I thought perhaps if I gave you a hint, you would remember, but when I told you I wasn't your wife, you thought I was being . . . I don't know . . ."

"I thought you were afraid of what we had together. 'Tis a powerful thing, this craving between us. But . . . when men want to be insulting about women and how they're all the same in bed, they say that all cats are gray in the dark. Am I a gray cat indistinguishable from my cousin?"

She twisted her fingers together. "No. But it had

been . . . nine years, and I thought you . . . he . . . had had much practice and learned well from other women."

"Am I supposed to be flattered?" he roared.

Indignant, she shouted back. "I don't care if you're flattered!"

She heard the crunch of his footsteps as he paced away, then returned. In something less than a mutter, he said, "Humph."

Apparently he listened when *she* yelled at *him*. She should remember that . . . except that they would not be together. In a lower voice, she admitted, "Physically you were much different, but I expected that. I was . . . was *fooking* a man who'd suffered through an explosion and almost died. I would have been surprised if your body had been the same!"

"Why didn't you tell me that night? That night you realized I wasn't Stephen."

"Someone had just tried to kill you in a fire, after doing a good job of almost killing you in an explosion." Just as MacLean had predicted, the light was growing. She could see his outline, tall and grim, against the sky. "I didn't know if I would put you in more danger by telling them what I knew. I didn't know if Mr. Throckmorton himself realized the truth."

"He knew." No doubt existed in MacLean's voice.

"I suppose." Bitterness rose in her. "In the large scheme of things, one woman's heart and body don't count for much."

"Not when weighed against the good of Britain. Men like Throckmorton do everything to advance England's cause."

"And you?" She tied the blanket around her like a cape. "What were you doing in Crimea?"

"Looking for my reprobate cousin Stephen. How did they get you to come and care for me?"

"They told me Stephen had been horribly injured and dying, so I—"

"Came in hopes of a legacy?" MacLean mocked.

Between gritted teeth, Enid said, "I grow weary of being called mercenary."

"Mercenary? You? The orphan girl who married my cousin? Answer me this, Enid—did they pay you to care for me?"

She saw the trap, but by now she was so weary she didn't care. He'd already made up his mind. "Yes. Lots."

"Did they pay you well enough to seduce me when I thought of leaving?"

She caught her breath. She *did* care, or his disdain would not have stabbed so deeply. "Bastard," she whispered.

"If I remember correctly, *you* are the bastard."

She swallowed the lump of splintering pain. She'd been called a bastard before; she could survive that. And surely she would survive him calling her a whore. She'd even half expected to hear it.

She hadn't expected to bleed and die. Not from the insults of a man she refused to love. With only a small catch in her voice, she asked, "Shall I stay on the beach and make my way to the harbor in the morning? I'm sure I can catch a fishing boat back to the coast."

He wrapped his arm around her so quickly that she

might have been the snake's first meal. "You're not getting out of this so easily, lass. You've come this far. You can face the MacLeans with your sins writ fresh on your face."

Chapter 20

"So you came racing to my side—or rather, Stephen's side—not because you wanted the money, but because you truly loved me . . . him?" As they marched through the dark wood and damp meadow toward Castle MacLean, Kiernan kept his arm around Enid.

She struck with her elbow into his ribs.

He winced but kept moving as he struggled to master his disappointment. But to discover the woman he had depended upon, cherished, laid claim to, was not his wife! He had his old memories back, yes. But he had new ones, too. He remembered living with Enid, talking with her, having her nurse him, help him, jest with him and fight with him. He knew of her sharp tongue, her golden laughter, the way she yawned just before she fell asleep.

He knew how she looked naked.

She had been his wife, and he wanted her still to be his wife.

She strode along beside him, matching his great

strides, and matching his anger, too. "I came to nurse my husband because of duty. Mr. Kinman acted shocked that I didn't care. Lady Halifax insisted I rush to your side . . . Stephen's side . . . and behave like a proper, caring wife. And I did. I brought you back from the brink of death, you ungrateful swine, and don't you forget it."

"For payment!"

"I could have let you die and still received payment, and saved myself heartache and sore feet in the bargain."

Damn the woman. Didn't she realize she had cut him to the quick? She had mistaken him for Stephen! For his worthless, reprobate cousin, Stephen. She hadn't been able to tell them apart. "I'm honored that you didn't kill me for a legacy."

"A legacy? Stephen never had a pot to wizzle in or a window to throw it out of, and when he abandoned me, he left me only his debts. I had no reason to believe this time would be any different. And I certainly knew I wouldn't receive a legacy from you, almighty laird of the castle. You made that clear enough in the letter you sent on the happy occasion of my marriage."

He remembered that letter. He had been livid with Stephen for marrying beneath him. When his aunt Catriona had wailed about her poor gullible son, MacLean had remembered Stephen's susceptibility to flattery, and so a portrait of Enid the seducer and opportunist had built in his mind. "Stephen didn't abandon you. You abandoned him when he couldn't provide the pleasant living you were expecting from a lord's nephew."

"I'll wager Stephen told you that."

"He did." Honesty compelled him to add, "I suppose he was lying to save face."

"I suppose he was," she said sarcastically. "I've had one MacLean husband. I don't want another. So please don't worry that, after our intimacy, I have designs on *you.*"

She didn't have to deny her interest quite so emphatically.

In a quieter tone, she asked, "So I'm right. Stephen was killed in the explosion?"

"He was." Poor sod. "Well rid of him, heh?"

She gave a brief sigh. "I never wanted Stephen to die, I just wanted to be—"

"Free of him?"

"Yes," she admitted. "I wanted to be able to live without knowing that someday Stephen could arrive and destroy my life once again. I didn't want to be ashamed anymore."

"So you admit you had reason for shame."

"Indeed. I married poorly."

My God, the woman pricked at his pride, at his heart, at his mind. "Stephen was a MacLean!"

"Stephen was a cad."

"You are a cold fish."

"I am. Cold and smelly, but you're a fool if you believe any tale Stephen ever told about me."

Everything she said was true, but this was not what he wanted. Yes, he wanted to be Kiernan, laird of the MacLeans, but he wanted to be Enid's lover, too. He wanted to bring her to his castle, hold her close to his side, introduce her to his mother and his sister, have her smile at them and at him. And when the welcoming was over, he wanted to take her to his bed and love her as she deserved to be loved. Instead, all he had was acrimony and regrets.

"Come on. I don't want us to be late, or we'll have trouble rousing anyone." More important, uneasiness slid its cold finger along his spine. Someone did, after all, want them dead. Pulling her close against his side again, he set off once more through the last bit of woods.

The forced march must have heightened Enid's resentment, for she demanded, "*When* did Stephen tell you lies about his marriage? When he came running home to ask for money? Or was it in the Crimea, when you went to rescue him from his own recklessness?"

MacLean went on the alert. "What do you know about his recklessness in Crimea?"

"I was married to Stephen for three months. I knew that man. If he went to the Crimea, he went to make some money and have a frolic, and got involved with something more than he could handle. So there you came, his beloved cousin, saving him from his own folly once more, and you both got blown up. Isn't that what happened?"

MacLean's heart pounded to hear her speak so heedlessly about what should only be whispered. "You know too much for a nurse."

"As Harry said—I'm not a fool." She breathed hard and kept her hand at her side as if she had a stitch. "What I don't know is—who was Stephen spying for? For Britain, or for Russia?"

"You tell me. He was your husband."

"At least I know his treachery didn't stain *my* family."

Audacious woman! "Are you saying I am tarnished by my cousin's actions?"

"*I'm* not related to him by blood."

No wonder Kiernan desired Enid so thoroughly. She didn't care who he was or what position he held. She wouldn't let him trample on her. She stuck up for herself. He wanted nothing so much as to kiss her, but . . . he lifted his head, then slowed his onward rush. "Sh."

"Why? You don't like to hear the truth? I could tell you tales of Stephen that would make your hair—"

Stopping, he put his hand over her mouth. In her ear, he murmured, "Be quiet."

She had the good sense not to fight him. Pushing his hand away, she stood still as he strained to discern that one, odd, sharp sound that made him think they were being stalked.

He heard nothing. Wrapping his arm around her again, he moved cautiously forward, toward the castle. They had less than a mile to go. He wouldn't let something happen to her now. Lifting his head, he gave the long, low call of an owl.

And he got an answer. Not far from him, a little to the left, toward the deer blind.

Changing directions, he started toward the noise, calling again.

Again he heard an answer. He recognized that particular call! That was young Graeme MacQuarrie. The whole MacQuarrie clan might be a wretched pain in the arse, but they were the other clan on the island and he would be damned happy to see them.

Enid, smart lass, kept silent and stayed close to him.

She made more racket than he did, but what could a man expect of a Sassenach with sore feet and a full set of petticoats?

The calls got closer and closer together until Graeme leaped from the blind to pound MacLean's back. "I can't believe ye finally made it, ye auld muttonhead!"

Graeme's thick Scottish accent was quite the sweetest sound that MacLean had ever heard. "And to find you here on MacLean land when I've whipped you time and again and told you to run along back to Mama!" Releasing Enid, MacLean pounded Graeme in his turn. "How are you, Graeme?"

"Good, for a man who's spent every chill night waiting to help ye limp along home! What ha'e ye been doing all this time? Whimpering like a lass aboot yer delicate constitution?"

Without showing an ounce of compunction, Enid lied. "He's done nothing but complain. First he whined about the heat, then the cold, then his feet hurt, then he complained of being hungry."

Astonishment kept Graeme silent.

"Woman!" MacLean said in the voice he used when he made lordly judgments. "You know how to try my patience."

"I would hope so. I've had enough practice." Enid leaned against a tree. "Are we close to the castle?"

Graeme snapped to attention. "Yes, miss. We were told a lady would arrive wi' the MacLean, but no one told us ye'd be so charming."

By that, he meant that no one had told him she would tweak the tail of the lion of the MacLeans. By her insolence, she had already proved her mettle and raised herself from the position of a cipher to a woman of consequence.

And she was leaning against the tree, which meant hunger made her weak.

Wrapping his arm around her once again, MacLean headed toward the castle. "She's not eaten since breakfast, and a poor one it was."

"And she doesn't like being discussed as if she wasn't here, any more than she likes being toted about like a package!" Enid snapped.

"When she gets peckish, she gets a wee bit choleric," MacLean explained.

"Any lass who has walked across Scotland can be as choleric as she wishes." The damned fool Graeme sounded respectful. "Would ye like me to carry ye, miss?"

"No, she wouldn't," MacLean said.

"Ah." Graeme fell back a little, and MacLean could tell he was smirking. "Is that the way the wind blows?"

"No!" Enid answered.

Graeme cackled.

MacLean would have set the man straight, but he had a more imperative question on his mind. "Is there someone else out tonight?"

"Sure. We've got Jimmy MacGillivray on the east, Rab Hardie to the north, and that Englishman, Harry. He's a spooky one, wouldn't want to cross him. We didn't know how ye'd come in, but the Englishmen were sure ye would get here and worried ye'd be attacked on the way." Graeme laughed to indicate his scorn.

"Tonight, as we were passing through the meadow, I thought I heard a rifle cock," MacLean told him.

Enid tripped.

He held her up and kept her moving.

"God's teeth, MacLean! No one's out here wi' guns," Graeme said tersely. "Not on a night wi' a bit of a cloud. Not when it's nigh on midnight!"

"How much further?" Enid asked.

"You can see the lights. There." Halting at the edge of the woods, MacLean pointed up to the knoll where the jagged battlements shone against a night sky shredded by clouds. "That's Castle MacLean."

"It's beautiful," Enid said.

MacLean grinned. Romantic sight the castle might be, but he knew otherwise. "Wait until daylight before you pass judgment. The castle's been through some hard times."

"Ye've salvaged the best of it." Graeme heaped praise as he got close to food and fire.

MacLean gave the owl call again and stopped beneath a tree until the great double doors opened.

His mother, Lady Bess Hamilton, stood in the doorway with the lights of the great hall shining bright behind her. He recognized her by her shape, which was voluptuous beyond propriety, by her turban, and by the lit cigar she held in her outstretched hand. "Kiernan?" she yelled. "You get in here right now!"

Ah, he had his problems with his mother, but right now her husky smoker's voice sounded as sweet as the call of a lark.

"We're going to run," MacLean told Enid. "Do you think you can do it?"

"I'll have to, won't I?" She sprang across clearing like a doe.

MacLean and Graeme uttered identical curses and raced after her.

They caught up with her, of course, then stayed behind and swerved from side to side to confuse any watching gunman.

"Come on, lass," his mother shouted, "you can outrun those two sluggards!"

Three men bearing torches stepped out of the door and started toward them, Kinman among them. Just when MacLean had about decided that only an idiot would dare shoot in such a company, a rifle roared. Graeme fell.

With a shout of fury, Lady Bess raced down the path toward them. The men with the torches began running. More men streamed out the door.

Enid tried to stop and kneel beside Graeme.

MacLean pulled her toward the castle.

She twisted in his grip. "MacLean, he needs my help!"

"We'll bring him to you. There's a villain with a rifle out there."

"He's used the bullet!"

MacLean didn't bother to explain that there could be more than one man, or more than one rifle. She was a smart lass. She knew.

"I've got her." Lady Bess, almost his height, took Enid firmly in her grasp. "Go help Graeme."

"No!" Kinman took an equally firm grasp on MacLean. "We can't take a chance with him."

"Bugger off," MacLean said, and turned back toward the group of men around Graeme.

Enid twirled away from his mother. "I'm not going inside if you don't."

MacLean glared at her. "You'll do as you're told!"

"I didn't cure you to have you shot a hundred yards from your own home!"

Lady Bess whistled. "So that's how the wind blows."

"No!" Enid answered.

"He's up!" the men around Graeme called.

MacLean saw Graeme staggering along, two men holding him erect while Graeme grinned and wiped blood off his forehead.

MacLean surrendered. "Come on, then!" Hooking his arm in Enid's, he hurried her up the hill without a care for her exhaustion. After all, she had made a fool of him in front of his friend and his mother, and that in the first hour of his return.

He could hear his mother laughing and coughing as she strolled toward the castle. His mother feared not a mere gunshot.

Kinman galloped just behind MacLean, swerving as MacLean and Graeme had done with Enid.

The old housekeeper, Donaldina, stood at the door waving them in.

And for reasons he understood only too well, MacLean swept Enid into his arms and carried her across the threshold.

Chapter 21

"MacLean, put me down." Mortified, Enid thrashed in MacLean's arms as they stepped across the threshold into the towering chamber aswirl with shouting humanity. "MacLean, I said put me down! It's a little late for chivalry now."

Then the noise died. She ceased struggling and looked out into the crowd.

Torches and candles lit the great hall. Long tables lined the walls, and comfortable seats were placed in clusters around the two huge fireplaces. The men held claymores and shields. The women held rifles and powder horns. The weapons drooped in their hands as they stood silent and open-mouthed, gawking at their laird—and at Enid.

The only sound came when one of the dogs, a great, leggy beast, laid eyes on MacLean and, with a yelp, ran forward, tail wagging.

A tiny, toothless, birdlike woman broke the silence. In the thickest Scottish accent Enid had yet heard, she said, "Ohh, look what th' master carried in. She's a pretty thing, m'lord. May we keep her?"

Everyone in the crowd nudged each other, exchanging grins and nods.

Enid wanted to hide her head in MacLean's shoulder, do anything to shut out the staring eyes. Dear heavens, she recognized some of them—about a dozen of Throckmorton's men, and that added to the humiliation.

Instead she lifted her chin, "For the love of God, MacLean, put me down."

He did, but slowly. Keeping his arm around her, he swept the room with a gaze filled with menacing possession.

He might as well have put a sign on her forehead— *Property of the laird of the MacLeans.* She had hoped to survive this stay with a modicum of dignity intact. MacLean had made that impossible.

MacLean turned to the old woman. "She's hungry. She wants a bath and a bed." To Enid, he said, "Go with Donaldina. She'll tend you."

The old woman curtsied. "Aye, m'lord, she'll ha'e th' best."

"I need to look after Graeme," Enid said stubbornly.

"You'll do as you're told," MacLean said. "You're starving."

She was, and dazed by a rather odd light-headedness. Something seemed very different here.

"This way, miss," Donaldina said kindly.

Enid didn't move. Very different indeed.

Mr. Kinman caught MacLean's shoulder. "We've been worried. My God, what has happened?"

"Later. For now, find out who did the shooting."
MacLean leaned down to scratch the ecstatic dog.

"Your men are after him." Mr. Kinman looked five
years older and ten pounds thinner than two weeks before. "We need to know where you've been!"

MacLean viewed him sternly. "Later. We'll talk
later."

Mr. Kinman almost danced with impatience, but
MacLean ignored him without compunction. Ah, that
was the difference Enid had noted. She had never seen
MacLean as laird. He danced to no man's tune but his
own. He looked taller, grimmer, stronger, with an aura
of authority that would have frightened her had it not
appealed so strongly to her every feminine sense. Dear
heavens, she'd slept with this man! And when his gaze
met hers, she knew he wanted her still. Without moving a muscle, he summoned her to his side, drawing
her with a dark enchantment that made nothing of dis-
agreements and difficulties. He was laird. She was an
English bastard. But the difference in their stations did
not matter when weighed against the desire that burned
between them.

She had taken a first, helpless step toward him when
shouting woke Enid from her trance. Two men supporting Graeme burst through the door, trailed by Jackson and one of the guards from England. Tearing her
gaze away from MacLean's, she said, "Graeme needs
my help."

"He's fine." Lady Bess's smoky voice sounded in
the doorway. " 'Twas only his head, which he doesn't
employ for much."

Loud laughter broke out.

"Ye're ungrateful, my lady." Graeme staggered as they escorted him to a chair.

Oh, dear. The Scotsmen wore skirts. What had Stephen called them? Kilts. In the dark and confusion, Enid hadn't noticed. Now she averted her eyes from their bony, hairy knees.

" 'Tis yer own son's neck I saved," Graeme said.

"By getting in the way!" MacLean said.

"But a neck worth saving." Lady Bess gestured to a manservant, who thrust a tankard into Graeme's hand. "I thank you."

Enid blinked as she got her first good look at MacLean's mother. Like him, she was tall, but there the resemblance ended. Eccentricity would have explained the cigar burning between her fingers. Nothing could explain the clothing, the cosmetics, the sheer outrageous appearance of a woman of . . . what? Forty-five years?

Obviously, she scorned both corset and petticoats, wearing a garment more fitting to the days of her youth than to current fashion and bespeaking more scandal than good taste. The sheer fabric gathered beneath her breasts and dropped straight to the floor, unhampered by anything so proper as an undergarment. Indeed, as Lady Bess passed in front of the light, Enid could see the silhouette of her legs, and the fabric clung in places it absolutely should not. At least . . . not for propriety's sake.

The lady moved to her son's side and asked, "After such an absence and all this excitement, will you give your poor, worried mother a hug?"

"Of course, madam." MacLean hugged her, but with what Enid considered an abominable lack of affection.

So she ignored the nasty beast and went to examine Graeme.

A serving boy held a branch of candles high to give her light.

She thanked him with a smile.

Pungent whisky wafted up at her when Graeme said, "I'm fine, ma'am. 'Tis nothing but a scratch."

"The scratch is bleeding all over your clothing." Enid brushed back his hair and examined the gash that cut through his scalp. "You'll heal better if I stitch it."

Graeme looked alarmed until MacLean moved to his other side.

"Let her do it, man," MacLean said. "She'll make you look good."

One of the kilt-clad Scotsmen brayed, "Is she a miracle worker, then?"

Another boisterous burst of laughter greeted this sally.

"She won't rest until she's satisfied you are cared for." MacLean stood at Enid's shoulder, bolstering her authority. "So sit still, Graeme, and take the discomfort like a man."

A man dressed in the rough garments of a woodsman said, "If he takes it like a man, we'll *know* she's a miracle-worker!"

The laughter was louder this time, but Enid now realized what had happened. Tables and benches were overturned all over the hall. Some of the men still held their claymores. They'd been warned of an attack on their laird, so they'd grabbed weapons and prepared for a fight. Before they could race into action, though, they'd been called back. Now all of them, servants, gentlemen and ladies, were restless and overexcited. If she needed proof she was no longer in England, this convivial, close-knit, mixed group of folk convinced her.

"Ma'am, here's a needle and catgut." Donaldina stood at her elbow and presented the professional-looking instruments on a silver tray. "Lady Bess usually does th' stitching, but she's none too mindful o' th' pain, so wee Graeme will be pleased o' yer services."

Obediently, Graeme said, "Aye, ma'am, that I will."

From her massive chair at the head of a long table, Lady Bess puffed on her cigar. "I'll remember that when next I'm called on to tend you, young Graeme."

He scootched down in the chair and looked so apprehensive that Enid asked him, "Are you hurt often?"

"If there's a stray arrow shot or a piece of broken glass to be had, our Graeme will find it, but this is your first bullet, isn't it, my lad?"

"First." Graeme grimaced. "And last."

"Make sure of that." MacLean laid his hand on the back of Enid's neck and massaged the stiff muscles. A small gesture, but everyone observed with bright eyes.

They observed, too, when Enid knocked his hand away and glared up at him. He didn't need to think he could pull his beguiling tricks on her.

MacLean smiled down at her with such open affection, she stood on her toes and whispered fiercely, "Would you stop that?"

"What?"

"Acting as if we have some kind of bond." She glanced around. Everyone in the great hall observed them avidly.

MacLean didn't seem to care. He didn't lower his voice. "But, lass, we do. Ye're my lover."

All around them, she could hear the whispers start, and she hissed, "You called me a mercenary bastard who slept with you for money. Did you think I would forget?"

He gathered her hands in his. He lifted them to his lips. He kissed first the backs, then the palms, then when she curled them into fists, he kissed the backs again. Looking into her eyes, he murmured, "That was wrong. Will you forgive me?"

She stood flat on her feet and tugged at her fingers. "No." Forgive him? She intended to cherish her grudges. That was the only defense she had against a pair of soulful green eyes and a winsome smile.

"Please. Enid. I was wrong to say those things."

"Why? They're true."

He lifted his brows in mocking astonishment. "You slept with me for money?"

"No, not that, but I'm a mercenary bastard and an Englishwoman to boot."

"Ah, we all have our faults." He started kissing her fingers one by one. "Forgive me?"

She had ten fingers. He had all night. "All right. I forgive you!"

He stopped kissing and allowed her to pull her hands from his. "I thank you."

She pushed her hair back from her hot forehead. Never before had she blushed so hard as to break a sweat.

MacLean gestured to Graeme, and in a respectful tone, asked, "Will you sew him now?"

"Could I have some of your whisky?" she asked Graeme.

With a grin, Graeme offered it up. "Aye, I knew

when I first heard ye speak to His Lordship that ye were a bonny lass."

"Ye can have yer own," Donaldina said. "Although th' liquor's usually a bit much fer our English visitors."

"I'll just use a little of his." So saying, Enid poured an ample amount over the wound, bringing a howling Graeme to his feet.

Laughter broke out again, and it took MacLean's heavy hand on Graeme's shoulder to push him back into the chair.

"That's the worst of it," Enid told Graeme and proceeded to stitch him up regardless of his squirming.

MacLean turned to Donaldina. "She'll eat as soon as she's done."

"Aye, m'lord." Donaldina curtsied. "Will ye ha'e a piece o' bread yerself?"

"When she's done." Followed by the dog, who nosed his hand at every opportunity, he moved among the crowd.

In between stitches, Enid watched him surreptitiously. He smiled and shook hands. More important, people waited in line to clap him on the shoulder, smile at him, have a word.

"Ah, 'tis fine t' ha'e him back." Donaldina still stood at Enid's elbow, ready with an extra strand of catgut. "We've missed th' lad. He's a good man t' help when there's trooble afoot, an' on an estate o' this size, there's always trooble somewhere."

Enid had been right when she'd told MacLean he shouldn't have believed the claims Stephen had made about her; now she realized she shouldn't have believed the claims Stephen had made about him. MacLean's people adored him.

She hated that. So much better to believe the cruel letter she'd received from Stephen's lord had been part and parcel of MacLean's general malice, and not specifically directed at her.

Yet tonight, in the woods, he'd called her a bastard. He might have apologized. He might even have really meant it, for he was not a cruel man. Yet it was true. She was an impoverished English bastard, and bastards did not wed noblemen. She needed to remember that.

"From th' look o' that face, the master's seen trooble aplenty since he left," Donaldina continued. "Did ye stitch him up, too?"

"No, that was done before they sent for me."

Donaldina stood on her toes and craned her neck to look at Enid's work. "Weel, that explains his scars. Ye—ye're a wonder wi' that needle."

"Thank you." Enid finished up and patted Graeme on the shoulder. "All done."

Standing, Graeme bowed to her. "Thank ye, miss, for yer kindness. If I can ever do anything for ye, ye've only to call on me."

"Thank you, Graeme." She curtsied in return. "I'll remember that." Indeed, she had reason to believe she would need all the friends she could find on MacLean's godforsaken island.

Seeing Enid was free, Lady Bess commanded, "Miss, come and sit by me. We'll talk."

Enid really wanted to eat, but she was a guest, one who had roused everyone's curiosity. So she made her way to the head of the table, followed by her serving maid with a tray of food, the lad with the candles, and · Donaldina.

Lady Bess looked over the procession. "You've acquired quite a following."

Enid refused to let MacLean's mother rattle her. After all, worse things had happened than being interrogated by the lady of the manor, and those events had happened this very night. "Set the tray down, please," she instructed the serving girl. To the lad, she said, "You've done well, I thank you." Donaldina sat herself on the bench on the right side of Lady Bess, which Enid found an odd sort of accommodation for a housekeeper. But since Lady Bess found nothing unusual about it, Enid seated herself on the bench on the left side.

At first, Enid applied herself exclusively to her meal, discovering that when she finished one item, three more appeared on her tray, each more appetizing than the last. It had indeed been a very long time since breakfast. Finally, replete, she had to lean back and wave away any further offerings.

Lady Bess had been observing her closely. "You've got a good appetite, I'll say that for you. Glad to see you're not one of those modern damsels who'll sacrifice a rib to possess a tiny waist."

"After the week I've had, my waist is as tiny as it's going to get," Enid said.

"Hm." Lady Bess tapped her cigar into an ashtray and smirked. "Aye, my son cares not for a tiny waist."

Irritated by the unwarranted assumptions everyone seemed to be making, Enid said, "I don't care what MacLean cares for."

"Don't you?" Lady Bess gestured toward him.

MacLean looked relaxed as never before. He stood among a group of men, waving a strawberry as he spoke. The men guffawed, even Jackson, whom Enid had thought a proper stick of a valet. Apparently Scotland had loosened him up . . . and frightened Mr. Kinman, who followed MacLean as if they were sewn together with a fancy stitch. When the outer door opened, two men walked in and went to MacLean, shaking their heads.

"Ah, too bad, they found nothing." Lady Bess sighed. "Still, it's grand to see Kiernan back. I'm a fair manager until the men fight, and then I want to knock their heads together until they ring. Kiernan can listen to their silly arguments and make good judgments, and they'll not grumble."

"They don't grumble aboot ye, either, m'lady." Donaldina drank a swig from the cup set before her and smacked her gums together.

"They're afraid of me. They respect MacLean." Lady Bess lounged in her chair. "Look. The MacQuarrie must have roused himself from bed to hustle over here and pay his respects to Kiernan."

"Th' auld fool," Donaldina said affectionately. "He'll be wanting t' spend th' night in my bed, I expect."

"I expect you'll let him, too." Lady Bess turned to Enid and pointed her cigar at the man who shook MacLean's hand. "See the elderly man with the hair that looks like seaweed? That's the laird of the MacQuarries. They didn't survive the troubles nearly as well as the MacLeans, so Kiernan has helped them with a loan or two."

Donaldina snorted into her mug. "I ha'e half a mind t' tell the MacLean where th' money came from."

"Never you mind that, Donaldina," Lady Bess said firmly. "Now look, Catriona has come down."

Donaldina turned to watch as the crowd around MacLean gave way for a lady older than Lady Bess and dressed in the finest and most modern fashion. "Do ye opine she'll ha'e one o' her fits?" Donaldina asked with interest.

"He's bearing bad news, so aye." Lady Bess told Enid, "That lady with the gray hair is Lady Catriona MacLean, Kiernan's aunt and my husband's sister-in-law."

Enid frankly stared. So that was Stephen's mother— a sweet face, round, dimpled cheeks, a button nose. Yet a perpetual frown puckered her brows.

Lady Bess continued, "She has seen great sorrow in her life. Her husband died before the birth of their son, and that son disappeared over a year ago. We all knew Stephen had found trouble when he didn't come home even to borrow money."

"Amen." Donaldina sank further into her drink.

Lady Catriona approached MacLean timidly, as if she were afraid he would reject her. Her trepidation surprised Enid; everyone respected MacLean, but no one else seemed the least intimidated by him.

Lady Bess watched her sister-in-law without fondness. "Kiernan, who suffers from an overdeveloped sense of familial duty, went to find Stephen."

"I wonder where he got th' overdeveloped sense o' duty, m'lady," Donaldina interjected.

"I said we weren't going to talk about it anymore, Donaldina."

"Aye, m'lady." Donaldina turned to Enid. "But we know, don't we?"

No, Enid didn't know, but she was curious. Curious about Lady Bess, and intent on watching Stephen's mother to see how she would respond to the news of her son's death. Stephen had spoken of his mother with open contempt. How did Lady Catriona think of her son?

"Kiernan disappeared for over ten months," Lady Bess said. "I assume from Kiernan's scars he found Stephen, eh?"

Enid nodded her assent.

"Too late to save him, I'd deduce, and Kiernan got injured trying to get that feckless boy out of trouble. Eh?"

Enid nodded again, her gaze glued to the drama taking place in the middle of the great hall.

When MacLean realized his aunt stood there, he gestured her over. She hugged him with what appeared to be coy affection, hung on his arm like ivy, and spoke.

Wrapping an arm around her shoulders, he escorted her to a chair. Kneeling beside her, he shook his head, and said only a few words before she burst into tears, knocked him away, leaped up and fled the room.

"Weel, there it is." Lady Bess puffed at the noxious cigar until smoke wreathed her head. "It's not kind of me to say so, but Stephen's death is no great loss. Catriona indulged the lad dreadfully. Thought everything he did was perfect. And cling! She never gave him room to grow into a man. No wonder he turned out to be a wastrel and a coward."

How very interesting. From Stephen's comments about his mother, Enid had deduced that very thing.

"If Stephen had gotten my son killed," Lady Bess

continued, "I would have chased him to hell to kick his arse."

Enid stifled an inappropriate laugh. "Someone needed to kick his . . . um . . . arse."

Lady Bess straightened her shoulders.

Donaldina sat upright.

They exchanged glances.

In a cordial tone that didn't fool Enid, Lady Bess said, "You know, dear, I'm an auld woman whose hearing's not too good, and I don't recall hearing your name."

MacLean hadn't given her name, as Lady Bess knew very well. But Enid couldn't put off this terrible moment; it had to be faced with courage. So in a clear voice that carried halfway down the table, Enid declared, "I'm Enid MacLean. I'm Stephen's widow."

Everyone had gone to bed except the little contingent of Englishmen. Kinman, Jackson, and five of Throckmorton's best men sat before the fire, legs stretched onto the ottomans, smoking cigars and waiting their turn to speak with MacLean.

Before he got to them and answered their impatient questions, he had one more conversation. His mother sat alone in the master's chair. A cigar smoked in the ashtray beside her, and she shuffled playing cards and laid them out in tidy piles in preparation for solitaire.

She had always loved cards. When Kiernan was a child, she had taught him all sorts of games, games that sharpened his skills at adding and subtracting, then at strategy and intelligence. She taught him how to read his opponent, how to win graciously, and how to lose without obvious regret. He utilized those skills every day.

Yet he never played cards with her anymore.

She rose as he strode toward her; he pressed her down and pulled out one of the benches beside her. "You've earned your place at the head of the table," he said. "I heard about Torquil and Eck and their fight over the long-eared racehorse."

Waving an indolent arm, Lady Bess said, " 'Twas nothing. Took no more than the wisdom of Solomon to make them see sense."

MacLean knew them. She did not exaggerate. "They're stubborn men, both," he acknowledged.

"Stupid men . . . but aren't they all?" She poked fun at him, as she always did.

She said things to him she would never say to another soul, things that made him want to say things best left unsaid, for she was not without sin, blast her. But she was his mother, and worthy of respect, for she had done a marvelous job tending his estate. "You know what I came to ask," he said.

"That's why I stayed here when your English gentlemen are chomping at the bit." She smiled at Kinman, who was peering around his chair at them.

Kinman blushed and ducked away.

"Where's my sister?" MacLean demanded.

His mother ground out her cigar. "It's not good news this time."

"When is it ever?" He thought savagely of Caitlin, long-legged as a colt and just as wild.

"This is the worst." Lady Bess looked down at the cards. "She's gone off to avenge you."

MacLean hoped he hadn't heard properly. "Avenge me? What do you mean, avenge me?"

"We feared you were dead. Caitlin was broken-hearted, and so enraged that she ran off, determined to trace your footsteps and punish your killer."

"No." Not that he didn't believe his mother. Only that the thought of his little sister out in the world looking for trouble made him ill. "How does she think to avenge me? No—please don't tell me. Just tell me you've searched for her."

"She wrote us from London. She said nothing of her quest to avenge you, and I want to think she went to that great city and abandoned her mad idea." Blindly, Lady Bess moved a card.

"I want to think that, too." But he didn't, and in truth, neither did his mother. Caitlin was as stubborn a lass as any to be found, and she had the persistence of a bulldog. "What is she doing in London?" A new worry sprang to mind. "How is she supporting herself?"

"She's not still in London. She found a position through the . . ." Lady Bess reached into her cleavage and pulled out a well-folded sheet of paper. ". . . Through the Distinguished Academy of Governesses."

Hope glimmered. "That is the agency which found Enid her position with Lady Halifax. A respectable agency. They would not send her into danger."

Leaning forward, Lady Bess gripped his arm. "Truly? You know this?"

For all her indolent appearance, she was, he realized, deeply afraid for her daughter. "Truly. Have you written them?"

"I sent them a letter, and I got a polite letter in return from a Lady Bucknell. She said Caitlin seemed sensible enough, had good references, and claimed to be twenty-five, which she is, so Lady Bucknell sent her out on a job in the Lake Country. She said she would write Caitlin and ask that she contact me, but that she couldn't demand the child return."

"The child is a woman." Leaning across his mother, he moved a red queen onto a black king.

Lady Bess lightly slapped his hand.

"It doesn't sound as if she's in danger. Did Lady Bucknell give Caitlin's location?"

"In the island nation of Rasnull. I sent a messenger to find her when we discovered you were alive. Perhaps that will bring her home."

"Yes." He stroked his chin again, and in a low voice, said, "And perhaps she will stay where she is and there find happiness."

Moisture shined in Lady Bess's eyes. "Kiernan!"

For the first time, he said what they both knew. "My lady mother, she can't find contentment here. No matter how hard we try to protect her, everyone whispers about the scandal and she hears it."

"I know." Lady Bess laughed without humor as she considered her own scandal. "I do know."

But you deserve the whispers and the slander.

He didn't say it, for Caitlin deserved the whispers and the slander, too. She had been the spoiled daughter of the clan MacLean, and she had wantonly thrown away her good name on a viper, a scoundrel . . . a man he had cherished like a brother.

"So, for the moment, we will assume that all is well

with her." Lady Bess picked up the cards, reshuffled, and laid them out again. "You have grown great in wisdom." She seemed serious, then she smiled at him, mocking him in the old, familiar way. "A man as great in wisdom as you must recognize that it's time you married."

Slowly he leaned back. "You think so?"

"Taking care of matters while you were gone showed me I'm too old for the burden of such responsibilities."

"You're not too old," he snapped. She wasn't. She had given birth to him when she was but sixteen, and he never remembered a time when he hadn't thought his mother a beautiful woman. Also outrageous, burly, difficult to live with, and a frequent embarrassment.

"Weel, *you* almost are." She shook her head over the cards and gathered them up once again. "There's not many women who'll want to marry an auld geezer like you, especially one who's not been broken in by a first wife."

"Do you have anyone in mind?"

"Let's not play games, son." Lady Bess rapped the deck against the table. "You made your claim on Enid clear tonight."

"Does it not bother you that she is my cousin's wife?"

"Stephen's *widow*, and obviously she is none of the terrible things he claimed. He lied to keep Catriona happy." Lady Bess's lip curled with the scorn she always showed when she spoke of his aunt. "Catriona would never allow another woman in her son's life."

MacLean remembered how Catriona had struck him aside as he'd tried to comfort her on the loss of her son.

The woman had adored Stephen with a zealot's fervor. As it was, even in his death he had brought them disgrace. "I know." He fumbled for his mother's hand. "So you . . . like Enid?"

She squeezed his fingers. "Marry her and give me grandchildren, and I'll adore her."

A wisp of warmth curled in his gut. He shouldn't give a damn what his mother thought. He should just take Enid and make her his wife . . . he took a breath. Ah, so that was his plan. He had to have Enid, so he would marry her.

"Will you do that?" Lady Bess asked.

And he wanted Lady Bess to like Enid. Obviously, she did or that plain-spoken woman would have made her feelings clear. "Enid doesn't care for me much right now."

"Not that you've ever had to bother before, but you could court the lass." As she rose, she ridiculed him with her smile. "Ask me if you need advice."

"I will not."

"You would never ask your wicked old mother for advice." She touched his cheek. "The more fool, you."

MacLean watched as she drifted through the great hall toward her bed, attracting the gaze of every able-bodied man still awake.

Damn the woman. She poked fun at him, and he responded with instinctive defiance every time. She always raised his hackles, she always laughed at him afterward, and he always felt the fool she called him. No, not a fool—a child, chided by his mother for not seeing through to the truth. But he knew the truth about her . . . didn't he?

Making his way to the fire, he sank down on one of

the comfortable chairs. He was tired, so tired he was staggering, but with a glance about the circle of Englishmen, he announced, "My memory has returned." At their gasp, he glanced around with a grin. But as he noted the obvious absence, his grin became a scowl. "First, tell where Harry has disappeared to."

Chapter 22

Enid woke in a huge, luxurious bed in a massive, luxurious bedchamber, clad in the lovely lace nightgown Celeste had sent for her. Covering her eyes against the morning sunlight, Enid groaned.

Last night had proved the ultimate humiliation. MacLean had carried her across the threshold of Castle MacLean as if she were a weakling or a . . . bride.

Then after breaking bread at the MacLean table, to have had to introduce herself to the family. For the second time that night, a silence had fallen, one that had rippled out from her and reached the very outskirts of the hall. More than that, heads had turned from her to MacLean, and back again.

But she had to hand it to the MacLeans. Even after that stunning piece of information, everyone had remained cordial. They'd filled her wineglass. They'd told her tales of Kiernan MacLean's youth. Tales that had made her laugh a little too hard. Well. She had been exhausted, and the wine had been potent.

When the MacLeans and their guests and servants had been told in no uncertain terms—by the MacLean himself—of Enid's fatigue, Lady Bess herself had led her upstairs to a bath and a bed. Although Enid had been almost asleep on her feet, she vaguely remembered Lady Bess explaining that in this chamber, Robert the Bruce had slept.

Enid hoped her wine-soaked brain had invented that fantasy, but in sitting up and looking around, she feared she had heard correctly. The sheets rustled like the finest cotton. The high posters on the bed, the ornately carved headboard, the paneling that covered the walls up to the chair rail, all was glorious, polished cherrywood. The coverlet, the bedcurtains, lofty canopy, and the drapes were deep green damask. Even the high ceiling with its painted clouds and plump cherubs suggested royalty.

Oh, how soon could she leave this hellhole and get back to her real life?

The sterling silver doorhandle rattled wildly, and Enid drew the covers up to her chin. "Come in," she called.

The doorhandle rattled again. Supposing it was a serving girl with the breakfast tray, Enid climbed out of bed via the steps and walked toward the door, which sprang open, spilling MacLean into the chamber in a facedown sprawl.

She yelped and snatched the new burgundy red brocade wrapper off the chair. Holding it before her like a shield, she looked him over and decided he hadn't hurt himself. He had landed on a very plush carpet. He wore the same clothing he had worn all the way through Scotland, and he was obviously the worse for drink. His head probably ached. He was probably sensitive to light.

Going to the windows, she opened the drapes.

And loud noises.

She yelled, "You're not my husband. Get out of here!"

Surprisingly enough, MacLean rose right to his feet and looked her over with squinting deliberation. "You look much better this morning." He waved his hand at his own face. "Last night you had big rings under your eyes and your mouth was all pinched and wrinkly."

Half-insulted, half-amused, half-desperate—that was too many halves, but she had never done well at mathematics—she said, "What a silver-tongued knave you are. Now get out." *Get out because you look too good even covered with filth and smelling of whisky.*

"You'll want to know what's happening." He tapped his lips. "Do you know I've been up all night talking to the Englishmen?"

Turning her back on him, she pulled on her wrap.

He didn't seem to notice that it looked superb on her. "I told them everything I remembered."

Marching to the door, she held the knob and pointed. "Out."

"But it was the most interesting thing. Just when I got to the good part, I didn't know anything!"

She stopped waving him out and stared at him instead. "What do you mean, you didn't know anything?"

"Better shut the door." He shushed her with extravagant care. "This is secret stuff. I'm not supposed to tell a soul."

"You're telling *me*."

" 'Course I am. I sleep with you."

Why had she ever considered this man appealing? She opened the door wider. "No, you don't. Get out."

"I can't remember the explosion."

She hesitated. She looked down the corridor to make sure no one was listening. She looked back at him, scruffy and casual. "The explosion that killed Stephen?"

He nodded.

"What *do* you remember?"

"I remember going to England to find Stephen, for I suspected he had fallen into bad company. Stephen always did. I found Throckmorton. He sent me to the Crimea to get Stephen and then"—MacLean shook his head sadly—"nothing. I remember nothing."

It shouldn't matter to her. She shouldn't care about MacLean's safety, or about this intrigue, but she had been involved. She was curious. "So you believe that the person who tried to kill you in the Crimea is trying to kill you now?"

"That, certainly."

"You think you were followed such a distance?"

"Why not? Train travel is easy, and if he can silence me before I declare him, he is safe." MacLean flung himself into a delicate chair so violently the wood groaned. "Harry almost shot me."

"What?" She gave up and slammed the door. "When?"

"You know Harry. Tall, dark." MacLean imitated a ferocious frown. "Always serious."

"I know who you mean, and I have long suspected he was the assassin."

"No, no, no. Not him. He came in last night long after everyone else, and he had a rifle." MacLean coughed as if he had a scratchy throat.

Walking to her bedside table, she poured MacLean a glass of water. Old habits died hard. "Why did Harry have a rifle?"

"Kinman and I had been talking about the shooting. You remember last night's shooting?"

She wanted to shake him to hurry the story. Instead she extended the glass. "I remember the shooting."

He considered her through red-rimmed eyes and fingered her robe. "That is a very pretty wrapper. Did you wear it for me?"

"No. Drink your water." She thrust it into his hand.

"No." He leered with ludicrous exaggeration. "For me, you would wear nothing."

Swiveling, she marched to the window. "It's a shame Harry didn't shoot you."

MacLean had the audacity to look wounded. "Cruel. You are cruel. If you're not nice to me, I'll leave."

"Let me hold the door for you."

"You jest." He slumped in the chair. "Harry hunted out of doors until he found the rifle, and he was angry. That really is a beautiful robe. It makes your hair look . . . wavy."

"My hair *is* wavy." She caught herself. "Why was Harry angry?"

"Because it's an English rifle." He took a long drink that drained the glass. "Stolen from Throckmorton's own personal collection and brought here, just to shoot at you."

"At *me*?"

"And at me."

"But Harry doesn't know who did the shooting."

"No."

They still weren't safe, but she deduced, "We know more than we did. We know it's one of the guards."

"They're going home today. All except for Harry, Kinman and Jackson."

Surprised, she questioned, "Jackson? You're allowing the valet to stay?"

"He has impeccable references from Lord and Lady Featherstonebaugh, so Kinman assures me Jackson is safe." MacLean managed to look both piteous and engaging. "And he shaves me so well."

Enid considered MacLean's scarred, scruffy, bewhiskered face. Yes, he would treasure Jackson for his way with a razor. "You ought to have him shave you now."

MacLean wiggled the glass. "Can I have some more?" As she drew near, he caught her fingers. "You have on a lace nightgown."

"I was asleep when you arrived." A lie, but she didn't care.

"I saw it before you put that ugly robe over the top of it. The nightgown is pretty." He tugged her close.

If she hadn't resisted, he would have pulled her into his lap. Fueled by anger that he thought she was so easy, and panic, because she wanted to be easy, she said, "You don't like me, remember? I'm Stephen's mercenary wife."

"Mercenary." He scowled, but he didn't drop her hand. "But not like my mother."

"Your mother?" Lady Bess? Mercenary?

"She and I talked about this last night. She thinks I ought to wed you."

Enid didn't know what to think. How to respond. "She's wrong. We will never marry. You're not wise enough to propose. I'm not desperate enough to accept. Why do you think your mother is mercenary?"

His face contorted as if he were in pain. "When I was young, she was a good mother. Then she betrayed the memory of my father. For *money*."

If MacLean weren't drunk, he would never speak so frankly. But he was drunk, and Enid had stumbled upon the reason MacLean despised her so much. She hesitated, for she knew to pry into Lady Bess's life was despicable, but curiosity conquered her reservations. "What did your mother do?"

"My father hadn't been in the grave for two months when she went off to Edinburgh and found herself a merchant." His voice vibrated in disgust. "He was old, absolutely vulgar, and very rich."

The thought of Lady Bess, vibrant and affable, lost in the arms of an ancient, uncouth parvenu jolted Enid. "Did she say why?"

"My mother has never explained herself to anyone, and certainly not to her fifteen-year-old son left in charge of his tearful, eleven-year-old sister."

"Oh, dear."

"Mother and her husband went off to London. She provided his entry into society. People laughed at her. Even up here, we heard how they ridiculed her." MacLean looked down at their entwined hands. "My sister and I stayed here, missing her, while I took charge of the estate and Elizabeth kept the house. Mother flitted about London, dressed in the finest clothing and ignoring her obligations."

Enid could see Lady Bess flitting, but she couldn't believe Lady Bess had ignored her obligations.

"Then, within the year, the old fool died, and my mother came back, expecting a warm welcome." MacLean shook his head, his rancor still fresh. "She gave me her newfound fortune to tend and thought I would thank her. But *I* would not be so easily bribed."

"Good for you. That's the spirit!" Enid said sarcastically. "That's probably because you've never been in need of money."

"As usual, you are wrong." Apparently, he'd recovered enough wit to return her sarcasm. "The troubles in the Forty-five hit my family hard."

By that she surmised the MacLeans had been involved in last century's futile uprising.

"The MacLeans have been recovering ever since. When my father died he left almost nothing except the lands and castle, and we counted ourselves lucky to have that. In need of money? Aye, I was fifteen years old and frantic."

The truth burst on Enid. A truth so obvious MacLean had to be deliberately blind not to see it.

Blind . . . or trapped in a fifteen-year-old's pain and disappointment. "Wait. Wait." She squeezed his fingers to get his attention. "You're telling me your mother married a decrepit old man for his money. You're saying she did this to get away from her responsibilities here at Castle MacLean, to live the good life in England while you struggled trying to survive on a pittance. You're telling me after the merchant's death, she came back with his fortune in her palm, threw the entire amount into your lap, told you she was too lazy to care for it, and now never leaves the Isle of Mull?"

Straightening his shoulders, he looked at her with chilly directness. "Yes."

"And you attribute her actions to selfishness?" Furious, she snapped her hand free from his. "You ought to know, you cold fish. You selfish swine. Your mother fixed it so *you* wouldn't have to wed some disgusting heiress to save your estate!"

His green eyes narrowed, and he snarled, "That is not true!"

She brushed at the air. "Don't talk to me. If you can't figure out that your mother should be cherished just for being your mother, much less for being a good mother . . . you're not just drunk, you're stupid!"

He got to his feet looking much more sober. "No one else thinks as you do."

"Is that what influences you? What everyone else thinks?" Enid thrust herself right under his nose and shook her finger at him. "I can assure you, everyone knows what your mother did. Ask Donaldina what she thinks."

"Donaldina was my mother's wet nurse." He said it as if that explained everything.

"Fine. Ask one of the men." Enid gestured freely. "Graeme complains about her. Ask Graeme what he thinks of your mother."

"She sews him up. He likes her." MacLean was groping now, unable to face the truth.

Enid didn't care. She wanted justice for Lady Bess, and she needed MacLean to admit the truth for his own sake—and for Enid's. "Everybody likes Lady Bess.

Everybody worships her. She brought me up here personally, fed me some twaddle about how Robert the Bruce slept here—"

"He did."

"—And I cried myself to sleep because I never had a mother like yours. I never had a mother at all, and you're whining because your mother sold herself to save you from marital bondage. You ungrateful wretch." Enid wanted to stomp her foot. Instead she straightened her shoulders and grasped for her rapidly slipping dignity. "So don't you compare me to your mother. She is a wonderful woman, while I—I am as mercenary as you fear."

"I sent someone to take the fishing boat back."

"What?"

"The fishing boat we borrowed to get here."

"Good." He twisted her in knots with his convoluted conversation, and now she knew he did it on purpose. He did it to distract her. He would not succeed. "As long as I've got you here, I want to say—everyone knows we're not married, so I'm in no danger. I want to go home."

He looked less intoxicated, less tired, and more like the commanding jackass she'd come to know. "You are not leaving until I have remembered everything."

"You might not ever remember everything."

"Then you will be here for a long, long time."

She pointed at the door. "Get out, and don't come back."

This time, he went.

*   *   *

"You can never go out alone." Kinman leaned forward, hands clasped at his knees, and looked earnestly at MacLean.

MacLean nursed his hangover. "You're right."

The fire crackled in the fireplace, releasing the faint scent of pine into the air. The great hall rang with after dinner conversation and laughter. All was as it should be, for MacLean sat with the three Englishmen, and Graeme MacQuarrie, Jimmy MacGillivray, and Rab Hardie, and the women sat at the other end of the hall beside their own fireplace. There Donaldina attempted to teach Enid to spin wool with a spindle, apparently with little success by the sound of the laughter. Everything was appointed just as MacLean liked it. Man talk for him, wench duties for them.

"We shipped off most of our men today," Kinman said, "but whoever is after you is desperate, and there must be more than one."

Although Jackson sat on the outermost edge of their group, they included him in their counsel. He stayed, by nature of his disposition and his appearance, almost invisible, but now he lifted his hand. "May I ask, Mr. Kinman, how you know that?"

"The man you shot in the attack on the train—"

That was news to MacLean. "Jackson shot someone?"

"An Englishman, an officer in the militia with a reputation for fierceness in battle," Harry answered.

"Apparently someone else owned his loyalty," Graeme said.

Kinman bristled as if Graeme slurred all Englishmen.

Harry nodded, calm as always. "Apparently. He was on board as one of our defenders. He killed the engineer and stopped the train. Jackson fired when he burst into the car."

MacLean eyed the dull, fastidious Jackson with new respect. "You can shoot?"

Jackson picked at a piece of lint on his sleeve. "My former master shot birds at his estate near Edinburgh, and he insisted I learn."

"I thought your former master was a friend of Throckmorton's. Lord Featherstonebaugh, was it not?"

Jackson turned his unremarkable blue eyes on MacLean. "I have worked for several gentlemen at different times in my life."

Fascinating. MacLean would send to Throckmorton and ask that he investigate the valet's past more closely.

A burst of feminine laughter distracted MacLean, and he glanced across the hall once more. He'd been with Enid perpetually for months. He couldn't miss her just because they'd been separated a day—and not even a whole day.

He winced as he remembered his arrival in her bedchamber this morning. He couldn't believe he'd been so inebriated that he'd sought her out. He had told her every family secret because, in some twisted place in his mind, he had decided she deserved to know.

Even now, while in his right, but hungover, mind, he thought she did. She had been with him almost since the beginning of this adventure. She was in danger because of him. Surely such devotion justified informing her of the day-to-day happenings of the castle. Even the little things that seemed of no importance.

Kinman dragged the conversation back to the topic at hand. "The other men boarded the train when it stopped."

"I saw only two," Jackson said.

"But in the dark and confusion, it was impossible to count. I know at least one more entered MacLean's car, probably just after he escaped," Harry replied.

Kinman grasped MacLean's arm to recapture his attention. "So you see, MacLean, we do know someone will come after you again. Someone will try again to kill you. Someone will ambush you."

The men glanced at each other with the kind of narrow-eyed determination men showed before battle.

"I know you, MacLean," Kinman said earnestly. "You'll balk at restrictions, but you must see they're a necessity."

"A complete necessity," MacLean said. He couldn't sneak into Enid's bedchamber for conversation, because this morning he'd managed to get himself thrown out. Of course, they weren't yet married. She didn't yet know his intentions, and she'd made it clear she wouldn't welcome his suit. He had no right in her bedchamber, but . . . he wanted to win that right.

Unfortunately, his mother was right. He didn't know how to court a woman. He'd never had to; as laird, women had courted him. Of course, he knew the basics: how to flirt, how to tell a woman lies. But never before had he wanted a woman who didn't want him. Never before had it mattered so much.

"You have to appear to be casual, and at the same

time always be on your guard." Kinman squeezed his hands together and looked as nervous as ever that large gentleman could look.

"Absolutely." If MacLean hadn't recovered his memory, he would have undoubtedly got her with child.

He sat up straight.

Perhaps a child already grew in her womb. In which case they would have to wed, regardless of her lack of enthusiasm.

Kinman had said it before, but now he said it again. "We don't know what information you have hidden within the depths of your mind, but the traitor has proved its importance by doing everything in his power to eliminate you."

"You're right," MacLean repeated in a daze.

A child . . . with Enid? His gut and his heart leaped at the idea.

Kinman jumped to his feet. "Blast you, MacLean, you're not listening to me!"

MacLean blinked at the huffing, red-faced Kinman. "I've agreed with everything you said!"

"And how unlikely is that?" Kinman complained.

Now that MacLean had his memory back, he remembered Kinman. They had grown to know each other when MacLean had gone to England to trace Stephen. Kinman was a conscientious, kindly, dutiful man who could fight with the best of them. His shambling appearance hid a sharp mind, and MacLean respected him.

But Kinman seemed to believe MacLean was intractable, and MacLean willingly reassured him. "I'm not to go out by myself," MacLean recited. "Most of the English guards are gone, but I'm still not safe. We don't know what I know, but the killer has proved how important that bit of knowledge is by torching the cottage, stopping the train, chasing me through Scotland, and shooting at me."

Kinman looked down at his feet and shuffled them. "Perhaps there is more than one killer after you."

"That's obvious." MacLean looked around at the serious faces. "I'd call myself brave, but I'm not stupid. I can't stop a bullet, and I'll not go haring off outdoors without men guarding my back. Does that satisfy you?"

They all nodded.

"Good, then." He stood. "I'm off to talk with the ladies. Come if you like. The worst any of them will do is stab me with her spindle."

Harry lounged in his chair. "And we know who she would be."

MacLean threw him a black look and headed across the great hall. The men trailed him, not to protect him, as MacLean well knew, but for the amusement of seeing the MacLean join the ladies.

All except Harry, who stayed where he was and stared into the fire.

By the time MacLean had crossed the room, the serving women were nudging each other and grinning, and his mother was shuffling her well-worn deck of cards.

MacLean almost paused to touch her shoulder.

Enid couldn't be right about Lady Bess. His mother dressed disgracefully. She flirted constantly, and with younger men. She smoked too much, drank to excess, played cards. She couldn't have sacrificed herself for

him and his estate. It was impossible that he could
have been so dim-witted as to overlook her selfless-
ness.

"Mother . . ."

She glanced up at him. "Son?"

He looked around to see everyone observing him.
He couldn't question her here. "Nothing," he said. "It's
of no moment."

Planting himself in front of Enid, he wondered what
he should say. He could scarcely demand if she'd had
her menses. So instead he stared at her downturned
head and noted how the candlelight flickered on the
dark waves of her upswept hair, how wisps slipped
down her slender neck, the way the new white gown
Celeste had sent clung to her curves. Enid was beautiful. He wanted her. His body and his very instincts
identified his gentle, perfect mate.

Looking up, his gentle, perfect mate snapped, "Either go away or sit down. You're standing in the light."

Chapter 23

What had Enid been thinking when she'd thrown MacLean out of her bedroom?

Of course, she knew. She'd been thinking she would go home soon—wherever home was. It was certainly not here at Castle MacLean, where an Englishman lurked in every corner and a Scotsman lurked behind each of them, and Enid ran into all of them with suspicious regularity. In the four days since her arrival, she'd begun to suspect they were following her.

Turning swiftly, she peered behind her. Shadows filled the long upstairs gallery, but nothing could account for her attack of nerves. She glanced at the marble bust set on a pedestal. She examined the window alcoves. Nothing. All she could see outside was the constant, drenching rain and the advent of purple evening.

She had to take herself in hand and remember who she was. Enid MacLean, a female who would soon be back in a dull job where one day would follow another without change or excitement—or futile yearning or long evenings in the great hall wherein Kiernan MacLean sat, staring at her and brooding.

Everyone in the castle observed his preoccupation with obvious glee.

She avoided looking at him at all costs. But she always knew he sat there, in the traditional Scottish garb with the hand-knit wool stockings gartered at the knee, his precious sporran, tied about his waist, and a kilt that allowed for occasional, breathtaking glimpses of his muscled thighs—and beyond.

She sighed. That explained why she dragged her feet on her way down for supper. For four days she'd dealt with this constant, tiresome scrutiny, and she was starting to spill things, to forget what she'd been saying, to blush for no reason. The whole situation was wearing on her.

If only something would happen. If only the villain would reveal himself! But while none of the men would discuss the situation with her—they didn't want to upset her delicate, female sensibilities—she knew they must be pondering the probability that their criminal had left with the English guards. How long would they wait before declaring MacLean out of harm's way and her able to return home?

Sometimes, she wondered whether MacLean kept her here for the pleasure of tormenting her. He knew the location of her bedchamber, and although she now kept the door locked, he could obtain the key. She was determined to bar him from her bed. But, oh! How she wished to avoid that test, for at night her body yearned for his touch. When she slept, her mind wandered through the Scottish hills in his company, and always they found a small hut where the wind was still and the sunshine warm, and they made love while the very mountains hummed their approval. She imagined that, somewhere in the castle, MacLean sent tendrils of desire chasing after her, and it seemed that every night he commanded with ever-increasing vigor that she come to him.

That was why she imagined someone watched her. Always, she hoped it was MacLean.

Hands clasped behind her back, she again started down the gallery, looking up at the walls crowded with portraits of long-dead lairds, their dogs, their horses, and their wives.

The portrait on the end in particular attracted her— the painting that showed the last laird with his wife, Lady Bess, their children, Kiernan and Elizabeth, Lady Catriona . . . and Stephen. Enid stared at the two lads, standing together as if they had been friends. Stephen had been older than Kiernan, seventeen to Kiernan's eleven, but already Kiernan topped Stephen in height and breadth. The artist had well captured the charm Stephen cultivated and Kiernan's rough impatience at being constrained. Two MacLeans, raised together, yet so different.

"He was handsome, wasn't he?" a breathy feminine voice asked beside Enid.

Enid jumped and turned.

Although she hadn't laid eyes on the lady since the first night, she recognized Lady Catriona. Lady Catriona's gray hair was swirled in a knot and topped with a black lace widow's cap. Her face was worn, her garb unremitting black, and she crumpled a handkerchief in her nervous fingers. She couldn't have been much

older than Lady Bess; indeed, Enid thought she should
be younger, but the years showed on Lady Catriona in
her stooped shoulders, her stout figure, and the wrinkles around her drooping mouth and red-rimmed eyes.

"Did I startle you?" Lady Catriona came up no further than Enid's chin. "I didn't mean to. You were so
absorbed in my dear boy's portrait."

"Yes . . . I was." Enid supposed she had been, but
Lady Catriona must be able to glide without a sound to
have crept up on Enid so completely.

"I'm Lady Catriona MacLean." She extended her
trembling hand. "I apologize for not having greeted
you sooner, but I have been in seclusion. In mourning."

"Of course." Enid couldn't have felt more awkward.
She was the widow of this woman's son, but her own
mourning had not occurred. "I'm sorry for your loss."

"Thank you." Lady Catriona's faded blue eyes filled
with tears. "But it's *our* loss, isn't it?"

"Yes. Thank you." Although Lady Catriona hadn't
exactly offered her condolences.

"I haven't felt up to dining with the family. They
have been so utterly without the proper sentiments at
this sad time."

"Oh. Yes." By that, Enid supposed, she meant that
no one showed regret for the absence of her son. "But
Stephen has been gone from here for so long, I'm sure
they mourned his loss before."

"Don't excuse their behavior. They are a disgrace."

As was Enid, she supposed, since she defended the
family. On the other hand, Lady Catriona slyly casti-
gated Enid, also, whose velvet ruby red gown could
never be called mourning garb. Enid almost said, "I
lost all my clothing in a fire," but she would not excuse

herself to Lady Catriona. This woman had never made any attempt to contact Enid after the wedding, never made the effort to welcome her into the family, never before extended a hand in friendship. The fault in decorum was not Enid's alone.

When Enid did not speak, Lady Catriona said, "I've known Kiernan since he was a babe, and he is the worst of the lot. A sly bully who always thought himself better than Stephen because of his title."

"Really?" Enid's lips felt stiff. "I would not have thought that of him."

"That's because Stephen never complained. Stephen was always the gentle, caring older cousin." Lady Catriona's voice lingered over her son's name, then her eyes flashed as she said, "And Kiernan was always an ingrate."

Driven to protest, Enid said, "Kiernan went to rescue Stephen."

Lady Catriona lifted her head and smiled with still, chill politeness. "You call Kiernan by his first name?"

Was this whole conversation filled with traps? "I named him as you did. I call him MacLean. The MacLean, everyone calls him here."

"Ah." Lady Catriona looked away to the portrait. "Well, Kiernan didn't rescue Stephen, and my poor mother's heart wonders if he failed on purpose."

Enid didn't even think. She snapped, "Lady Catriona, what a dreadful thing to say. MacLean would never deliberately fail in any mission he undertook!"

"I should have known you would take his side. Stephen couldn't even count on his own wife to champion him as he deserved." Tears swelled in Lady Catriona's eyes, and she dabbed at them with her handkerchief. "I am the only one who ever understood my darling son."

This woman was a manipulative spider, and Enid had allowed Lady Catriona to maneuver her in ways she had never imagined. She wanted nothing so much as to get away. Instead she asked politely, "Will we have the pleasure of your company tonight?"

"No." Lady Catriona sighed. "No. I did want to meet you, but I fear this heavy sorrow has worn me out. I'll go back to my chamber. I'll have a tray, although I have scarcely managed to choke down a bite."

Enid watched as Lady Catriona wandered off, a lost soul in the gallery of prodigiously vibrant MacLeans.

Then Enid again looked at Stephen's portrait, and for the first time in nine years, Enid felt sorry for him.

Supper in the great hall of the Castle MacLean was a huge, blithe meal, with laughter, the occasional argument and frequent flirtation. Only the head table was quiet. There MacLean and Enid sat in a pool of silence. Silence, because MacLean seemed unable to carry on a conversation. When asked questions, he would answer yes or no. He could even on occasion form entire sentences. But for the most part he stared at Enid as if trying to discern some great issue relevant only to him.

When the covers had been pulled away and the brandy poured, Enid had at last had enough of MacLean's ominous gaze. In a clear tone, she announced, "I met Lady Catriona tonight."

The clatter of silverware against plates dwindled. Conversation died. Enid looked up from her plate to see every Scottish face turned to her, all wearing identical expressions of chagrin and sympathy.

Lady Bess, usually so outspoken, said nothing but, "Oh, dear."

Driven to speech at last, MacLean asked, "What did she say?"

Enid straightened her napkin in her lap. "She wanted to meet me so we could share in each other's sorrow."

"That was good of her," MacLean said. "Now what did she really say?"

Enid fussed with her napkin again. "I fear I have offended her by not donning mourning."

"We have all offended in that matter." Lady Bess lit one of her stinking cigars.

"It is impossible not to offend my aunt." MacLean nodded solemnly to Enid. "If she has insulted you, I beg your pardon on her behalf."

"No." Now Enid felt like Lady Catriona herself, manipulating MacLean for her own satisfaction. "I thought her unhappy."

Lady Bess blew out a stream of smoke. "Perpetually."

"And a little . . . unsettled," Enid concluded.

"Daft as a hatter, just like the rest of her family," Lady Bess agreed. "I've always thought so."

MacLean turned to his mother. "Is she eating?"

"Oh, please." Lady Bess pulled a long face. "When have you ever seen Catriona so melancholic she couldn't eat?"

"Then I won't worry that she will waste away." MacLean pushed back his chair and stood. "Shall we adjourn to the fireplace?"

"No." Enid stood also. "I'm weary." And irritable and depressed—all sure signs her menses were in full strength. "I am going to my chamber."

MacLean replied, "I'll walk you."

"What?" Enid glanced about at the company, all present to hear MacLean make his remarkably compromising statement. "Why?"

"It's a long, dark staircase and a long, dark corridor. You need an escort. Someone to carry your candle."

She primmed her mouth. "It is not proper for you to accompany me to my bedchamber."

With a placid smile, Lady Bess said, "My dear, this isn't England with all its fancy rules and high etiquette. In fact, in Scotland we have an institution called a handfast, where a couple is married for a year and a day and if a bairn results, the marriage is binding."

"And if a child doesn't result, what is the woman to do? Declare herself a failure and slink away?" Blood burned in Enid's cheeks. She had been the wife with a failed marriage. She knew what it was like to suffer pity and disdain. "Why would any woman consent to such an arrangement?"

"Lass, it's not exactly a matter of obtaining the female's consent," MacLean said. "The handfast is a legacy of days gone by when a man carried off his bride regardless of her wishes."

Enid did not care for his tone or his words, and she crushed him with a firm "Thank heavens we live in enlightened times."

He appeared to be uncrushed. Indeed, the slight smile that played about his lips made her worry he considered such a drastic action. But no. No. He didn't wish to wed her. Bad enough that she had fornicated with him, and not just once . . . she cupped her forehead in her palm. Fornicated with him time and again when she had known his true identity!

"Do you have the headache?" He rested his hand on her shoulder, and he used that caressing tone that recalled that day in the Scottish mountains.

She ducked and stepped swiftly away. "I'm fine!" she snapped.

He smiled again, and the way he looked at her, all strength and dominance, made her think he had truly been exerting his will to bring her to his bedchamber.

Turning to Lady Bess, she said, "I'm not Scottish and as such am not subject to your handfast laws."

"Weel, yes, dear, you are." Lady Bess laughed heartily. "But that's not in question."

"No. What is in question is my ability to carry my candle," Enid said tartly, "and I have been doing so successfully these four nights. I can do it again tonight."

"Nevertheless, I will escort you," MacLean said with uncompromising certainty.

If she said she'd been jesting, that she wasn't really going to go to bed, that would merely postpone the inevitable. Eventually, he would escort her. Since she knew his mind, she knew there could be no question. He would also escort her only as far as her door. Of that she was determined.

So she smiled, a brief, tight grimace with no warmth. "As you wish, my lord." She started toward the stairway.

He started after her.

She halted. "MacLean? You have forgotten the candle."

He scowled, and she waited for him to say he didn't want to be bothered about the blasted candle. But when a smiling serving girl offered him a single lit taper in a holder, he accepted it and followed Enid as she made her way up the stairs and along the portrait gallery.

"Do you like the castle?" he asked.

She blinked and wondered why he would care what she thought. "I do, indeed. There's an overwhelming sense of history here."

"Fifty generations of MacLeans have made their home on this rock outcropping. The original Mac-Lean came in on the tide and hunkered down on the first place that he could defend. We never left." As if the words had dried up, MacLean stopped talking.

But he'd said more to her tonight than he had on the previous four nights, so she encouraged him. "The castle is so large, I can't even tell how many levels there are."

"Four." He cleared his throat. "Four levels. A multitude of lairds added onto the castle. The original building was wood, with a moat, and all was for war against the English and the Northmen. Then the castle was rebuilt in stone, with battlements that looked out over land and sea."

Now that she had stayed here, she better understood MacLean's limitless arrogance. Or, call it what it truly was—his conceit.

Although he seemed to be paying attention only to the candle, he now asked, "Why are you smiling?"

She hadn't realized she was smiling, but she had no intention of provoking him. "So the MacLeans have repelled the enemy for all these years."

"Yes . . . but the MacLean women always got their way, too. That's why there are carvings." He pointed at a battle scene hewn from a walnut slab and hung in the middle of the gallery.

Enid examined the depiction of decapitation, of

blood spurting, of enemies dragged beneath a horse. "Very feminine."

"You're being sarcastic. All right." In a belligerent tone, he said, "How about that? A vase."

A Chinese Ming vase on a marble pedestal. "Incredibly beautiful."

"No MacLean male bought that." He nodded. "Some MacLean wife who wanted it, and her husband couldn't say no."

Enid subdued her amusement. "I suppose that explains the carpets and tapestries, too."

"Yes, it does. MacLean men have no appreciation of beauty, but they spoil their women without ceasing."

"Then I would suppose they usually marry ugly women."

"What? No!" He looked directly at her. His gaze softened. His voice became that purr of blandishment that sent shivers up her spine. "No, MacLean men recognize beauty in their women, and once they find their one true love, they see beauty nowhere else."

Her smirk abruptly disappeared. His commentary on the castle was more than just a man's poor attempt at entertainment. He was indicating interest in her. *He was courting her.*

With a well-pleased smile, he said, "Lass, you look a little flabbergasted. Are you well?"

"I am well, thank you." But she whispered.

He was courting her.

But no. She was mistaken.

But he was presenting his home to her like a jewel on a silver tray.

But he had said in no uncertain terms that she was a

mercenary unworthy to wipe his feet. He'd called her a bastard. He'd asked if Throckmorton had paid her to sleep with him.

But he'd apologized. Enid rubbed her forehead. This couldn't be happening. She had been unhappy before. Now she was panicked, afraid, almost sick with the need to run until she could run no more.

And why? All she had to do was say no. There were no hidden traps; she knew them all. She'd sprung them all.

"You *do* have a headache." He positively crooned.

"No." She certainly did not have a headache. She was well. She was strong.

"Let me stroke your temples," he said.

"No!" This panic roiling in her stomach could be subdued once she faced the truth. She might find the idea of living under MacLean's largess superficially appealing, but if she consented to be his wife, she would always know he was disappointed in his choice of an English orphan, and always on the look-out for a return of her greediness.

Greediness . . . she glanced around at the portraits, the vases, the security encapsulated by the sheer display of wealth. He *did* have a great house. A noble family. If she wed him, she would always be secure. She shook away temptation.

So she would survive this ordeal by summoning such wit as she had acquired in the difficult circumstances of her life. She would change the subject. Pacing again down the gallery, she said, "I have a question about your Scottish customs."

"Do you now?" His accent settled on him like a

well-fitting cloak. "It's good that you wish to know about Scottish customs."

He made it sound as if she were asking to learn more about his ways. She wasn't. She just needed something to fill the silence. Hastily, she asked, "Why do you wear the sporran and the kilt? Stephen told me they were obsolete."

As MacLean looked down at her, he looked broader and taller than ever. An illusion, of course, for while his daily walks about his castle, accompanied by the Englishmen and his Scotsmen, had probably contributed to his well-being, he was far too old to change either his physiognomy or his way of thinking.

"After the Forty-Five, the British tried to wipe out the traditional dress, as they tried to wipe out the clans themselves. They especially objected to the sporran, since a man could keep a weapon hidden within." MacLean fingered the scorched fur. "The explosion ruined mine, yet since it was my father's, I'll carry it forever."

"An admirable sentiment." Her heartbeat calmed.

"Memories are long here, and while we've been forced to learn to live with the English, we don't forget our traditions." He smiled faintly. "Funny, that. We are now 'allowed' to wear our tartans and our kilts, and they're becoming the fashion among the English who visit." MacLean leaned closer. "Some would tell you the reason a Scotsman wears a kilt is that it's easy to lift for the lassies. Shall I lift mine for you?"

She had asked an innocuous question, and somehow he had turned the conversation into channels sure to shock. Not that she was titillated. She crossed her arms over her chest and said, in oppressive tones, "I am sure you wear some kind of undergarment beneath."

Lips puckered, he shook his head. "It's tradition. You wouldn't want me to break with tradition, would you?"

"That's . . . scandalous!" And she was scandalized at herself for the number of times she had wondered. Shooting him a loathsome glance, she took extra long strides to hurry him along the length of the gallery.

It didn't work; he took her arm to slow her down. "Now *I* have a question for you. We were living as man and wife."

His hand held her arm against his side; the warmth of him heated her whether she wished it or not, and her heart rate quickened. "Yes."

"For more than a fortnight, we were together, and by my reckoning, we made love six times."

"Perhaps. I didn't count." Exactly six times.

"So I must ask the question any man would ask a woman he's known—"

He was going to ask her to marry him. She feared this intimacy . . . this enticement. "No, please don't."

"Are you expecting my bairn?"

She froze. She blushed at her own gullibility. She wanted to close her eyes and bang her head against the wall—because of the relief, of course. She was relieved. The mystery was solved. He had insisted on accompanying her not to propose marriage, not even to seduce her, but to discover if he'd accidentally fathered a child.

And if she had continued on this course of falling weak-kneed into MacLean's arms, she would repeat her mother's mistake. She would produce an illegitimate baby. For some reason, during the turmoil and the travels, the idea of a babe had never occurred to her. In her quietest voice, she said, "No. I am not with child."

"You're sure?"

Her hand formed a fist. His questioning would have exasperated her at any time, but at this time of the month, he made her want to box his ears. "Yes. I'm very, very sure. I couldn't be more certain."

"Ah." He nodded.

Which also made her want to box his ears. How dare he act so knowing, as if he comprehended the workings of her body? Even she didn't comprehend the workings of her body, with its cramps and its aches, and its illogical desires which, if she weren't careful, could drive her to do something stupid, like again falling in bed with MacLean.

They had reached the end of the gallery, and without looking at him, she took a grip on the candle holder. "You've found out what you came to discover. Don't bother to accompany me farther."

He didn't let go of the candle. "That isn't why I walked with you."

"I understand. You're an honorable man. You were going to offer support for the child." She gave the candle a tug. "I appreciate your thoughtfulness."

He hung on like a man who saw too much and didn't like what he saw. "You are comparing me to your father."

"Of course I'm comparing you to my father! Honorable men, both." Too bad she had told him what she really thought of her father.

"Your father was a coward."

"He paid for my education. What else could I expect

from him?" She retained control of herself, she kept a grip on the candle, and she was very proud of herself.

"A welcome to his family? An occasional visit? At the least, an inheritance on his death?" MacLean's voice rose.

So her voice rose. "Would you be so kind to our child?"

"Our bairn will have the comfort of a father with him all the time."

"I would never allow you to take our child from me."

"I'm not taking our bairn from you," he protested. "I'm marrying you!"

"No . . . you . . . aren't." She yanked at the candle. "Now let me go!"

Moving so swiftly that she didn't realize his intent, he wrapped his arm around her waist, pulled her close and kissed her.

No. No, she didn't want this. Every time he kissed her, she came closer to the edge of disaster. The ground was already crumbling beneath her feet. She didn't want to fall over that cliff.

But . . . heat. Closeness. Need. She tasted them all on his lips.

And she . . . she was angry and upset, and those emotions transmuted into passion far too easily.

Nothing could match the seduction of pressing her palms against the chest of a strong man and feeling his heart thunder. The glory of knowing he wanted her so much was an inducement in itself. Their breaths matched; their bodies moved together in the ancient, primal dance of desire. She crumpled his supple linen shirt between her fingers, enamored of the texture of the cloth, of the muscled chest beneath. Here in his arms she felt safe, and no amount of denial could change that. She leaned against him, wanting him. Fearing him and the temptation he presented.

He trembled.

She exulted.

Then he flinched and gasped.

At once, she pulled back. A blush scorched her cheeks and climbed to her forehead. She had kissed him as soon as the opportunity presented itself. He had not been as captivated as she; he had caught himself.

Hastily he placed the candle on the pedestal. "Damn, lass, you made me forget the light!" He peeled the still-soft wax off his wrist.

"Oh." She shouldn't have laughed, but she was so relieved that she couldn't help herself. "You were distracted."

"Always around you." He smiled at her, and while it was madness to think so, he looked at her as if she were the most precious of beautiful objects. The only object of beauty that MacLean male could see.

She couldn't be the object of his veneration. She would not become his wife.

He caught her back to him.

She shoved against his chest.

Paying her no heed, he embraced her, kissed her once again.

She turned her head away. "No!"

Catching her chin, he brought her face back to his. He pressed his lips to hers, soft, soothing little motions. He liked kissing her. Curse the man! He appeared to like kissing even when he knew she couldn't welcome him into her bed. He ran a hand up her back, massaged the nape of her neck.

Surely she could find nothing to fear in this embrace. This was not pursuit. This was closeness. This was pleasure. Softening against him, she felt the fullness in her breasts and her heart.

She didn't know how it happened. Somehow, she opened her lips to his, she gave him her tongue and sucked deftly on his. She reveled in the dampness, the passion, the glory of MacLean. As always when in his arms, the future vanished, and he routed the spectre of her fears.

Then, in the quiet of the gallery, the click of a rifle's flintlock echoed from one end to the other.

MacLean wrenched his head up.

A man shouted, "MacLean, get down!"

MacLean knocked Enid to the floor. He landed on top of her, covering her with his body.

The shot roared, echoing down the gallery.

Someone toppled to the floor, screaming in agony.

Heels clattered on the hardwood, and a distant door slammed behind their would-be assassin.

Lifting his head, MacLean asked, "Enid, are you all right?"

He weighed approximately as much as a wild boar, and he'd tossed her to the carpet, then thrown himself atop her. "Yes," she gasped. "Who is screaming?"

Leaping off of her, MacLean ran down the gallery to the writhing victim.

"Harry," she heard him say. "Harry!"

Chapter 24

MacLean waited until the gladsome greetings had died down, the men had dispersed, and Harry had settled before the fire in the great hall before making his way over, tray in hand.

Enid still fussed over the invalid, but she straightened at once and looked MacLean over haughtily. "What do you want?"

Ah, she was a beauty, with her proudly tilted chin that warned a man off and her glorious breasts that invited him close.

Those breasts were one of the reasons he wanted Harry to recover, and quickly. She didn't need to be extending unwitting invitations to other men. "I want to chat with our savior."

She rested a hand on Harry's good shoulder. His other arm was wrapped tight against his body; his collarbone had been shattered by the bullet. "He did save us, and since today is the first day I've allowed him to rise, you'll refrain from upsetting him."

"Yes, ma'am."

Harry grinned at MacLean's meek answer. "That's right, MacLean. I took a bullet for you, and by God you owe me."

"And me." Enid tossed a rug over Harry's knees.

Harry's voice softened. "Although you're a tyrant in the sickroom, you've paid your debt."

MacLean didn't like his tone, didn't like to be reminded that Enid had just spent six days tending Harry. MacLean had come to think of Enid as his. His nurse. His woman.

"I do know what a tyrant she is." Taking her hand in his, MacLean kissed her fingers. "But a tyrant I live to obey."

"Balderdash, MacLean," she said briskly, and gathered her spindle. "I'll leave you gentlemen to talk."

MacLean retained her hand. "Stay."

She paused. She trembled. Without looking at him, she said, "I think it would be better if I leave you alone."

In the low, vibrant tone he saved only for her, he asked, "Lass, do you always have to be contrary?"

Her gaze flew to his, and for a moment he thought she appeared to be frightened. Frightened. Of him. Why?

Wrenching her hand free, she backed up a step.

"Harry and I are going to talk about who pulled the trigger last Tuesday and how we will capture him. You're interested, aren't you?" he coaxed.

Still she struggled with indecision. "Surely Harry will not wish me to stay."

"You're caught in the middle of this situation, and if

you've not been told all the truth, I'm sure you've drawn the right conclusions," Harry said. "And I'd be interested in your opinions on how to capture the culprit."

Subsiding into a chair opposite Harry, she said, "As you wish."

MacLean had heard that phrase from her too seldom—and right now it made him want to grind his teeth. She required *Harry's* permission to remain with them? Had she and Harry drawn so close in so little time?

"I brought you a glass of ratafia." MacLean extended the tray to her.

Taking one of the crystal goblets from the tray, she said, "Thank you."

MacLean asked, "Whisky, Harry?"

"I'd rather have a good burgundy."

Indicating the second goblet, MacLean said, "I thought you would."

Harry pierced MacLean with his dark gaze. "So you recall my drinking habits in the Crimea?"

Enid gasped faintly.

Astonished, MacLean paused in the act of sinking onto the wooden footstool at Enid's feet. "You were in the Crimea with me?"

Harry sounded as if he would command MacLean. "You *must* remember."

"I don't." MacLean seated himself. The footstool was low, hard, and uncomfortable on his rump, but he was very aware of the picture he and Enid made as he leaned his elbow against her chair. She held the MacLean suppliant at her feet. Certainly Harry understood the symbolism of that.

Surely Enid did, too. Yet she shifted her legs away from him.

What was wrong with the woman?

"Do you trust me now?" Harry indicated his wound.

Harry had seen the rifle barrel thrust from behind the drapes, yelled his warning and run toward the assailant. He'd been shot for his trouble. "You have my trust." MacLean indicated Enid. "You saved me and you saved Enid, and you have won the eternal gratitude of the MacLean."

"I don't want gratitude," Harry said impatiently. "I want you to remember. Do you realize what's at stake here? Not just your own safety and the safety of Mrs. MacLean, but the safety of our agents in the field. The future of England. All this depends on your memory."

MacLean shook his head. "The trip is foggy from the moment I left England until I set foot on the Isle of Mull again." Although he didn't tell the whole truth. He did have shards of memory scattered like broken glass in his mind. Yet when he reached for the memories, pain streaked through his head and he broke out in a sweat. Something lurked hidden in his brain, probably the identity of the traitor, and he feared its unveiling— for he worried it was his mercurial cousin. He worried Stephen had tried to have MacLean killed and instead had gotten killed himself.

Beside him, Enid spun her spindle, and a long, uneven thread of yarn drew forth from the wool in her lap. Although she appeared to be totally concentrated on her activity, MacLean felt the tension quivering through her. She listened to every word, and he suspected she feared the same thing he did. She feared her husband had tried to murder his own cousin.

"Throckmorton wouldn't like what I'm about to do, but nothing else is working and I fear we're running out of time." Harry took a breath. "So I'll help you. Tell me what you do remember about that trip."

MacLean lounged in his chair, but his blood pulsed through his veins. This was it. Surely, with Harry's help, he would remember. "I traveled to the Crimea—alone."

"I was already there. You brought me Throckmorton's letter of introduction."

MacLean sat up straight. "That's right. You said, 'Another damned Scotsman.' "

"So you put your fist in my face."

"I was still in my right mind then."

Harry laughed, then flinched and held his shoulder. "I'd been supervising your cousin. At first, Stephen had been brilliant. A great gambler and a drinker, the kind of man who could visit a tavern and learn every secret from every Russian officer within an evening. Then, after about a year, the information began to stink. Not all of it, not all the time, but when it counted."

Enid's spindle spun slower.

"I'm the one who applied to Throckmorton for assistance, and he sent me you." Harry grinned, a baring of his teeth. "Another damned Scotsman."

"I didn't know any of that." Throckmorton certainly hadn't told him. "Stephen's mother drove me mad with her fears for his safety, so I traced him to Throckmorton and demanded he be sent home."

"And Throckmorton sent you out to fetch him."

"Yes." MacLean struggled against the fog that enveloped the past. "Yes, I gave you the letter of introduction. You looked me over and weighed me with your gaze."

"You didn't care what I thought of you. That's why I decided Throckmorton was right. You could be trusted."

"So you trusted me?"

"As much as you trusted me."

"As much as you trust anybody."

Harry's mouth curled. "Perhaps. I only know that when Stephen saw you, he looked hunted. Then I knew without a doubt he was guilty."

MacLean sipped the whisky and tried to keep reproach from his voice. "I wish you'd told me what you suspected."

"I wish I had, too." Harry's teeth gleamed white as he grimaced. "All the way back from the Crimea, when you were torn to pieces by that bomb and I thought I would lose you at any moment, I kicked myself for hiding the truth from you. If you had known immediately, you might have been wary enough to avoid the trap."

MacLean feared he knew the answer, but he had to ask the question. "But why did they want to kill me?"

Harry surprised him. "Not you. Stephen."

Enid's spindle dropped in her lap as she gave up any pretense of spinning.

"At once it was obvious that you held great influence over your cousin, and you were incorruptible." Harry watched MacLean as he spoke. "Stephen was easily influenced, and the Russians feared that you would bring him back to the English side. He knew too many of the Russian operatives. He probably knew the other English traitors. They couldn't afford for him to give you names. So they planned to assassinate him, and if you were caught in the blast, so much the better."

"I remember walking along a street, arguing with Stephen. I thought . . . I feared . . . Stephen was always the wild one, with no more morals than an alley cat. I feared he had betrayed England. Mind you, not that I'm fond of the English."

"No," Harry said, "but I thought that once you had declared your loyalty to Throckmorton, you would not waver."

MacLean nodded. "There is that. Throckmorton has a way of engendering allegiance. But those slippery Russians are not even my enemies. They are nothing to me, and when I drank with them . . ." He vaguely recalled a bar filled with men with harsh accents and drooping mustaches, and only too clearly he recalled hating their arrogance and the way Stephen paid court to their leader. "The Russians are a bunch of condescending bastards."

Harry grinned and nodded. "When I started, I hated the Russians because they thought to compete with England. Now that I've met them, it's personal."

MacLean nodded. Memories were dropping into place as Harry spoke.

Harry scowled and stroked the side of the cut facets. "I was following you at the time of the explosion."

MacLean's heart took a leap. "Why?"

"You asked me to follow you and your cousin. Someone wanted to meet you."

"Yes . . . that set ill in my belly." Even now, it sat ill. "What did you see? What do you know?"

"You were arguing with Stephen. He tried to hush you, to tell you something."

MacLean remembered this. God, he remembered now. "He had a list of Russian agents in England. He wanted to tell me where, but I was so angry. I wasn't listening to a word he said." MacLean pinched the bridge of his nose. "A damn fool am I."

"I'll not argue," Harry said.

"He didn't know what would happen!" Enid protested.

The two men stared at each other. Bless her, Enid defended MacLean, but if he'd kept his reprimands to himself, perhaps they would know the location of that list.

"In the Crimea," Harry continued, "when you got to the meeting place, it was a deserted street corner with a broken-down wooden wagon and barrels stacked about. But no one was there. I was behind you. I don't know what Stephen saw, but he knocked you behind the wagon and picked up one of the barrels to throw it—"

"—And it exploded in his hands." MacLean covered his face, but he still saw the terrible scene. The memories cut at him. His stomach heaved as he lived the moments of bewilderment and terror. "He hit me, no warning, I didn't know why, but I lifted my head and saw—"

Enid put her arm around his shoulders. "Don't."

If only it were that easy, but now he couldn't shut off the memories. "Stephen just . . . blew apart. The blast lifted me, burned me, blasted me with pain. My leg splintered. Blood splattered everywhere. Mine. Stephen's." The carnage exceeded his most horrific nightmares.

This was the memory he had avoided for so long. He fought the tears that dripped between his fingers. Enid pressed a handkerchief into his hand. He struggled to maintain control. Somewhere in this hall, someone watched him. If they knew he had at last remembered, they would kill with blithe indifference.

Yet his cousin was dead, and MacLean grieved. To see it in his mind, to know that they had played together as lads, that Stephen had come to such a bad end . . . yet . . . "He didn't betray me," he whispered. "In the end, he saved me."

Beneath her breath, he heard Enid say, "Thank God for that."

Was she thanking God that he was alive? Or that her husband had had honor after all? MacLean swallowed. Hopefully, both. Probably, both. "After that . . . I really do not remember anything at all."

Harry picked up the story. "You were unconscious. I picked you up and ran. I thought you were going to die in my arms. I got you back to my house, got an English doctor, who shook his head and said you had no chance. I got a different doctor, an Arab, who put you back together and set your leg. One of Throckmorton's ships was in the harbor—that was my only piece of luck that day. The Arab gave me instructions on how to care for you. I did, and barely got you back to England."

In a low voice, Enid asked, "Who decided to bring me under the guise of being his wife?"

Harry flinched a little. "Throckmorton and I dreamed up the scheme. MacLean was so badly hurt, no one could recognize him, and we thought it would be better if the Russians believed Stephen had lived."

"Why?" she demanded.

"Once Stephen was back in England and not under MacLean's influence, he had reason to conceal his traitorous activities from us. MacLean, on the other hand, would tell us everything as soon as he regained consciousness. We thought he'd be safer as Stephen." Harry looked at MacLean. "Of course, we didn't figure on the loss of your memory."

The two men were silent as they contemplated their great quandary.

"It doesn't matter, does it? Whether or not I know anything, the Russians fear I do, and they'll not stop until they kill me."

"No!" Enid leaped to her feet, and in a low, intense voice, said, "I won't wait here for them to kill you. We're going to flush them out."

"Good idea, Mrs. MacLean," Harry drawled sarcastically. "Any idea how?"

Lifting her chin, she smiled coldly. "We're going to hold MacLean's funeral."

MacLean stared at her.

Harry stared at her.

She stared back at them, chin tilted, mouth compressed.

Harry slapped his knee and crowed. "Blast me, Mrs. MacLean, that's brilliant!"

"Brilliant," MacLean said quietly. "Or at least—half brilliant."

Now Harry and Enid stared at him.

"On the day of the funeral—"

"Day after tomorrow," Harry declared. When Mac-

Lean and Enid turned on him, he shrugged. "Why wait?"

MacLean inclined his head. "Why, indeed? On the day of the funeral, you'll declare that I begged to be buried with my sporran. You'll explain that everything valuable to me resided therein. Of course, since my sporran was in the explosion, the leather clasp was fried shut . . ."

Eyes alight, Harry said, "You'll wear it in the coffin, and when our villain tries to take it off of you—"

"No. This is foolish. This is dangerous." Enid leaned toward MacLean. "I want the villain to think you're dead so he'll leave you alone. If you're already dead, no one will try and shoot you."

MacLean leaned toward Enid. "Lass, you're assuming the villain is an Englishman, someone who'll go away and never return. But it could be a Scotsman, and anyway, that's not the way these people work. They buy people. They hire people. They watch, and they wait. The only way I can be free of this threat is to reveal the villain and give his superiors reason to believe I know their names—and that I have passed those names on to others."

Their heads were almost touching; they spoke in furious, hushed voices.

"You'll be lying in a coffin and vulnerable to attack," she said.

"No one's going to attack a dead man, but the spy will steal from a corpse if he thinks he can keep that list of agents out of English hands."

"But you won't really have the list. They'll send someone else after you."

"Perhaps, but we'll have captured the one agent, and perhaps to save his life we can convince him to confess." MacLean gazed into Enid's drawn, anxious face. "You know I'm right. You know this is what I have to do."

Enid looked at him, then slowly drew back. "I know. You're right. Do what you have to do." Under her breath, she added, "And I'll do what I have to do."

Chapter 25

"Poor Lady Bess." With a pathos that broke Enid's heart, Graeme MacQuarrie wiped a tear off his cheek with his sleeve. "I've ne'er seen a woman so distraught. She won't leave the MacLean's side, won't let any of us take the death watch."

"Aye." Jimmy MacGillivray stood and stared up the stairs. "Poor lady. To lose her daughter in such a manner, and when she finds her son again, to ha'e him die—" His voice cracked.

What a long, dreadful day it had been! Enid could scarcely bear to watch the men as they tried to deal with their grief. And the women, with their eternal weeping—they were driving her crazy. She wanted to shout, to tell the wretched women and grieving men that MacLean was fine. He had merely spent the day hiding in his bedchamber. On the morrow he would climb, under his own power, into his coffin and lie in wait for the traitor to reveal himself. But to tell the truth would ruin her entire splendid plan—and it was splendid.

Although she despised MacLean's part of the plan. He dismissed the danger; she knew very well that a man who impersonated a corpse could be murdered before he opened his eyes.

"Last night when he complained o' a pain in his gut an' sought his bed early, I suspected trooble. That lad is ne'er ill." Donaldina had helped Lady Bess hide the truth from the others. Now she played the drama for all it was worth. "An' this morning, when Lady Bess went up t' check on him, her scream fair chilled my blood."

"Th' poor dear master. I'll ne'er forget th' sight o' him on that bed, all cold an' white." The serving girl dropped her head into her hands and wept.

He was white because Lady Bess had applied a careful coat of powder on his cheeks. The cosmetics wouldn't have stood up to a vigorous scrutiny, but Lady Bess had proved her worth as an actress. As Enid had gone to the bedside, Lady Bess had flung herself about in a frenzy of grief and commanded the center of attention.

The people who had crowded into MacLean's bed-chamber had held their breath as they'd awaited Enid's confirmation. She had looked at his still face, and her gut had drawn up tight with panic. She had had to touch the warmth of his cheek to confirm for herself that he did indeed still breathe. Only then had she been able to play her part, turn to the crowd and nod solemnly to confirm the sad news. Her gesture had brought forth such a flood of lamentations she'd wished she had never suggested a funeral.

But how else to draw out the villain who skulked and hunted? If they didn't discover his identity, she would never get to go home. If they didn't find the assassin, MacLean would never be safe. She wanted to leave. More, she didn't want to have to worry about MacLean. In fact, she never wanted to think of him again.

"In Suffolk, when he was so ill he thought he would die, he requested that he be buried in full Scottish costume." Harry projected his voice to reach the edges of the crowd. "Even though his memory was gone, he asked that he wear his sporran, his most precious possession."

The Scottish men and women nodded solemnly.

" 'Twas his father's," Rab Hardie said. "Made from a badger the old MacLean killed wi' his own hands. Kiernan MacLean took it wi' him always."

"I never heard him say anything about his sporran," Mr. Kinman protested.

Poor Mr. Kinman. He was bewildered and apparently grieved, but Harry said the fewer people who knew, the better, and MacLean agreed.

Graeme took it upon himself to explain. "A Scotsman's sporran is one of his most important possessions. There he keeps a lock of his mother's hair or a letter from his dearest love."

Enid looked sidelong at Harry and found him doing the same to her. All unknowing, the Scotsmen were doing their part to deceive and direct the traitor.

Enid nudged them on. "Did he keep his secrets there?"

Donaldina proclaimed, "Th' MacLean had nae secrets. Nae secrets at all."

"But whatever the MacLean prized he kept in his sporran," Graeme said.

"I wish I had my poor Stephen's sporran. I wish he could have been buried on MacLean land. If only I could have had a funeral for Stephen." When the sound of crying had reached her bedchamber, Lady Catriona had drifted down and hung about the great hall like a ghost seeking solace in misery. "If only I had anything to remember him by. The grief is tearing me apart." She dabbed at her eyes with her handkerchief.

"I'll go to MacLean in the morning and shave his poor, shattered face." Jackson held himself erect, but he trembled as if he were only a moment away from weeping. "He was a good master. It's the least I can do for him."

Enid struggled against her dismay. If Jackson got close to MacLean, he would know the truth, and Jackson was one of the highly suspect Englishmen.

Then Lady Bess spoke from the top of the stairs. "No. I could never bear to have someone else care for him in this, his last moments in Castle MacLean. I have shaved him already. He's ready. All except for his sporran. Tonight I'll lock myself into my chamber with it and cry over that last keepsake I have of my son and my husband. Tomorrow I will place it on Kiernan's poor, dead body so he can be buried with it."

The fresh outbreak of crying found Enid gulping back her own tears. For some reason, this sorrow was infectious. Although she knew MacLean remained hearty and well above stairs, still the thoughts drifted through her mind. What if she knew he were gone from this earth? How could she bear the thought that that man, the one she had dragged back from the brink of death, was no longer smiling, boisterous, witty, sarcastic, arrogant? What would she do if she could never see him again?

Lady Bess drifted to Enid's side. "I have a request." Determined to play the part, Enid dashed a tear away from the corner of her eye—playacting, only—and patted Lady Bess's fingers. "Anything, my lady."

"I want you to take the role of chief mourner."

Enid almost choked. "Ch . . . chief mourner? But, my lady, I'm not MacLean's . . . anything."

"You love him. It's obvious for all to see. You cared for him all those months. You fled with him across Scotland to bring him home. You deserve the honor."

"I'm not . . . I can't . . ." Enid darted a panicked glance about.

The Scottish folk nodded, and a few smiles broke through the tears.

Mr. Kinman and Jackson stood with hands folded and eyes cast down, but they, too, nodded.

Only Lady Catriona drew herself up to her full, outraged height. "Bess, that is a disgraceful suggestion. Enid is Stephen's widow, and she hasn't had the decency to don mourning for him. Now you want her to take your place at your son's funeral? Do you cherish no proper feeling at all?"

Lady Bess charged into the fray. "If Enid had realized a man like Kiernan lived anywhere in the world, she would have searched until she found him. She settled for Stephen, and now she deserves to take her place as Kiernan's wife of the heart."

Enid tried to intervene. "Please, ladies . . ."

With a huff of fury, Lady Catriona spat, "This Enid creature could never have done better than my Stephen. She didn't deserve my Stephen."

Enid had thought the long, dreary day could scarcely get worse, but abruptly, it had. Once again, Lady Catriona had sunk her claws into Enid, and scratched at Lady Bess. "Lady Bess, I would be honored to be the chief mourner at MacLean's funeral. Thank you for asking me." With a toss of her head, Enid started up the stairs.

After all, it wouldn't harm her to pretend to cry for MacLean. She knew he wasn't really dead. On the morrow, if all went well, she would be on the train back to London and nothing could ever make her return to Scotland. Nothing. Not ever.

Going to her room, she shut the door behind her and leaned on it. She looked about her. The chamber looked much as it had the first day; too large, too grand, too royal. If she didn't get back to her lot as a nurse-companion soon, she would come to think she had the right to live in such splendor.

Nightfall was close, and one of the maids had put aside her grief long enough to light all the candles within. But women like Enid didn't have servants. What frightened Enid most was the knowledge—oh, she was almost sure of it—that if she wished, she could have MacLean as a husband. Some eternally wistful part of her wanted him to hold her and say words like "Forever," as he had in the Scottish mountains. How was it he had laid claim to her?

The blood in your veins, the marrow in your bones. I'm inside you, supporting you, keeping you alive. I am a part of you. You are a part of me. We are forever.

Turning to face the door, she stroked the smooth wood. At that moment, he had meant every word, and she had thrilled to hear him.

Only two doors down the corridor was MacLean's bedchamber. In the weeks she had lived here, she had taken care never to discover its location. But this morning, she had had to troop along with the whole household to view his unmoving body, and now she knew where he slept—or, tonight, where he paced.

Without being told, she knew the inactivity grated on his nerves. She could imagine how much he wanted a report on the state of the household. She did not doubt that the tendrils of his will curled like smoke along the corridor and through her door, commanding her to come to him.

He wanted her to come to him. He demanded she come to him.

Leaning against the door, she rubbed her forehead against the cool wood.

Not to question her about the day, or who had behaved suspiciously, but because he would take her to his bed and punish her for all the nights she had withheld herself from him—as she continued to do.

Whirling away from the door, she removed her black dress and donned one of her plainest white cotton nightgowns, buttoned down the front and ornamented only by tiny, vertical pin stitching at the bosom.

If she went to him tonight, she knew one night's compliance wouldn't satisfy him. He would expect more. He would view her appearance as capitulation, and he would think he had her to command for all of his days. She had to resist . . . even though resistance brought her suffering.

Blowing out the candles, she separated the heavy curtains and looked out across the moonlit landscape. Her bedchamber faced the sea. Below her the castle wall plunged straight down to the cliffs, and the waves thundered at their base, clawing at the rocks. The wild, glorious view suited the MacLean and his clan of madmen and eccentrics. Pressing her cheek to the glass, she absorbed the smooth comfort.

She wanted to go to MacLean's bed. She craved the pleasure he brought her. Her womb ached and pulsed with need. She hungered after his body with an insatiable passion that could never be fulfilled.

Below her, the sea rose and fell in a primitive rhythm, each movement an enticement. From across the corridor, MacLean called to her, his desire a warm and misty command.

She was leaving tomorrow. No matter what happened, she was leaving tomorrow. What harm . . . ?

But no. She needed to get back to England. If she stayed, she would lose everything: dignity, honor and self-esteem.

Compared to desire, of what value was dignity? Honor . . . she'd lost honor already when she'd knowingly cavorted with a man not her husband. And self-esteem . . . as Lady Halifax had pointed out, Enid had survived and prospered where others would have surrendered to despair. If Enid chose to spend the night with MacLean, she would still hold herself in high regard.

She let the curtains fall and drifted toward the door.

She was a fool.

She would never have this chance again.

She could have a child.

She turned back into the room.

But she had just finished her menses not two days ago. She couldn't get pregnant.

Her wrap was a rich splash of burgundy brocade cast across the chair. Picking it up, she slipped her arms into the sleeves.

She was going to him.

Her bare feet made no sound as she hurried through the dim, empty corridor toward her goal. The door should have been locked to protect the very alive MacLean from discovery, but the knob turned easily.

He was expecting her.

Pushing the door open with a gentle hand, she slipped inside and shut them in.

Stretched out on the massive bed, his arms behind his head, MacLean watched her, face clear of powder, from the only pool of light within the room. The royal blue drapes were drawn across the windows, shutting out the night. The oak paneling muffled any sound from the other chambers. The wide spread of rich blue and rose carpet lent the room a preternatural silence, and in that silence Enid heard her own hurried breath.

The candlelight should have softened his mien, but in fact he looked as stern and rugged as the cliffs outside her window. The crisp white sheets beneath him hugged his long form. He wore only a kilt, and above his chest rose in gleaming ripples of muscle well-dusted with curling auburn hair. The candles cast shadows across his scarred, tanned features. His green eyes glowed, with the golden streaks that did, indeed, look like lightning bolts.

He had been waiting for her, and her resistance had frustrated and enraged him. "Lock the door," he said.

He reclined with the taut intensity of a great tawny cat, waiting to pounce on its prey. Behind her back, she fumbled with the key.

He remained still, and she realized his intention. He would not come for her. Without any kind of urging, she would approach him.

His attitude incensed her. He was angry? Well, so was she. She had been betrayed in every way possible by everyone possible—and now her own body had turned traitor. She ought to leave. Now. Before she went any further.

But she couldn't. She wanted him so much the craving scorched her mind and drove her to take that first, reluctant step.

Immobile on the bed, he watched.

His gaze stripped her bare, scoured her skin, saw inside to the jumble of longing and impatience.

She took another step. Her toes dug into the tightly woven carpet. She wanted to turn and flee, but his will commanded her as surely as words.

How dare he command her?

Why did she obey?

She took another step. Her heart beat heavily. Her breasts ached with tension. She wanted to smile, to soften his severity, but her trembling lips wouldn't obey her.

She moved toward him, enraged by his ultimatums, furious with herself, yet wanting him with a passion that propelled her forward. The step onto the dais was the highest she'd ever taken. Halting at the edge of the bed, she bided there, expecting him to speak, to stir.

He didn't. He remained still, his expectations palpable between them.

Tonight, only tonight, she would fulfill those expectations. Unbelting her wrap, she allowed the rich brocade to slither down her arms.

His gaze dropped to her bosom. His nostrils flared.

Her gown was plain, yes, but the cotton was thin and soft, and her nipples lifted the material in small puckers that told him too clearly her state of agonized desire. Hiking up her nightgown, she leaned one knee and both hands on the plush mattress.

His gaze drifted back to her face. Still he displayed no sign of helping her. Of yielding.

She crept to the center of the bed, where he reclined on a tumble of pillows. Seating herself on her hip, she gazed at his body, seeking nerve, seeking inspiration. The muscles and the beautiful, marred skin tempted her to touch, to love. Even the erection that lifted his kilt beckoned.

But she knew that when she looked in his eyes she would see more than simply his desire. Reflected there she would see obsession, a pure passion, a madness of insatiability. She knew, because she suffered from the same insanity that afflicted him.

Filled with trepidation, she extended her hand over his chest, over his heart. Bit by bit she lowered her palm onto the mat of auburn hair, and down to his skin. The texture of his hair, the warmth of his body, the power that hummed through him: they beckoned her. She craved him, needed him, and as much as she hated it, no other man could fulfill her need.

Taking a daring breath, she looked into his face.

His eyes glowed with power. She had surrendered

herself to him, and he wouldn't allow her to retreat, or to change her mind, or to pretend differently. He held her in his grasp, and he would keep her.

Without further delay, he wrapped her in his arms, rolled her beneath him, and pinned her beneath his weight. He wasted no effort on subtlety; his every movement was aimed at domination.

He had won. She had come to him.

Now he would impress on her that she was his.

She panted with the onset of panic. She had made the decision to come to him, but now, with his body trapping hers, she thought better of her decision. She was afraid . . . no, she was angry.

Looking into her face, he saw the fragments of emotion, but his patience had run out. With a forceful thrust of his knee, he separated her legs.

No, she wanted him so much that no other emotion could exist within her.

With no preliminaries, he placed his hand there, on her most feminine place.

The intimacy . . . too soon. Too much. Too forceful. She was shocked, and when he molded her firmly with his fingers, she gasped and shrank away.

He wouldn't allow that. The cloth of her nightgown formed no barrier to him. He found the opening to her body and dampened the material with her pleasure. Sliding his thumb up, he stroked her most sensitive bud, and yearning blossomed in her womb. She moaned, the soft, low moan of unexpected desire.

He forced bliss on her with a light hand, stroking her between his fingers, igniting a fire in her loins. The cotton pulled and rubbed, and the material added an earthy texture that hurdled her toward gratification.

She couldn't believe this was happening. So quickly. Without warning. She tried to twist away. He gave no quarter. He allowed her no respite. Climax struck, rendered her blind and insensate to anything but him and his caress. She convulsed in mighty spasms of glory . . . then, slowly, she subsided. Humiliating, to let him know how much she wanted him, how easily she responded to his touch. She thought he might laugh. She thought he might taunt her. But when she opened her eyes, she saw that he was not amused. He watched her with all the intense passion of a man enthralled, clothed in dark menace and nothing else. He'd rid himself of the kilt, and his cock thrust up at her, blue-veined, softly capped, rigid and demanding. His muscled hips moved against her belly, forewarning her, preparing her.

While he held her weak and captive still, he flicked open the buttons of her gown—all the way down to her toes.

The beat of her heart had begun to subside. Now it picked up again. She wanted to protest his methods, but she didn't dare. She didn't fear him; not exactly. But the man who held her so securely was a conqueror, a warrior who had surmounted great obstacles for his lady. He would brook no defiance.

And she . . . she had done nothing but defy him. She had laughed at him, flouted him, scorned him. Tonight nothing remained between them except the struggle of male and female for supremacy.

The conclusion was foregone, but she had to fight . . . with a tender stroke to the scars on his chin and his cheek, or a finger caressing his earlobe.

His eyes half-closed, a creature luxuriating in sensuality. Lowering his head, he softly bit her lower lip, and when she cried out, he licked the little wound.

His breath smelled of mint and tasted of lust. At his unspoken command, she slid her hands into his hair and opened her mouth to him. He kissed as if he would devour her, slanting his lips to fit hers exactly, thrusting his tongue deep. Tears started to her eyes; given his choice, he would leave her nothing of herself.

He kissed her eyelids, slid his lips over her cheek and slid his tongue into her ear.

She stroked his broad shoulders, soaking up the primitive awareness that this male was intent on subjugating her. And she was willing. Oh, so willing.

Strange. When she thought of herself, she imagined herself to be a strong, upright woman of character. When he touched her, he found all the soft places, the female places, those pieces that disarmed and relaxed her.

His wicked breath thrilled her even as he slid his hand inside her gown and cupped her breast. His thumb rubbed her nipple, over and around, and her breath staggered and caught. She brought her knee up, parting the buttons, baring one side of herself. Rearing above her, he looked at her half-draped form and growled. Actually growled like a beast presented a banquet.

He bent to catch her nipple in his mouth, and the suckling drove her to wrap her leg around his hip, to rub herself against him.

He laughed faintly. Damn him, now he laughed against her skin, and his hand skated down her spine to the cleft of her bottom. He urged her closer, pressing his thigh firmly between her legs and providing delight with the long, deliberate stroking before and the light, unhurried friction of his fingers behind.

She arched her back. Her head thrashed on the pillows.

He suckled at her other nipple. Rapture built to unbearable proportions. Every part of her body thrummed, demanded, yet when she tried to push his head away, he took her wrist and pressed it against the mattress. Then he licked her palm, and the nerves beneath her skin jumped and rioted. She moaned deep in her throat.

He shushed her.

For a mere moment of sanity, she rose from the deep, sybaritic well and realized that he was right. They couldn't cry out with enjoyment. No one lingering in the corridor could know that MacLean yet lived, and the sounds of love could never be mistaken for anything else. So except for their hurried breaths and their faint, untutored whimpers, they must skirmish in silence.

One by one, he sucked on her fingers.

This was the way it felt for him inside her. The warmth, the rasping, the iniquitous motion that brought paradise to earth.

As he assaulted her with pleasure, euphoria built in her mind, in her body. The silence built in the room. Their restraint became almost an aphrodisiac. She wanted him on her, in her. She needed to be filled.

"Now," she whispered in an agony of need. *"Now."*

He ignored her, the bounder. He wanted her. She knew it, for his cock twitched against her. Yet he held off, tormenting her to prove who held the control. He kissed her lips but didn't allow her to kiss him back.

He nipped her ear and chuckled when she moaned. He took a breast in each hand and circled the nipples, over and over again. He slid two fingers inside her and imitated coitus. Imitated it so well that she bit his shoulder in animal delight.

His discipline broke. Tossing her onto her back, he spread her legs and mounted her.

There was nothing of elegance in his conquest. He found the entrance to her body and invaded, driving hard against the tender tissues, making a place for himself without regard to her delicacy.

She didn't care. Her body yielded because he had made her wet for him with the artistry of his touch.

She loved this. The heat, the lust, the desperation. Spreading her legs wide, she wrapped them around his hips and gave herself up to him.

He set a fast rhythm, a glorious motion.

She dug her nails into his bottom, wanting everything he had to offer.

Like a rampaging stallion, he pulled back and plunged, giving everything in a ravishment of the senses, of the will.

She whimpered, a soft, steady whimper that conveyed too clearly her desperation. Climax built and built, always just out of reach. He never slowed enough for her to grasp it, but it was there. So close. So fierce.

Just when she thought she could bear it no longer, he seized her hips, paused, hung above her. For one trembling moment, he stared down at her, his eyes crackling with the golden lightning that seared her with his brand.

She wanted to close her eyes against him. She couldn't.

He bore down on her. His penis jerked. His sperm filled her, a mighty splurge of intemperance and dominance. Then he lunged again. Over and over.

Climax, too long delayed, lashed at her.

He pressed his hand over her mouth to stop her betraying scream, all the while thrusting in and out with a pace that prolonged her pleasure beyond reason, beyond temperance, beyond bearing. She rippled and shuddered, every muscle in her body tensing, and deep in her womb the spasms gathered strength until she attained a peak of satisfaction so sublime she would never reach it again.

Except with Kiernan, she knew she could.

The pillows were scattered. The sheets were ripped from the mattress and damp from their exertions. The place between her legs throbbed, and the evidence of his orgasm and hers smeared on their bodies like some ceremonial ointment.

Gradually, the spasms subsided. His motion slowed, then stopped. He caught her chin in his palm, lifted her head toward him.

She hadn't recovered. Could never recover, but she knew enough to jerk her chin free. She half lifted herself, wanting to escape that piercing gaze, his wordless demand.

He wouldn't let her rise. Wouldn't even leave her body.

She searched for some way to end this.

Someone had to say something.

Someone had to break.

Of course, it was her. "I love you," she whispered. "I love you."

Chapter 26

In the early morning hours before dawn when the night candles sputtered and dark wrapped the castle in its velvet cloak, Enid made her move. Slowly, so slowly, she slipped out of the sleeping Kiernan's embrace. Barely breathing, she inched across the bed, lowered first one foot, then the other, to the floor. Slithering off the mattress, she groped for her robe, listening all the while for him to wake, to realize she had escaped him.

But he was exhausted from his efforts, and he imagined he had conquered her beyond all denying.

Creeping along the floor, she pulled on her wrap, and when she came to the door, she reached for the key and prayed that the lock was oiled. Her heart thundered as the tumblers fell into place, but although MacLean tossed for a moment, he settled back into slumber.

For one moment, she wanted to go back to him, crawl in beside him, and let his will guide her. Yet she couldn't. She just couldn't.

The corridor was empty. The door opened, then shut behind her, and she scurried to her own bed. Pulling the covers up to her chin, she stared into the darkness. She was still staring, wide-eyed, when morning slid golden sunshine through the gaps in the curtains and brought her to a sitting position.

She knew Kiernan. He was a man of power and strict morals, and he had made his intentions clear. Although she wasn't expecting his child, he wanted her in his bed. He had forcefully proved that time and again. She didn't for a moment suppose he offered her a position as mistress. He was so upright he irritated her like a hair shirt. No man had the right to be so honorable, especially not Stephen's cousin. Yet MacLean wanted her as his wife, and she, who had spent her life looking for a home, a fortune, a family, a mate, could have all those things in him.

The mere offer choked her with panic. She was more frightened now than when the fire had broken out, or when she'd realized he was not her husband, or the train had been stopped. And why? She didn't even understand herself.

Yet she was. When she thought about his plan to trap the villain and the danger that stalked him, she wished so strongly to be away and safe in London that, like a child, she closed her eyes and imagined she could transport herself there.

Instead Lady Bess herself rapped on her door. "Enid, it's time to get ready."

Overcome with resentment, Enid pounded her hand on her pillow.

Lady Bess had come to assure herself that Enid had

not defected. Lady Bess was an intelligent woman. "Enid?" She knocked harder. "You promised you would be the chief mourner. Remember?"

"Yes, my lady," Enid called, and she marveled at the clarity of her own voice.

Of course, the last time she'd used her voice, she had been clear enough. *"I love you,"* she had told MacLean.

Trying to escape the memory, she tumbled out of bed. *"I love you."* Could she have said anything more likely to cause herself trouble? MacLean thought he had won all, because he had won her heart.

He had won nothing, and she could only imagine his wrath when he woke this morning and found her gone. She was surprised he hadn't frightened the whole castle half to death and ruined their plan as he rampaged toward her chamber.

Lady Bess knocked again. "Let me in. I'll help you prepare."

Enid unlocked the door, opened it, and ushered Lady Bess inside.

As Lady Bess bustled into the room, Enid saw that she had overcome the austerity of her black clothing to look appallingly cheerful. "I am so glad this farce is almost over. I'm tired of being worried about the lad, and about you." Peering into Enid's face, she added, "You look as if you didn't sleep a wink."

Enid touched the skin beneath her eyes. Puffy and sore. "No, I didn't." Although not for the reasons Lady Bess imagined.

"Good. A chief mourner should look the part." With brisk resolve, Lady Bess got Enid into her black, light wool mourning clothes, pinned a black hat to her head, and draped a black veil over her face. She tucked a black handkerchief up Enid's sleeve. "Of course you won't really need a handkerchief, but you can cover your face with it and no one will ever know you're not crying."

Enid nodded politely. "Is the MacLean already in his coffin?"

"Indeed he is, wearing the MacLean tartan and his father's sporran. His father would be proud of him for being so brave, and proud of you, too, for thinking up such a clever plot." Lady Bess lowered a black veil over her own face and shepherded Enid down the stairs, whispering, "But we have to get this funeral going, because we can't wait forever. Sooner or later, Kiernan's going to have to take a piss."

Enid didn't suffer even a twinge of amusement at Lady Bess's plain speaking, nor did she notice Lady Bess's sharp look.

The chapel was plain and old, and filled with a surfeit of humanity. Everyone was standing, and each person wept softly or sobbed loudly or simply wiped their reddened eyes. The servants stood in the back rows and bobbed curtsies as Lady Bess and Enid walked down the aisle. Donaldina managed to look both grieved and strong.

"That old woman could have gone on the London stage and made her fortune," Lady Bess murmured to Enid. "Look, to your right. The MacQuarries came in full force. Curtsy to the laird. Ah, he looks upset. Fond of Kiernan, he is, but you'll see a royal tantrum when he realizes the trick we've pulled. There's Graeme, and Rab beside him. Since the Englishmen are not only our guests but our primary suspects, we put Mr. Kinman in the front pew with Harry and Jackson."

Enid looked sharply at Harry. He was pale and still wobbly from his gunshot wound, but he was standing beside the other two men.

Mr. Kinman's cheeks were the color of parchment, and he stared at the coffin and periodically shook his head. His lips moved. She saw the words. *"I don't believe it."*

Jackson wore a sharply pressed, perfectly proper black suit. His hands were folded before his stomach. His face was arranged in an appropriately somber expression, and he stared at the floor before him.

"And on the other side of the front row with us"— Lady Bess sighed—"Lady Catriona."

The plump, petite woman wore the same unrelieved black as everyone else, but she managed to make it more dramatic with the addition of acres of heavy lace and a veil that extended from her hat all the way to the floor.

"I don't suppose you could keep her away," Enid said dryly.

"I don't suppose, but in truth, I had hoped she wouldn't come." Lady Bess fingered the ebony cross that hung about her neck. "Still, it's good that she's here. Our minister's old. Mr. Hedderwick saw the lads grow up, so he'll talk about Stephen as well as Kiernan. Everything about Stephen's character will be whitewashed, of course. Death has a tendency to do that for people."

Enid stepped into the MacLean family pew ahead of Lady Bess. She nodded politely at Lady Catriona.

Lady Catriona replied with a disdainful sniff.

"My wager's on Kinman," Lady Bess whispered.

Startled, Enid glanced at her. "What?"

"Kinman is our villain. He's too bluff to be real. All that blunt-nosed honesty makes him a suspect."

Dismayed, Enid protested, "Oh, no. Not Mr. Kinman."

"Harry took a shot in the shoulder for MacLean." Lady Bess kept her eyes front as she spoke softly. "The valet is too bland and proper to care for intrigue. So it has to be Kinman."

Patriotism and exasperation drove Enid to say, "It could be a Scotsman."

Lady Bess leaned her head on Enid's shoulder as if overcome with emotion. "I think that may very well be, but an Englishman's in charge."

Astonished at Lady Bess's admission, Enid took a long, measured breath and let it out. Nerves tightened in her gut. It was true. Everything that Lady Bess said was true. For the first time, she was forced to acknowledge that one of the men she knew so well was a murderer. As the stern-faced, black-clad minister tottered in from the side door beside the altar, she looked again at Mr. Kinman, Harry and Jackson. Today she would face the traitor at last and know that, whoever he was, he had tried to kill her and MacLean in three different attempts at cold-blooded slaughter.

The congregation quieted as Mr. Hedderwick began his discourse.

Enid didn't want to look at MacLean stretched out in his coffin. To see him would recall last night and all its wickedness, all its pleasure. All the anger, the lust . . . her own betrayal of herself.

In that madness of delight, she'd told him, *"I love you."* Her fingers trembled as she wiped her damp palms on her skirt. If she thought about her impetuous confession right now she would faint. If she thought about MacLean and how his sporran rested on his body, an enticement to a ruthless killer, her head would burst.

Instead, surreptitiously, she looked about her.

The chapel had been built so long ago that the stone steps onto the altar were worn. Fine stained glass windows rose toward heaven. Tall iron candle stands stood on either side of the podium, a podium so old it had heard centuries of sermons.

And MacLean's coffin had been placed right in the middle, where morning's light could shine onto his still form.

He looked amazingly . . . dead.

"I covered his face with powder again this morning," Lady Bess murmured in Enid's ear.

Enid glanced away. She had resolved not to think about MacLean right now. Even though she knew the truth, she didn't like to see MacLean in these circumstances. False though this funeral was, it nevertheless reminded her of all the funerals she had missed.

Less than a month ago, Lady Halifax had died, and Enid had sincerely mourned her . . . for a few hours. Until she had sought comfort in MacLean's arms, and been chased out by a fire, and been sent to Scotland. Enid had scarcely thought about the old lady since that first night, yet . . . she had loved Lady Halifax. At one time, she had imagined she would have the chance to attend Lady Halifax's funeral, to listen to the hymns and say a prayer. She could almost hear Lady Halifax's acerbic voice saying, "Enid, the Lord will listen wherever you choose to pray, so don't make excuses."

Bending her head, clasping her hands, Enid said a

prayer for Lady Halifax and tried to ignore the tightness that clutched at her throat.

Tears. The memory of Lady Halifax had brought her close to tears.

Swallowing, she glanced at MacLean, dressed in his crisp white shirt and lacy cravat, draped in a length of his family plaid and clad in a kilt. Oh, Kiernan, how can you conceal your vibrancy in this deathlike pose?

Hastily, before a sob could escape, she turned her thoughts elsewhere.

To her husband. Of course, to Stephen. The minister reminisced about Stephen now, of his bravery and sacrifice for his cousin at the moment of the explosion. The minister remembered that Stephen had been a charming lad who had brought happiness and solace to his widowed mother.

Lady Catriona sobbed aloud.

Stephen had been mischievous, full of laughter, always quick to join in games and lead his team to victory. He had joked about his big ears and had always been a favorite of the ladies, young and old.

As the minister spoke, a portrait of Stephen rose in Enid's mind. When she'd met him, he *had* been charming. So charming. He'd taken an orphan, a girl living a never-ending nightmare, and taught her to laugh.

That was why she had married him. Because with him, she had learned to laugh.

Ah, the laughter hadn't lasted long, but for a few brief, glorious weeks, she had lived for the moment and loved with all her heart. Now he could never return. After nine years of loneliness, of days when she'd cursed his name, of nights when she'd refused to remember that there had indeed been good times . . . he was truly gone forever from this earth. "Oh, God," she whispered.

". . . Survived by his beloved mother, Lady Catriona MacLean," the minister droned in his tremulous voice, "and his faithful wife, Enid MacLean."

How strange to discover that the death of a delinquent husband was almost as devastating as the death of a beloved mentor.

Enid sniffed, trying to control her errant emotions, but a tear escaped her control and trickled down her cheek. Furtively, she slid her handkerchief under her veil and swiped it away.

Beside her, Lady Catriona elbowed her, and when Enid glanced at her, Lady Catriona shot her such a venomous stare that Enid sidled closer to Lady Bess.

Why was Lady Catriona angry? This was the funeral she had wanted for her son. Enid wore black, she cried for Stephen . . . but of course, Stephen shared this service with MacLean.

MacLean . . . the coffin swam in a blur of tears. She wanted MacLean to rise, to prove he was alive!

In a voice so quiet it scarcely reached Enid, Lady Bess said, "Catriona always wanted all of Stephen. She can't bear that you had him even for a moment."

The minister lifted his hands toward the heavens. "Let us pray. We beg that our Father take Stephen to His bosom . . ."

Our father.

Enid's father.

Another funeral not attended. Another grave never visited. Her father. Ah, now there was a man who deserved nothing in the way of respect or affection. Yes, he had supported and educated her when he could have left her to the workhouse. She would have died there, of course. Most children did. Instead he had thrust her into a school and abandoned her. The other girls had gone home for Christmas, for months in the summer, but Enid had stayed, month after month, year after year. And although, as she grew, she understood why she was condemned to a life lived in empty, echoing corridors and lonely dormitories, she could never forgive her father for being so weak as to leave his daughter bleakly forlorn when his had been the sin.

She would never be as weak as he had been . . . but she had. As the full horror of that truth sank in, she covered her face with her black gloved hands. The day in the mountains she had slept with MacLean and never considered the consequences. Worse than that . . . last night, although she knew well many babes had their start at the wrong time of the month, she still had succumbed to his allurement. Last night, she had lain with him in debauchery and pleasure not once, but three times.

She released a quivering sob. So the faceless man who had been her father was only a creature like herself, driven by passions beyond control. And she wanted to tell him so, tell him she understood . . . but she couldn't. He was dead. He was dead, and she'd never even met him.

Enid's knees gave way, and she collapsed onto the pew. Her hands trembled as she searched for the handkerchief in her sleeve.

The minister's words intruded on her fumblings. "To speak of our laird, Kiernan MacLean, is to speak of a man driven by honor."

Enid caught her breath on a pain so razor-sharp it cut at her lungs. MacLean rested in his coffin.

But he wasn't dead. She knew he wasn't dead.

"Our laird cared for us, each and every one, with a deep and abiding sense of duty and, more than that, a love that went bone-deep."

Love. Enid shook her head. Not love. Not from him.

"Kiernan MacLean never gave his trust, his friendship or his love easily, but once given he could be depended upon forever."

Forever. *I am a part of you. You are a part of me. We are forever.*

She sobbed again, louder this time, and pressed the handkerchief to her lips to subdue the wailing that threatened to escape in a massive flood of sorrow.

Lady Bess rubbed Enid's back, leaned over and whispered, "Very good."

"Beloved son. Beloved of our sister Enid . . ." The minister glared at Enid as if he knew she had spent hours in MacLean's arms, kissing him, loving him.

Loving him.

Enid's chest hurt, her throat ached, her eyes burned, and painful tears dripped, one at a time, down her heated cheeks.

Love. She loved him, and she knew better. She knew that all that could follow such a love would be anguish. In all her life, no one had ever loved her enough to be with her. If she loved MacLean, if she married him, if she lived with him, someday she would be facing this moment in truth. Someday they would be separated by quarreling, by abandonment, by death, because no one ever stayed with her.

"Enid?" Lady Bess put her hand on Enid's shaking shoulder. "Are you all right?"

Enid was not all right. She was in agony, weeping for the relationships that had never been, that would never be . . . weeping for herself. She loved MacLean. If she didn't get away soon, this love that trapped her would deepen and flourish. She would give her whole heart and everything that was in her to MacLean. Then she would spend her life waiting for him to die or leave her. Never had she seen a love that was worth the pain at the end.

Never.

She had to get away.

MacLean reclined in the coffin, unmoving, on guard, waiting for the assassin to make his move . . . and livid with Enid. With nothing to do but wait, her defiance preyed on his mind..

Last night, for the first time since he had arrived back home, he had slept a deep and peaceful sleep. He had staked his claim on his woman. Enid understood her place was at his side. She would quarrel with him no more. She would settle down and behave. Or so he had thought.

In the chapel, he could hear the sobbing of the women, the snuffling of the men. One female, especially, cried as if each breath hurt her lungs, and for a sweet moment, he imagined it was Enid, coming to her senses. She *had* to come to her senses.

When he thought of her, he didn't think of her background or her faults. He remembered only how she'd pulled him back from the brink of death, of her bravery in the face of danger, of her kindness to his family and

her pleasure in simple things. Everything about her
character would bring honor to the MacLeans. The
thought of her living far away, moving from one sickroom to another, always at the beck and call of some
invalid, made him furious. Enid deserved the best. And
she would get it, because she was going to get him.

She'd finally admitted she loved him. He had forced
the issue, yes, but she'd needed to confess, to understand her own emotions before she could settle into her
life here.

Yet then she had run. If he had not had this part to
play, he would have gone and dragged her back.

The minister stopped preaching. MacLean concentrated as the congregation queued up to pass by the
coffin. He couldn't see, but he allowed his other senses
to roam, listening for a guilty cough, sniffing for the
scent of nervous sweat.

Feet shuffled past. At the head of the coffin, a
woman stopped and sobbed as if her heart were breaking.

No. It couldn't really be Enid. Why would she cry
with such passion?

He wanted to stand up, to see, but the line snaked by
him interminably. He was especially aware of his
sporran, attached around his waist with a leather strap.
If Enid and Harry had done their job correctly, the spy
would believe that any information passed from
Stephen to MacLean would be contained therein.

Hands reached out to touch him. Some people mentioned that he still felt warm. Some exclaimed that he
looked like he was sleeping. Some pitied his mother
and that poor lass who so loved him and who wept so
terribly.

So it *was* Enid who was crying. Why? Did she imagine he would let her go? He had carried her over the threshold of Castle MacLean. She was his bride.

As the chapel emptied, nothing happened. In a secret part of him, he almost hoped the funeral would fail to flush out the traitor. Then he would have an excuse to keep Enid at his side, to keep her safe.

Yet he knew the danger would remain and they could never be free to fight and love as they should.

He waited and waited. Most of the line passed. The chapel grew quieter as people proceeded toward the lawn where the funeral feast had been set up. Only Enid's crying continued unabated. His mother whispered comfort, and MacLean could only imagine Lady Bess's incredulity. Even he couldn't believe Enid mourned for him, for a man not dead . . . but if not for him, what did she mourn for? He feared he wouldn't like the answer.

Then fingers slid across his belly, grasped his sporran, sliced his leather belt.

Opening his eyes, he seized the arm.

For one incredulous moment, Jackson stood looking down at him, wide-eyed with horror. Then he screeched in fear.

MacLean grabbed at Jackson's throat.

Jackson threw himself backward, toppling the coffin from its stand, spilling MacLean onto the stone floor . . . rebreaking one of his ribs. For one essential moment, MacLean doubled over in pain.

In the swiftest recovery MacLean had ever seen, Jackson realized the ruse and threw himself into the fight. On his knees, he slashed with the razor, his blue eyes cold with determination.

He had the reflexes of a killer.

Lady Bess dragged Enid away from the coffin. The minister exhorted the men to peace. Of the two remaining mourners, one was a footman who ran shrieking from the chapel, calling for help. The other, a maid, plastered herself against the wall.

Holding his ribs, MacLean dodged backward, then lunged at Jackson from the side. Swift as a snake, Jackson sliced the air just above MacLean's throat. MacLean seized Jackson's arm again, but he couldn't win using only one hand. So although it hurt to move, to breathe, MacLean let go of his ribs and punched Jackson in the face with his free hand.

Jackson's nose broke beneath his fist.

Jackson punched back, aiming right at MacLean's broken rib. MacLean danced backward, loosing his grip on Jackson's arm. Jackson slashed again. MacLean kicked out, tripping Jackson. Grabbing the razor arm again, he held Jackson, knowing that if he didn't win this contest, he would be back in the coffin for good.

They swayed, trying each other in a brief test of strength. Jackson leaned his whole weight toward MacLean. MacLean pressed against Jackson. White powder flaked off MacLean's face in a shower. Their arms shook from the strain, but MacLean narrowed his eyes at Jackson and smiled. A confident little smile, one to shake his opponent's confidence. "You're on my land. You can't get away."

Jackson answered with a lunge at MacLean's throat.

Enid screamed.

But MacLean clutched him still, and that lunge was Jackson's last big effort.

"You can't win. Give up," MacLean said to him. He had just begun to inch Jackson's arm back, forcing the razor toward Jackson's throat, when Enid, red-eyed and wild, appeared behind Jackson. Lifting the tall iron candle stand from the altar, she smacked Jackson in the back of the head. The force compelled Jackson forward. The razor sliced MacLean's throat.

Unconscious, Jackson slithered to the ground.

Wrapping his arm around his middle once more, MacLean stared at Jackson, face bloodied by his nose, the back of his head split.

MacLean touched his own neck, and his fingers came away crimson and sticky with blood. Taking a huge breath, he shouted, "Damn, woman, I was doing fine. Now, thanks to you, I've got my throat cut."

Chapter 27

"You're welcome!" Enid shouted back. The man was an ungrateful wretch. She didn't know why she had ever cried for MacLean. She didn't like him at all. "Why are you holding your chest? You broke your ribs, didn't you?"

"Not many!"

Pointing to the front pew, she said, "Sit down so I can wrap them."

Still holding his side, he limped over and eased himself down. "I was winning the fight."

"None too quickly," Enid snapped.

Harry looked into the chapel, and hearing the shouting, vanished again.

Turning to the open-mouthed Lady Bess, Enid asked, "Could you get me a long roll of bandages?"

Lady Bess nodded silently.

"And Mother, get someone to pick that piece of trash off the floor." MacLean pointed to the inert Jackson.

"Right away," Lady Bess said.

"Fighting in the chapel. In God's house." Mr. Hedderwick shook his white-wigged head. "You were always such a good lad, Lord MacLean. What's happened to you?"

Enid tossed back her veil and considered the old minister. He had seen a man rise from his coffin, and all he could say was that he shouldn't have fought?

"Mr. Hedderwick, won't you come with me?" Lady Bess tucked her hand in his arm. "We'll get bandages for Kiernan's ribs." She looked at the gaping serving girl. "We'll *all* go get bandages for Kiernan's ribs."

The serving girl curtsied and scurried down the aisle, racing to tell the others that the MacLean was alive.

"I'll keep everyone out," Lady Bess said to Mac-Lean.

"Thank you, Mother." He bit off the words.

"He wouldn't be hurt if he hadn't been scrapping." Enid heard Mr. Hedderwick's querulous voice fade as Lady Bess led him from the chapel.

Hands on hips, Enid stood over MacLean. White powder smeared his clothing and unevenly dusted his face. He glared at her and grimaced in pain at the same time. And he was alive. Thank God he was alive. "You weren't supposed to fight!"

"How the hell else did you think this would end?" MacLean dabbled his fingers at the oozing cut on his throat. "How bad is this?"

She glanced at it. "It's just a scratch, but I can put a tourniquet on it if you like." She grinned evilly at the idea of tying a bandage tightly around his neck.

"Funny."

She handed him her handkerchief. "Press it on the wound." Without drawing breath, she returned to their argument. "I thought Harry would get him."

"Because Harry is well enough to fight?"

MacLean's logic infuriated her. "Then Mr. Kinman."

"May I remind you, we didn't know if Kinman was the blackguard and we didn't tell him I was alive."

"All right. You're right! You're always right."

Her sarcasm went right over his head. "I wish you'd remember that."

The serving girl came scurrying back up the aisle, a roll of bandages in her hand. She viewed MacLean as she might view a phantom, handed the bandages to Enid, and backed up the aisle as fast as she could go.

"You could have been hurt," Enid said.

"I was hurt."

He was so stupid. "Badly hurt," she explained. "Killed!"

"Would you have cried for me again?"

She didn't want to answer that.

With gentle insistence, he asked, "Enid, why were you crying? You knew I wasn't dead."

Enid untied his blood-stained cravat. "Ease your shirt off your shoulder."

"You're going to have to answer me someday."

Steadfastly, she ignored him. "Which ribs?"

He must have been in real pain, because he gave up and answered, "I don't know. It hurts enough to be all of them."

His bare chest too easily recalled the night before,

and the criss-cross of scars reminded her how close he'd been to death not so long ago—and today. She had to get out of here. Before she cried again. Before she gave in to temptation. Before she ruined her life.

But first . . . kneeling before him, she stroked her fingers over his skin, probing for breaks. She knew she'd found one when he sucked in his breath harshly. He didn't complain, but she hated to see him so hurt.

In sharp, jerky movements, she searched for the end of the roll of bandages. "At least two are broken. They'll not hurt so much once you're bound."

He put his hands over hers. "I've been bound for quite a while, lass, and by you. You just don't seem to realize it."

She stilled and muttered, "Don't."

"Don't?" His voice rose again.

Good. It was easier to deal with his anger than his hurt.

He continued, "I spend the night convincing you you belong in my arms, and you say, 'Don't'?"

She had reached the end of the roll. "What do you want me to say?"

"Aye! I want you to say aye."

"To anything you propose?" Leaning into him, she placed the bandage flat on his rib. "Hold that."

He placed his hand on it. "I'm proposing marriage."

So he'd said it at last. "Marriage."

"Marriage. The institution of holy wedlock, wherein our two souls are united for all time."

Dear God. He spoke words of extravagant passion, words that could have mocked and hurt—and he meant them! He wanted her for his wife, and he saw no shame in declaring himself in all seriousness. But she . . . she couldn't marry him. He might pretend to forget her circumstances, now, but no man ever truly forgot.

The strip went over his fingers, holding the end in place. "You called me a bastard."

"I was angry. I apologized."

"Let go now." When he did, she wrapped her arms around him, bandage in hand, and wound the broad strip of cotton around his rib cage. "You asked if I slept with you for money. You called me a whore."

"I was very angry—and I apologized."

Her fingers trembled. "So every time you're angry, you'll call me a whoring bastard?"

"When I'm angry, I'll shout and rage, and you'll shout and rage in return, but I know you're not a whore, and I don't care that your parents weren't married." He tried to lift her chin so he could look in her eyes.

She jerked away. She would have run, but she was tied to him by a bandage and by words spoken in passion. *I love you.*

"I was hurt. For the first time in months, I knew who I was, and I realized the woman who had guided me through the darkness wasn't my wife. I feared you'd misled me on purpose. And I couldn't bear that." He stroked the side of her neck. "Enid, I was a fool."

"Yes, you were." Her lips trembled. She was ready to cry again. Cry over a bit of name-calling done days ago. But MacLean had done the name-calling, and the ache subsided only to rise again.

"I'll never hurt you like that again. Enid—" He shifted, slid off the seat.

Alarmed, she tried to shove him back into place. "What are you doing?"

"When I apologized, you said you forgave me, but you didn't forget." He faced her on the hardwood floor. "So I'll kneel to beg your pardon."

"What? No!" Oh, she didn't want his face so close to hers! "I'm wrapping your ribs."

"No, you're not. You're crying." With a grimace of pain, he bent to peer into her face.

She whisked the tears away with her free hand.

"I apologize for making such hurtful accusations. In this holy place, in the presence of God, I vow I will never make them again, nor even think them."

She avoided his gaze.

"To me you are everything that is courageous, compassionate and loving."

"All right. All right!" *Just stop talking like that. Stop sounding sincere. Stop using words like* vow. "Now sit back on the pew so I can finish your ribs."

He didn't stir. "Do you believe me?"

"I believe you. You always tell the truth." It was almost a failing, the way he always told the truth.

"Do you forgive me?"

Forgive him? Ah, now that . . . that was not easy. But he wasn't going to give up. Not until she had forgiven him, really forgiven him. And could she? He'd wounded her with his malevolence, driving a stake into a heart made tender with caring. Yet . . . yet when she thought about it, she understood how a man who discovered he'd been lied to about his very identity could lash out in rage. He would never hurt her so again. He had made a vow, and she trusted him to keep it.

She had to take a few breaths before she could answer. "I forgive you."

"Truly this time?"

"Truly."

"Will you marry me?"

"Sit up on the pew. I can't wrap your ribs until you do."

In a deep, vibrant tone that reminded her of love-making and love-having, he asked again, "Will you marry me?"

And he would ask again and again until she convinced him she would not. She needed to get done and get out of here. "Why me, when you can marry a proper Scottish girl with lots of money and become a proper Scottish laird with proper Scottish children?"

"Because I wouldn't be happy."

She waited. At last she realized that that was it. He had decided he would be happy with her. He accepted her as she was, and the doubts and fears that plagued her didn't exist for him.

She *had* to get out of here. "Sit up on the pew. Please. My knees ache from this floor."

He did, but he moved carefully like a man in pain.

Pulling the bandage to drive his ribs back in place, she wound with greater briskness. When she got to the end she pulled it tight and tucked it in. "Is that better?"

"So much better." Before she could rise, he slid his fingers under the veil that drooped down the back of her neck. Lifting her chin with his other hand, he looked into her eyes. "You're trying so hard to escape me. A normal man might think it was him, but you shout at me, you stand up to me, you cleave to me in glorious passion."

He gazed at her so solemnly, his beautiful eyes alight with not just possession but some deeper emotion as well. She felt she could sink into his soul and rest there, safe and at one with him, forever. *Forever.* He'd promised forever. She could almost believe him.

On the floor behind them, Jackson groaned.

Enid wrenched herself away from MacLean.

"No!" MacLean tried to catch her but stopped. The moment was gone, and he knew it.

Saved. Enid could scarcely breathe for relief. Jackson's return to consciousness had saved her from the most frightening, impetuous step she could ever imagine.

"Damn him for a blackguard!" MacLean half-rose. "There's a coil of rope in the coffin. Hand it to me and I'll tie him."

"I can tie a knot," she said in irritation. The rope had spilled out of the overturned coffin, and without hesitation she tied Jackson's wrists behind his back, then his wrists to his ankles.

A reluctant smile played about MacLean's mouth. "Where did you learn that?"

"From Dr. Gerritson. We used to castrate calves."

When Jackson opened his eyes, MacLean chuckled. "From that look of panic, I'd say Jackson heard you."

"Good. When I saw that razor in his hand . . ." Her voice shook as she recalled that moment of terror.

MacLean took her hand and stroked it. "A razor is a good choice of weapon for a valet. No one seeing him with it would be suspicious."

From the floor, Jackson spoke. "I was after the sporran."

"And you would have slit my throat if you'd known I was still alive," MacLean said.

Jackson twisted to look up at MacLean. "So the sporran was a trap. There was nothing in there after all."

With a smile, MacLean said, "But there was."

Enid's head snapped up. "What? No!"

"After you suggested we hold the funeral, I began to think. Stephen knew the sporran was my dearest possession, and that I would never let it out of my custody. If he wanted to pass a message to me, he would surely use that sporran somehow." MacLean smiled grimly. "The blast sealed the clasp, so I slit the seam and turned the sporran inside out."

Enid understood at once. "The badger skin is tanned leather on the inside."

"On it, Stephen had written the names of all the spies in England." MacLean's smile faded. "Including Lord and Lady Featherstonebaugh, the nobles who recommended Jackson for this position."

Enid remembered the old couple who had been such gossips—who had been such trusted friends of Throckmorton. "Are you saying they're spies?"

"Very important ones."

"Have you sent a message to Throckmorton?"

"Last night. He should know by now." MacLean rose to his feet and strolled over to Jackson. "You tried to kill me, and more important, you tried to kill my lady."

Instantly, Jackson said, "I didn't shoot at you in the gallery."

"Do you really think we're going to believe that?" Enid exclaimed.

"I set the fire, I stopped the train, I shot at you when you ran to the castle, but I didn't shoot at you in the gallery." Jackson wiggled in indignation. "I don't know who shot at you, but he was a fool."

With her fingers worrying the black cravat at her throat, Enid said, "Jackson, you had to be the one who fired that shot." For if he had not, the assassin remained at large, and she—and MacLean—were still in danger.

"If all had remained quiet, you would have dropped your guard, and I"—Jackson glanced up at the narrow-eyed MacLean—"I would have discovered the list."

"You would have killed me." MacLean nudged him with his toe. "If you didn't shoot at us, who did?"

From the door at the side of the altar, a woman's voice spoke. "You were a stupid lad, and you've grown to be a stupid man."

MacLean and Enid swiveled to face Lady Catriona—and the rifle she held against her shoulder.

Enid took a useless step backward.

"My God," MacLean said hoarsely. "Aunt Catriona, what are you doing?"

"Getting justice for my lad."

Catriona was daft as a hatter, Lady Bess had said. It appeared she was right, and Enid's heart thundered as she faced the ugly black eye at the end of the barrel.

"Neither one of you deserved to have my Stephen wipe his feet on you." The muzzle roamed between MacLean and Enid. "He was a good lad, and neither of you appreciated how lucky you were to have him."

She was far too steady in her aim.

Moving slowly, MacLean took Enid's hand and led

her to the pew. They sank down together to present a smaller target.

"Does she shoot?" Enid whispered.

"Every season she bags a hart," MacLean answered quietly.

Jackson wiggled like a worm as he tried to get out of the way.

"She shot at us in the gallery?" Enid could scarcely believe the petite woman could deal death so callously.

"I would have hit you, but that Harry creature stepped in the way." Lady Catriona hated with profound malice.

"Harry never harmed you, Aunt Catriona." Mac-Lean spoke in a soothing voice.

"He was a friend of yours, and besides, I had to shoot him, or he would have revealed me." Lady Catriona took a few steps into the chapel, and the barrel moved toward MacLean. "And I want to kill you so badly. You were with Stephen when he died, Kiernan. You probably killed him."

MacLean was clearly shocked. "How can you think such a thing?"

Lady Catriona's pointed the rifle toward Enid. "But you . . . you're the one who truly betrayed Stephen. You were his wife. You rutted with his murderer."

It was a useless protest, but Enid had to try. "Lady Catriona, Kiernan didn't kill Stephen."

"Perhaps not. Perhaps he only failed to save him. But you *did* fornicate with Kiernan, and Stephen barely cold in his grave. I hate you both so much, I don't know which one of you to shoot—but I know whoever is left will be miserable." Catriona's finger tightened on the trigger.

MacLean shoved Enid to the floor. He landed on top of her with a grunt of pain.

The rifle roared, and before the echo died away, Lady Catriona screeched. The rifle clattered to the floor.

Harry said, "Got you, you bitch."

Harry. Thank God for Harry.

MacLean stared at Enid. She looked all right, and although his ribs ached, he was all right. Together, the two of them lifted themselves cautiously to peer over the pew.

Harry held Lady Catriona's arm twisted behind her back, and she made little squealing noises as she struggled against his grip. "She shot me in cold blood," he said. "It's time to put her away."

"Yes," MacLean said. It was time she went back to her family. Her family was used to dealing with people like her; there were enough of them. "Take her to the north tower and lock her up. We'll send her away tomorrow."

Turning to the crowd gathering behind him, Harry said, "Kinman! Take her." He shoved Lady Catriona away. "And get Graeme and Rab and carry Jackson out of the chapel." In answer to an inaudible question, he said, "No, you can't stop to talk to MacLean. Can't you see he's busy?"

While MacLean and Enid rose to their feet and dusted themselves off the two Scots and a grinning but silent Mr. Kinman hauled Jackson away.

Enid would have escaped with them, but MacLean wasn't about to let her go. Not after so unsatisfactory a conversation. Catching her arm, he brought her to a halt. "Last night, you said you loved me."

She flinched, as if he had hit her. "But I don't want

to love you." Her voice got higher, a sure sign she was nervous. "Love is nothing but an ambush, a trap, and you can't run far enough to get away from the pain and the heartache."

"But there's joy, too. There's having someone for your own. There are whispers in the night and raising a bairn and love that stretches to eternity—"

"It doesn't stretch into eternity. That's the trouble. We'd argue. You'd leave me because of who I am."

Enunciating each word clearly, he said, "I ... would . . . not."

"Or you'd . . . you'd die!"

Her outburst surprised him. He glanced at the coffin and looked back at her. "I'm in reasonable good health, my dearling, and any man who survived what I have has proved his hardiness."

"Or used up his luck!" She clenched her fists. "I'm so angry at everything that has happened."

"It seems as if you're always angry." He was beginning to understand. "But you're not. You're scared."

The color bleached from her face. "No."

"Scared to death." He studied her, seeing for the first time the truth behind her defiance, her self-defensive wit, her sarcasm. "Of having a man, and expectations, when life is uncertain at best. You've been trained to expect the worst of love."

"The worst is the truth," she snapped and backed away from him.

He followed. "No. From the first moment I saw you, I wanted you desperately. I couldn't even lift my head from the pillow, and I managed to kiss you. There can never be another woman like that for me."

She moved more quickly. She stumbled on the carpet.

"You want me, too." He knew it. "You came to me last night. You said you loved me."

"I do love you. But I can't stay. I won't stay."

He didn't even know he could say the words, but when she turned and walked up the aisle, he blurted, "Enid, I love you."

She never slowed. She disappeared out the door.

"I love you!" She must not have heard him. He hurried after her.

Lady Bess stepped into his path and grasped his arm. "Let her go."

"I can't." Enid was leaving him. She was all he wanted. She loved him, and he loved her, and she was leaving him!

"If you force Enid to stay, you'll have only ashes in your hands. Let her go."

MacLean could scarcely bear to listen to his mother, but so far nothing he had done had succeeded. He dragged Lady Bess along until he could see Enid's fleeing form. Then, although it killed him, he stood still and watched her take flight, thinking she tore out his heart as she went. His breath was harsh and deep, and his voice was guttural when he asked, "Mother, is it true you wed the Englishman to save me from having to wed an heiress?"

"Well, yes, dear."

He looked down at her, his beautiful, eccentric mother, still clinging to his arm. "Why didn't you tell me?"

"You're a smart lad. I knew you'd figure it out sooner or later."

Taking her head in his hands, he kissed her hair. "Thank you, Mother."

With a smile, she dug a cigar out from between her breasts. "Enid's a smart lass, too. She'll figure out that she loves you sooner or later."

"Sooner?" he asked, needing comfort, no matter how indeterminate.

"Or later," she confirmed.

Chapter 28

The London solicitor bowed in a most respectful manner as Enid left his office, but Enid scarcely noticed. She was in shock. In her hands she held a letter from Lady Halifax, written in the last days before her death, and in a velvet-lined box was the silver-backed brush she had used to brush Lady Halifax's hair.

In a daze Enid wandered toward Hyde Park. She would sit on a bench and read it there, and then all would become clear. Surely then she would know what to do.

"My lord. My lord!"

The afternoon sun shone down on MacLean's bare shoulders as he stuck his shovel in the earth of the newly plowed herb garden and waited until a panting Graeme reached him. "What?"

"She's back." Graeme leaned his hands on his knees and gasped for air. "Enid has returned to Castle MacLean and—"

MacLean dropped the shovel handle and started toward the castle at a run.

"She's bargaining wi' yer mother for yer hand in marriage," Graeme called. "I thought ye'd be interested!"

MacLean was interested. He was more than interested. He burst through the front door of the castle and saw Donaldina.

"They're in th' east library," she informed. "An' my, doesn't Mrs. MacLean look elegant!"

Elegant? Why did Enid look elegant? Better she should look haggard, as he did, from waiting a whole month to hear if the woman of his heart would wed him. Elegant, indeed. Better she should look hot and dirty from planting an herb garden as an enticement to a woman who'd been off to London buying clothing so she could look elegant. He strode up a flight of stairs and into his mother's study—and saw Enid.

She *did* look elegant. She wore the newest, most fashionable travel costume made of dark purple satin with a matching hat and a silly feather that bobbed when she turned her head. He was ready to go over and shake her, but she smiled at him with such warmth that he stopped in his tracks. She smiled at him, and he would have sworn his broken heart played a bagpipe tune.

"We were just talking about you, son." Lady Bess sat behind her desk, her book of household accounts open before her, twirling her pen. "Enid has made an offer for your hand."

When her words finally penetrated his daze, he stared at his mother with her wrinkled brows and somber mien. "What?"

"She has made an offer for your hand," Lady Bess repeated. "I think I speak true when I told her you would be happy to wed her . . ."

"Aye." As a gender, women were stark, raving mad.

"Enid is offering us a dowry."

"A dowry." He turned back toward Enid. "Damn, woman, I don't care about a dowry. I just want you!"

Lady Bess cleared her throat and frowned. "Nevertheless, we're getting a dowry. She has offered two thousand pounds. I won't allow you to wed for less than twenty."

"Twenty thousand pounds!" MacLean shouted. Stark, raving mad. "Where would she get twenty thousand pounds?" He gestured toward Enid. "Where would she get two thousand pounds? She's a nurse-companion."

In an insulted tone, Enid said, "I'm offering two thousand pounds for you."

Two thousand pounds! What had Enid been doing? Concerned, he demanded, "You didn't rob the Bank of England, did you, lass?"

Enid laid her arm across the back of the sofa in an elegant arch. "Not at all."

"She seems to have come into some money," Lady Bess said. "She has offered a dowry, and we're going to take it."

"We don't need a dowry." This smacked of buying a husband. Of buying him.

"Don't tell me what we need and what we don't need." Lady Bess tapped the book of accounts. "Twenty thousand pounds would buy us that strip of land the MacLeans had to sell off after the Forty-Five."

Enid shrugged with fine disdain. "That's too bad,

because I can't afford more than three thousand pounds."

MacLean stood, staring at Enid, hands dangling at his side. The first words he'd heard her say in over a month, and they were about money?

Lady Bess seemed to find nothing unusual in the scene. "Kiernan is the laird of a powerful Scottish clan. He's worth twice twenty thousand."

Enid looked him over, at the dirt on his kilt and his bare, sweaty chest, and her lascivious appreciation made him flush. "He is that, and not because of his clan."

"Aye, he's a handsome lad," Lady Bess agreed. "In good health, with all his teeth, but a few scars from his recent ordeal. So you'll pay twenty thousand?"

"Mother!"

Enid shook her head. "Four."

"Fifteen."

"Seven."

MacLean wanted to punch his fist through the wall. "Why are you two doing this?"

Lady Bess glared at him meaningfully. "Don't interrupt the negotiations. Enid will not wed you any other way."

Once more, he gazed on the woman he loved. He was, as his mother said, the laird of a powerful clan. Enid was an illegitimate orphan, and when he'd discovered his true identity, in his rage he had accused her of being a liar. Of being mercenary. Of being a bastard and a whore, and he had hurt her so much that he would spend the rest of his life trying to make it up to her.

Now, somehow, she had discovered a way to bring something besides her own self to their marriage—and he would let her.

He needed only her.

She needed her pride. "Go on," he said tersely.

"Twelve thousand pounds," his mother said.

"Ten," Enid countered.

Lady Bess stood and smiled. "I believe we have an agreement."

MacLean gave a gusty sigh of relief.

Enid did not stand. "Ten thousand over the next ten years."

Lady Bess's smile faded, and she sat back down.

His frustration came out in a roar. "For God's sake, women, by the time you get done with these negotiations, I'll be too old to consummate the marriage!"

Lady Bess struggled against a grin. "Perhaps, son, it would be better if you went to your room and bathed while we finish."

Patient. He had to be patient. Crossing his arms across his chest, he leaned against the cabinet. "You can just put up with the smell. I'm staying right here."

By the time they finished negotiations the tension had put him into a state of exhaustion.

Lady Bess and Enid stood and shook hands.

Lady Bess left and closed the door behind her.

He straightened. "Are you happy now?"

Enid didn't look happy. She looked a little like a female uncertain of her welcome. "Are you?"

"You're going to marry me?"

"Yes."

He allowed a grin to break over his face. He strode

over to her and without a care to her elegant travel costume, he pulled her against him. "Then I'm happy." He kissed her, and when he finished she no longer looked uncertain, and that damned silly hat had fallen to the floor.

"Let me show you something." Enid eased herself out of his arms, went to the sofa, and got her reticule. "Do you remember that I received the bequest from Lady Halifax?"

"Indeed I do." He began to understand.

She pulled a paper covered with shaky, spidery writing from her reticule. "This is the letter she wrote to accompany it."

He pushed it aside and pulled her into his arms. "Tell me what it says."

She didn't protest. Indeed, she snuggled close as if she liked half-naked, dirty men. "Lady Halifax said she liked me. Admired me. She left me five thousand pounds, and told me to conceal it from Stephen, to save it for the moment when I could achieve my heart's desire. But when I received it, I had just come back from Castle MacLean, Stephen was gone, and I no longer knew my heart's desire. I had thought I wanted to grow herbs on my own land, but in the last months that dream had grown acrid and unappealing. I tried to think where I would go, what I would do, now that I had the resources to make myself happy. I didn't know. I thought maybe I should buy a home, but where? And a family, but I couldn't buy one of those. Friends? I have friends, but while I have a fortune, they must still work for their living. I spent a fortnight wandering about London, looking for the truth in every park, on every street, in every garden."

"What made you come for me?"

"I read the letter again. Lady Halifax said to seize my heart's desire, and I realized—I could not see inside my own heart by looking about London. I had to . . . look inside myself."

"And what did you see?"

Looking up at him, she placed her palms on either side of his head. "You. And you. And you. There is nothing that I want except you."

He slid his hands over hers. "If you hadn't come soon . . ."

"What? You would have come to get me?"

"Aye. A handfast marriage would do for us—until you agreed to take vows in our chapel with all my people as witnesses."

She laughed a little. "I wondered. I kept looking behind me, thinking I would see you."

Clasping her hands, he pulled one to his mouth and kissed the palm. She tasted like woman. His woman. "There is one thing I don't understand."

Her eyes half closed with pleasure. "Yes?"

"You said you inherited five thousand pounds."

Opening her eyes wide, she smiled with excessive innocence.

"But you promised a dowry of ten thousand."

"Over a period of ten years."

"So you really are a liar."

"And I'm a mercenary."

"Who spent every pound of your fortune on me."

"A wise investment, for you could do your part and make a family with me, and your mother would consider our child as part of my payment."

"My wife is a beautiful, wanton trickster." Laughing

slightly, he slid his arm around her waist, bent her back and kissed her with all the pent-up passion of the last month. "A beautiful, wanton, mercenary liar who would do anything to get me."

"Anything," she vowed. "I would do anything."

Looking into her brilliant blue eyes, he repeated his vow, the vow he had made that day in the mountains in the sunshine. "I am the blood in your veins, the marrow in your bones. You'll never go anywhere without knowing I'm inside you, supporting you, keeping you alive. I am a part of you. You are a part of me. We are forever."

She wrapped her arms around his shoulders. "Forever."